The Monk

A **DS CROSS** THRILLER

TIM SULLIVAN

HEAD
ZEUS

An Aries Book

First published in the UK in 2023 by Head of Zeus,
part of Bloomsbury Publishing Plc

9 7 5 3 1 2 4 6 8

A catalogue record for this book is available from the British Library.

ISBN (HB): 9781804545607
ISBN (E): 9781804545584

Cover design: Ben Prior

Printed and bound in Great Britain by
CPI Group (UK) Ltd, Croydon CR0 4YY

Head of Zeus
First Floor East
5–8 Hardwick Street
London EC1R 4RG

WWW.HEADOFZEUS.COM

For Brian Worthington
who had confidence in my ability before anyone else
and introduced me to Henry James

Ora et Labora

George Cross was rarely shocked by anything he came across during his work as a detective sergeant in the Avon and Somerset police. He had quickly come to the conclusion, many years before, that people were capable of inflicting the most grotesque acts of violence upon one another. So, no matter how bloody or gruesome a crime scene was, he managed to view it objectively. The sight of a throat cut with a blade or slashed by a broken bottle, brain matter splattered over the ground near a shattered skull, was simply evidence, and should be thought of as such. As appalling a sight as it may be, it was just the first step in a process that would lead to the identification, arrest, charging and hopefully conviction of the killer. A sense of emotional outrage or disbelief were just obstacles to an investigation, in his view. An emotional reaction to a crime scene was an unnecessary distraction. In a sense this was easy for him to think, as empathy in any given situation was not one of his strong suits.

What confronted the Avon and Somerset murder team that morning in the woodlands of Goblin Combe was, though, without question truly shocking, as well as confounding.

If a murder scene wasn't easily accessible and, as in this case, necessitated a lengthy walk down a wet and puddled footpath, requiring a slow hopscotch to avoid wet feet, the sense of anticipation that built inside the stomachs of the murder team became increasingly palpable. It meant that some of them had to take pause before facing whatever horror awaited them that particular day. It had rained heavily overnight so the trees were laden with huge bulging berries of rain, which grew in size as other drops joined the party, before the surface tension was too much and they burst, falling intermittently with unerring accuracy on those below. The shoulders of Cross's beige mackintosh had dark, wet epaulettes. As he and Ottey approached the scene, the first thing they saw was the back of a wooden chair protruding from the ditch that ran alongside the path. Many people had walked past this chair in the past few days, doubtless bemoaning the lack of respect others had for the countryside and how fly-tipping had become something of an epidemic in Somerset. They couldn't have ignored the smell, however. That sweet and sour, sickly smell of human decomposition, so familiar to the squad. But, this being the country, they'd probably put it down to an animal carcass lying somewhere nearby. The actual source of it was taped to the chair with industrial duct tape. A man whose face was now dark purple from lividity, having been left facing downwards onto the ditch. Blood had also pooled round his wrists like gruesome dark bracelets. Gravity was pulling the body downwards so that the tape was stretched to breaking point. The man was dressed entirely in black. It appeared that he was wearing a black habit and hooded scapular. He hadn't been to a fancy-dress party or a T20 cricket match, though; he was in fact a Benedictine monk. They knew this because Dom Dominic Augustus of St Eustace's monastery, 15 miles away, had been reported missing two days earlier by the father abbot. It almost certainly had to be him. So, in a sense it wasn't exactly a surprise. Brutal, horrific and unexpected, yes.

Everyone was focused on wondering how anyone could do this to a monk. Cross's attention, however, had been drawn to the fact that the lifeless, chair-bound corpse in the shallow ditch below him had been savagely beaten prior to his death. His bruised eyelids were swollen shut. His lips were bloody and cut. Cross couldn't imagine why such a fate would befall a man who had made the decision to withdraw himself from everyday life and devote himself to one of contemplation and prayer. What could possibly provoke someone to do this to a monk? Or what could the victim have done to drive someone to such an act? What had been the purpose of the beating? He looked carefully at the monk's body and saw tiny ripples of movement under his cassock. This meant thousands of maggots had already colonised the body. Hundreds more were congregating at various orifices, his ears and nostrils and around his eyes. It also meant he'd been dead for at least twenty-four hours but Cross didn't know exactly how cold or warm it had been in the last few days. The body could have been in situ for two or three days depending on the life cycle stage of the maggots, which he would leave Swift to determine.

'Stag night gone wrong?' a nervous uniformed police constable had joked when he arrived at the scene.

'Are you aware that a monk local to this county has been reported missing?' Cross asked him.

'Of course,' he replied.

'So, presumably you thought your comment was amusing?' Cross went on. Ottey was about to intervene. But it was first thing in the morning and she decided she didn't have the energy for the inevitable lecture about appropriate behaviour at a crime scene.

'Sorry,' the constable replied.

'You should leave,' Cross instructed him.

'What?'

'Your presence is no longer required,' Cross said. So the young constable left. He probably thought he'd done nothing wrong and that Cross was just an uptight, humourless prick. Cross would've been unconcerned. He considered that kind of comment, coming from a policeman at a murder scene, unacceptable. To him it showed not just a lack of respect for the victim, but a lack of professionalism too, which he couldn't tolerate. He also hoped the young man might learn something from his dismissal.

'George, he was probably just trying to ease the tension,' said Ottey quietly.

'Then he might have been better suited to a career as a masseur,' Cross reflected. Ottey laughed. Cross looked at her, surprised.

'That was a joke, George,' she said. But he still looked at her blankly. 'Maybe not.'

Cross's attention was now drawn to the arrival of the forensic pathologist Clare Hawkins and forensic investigator Dr Michael Swift, who at six foot eight towered over her. Both were dressed in their white paper forensic overalls. They signed in with the policeman on the perimeter, then came over. Clare held out two paper suits for Cross and Ottey. He took his and walked away to put it on. Ottey declined hers.

'I won't be needing one,' she said.

'Seen enough?' asked Clare.

'Yep.'

'I've got some coffee in the car. Freshly ground. Piping hot. I can go get it if you want,' Swift said kindly, realising she might need a restorative pick-me-up.

'Maybe after you've done your stuff. Thanks,' she said and walked away towards a clearing in the trees. She walked through it to a view of the beautiful Somerset countryside which couldn't have changed in hundreds of years. That thought comforted her. Grounded her, in a way. Various tractors were working a hillside field opposite her. Probably tilling, destoning and maybe planting potatoes at this time of year. Clouds scurried across the landscape unnaturally quickly like speeded-up film. The fields were relatively small by modern standards, bordered by orderly hedgerows that had survived the wholesale destruction modern farming methods had inflicted on much of the English countryside. It was a beautiful April day. One of those on which it was difficult to decide what to wear. Warm when the sun came out, then suddenly cold as it retreated behind slow-moving clouds. Birds hovered in the wake of the distant tractors, swooping down to feast on any uncovered worms; the farmer obviously had good biodiversity in his earth. Ottey breathed in deeply in an attempt to remove the stench of death inhabiting her nostrils. It had stuck stubbornly to the tiny hairs inside her nose, like pollen on a bee's back legs. The air smelt of freshly grown grass and drying soil. It was filled with birdsong. They sounded excited, as if they were communicating to whoever was willing to listen that summer was on its way. A couple of hawks soared effortlessly on the thermals high above. A day of perennially renewed promise, except for one unfortunate monk. Ottey was a regular churchgoer, partly out of habit, but also because when she thought about it, she did believe in God. She had to. Despite the fact that her job often presented formidable challenges to maintaining any kind of faith. Like today.

A tent was erected over the monk's body. Hawkins and Swift then entered it to do their grim work undisturbed. Cross and Ottey walked back to her car. They wanted to tell the abbot at St Eustace's the news before he learnt of it third-hand, probably through the media. Their task made all the more urgent by the arrival of a couple of local news vans who parked up and quickly started to unload their equipment.

'They're quicker than blowflies when it comes to finding a corpse,' Cross observed.

2

St Eustace's monastery was in the countryside just south-west of Cheddar.

'Do you know something?' asked Ottey.

'I happen to know quite a lot of things,' Cross replied.

'I've never been to Cheddar Gorge or the caves.'

'People often take for granted things of interest that are on their doorstep,' he observed.

'Have you been?'

'Yes. Raymond took me there when I was a child. The caves are quite impressive. You should take the girls.'

'I will. Maybe Raymond would like to join us,' she said.

'Why would you ask him?'

'The girls like him and he's so interesting about stuff like that,' she replied.

'I also know lots of interesting stuff. Probably a great deal more than my father,' Cross said, trying his best not to sound defensive, which he failed at comprehensively.

Ottey didn't reply.

'Ah, I see. The girls don't like me,' Cross went on.

'That's just not true. They are both very fond of you. I just thought Raymond might enjoy it a little more than you.'

'You are, of course, completely right. I wouldn't enjoy it at all.'

'Now I can't tell whether you're joking or not,' she said.

He looked at her, confused. Hadn't he just agreed with her? 'Why would I joke about the tiresome nature of children?' he asked.

They arrived at the monastery which sat at the top of a small hill, shrouded by mature trees. There was a set of electronic gates and an entryphone system at the bottom of the hill.

'They obviously want to keep the outside world outside,' Ottey commented.

'Or the monks inside,' Cross replied.

Ottey pressed the intercom button which was mounted on a post at the driver's side of the vehicle.

'St Eustace's Abbey,' came a polite, distant voice through the speaker.

'DS Ottey and Cross to see the abbot,' Ottey replied.

'Yes, of course.'

They drove up a single lane winding through a canopy of trees that joined together over the road. It made it quite dark, as if preparing the visitor to leave the world behind them and enter a different place. They came to a Victorian Gothic structure that could easily have been mistaken for a small preparatory school. A monk was waiting at the front door for them. He smiled warmly as they approached, his arms folded under his scapular.

'Good afternoon, officers. Welcome to St Eustace's. My name is Brother Andrew. Please follow me.'

He had an open face that was almost line-free. Probably in his mid-twenties, Cross thought. They followed him into the enclosure and the abbot's office.

'Detectives are you here about Brother Dominic?' the abbot began, standing up behind his desk. He was in his late fifties, in an identical habit to Brother Andrew and the late Brother Dominic. The only difference being a large silver crucifix which hung from his neck, reaching just below his chest. He had tightly cropped grey hair which looked like it might be wildly curly, were it given the opportunity to grow. His light blue eyes betrayed his Scandinavian heritage. Father Abbot Anselm was originally from Denmark.

'We are,' said Ottey.

'Oh good. I was beginning to get a little worried,' said the abbot, smiling.

'A body was discovered this morning by a woman walking her dog,' Cross said. Ottey turned to him, horrified.

'DS Cross,' she said, shutting him up.

The abbot sat down slowly. This was unexpected and incomprehensible. It wasn't a scenario he'd contemplated.

'It's always a dog walker, isn't it?' he said quietly, as if he hadn't really taken in what he'd just been told.

'Dogs have thousands more receptors in their nose and on the whole have a much stronger sense of smell than humans. They are very sensitive to the smell of putrefaction,' Cross volunteered unhelpfully. Ottey looked at him again, in disbelief.

'I'm sorry to inform you, Father, that we do believe the body to be that of Brother Dominic who you've reported missing,' said Ottey trying to signal to Cross that this conversation would be better handled by her.

'I see. Where was this body found?' asked Father Anselm.

'In the woods at Goblin Combe,' Ottey replied.

'Really? Are you certain it's him?'

'That is a good question,' said Cross, jumping in. 'He will need to be formally identified.'

'Of course,' replied Father Anselm.

'The fact that you have reported one of your community missing and that the victim is dressed in a monastic habit, mean the chances of it being him are quite high,' Ottey replied.

If the abbot was upset by this news he gave little away to reveal it. He had an air of unaffected composure and preternatural calm about him.

'I will come and formally identify him as soon as is convenient for you. In the meantime, do you have a photograph of the dead man? If it appears to be Dominic I'd like to be able to tell the community. Your very presence here this morning will have set tongues wagging among the monks.' This was a surprise to Ottey. She found the idea of monks gossiping comfortingly amusing.

Cross reached for his phone and scrolled through the photographs.

'Father, the deceased was badly beaten,' said Ottey.

'Really?' came the weary reply, as if he couldn't believe things could be getting worse.

'His face is bruised and swollen.'

'I see.'

As Cross looked at the photographs, he realised that the bruised appearance of the dead monk's face was the least of their concerns. Every photograph showed the monk's face covered in maggots around his eyes, mouth and nostrils. He gave the phone to Ottey who immediately saw the problem.

'I think it's best you come to the mortuary once we have him there,' she said.

'I understand. How terrible. It's that bad, is it?'

'I'm so sorry, but it is.'

The abbot thought for a moment. 'Was he still wearing his shoes? Do you have a photograph of them?' he asked.

'His shoes?' asked Cross.

'It was the last vestige of his old life that he couldn't quite forswear. He liked to wear what you might call "elegant" shoes. He always had the same ones, ecclesiastical of course, but they were quite a sharp pair of tapered black suede shoes.'

Cross made a call to Swift.

'Cross here. Could you photograph the victim's shoes and send them to me urgently?' he asked, ending the call before Swift had a chance to answer. A couple of minutes later the abbot looked at the photograph Swift had sent to Cross's phone and sat back in his chair.

'Those are Dominic's shoes,' he said quietly before crossing himself and muttering a quick prayer. A bell sounded from the church.

'That's the call for Sext. Will you join us?' asked the abbot.

'Father, Sext will have to wait,' said Cross. 'We've just informed you of the murder of one of your community.'

'Indeed. What better time to pray for his soul, Sergeant. We are very strict in the observation of our daily offices. They take place at the same time every day come foul weather, illness or indeed death,' replied the abbot in a way that implied he would brook no argument to the contrary, murder or not. They followed him.

Ottey turned to Cross. 'I thought he said...' she whispered.

Though not quite as quietly as she thought, as the abbot said over his shoulder, 'Sext is the sixth hour at which we have prayers before lunch. Terce is the third hour.' He turned to them. 'It's derived from the Roman *sexta hora* and is quite different from what I understand to be the modern meaning outside of these walls. Which is to issue communications of a sexual nature to others via the telephone. Is that right?' he asked a little mischievously. Not in a risqué manner but in a way that said he knew a monk possessing such information would be a surprise to them.

Cross glared at Ottey for what he considered to be her immature comment, casting them both in an unprofessional light. He was also annoyed and surprised by the abbot's insistence on sticking to his timetable given their news. Time was always of the essence this early in an investigation. But he consoled himself with the fact that he could get his first look at the community.

As they walked up the hill, a file of monks processed up to the side door of the church. Cross noticed that the narrow road and turning circle outside the church had been recently resurfaced with barely worn tarmacadam. But then he imagined it could have been done a while ago as it presumably had very little traffic other than on a Sunday. The monks walked in single file, their arms folded under their scapulars. None of them spoke, not even to greet each other, as they joined the line. On entering the church they pulled their hoods over their heads. It occurred to Cross that he was looking at a scene which would have been identical had they observed it hundreds of years before.

The prayers were sung in Gregorian chant, in Latin. They were short, just over ten minutes in length. Cross thought the abbot looked remarkably composed, bearing in mind the awful news he'd just been given. Did that mean anything? he wondered. The abbot said nothing to the two police officers, nor looked in their direction as he followed the other monks out of the church and down the path back to the house.

Cross and Ottey followed the line down and into the refectory, without speaking a word.

'Please, before we begin lunch, be seated,' said the abbot to the roomful of monks. He didn't need to raise his voice in the slightest, such was the quiet in the room. It was very plain with two long tables and wooden chairs. There was a door at one end and a hatch which opened to a small kitchen where a monk had been preparing lunch. The monks sat obediently. None of them even looked at each other to question silently what was going on. Only one of them gave Cross and Ottey the most cursory of glances.

'I have the most dreadful news. About Brother Dominic. Our guests here are police officers. They have just informed me that Brother Dominic is dead,' the abbot announced calmly.

There was no reaction in the room from any of the monks.

'Murdered,' Cross announced with inappropriate volume, having been unable to resist the urge to clarify the situation and make sure that none of them were under any illusion about exactly what had happened to their friend. This did elicit a response. The monk who was cooking turned to go back into the kitchen urgently as if he'd suddenly smelled something burning. An elderly monk in a wheelchair looked down to the ground, closed his eyes and sought solace in the only way he knew, by praying. One younger monk turned to the brother sitting beside him and whispered, asking if he'd heard the father abbot correctly.

'These police officers will be here I should imagine quite regularly over the next few days. Please afford them your time when they request it. Let us pray for a moment for the soul of our lost brother and for DS Cross and DS Ottey to give them the strength to help us understand what befell Brother Dominic.'

Ottey couldn't help thinking she'd never heard of a murder enquiry described in such oblique terms before. The monks stood and looked at the floor in silence. But it was all too much for one of them who suddenly bolted from the room. Another older monk looked up to the abbot who gave him the most imperceptible of nods. The monk left the refectory to go after the distressed brother. Cross noticed a couple of other young monks looking at each other with knowing concern.

'Will you join us for lunch?' asked the abbot as if nothing unusual had just happened.

'No,' replied Cross.

'We can't. We have to get this enquiry up and running,' said Ottey.

'Of course. God bless you,' the abbot said, taking hold of both of Ottey's hands to comfort her. 'This must have been such a difficult morning for you. First bearing witness to what I can only imagine was a distressing sight. Then having to break such awful news to us. God bless you both.'

'We'll need to return tomorrow morning and interview each monk individually,' Cross informed him.

'Is that really necessary?' asked the abbot.

'Of course. Why wouldn't it be?' asked Cross.

'Well, you can't possibly imagine any of them had anything to do with it, can you?'

'Why would you ask that?' replied Cross.

'Because it's so obviously implausible.'

'Nothing is obvious nor indeed implausible in a murder enquiry,' replied Cross who had had enough and turned on his heels and left. The abbot watched him for a moment, then turned to Ottey.

'Well, see you tomorrow, apparently,' he said and began to walk away.

Cross turned back at the door and spoke, again, without thinking, again, loudly enough for the whole room to hear.

'Father Abbot, you reported Brother Dominic missing the day before yesterday. But the insect activity on the body would suggest his body had been at the deposition site for maybe three to four days.'

'We hadn't seen him for three days when Father Magnus reported it to the police.'

Cross nodded, acknowledging that this was all he required. As they walked back to the car Ottey turned to Cross.

'Did you really have to be so...' she began.

'So, what?' asked Cross.

'So, you,' she replied, deciding she couldn't be bothered to have the same old conversation again that morning.

3

DCI Ben Carson stared at the photograph of Brother Dominic's beaten face in the centre of the whiteboard. He then turned to the team of detectives and uniformed police in the incident room of the Major Crimes Unit (MCU).

'Who the hell would want to do this to a Benedictine monk? It makes no sense,' he proclaimed to the room. He was genuinely incensed. His outrage completely instinctive.

For Cross this was the wrong initial question. The right one, the one most likely to be helpful, was why? Was it an act of random violence? An act of deliberate violence against a religious figure? Or a case of mistaken identity? The fact that it was someone whose links with the outside world were presumably limited, made it all the more difficult and intriguing. He looked to Ottey who knew instinctively what he was thinking.

'I think it's more a question of why, boss. I mean, a monk?' she began.

'Okay, so let's begin with what we know,' Carson replied.

'Well, we don't have an official cause of death yet, although initial impressions would indicate blunt force trauma. We also don't have a murder scene yet, just a deposition site,' she went on.

'And we know that how?' asked Carson.

Ottey turned to Michael Swift.

'Not enough blood at the scene. There's no iron content in the grass around nor beneath the body,' answered Swift.

'Do we know how long the body had been there?' asked Carson.

'Based on the stage of development of the larvae on the body I'd estimate three days,' replied Swift.

'Murder weapon?'

'No.'

'Anything else, Michael?'

'We have a viable fingerprint on the back of the chair.'

'What the hell was he doing taped to a bloody chair? It's just too odd.' He thought for a moment. 'Couldn't the print just be from normal everyday use?'

'It's a bloody fingerprint.'

'Ah, okay. Good. George, you're very quiet,' said Carson.

As Carson hadn't asked a question, merely made an observation, Cross didn't reply.

'Any thoughts?' Carson persisted.

'About the case?' Cross asked.

'Well, obviously,' Carson replied.

'Well, no. Obviously,' said Cross, unintentionally causing a ripple of laughter.

'How do you think we should proceed, George?' said Ottey, stepping in.

'The beating is incongruous. He's a monk. The current forensic timings would suggest that he was tortured.'

'Could be a revenge beating,' Carson offered.

'It could, but wouldn't that be more instantaneous? One beating and done with it? Why hold him for two days? And revenge for what? It's more probable that someone wanted something from him. But what? We need to find out how long he was at the monastery, what and who, as it were, he was before he entered it,' Cross began.

'It would make sense if it was someone from his past life,' Carson commented.

'No more sense than if it were someone he'd come across as a monk, or a monk at the abbey, if indeed sense has anything to do with it,' Cross replied.

'Okay, while we wait for the autopsy results let's set up a

roadside canvas around Goblin Wood and see if anything comes out of that. Continue the fingertip search of the area. George and Josie, go back to the abbey and see what you can dig up on our victim. Let's do this,' Carson said, sounding as though this was a positive, well-thought-out plan of action. Which it clearly wasn't.

4

On their second visit to St Eustace's, Cross took in more details of the abbot's office. It was sparsely furnished with just a plain wooden desk and chair at one end. There were three armchairs and a small coffee table at the other, where Ottey and Cross sat with the abbot. The walls had some bookshelves on them with a small number of books, mostly historical at first glance. A large crucifix adorned one wall. There were arched leaded windows behind the desk, looking out onto the driveway. A great vantage point to observe the comings and goings of life in the abbey, Ottey thought. There probably wasn't much which got past the abbot in this monastery. The floor was a dark wooden parquet. The room smelt distinctly of polish.

'Excuse the strong smell of polish. Brother Jude likes to give the floor and furniture a good going over the first Tuesday of every month.'

'Beeswax?' Cross asked.

'Yes. How clever of you. But then again, I suppose you are a detective,' the abbot said, laughing, as did Ottey.

'My father's cleaner likes to use it,' Cross informed him, failing to see the joke.

'Oh really? We make our own. We sell it in the abbey shop. I can let you have a couple of tins,' replied the abbot.

'I would have to pay for them,' Cross insisted.

'Of course. We're not a charity, you know.' He laughed again. 'Actually, what am I talking about, that's exactly what we are.'

Ottey thought the father abbot looked a little drained compared to the day before. Possibly he hadn't slept. Maybe he'd been praying for Brother Dominic all night. His calm and composure of the previous day had doubtless been abruptly upset by the reality of Dominic's death slowly sinking in. Or was he hiding something? Did he know something that he hadn't told them, that was troubling him?

'How are you today, Father?' Ottey asked.

'In a state of shock, I think. We all are. It's difficult to imagine why anyone would do this to anyone, let alone a monk,' he replied.

'Why is that difficult?' asked Cross, pleased though, that the abbot was asking the right question.

'Um, not because our devotion to God makes us a special case, or sets us apart in any way, but because we are so withdrawn from society. It's difficult to imagine any connection to the outside world which would lead to this.'

'That, of course, presumes it happened outside the confines of the monastery,' Cross pointed out.

The abbot was taken aback by this thought. He looked genuinely alarmed but was it simply by the question being asked, or something else?

'That's the second time you've made that observation, Sergeant. What's your point?' he asked.

'What my colleague is saying is that nothing, however unlikely it might appear to be, is off the table at this early stage of an investigation,' said Ottey before Cross had a chance to reply and make matters worse.

'Of course. But I shouldn't want you to waste your time looking within the monastery when the killer is more likely to be outside these walls. You must remember we have no transport of any kind. So how would a monk have got Dominic's body up to Goblin Combe?' replied the abbot, making the same observation as Swift had.

'It's a good question, but not one that completely rules out the possibility. Most murders in this country are committed within a family. This community is a family,' Cross countered.

'Well, you are the experts in this field so what is the best way forward in this situation, detectives? It won't surprise you to know that a murder enquiry is new territory for our community,' said the monk.

'We'd like to build up a picture of Brother Dominic, and the life you lead here, to begin with,' said Ottey.

'How long had Brother Dominic been a monk?' asked Cross.

'Do you mean how long had he been with us, or how long had he been a monk?' Father Anselm asked. Cross was pleased with the abbot's need for precision. He might have asked the same question had he been on the other side of the table.

'How long had he been with you?' Cross asked.

'He joined us fifteen or sixteen years ago, as I recall.'

'So, he would have been in his late twenties?'

'Correct.'

'What was he doing before then?' Cross asked.

'I have no idea,' replied Anselm.

'Really?' asked Ottey.

'Really. Some monks are very open about their lives before they enter our cloister. They stay in touch with their families. But not all, and that would include Dominic. They want to leave their previous life and all its distractions behind them. To devote themselves to God.'

This was of immediate interest to Cross.

'Did he have any particular reasons for not disclosing it?' he asked.

'He would have disclosed it to the previous abbot, of course. It would have been between the two of them and as they are now both with our Lord, we'll have no way of knowing.'

'Could he have discussed it with other monks in the community?' Ottey asked.

'It's perfectly possible. You would have to ask them,' the abbot replied.

Cross and Ottey were now both thinking the same thing. Was the abbot being deliberately unforthcoming for some reason?

'I sense a feeling of disbelief in the two of you. So perhaps I might explain. We may not do police background checks on men wanting to answer the call of our Lord here, but our process is very effective in eliminating those who might be, shall we say, unsuitable.'

'Could you elaborate?' asked Cross.

'Well, there are certain initial requirements. A man interested in the monastic life must be a Roman Catholic, have been confirmed and be debt-free.'

'So you do check their financial status?' Cross asked.

'To an extent. But generally, we take their word for it.'

'That seems a little trusting,' Ottey commented.

'Because it is. But we find the process towards taking solemn vows – when someone actually becomes a monk – effectively self-eliminating. It begins with a few initial visits, then he will come and live with us for a month. If he is still convinced he has a calling from God he will have a postulancy of six months living at the abbey. At the end of this he enters a two-year noviciate in which he learns more about monastic life, the scriptures and Gregorian chant. He is free to leave at any point and may also be asked to leave. At the end of the noviciate there is a vote in the community as to whether he should stay. If successful he takes temporary vows. These last for another three years. Another vote follows, after which he can take solemn vows. All in all it's about five and a half years. So we like to think our vetting process, as you might call it, is very thorough.'

'You can say that again,' Ottey commented.

Cross looked at her. He saw no reason for the abbot to repeat himself.

'Was the vote in the community for Brother Dominic to stay, unanimous?' Cross asked.

The abbot looked at Cross in a way that was familiar to the detective. He was considering how to reply, in a way interviewees often did when they thought the answer might look incriminating when, in truth, it really wasn't.

'It was not,' he replied.

'Is that unusual?' asked Cross.

'It is.'

'Who voted against him?'

'That is a private matter,' the abbot replied tentatively.

'This is a murder enquiry. Nothing is private when it comes to solving murder,' Cross replied, not taking his eyes off him. The abbot held his look.

'It was a secret ballot,' he finally replied.

'Was Brother Dominic well liked within the community?' Ottey went on.

'Very much so. Which makes his loss all the more difficult to deal with.'

'Do all the monks have designated tasks in the monastery?' Cross asked.

'Yes.'

'What were Brother Dominic's specific tasks?' Cross asked.

'He helped look after the bees, worked in the bookbindery and did our accounts,' the abbot replied.

'You bind books?' Ottey asked.

'We have done since the foundation of the abbey in the mid-nineteenth century,' the abbot replied.

'What type of books?'

'We used to do everything, but times change. Now it's mostly ecclesiastical texts for church services, that kind of thing.'

'I read that you also repair and restore books,' Cross added.

Ottey was annoyed with herself that she hadn't done her research, but consoled herself with the fact that, as it was Cross, he wasn't scoring points.

'Oh yes. We've... well, in truth, Dominic became something of an expert in it. He dealt with valuable, sacred texts from all over the world,' said the abbot.

'Valuable financially or religiously?' asked Cross.

'Both. There is quite a market for ecclesiastical texts these days. But then again there seems to be a market for everything.

Dominic was frequently asked to value texts for insurance, probate and the auction houses. He did it for a fee, which was a good source of occasional income for the abbey.'

'Did that involve him travelling?' asked Cross.

'Not always, maybe two or three times a year. Mostly they were sent to us. Sometimes in an armoured security van, can you believe?'

'We'll need a list of any such trips in the last twelve months,' said Ottey.

'How did you keep them safe when they were here?'

'One of the auction houses donated a substantial safe to us for that very purpose.'

'I'll need to have a look at that,' Cross informed him.

'Now?'

'No, but at some point.'

'Were there other occasions when he had to leave the abbey?'

'Not really. He was quite involved in the local bee community but that was about it. He wasn't ordained, he had very little to do with the parishioners. Other than when he took his turn behind the till in the abbey shop.'

'While DS Ottey continues to speak with you I'd like to have a look around the abbey,' said Cross.

'Let me find a brother to show you around,' replied the abbot.

'On my own,' Cross stated.

The abbot didn't seem to have an immediate response to this.

'I'll ask for help if I need it,' Cross said and got up to leave.

'Of course, feel free. The only thing I'd ask is that if you want to look at any of the monks' cells you obtain their permission. None of them will decline and there won't be much to see. But it's the only personal space they have in life and so should be respected as such.'

'That goes without saying,' Cross replied.

'The other thing you should know is that we conduct most of our work in silence. A monk won't speak to you unless you address him first.'

Ottey thought Cross was going to feel completely at home in this place.

'Understood,' Cross replied. The abbot watched him leave then turned back to Ottey.

'George takes a little getting used to,' she said.

'We have a monk on the spectrum here, Brother Thomas, so you have no need to explain,' the abbot replied with a smile. Ottey was impressed with his acuity.

'Do you remember Brother Dominic's name before he took solemn vows?' she asked.

'I do not,' he replied, almost too emphatically, Ottey thought.

5

Cross walked through the abbey house. It was completely silent and felt a little colder than it was outside. The house was the centre of the monastic community, where they lived, slept, ate and studied. The air, while in no way stale, had an institutional taste to it. Almost as if the same air had been circulating in there for the last couple of centuries. He walked through a cloistered corridor whose windows looked out onto a courtyard with the most perfectly manicured lawn. It was a rich verdant green with perfectly symmetrical lines of dark and light. It would be the envy of any Oxford or Cambridge college, thought Cross. In fact, if you didn't know where you were, you could be forgiven for thinking you were in such a place. A monk was on his knees cutting the verge with what looked like a pair of nail scissors.

Back inside, another monk was washing the floor with a mop and bucket. He hadn't looked up when Cross walked in. He simply carried on with his simple task in a slow-paced rhythm. Cross turned to him.

'Is he cutting the edge of the lawn with a pair of nail scissors?' Cross asked.

The monk laughed quietly, put down his mop and came over.

'Brother Thomas and his lawn. No one has been allowed to walk on it for the last couple of years,' the young monk said.

'Well, he's doing a very good job of tending to it.'

'Yes. The truth is he's obsessed with it. Says it's his way of praising the Lord. He got so agitated when we continued to walk on the grass that he had Brother Jude make some small "keep off the grass" signs for him. Not really necessary when you consider there are only ten of us.'

'Nine,' said Cross, correcting him. The monk paused before continuing.

'Father Abbot negotiated with him that we could walk on it on feast days.'

'You can see his point. It wouldn't be nearly as perfect with the daily footfall of a monastic community, however small,' Cross commented.

'My name is Brother John,' the young man announced, proffering his hand, which Cross ignored.

'I'd like to see Brother Dominic's room.'

'Of course. Please follow me.'

Brother John led Cross upstairs to a corridor off which there were several doors. The young monk stopped and turned to Cross.

'These are our living quarters,' he said. 'This is Brother Dominic's room.'

He didn't open the door for Cross, but just stood back. Cross opened it and went in. Brother John stayed outside, as if he were still conscious of respecting Dominic's privacy, despite the fact that he was now dead. The room was small and barely furnished with just a single bed, a wardrobe, desk and chair, and a washbasin which probably dated back to the fifties. It had a small mirror above it and there was a wooden crucifix on the opposite wall. The window looked out onto the abbey vegetable garden where a monk was tilling neat rows of soil. At the far end were six beehives. It was idyllic. Cross was struck by the quiet of the whole place. He opened the wardrobe. Hanging inside were a monk's tunic, scapular and cowl. Also a pair of normal trousers and two shirts. Civvies, Cross thought to himself.

'Are these all his clothes?' Cross asked.

'Except for what he was found in, yes. We don't have need for much,' the monk replied. One less decision to make in the morning – what to wear – Cross thought. Everything about their life was designed for simplicity, with so few distractions, which meant they could concentrate on their devotion, he assumed. Cross then looked at the desk. He opened the drawer. In it was a beautiful bible, bound in leather with gold embossing and rings on the spine. It had several pieces of torn paper marking passages on various pages. He picked it up.

'Brother Dominic bound that bible. He did one for all of us. Identical.'

'He really was a master craftsman. It's a beautiful thing,' Cross replied, putting it back into the drawer alongside the only other occupant, a cheap Bic biro. It was almost out of ink, which struck Cross as unusual. He never managed to keep one long enough to run the ink down that far. He generally lost them, or they were irritatingly pilfered by other detectives in the MCU. He pulled the drawer out and held it up so that he could look underneath it. There was nothing there. He pulled the mattress up off the bed and looked underneath. He then pulled the wardrobe out from the wall, looked behind it and also underneath it. He tapped the base of the wardrobe. He then patted down all of Dominic's clothes and searched the trouser pockets.

'What are you looking for?' asked John.

'I have no idea,' Cross answered. 'Did you know Brother Dominic well?'

'Of course.'

'Why of course?' asked Cross.

'Well, as I said, there are only,' he paused, 'nine of us and we live in close proximity to each other on a daily basis,' replied John.

'Did you like him?'

'Everyone liked Brother Dominic.'

'Why?'

'He was always helpful. To everyone. A great listener if we had a problem,' replied the monk.

'What kinds of problems do you encounter in a monastery?' asked Cross.

'Monkish problems,' replied John with a smile.

'Is that a smile?' Cross asked.

'It is. I'm smiling because "monkish problems" was how he referred to them. Brother Dominic was central to our community. He was a confidant of the father abbot.'

'You must miss his presence here.'

'Yes,' the monk replied. He was about to go on, but emotion got the better of him and he concentrated on suppressing that, instead of elaborating any further.

'Why are you upset?' asked Cross. 'At this particular moment, specifically.'

'Because it's so horrifying and completely puzzling that he could die in such a manner.'

'You mean that he was murdered.'

'Exactly so. Poor you,' John said.

'I don't understand,' said Cross.

'This is an everyday occurrence for you. Something you have to deal with every day of your working life. How sad to have to view the world through the daily lens of death.'

Cross looked at the monk for a moment, trying to compose a response. He had never thought about his life in this way and wondered whether it affected how he lived.

'Where is the bookbindery?' was all he could come up with.

'Are the brothers free to come and go as they please?' Ottey asked the abbot.

'Yes and no. The main purpose of the Benedictine life is to isolate and spend our time in contemplation and devotion to God. But we have to go out to do our weekly shop, just like anyone else. We need to visit the pharmacy and, on occasion, family. But the monks have to ask my permission.'

'Is that every time they go out?'

'Every time.'

'Even for something as regular as the weekly shop?'

'Yes.'

'Do you ever refuse them?

'In my ten years as abbot here I haven't turned down a single request.'

'So what's the point, if you don't mind my asking?'

'Not at all. There are three Benedictine vows. Stability, obedience and *conversatio morum*.'

'What is that last one? What does it mean?' Ottey asked.

'*Conversatio morum*, well it's been open to interpretation over the years but I think the easiest way to explain it is that it's fidelity to the monastic way of life,' he replied.

'Got it.'

'St Benedict says the first degree of humility is obedience. This humility comes with the asking of permission. As father of the community St Benedict says, "*Christi agere vices in monasierio creditor.*" I am the representative of Christ here at the abbey. To obey me is to obey Christ.'

'And did Brother Dominic ask permission to leave before he went missing?'

'He did not,' replied the abbot quietly. 'Which in the light of what has happened confirms, I think, he didn't leave of his own free will.'

'Why do you use nail scissors?' Cross asked Brother Thomas, who was now sharpening the blades of a very old manual lawnmower in a corner of the courtyard. He was using a sharpening stone slowly and methodically down the length of each blade. Cross noticed the lawnmower might be old, but it was very well maintained.

'It's more precise. Easier to cut individual blades of grass,' replied the monk without looking up.

'Why cut individual blades?'

'For more precision,' he said with a hint of irritation, as if the answer was obvious.

'Did you know Brother Dominic?'

'How could I not? There were but ten of us.'

Cross realised that he was asking questions pro forma and should stop. They obviously all knew Dominic. He was mildly irritated. With himself.

'I'm a policeman,' he said. At this the monk looked up, shielding his eyes against the sun, and gave Cross a good inspection.

'I know. But you don't look like a policeman.'

'What do policemen usually look like?' Cross asked.

'That is a good question, and now you've asked it, I don't actually know.'

Cross got to his knees and with his eyes at grass level, looked down the length of the lawn.

'Almost perfect,' he commented.

'Almost?' asked Thomas, surprised. Cross stood up and walked towards the end of the lawn and pointed at the edge.

'You have a few unruly blades just here.'

The monk looked troubled, got up and immediately came over. He examined the area Cross had pointed to.

'Oh yes,' he said, gratefully. 'You have a good eye.' He got onto his knees and cut the offending stalks. 'Brother Dominic worked in the bookbindery and with the hives.'

'So I believe.'

'Well if you know that, I have nothing to add.'

'Why?'

'Because that's all I know about him.'

'Brother John said he was very popular in the community.'

'He was helpful to those who needed it, yes,' the monk agreed.

'Did you ever need his help?'

Thomas thought about this for a moment, giving it serious consideration.

'No,' he said and returned to his mower at the other end of the lawn.

6

The bookbindery was in an outbuilding a little further down the lane from the abbey house. It was a small stone building as old as the abbey itself, so probably mid-nineteenth century. A slate plaque by the side of the door was engraved in gold lettering, proclaiming it to be the Bookbindery. Cross knocked and waited for a response. There was none. He knocked again.

'Come,' said a voice from within.

Cross opened the door and went in. The voice inside belonged to Brother William, the young monk who had left the refectory in distress when they told the community about Brother Dominic's murder.

'Brother William.'

'Detective, good morning,' Brother William said quietly. 'How can I help?'

'I'm familiarising myself with the abbey and the community,' Cross replied.

'Of course.'

'Don't let me interrupt your work.'

'Are you sure? Thank you. I am a little behind, now that I'm on my own.' Cross noticed the monk take a small, sharp intake of breath as he said this.

The room was quite large with another door at the back. It was slightly open and Cross could see that the room beyond was filled with supplies. There was a lot of equipment crammed into the main room, which gave it the impression of being a lot smaller than it actually was. Bookbinding tools hung on one wall which had been covered in pegboard for that purpose. It reminded

Cross of his father's workshop walls when he was young. All the tools here were old and had the unique patina brought about by regular use, particularly around the handles and other areas where they had been frequently held. On one section of the wall hung a collection of wooden-handled embossing tools together with various chisels. Cross, as usual, quickly scanned them to see if any were missing. But those that weren't on the wall were on the table, obviously in use. His father had once made a joke about how Cross always glanced around any new room they went into as if he was looking for a murder weapon. It was true of him when at work, though. The embossers had small wheels on each end with different, intricate patterns. There was a large wooden press that looked like it could be Victorian, and a guillotine. Several sheets of paper were stored in deep, shallow shelves, as well as various sheets of leather in differing colours. The room smelled of leather, glue and paper. It had an air of quiet industry. There were also metal racks on which large pieces of marbled paper were drying. These were the patterned papers that often adorned the inside covers of books. Cross had always imagined that with most books such paper was mass-produced on printers, not made in the traditional way, individually by hand.

William poured a thick, glutinous clear liquid into a shallow metal tray.

'So, you do your own marbling?' Cross asked with sudden interest.

'We do.'

'Is that size?' Cross asked, referring to the liquid.

'It is.'

'Do you buy the size solution?'

'No, we make our own,' the monk replied, pointing to a tall white plastic bucket which contained what looked like dried vegetation and moss. 'It's organic Carrageenan Irish moss. We boil it down with water to make the size.'

Cross examined the moss carefully, feeling its texture with his fingers.

'Do you need to talk to me about Dom?' William asked.

'I do,' Cross replied, immediately noting the abbreviation of Dominic's name and no 'Brother' prefix. No one else had used it. 'But I've never seen paper marbling done by hand before. I would like to watch.'

If Brother William was taken aback by the almost childish insistence of the request, he didn't show it. But while Cross was indeed interested in the process, it was also a useful way of observing this young monk a little closer.

'Of course,' he replied affably.

He picked up a pot of blue ink and dipped a brush into it. He carefully flicked drops of ink into the size solution. The blue drops sat in small circles in the liquid, like oil in water. William followed this with green ink, then black and red. He took a thin piece of wood, which looked like a knitting needle, and drew it through the solution from side to side. The dots of ink began to form patterned lines. Finally, he took a long wooden industrial 'comb' and pulled it through the whole solution. A beautiful, intricate pattern emerged. Cross watched, fascinated, as the monk took a large piece of paper and laid it gently across the surface of the solution. He ran a palette knife across the paper, gently, and noticed Cross paying close attention.

'This is to remove any potential air bubbles,' he informed him. He then pulled the paper carefully from the surface of the solution and held it up. It was a beautifully symmetrical yet complex pattern.

'It's like a work of art. I feel I should applaud,' said Cross, genuinely impressed.

'That would be a first,' William replied, laughing.

'In that case,' said Cross, clapping enthusiastically. Such was his passion and fervour that it was a little embarrassing for the young monk. It also went on a little longer than perhaps was necessary. Someone of a less charitable nature might have thought the policeman was being ironic, but he wasn't.

'I'm not sure what I find more fascinating, the end product or the process,' said Cross.

'Then perhaps it's a combination of both,' replied William as he laid the sheet out on a drying rack.

'Presumably every sheet you do is unique?'

'Absolutely. Completely individual. Unrepeatable. Like DNA,' said William.

'What makes you say that?' asked Cross.

'Because like DNA each pattern, each sheet, is as you say completely unique.'

'That's an interesting thought. That a hand-marbled page in a book makes that book in itself, by virtue of the paper, unique. What if you're doing a series of books?'

'If we need more than one sheet then we'll—I'll,' he corrected himself, 'use the same density of solution, the same colour inks, obviously, and replicate the pattern as best I can. It'll be different, but not so much to the untrained eye. On close inspection, though, you'd see marked differences.'

Cross stored this information away, as he always did in the knowledge that it might well come in useful at some unknown point in the future.

'You called Brother Dominic "Dom". Why?' he asked.

'I don't know.'

'No one else does,' Cross went on.

'Probably laziness. We worked together every day. Dom is quicker than Brother Dominic,' replied William.

'So, a matter of efficiency rather than endearment?'

'What exactly are you implying?'

'I'm not implying anything. It's a simple question.'

'We're Benedictine monks, DS Cross.'

'How did he refer to you when you were working together every day?' William didn't answer. 'As Will, perhaps?'

'On occasion, yes.'

'Another abbreviation. Does anyone else in the community refer to you in the same way?'

'No. What's your point?' the monk asked.

'You sound a little defensive, Brother William.'

'Because you seem to be implying something.'

'I noticed how upset you were when the father abbot broke the news of Brother Dominic's murder,' Cross went on, ignoring him.

'I was. But no more than anyone else. It was very upsetting news.'

'More in the sense that you had to leave the refectory.'

'I needed air. I felt faint. Sick.'

'That would've been the shock,' said Cross.

'I suppose it was.'

'How long have you been here? In the monastery?'

'Six years.'

'Did you find it an easy transition?'

'From what?'

Cross saw the monk was getting irritated, but didn't know whether he was just an irritable individual, or whether he didn't like being questioned.

'Everyday, conventional life. The comfort, relationships. Did you have any relationships before you entered the monastery?'

'Well, I had family, obviously.'

'I meant romantic, sexual.'

'I have left that life behind, Sergeant.'

'So, you did have relationships? I've often wondered that about monks. Whether the abstention from such relationships is the most difficult thing about joining an order. The vow of chastity.'

'What is it you're after here, Sergeant?'

'Nothing. I'm just curious.'

'And what has your curiosity got to do with Brother Dominic's murder?'

'My curiosity? Well, I would say everything, wouldn't you? I would say the chances of our finding Brother Dominic's killer rely entirely on my curiosity.'

'Of course.'

'He was older than you,' Cross observed.

The young man faltered at the reference to his friend in the past.

'He was. You could say he was my mentor. He took me under his wing when I was a novice. Counselled and guided me as I got used to life here. Then I became his bookbinding apprentice.'

'Brother Dominic occasionally left the monastery for work. Was that to do with the bookbinding business?'

'Yes, sometimes to view a collection of books that might need restoration. He'd like to see a collection in situ to ascertain what conditions they'd been kept in.'

'Humidity, sunlight, central heating?' asked Cross.

'That kind of thing, exactly. But in the last few years he'd become known for his expertise in the valuation of rare books – particularly ecclesiastical. It became something of a speciality. It was often easier to go and see them where they were rather than have them sent here.'

Cross nodded slowly. 'I would like to talk to you further about your friend.'

'Why do you say it like that?'

'I'm not sure how else to say it,' replied Cross. The monk nodded as if consoling himself that he was overreacting. Cross turned to leave.

'Why would anyone want to do this to him? Do you have any idea?' William asked.

'Not a clue. Literally,' he replied and left.

Cross's last port of call was the abbey office where Brother Dominic often worked. A monk in his fifties was in there sitting at the desk which had the computer. His hair was thick and slightly wavy without a hint of grey. As he was a monk Cross assumed this dark thatch to be natural. He seemed familiar and Cross tried to work out why. Then it suddenly came to him. With his thick eyebrows all he needed was a thick moustache and he'd be a dead ringer for Groucho Marx. This was Father Magnus.

'I've had to take over the abbey email correspondence until we assign another monk to it. It was Brother Dominic's domain, really. As were all things computer-related,' he said.

'Is that where he sat?' Cross asked.

'Yes,' said Father Magnus immediately getting up.

'I need to have a look around,' Cross said in a way which suggested he wasn't asking permission, merely informing the monk what he was about to do.

'Yes, of course. Would you like me to leave?'

'No,' Cross replied. He busied himself looking at the email accounts that were open. There were only two, the abbey account and another for the abbot. That was it.

'I need to make a copy of all the email correspondence so it can be examined.'

'Of course,' replied the monk.

Cross inserted a USB into the back of the computer and started downloading all of the email correspondence. He would hand it over to Mackenzie to go through thoroughly. While this was happening, he looked through the drawers in the desk. They were filled with various office essentials. Envelopes, headed notepaper, a large book of stamps, a stapler. It was all very ordered and well organised which Cross instinctively approved of. He lifted up the mouse pad and examined it. He then reached under the desk and felt around with his hand. He stopped as he found what felt like a piece of paper. He pulled it off. It was a faded post-it note. On it was written a series of letters and numbers. He showed them to Father Magnus.

'Does this mean anything to you?' Cross asked.

Father Magnus read the sequence out, '"URSM02116ste2011". No, it means nothing to me.'

'I need to take it,' said Cross.

'No, of course.'

'You should write it down so you have a copy.'

The monk did so.

Cross put it into an evidence bag.

'What is it?' the monk asked.

'It looks like a password to me,' Cross replied.

'For what?' the monk asked.

'Good question,' came the reply. 'Where is the safe? The one the auction house supplied?'

Father Magnus opened a cupboard to reveal the safe.

'Is there anything in there at the moment?' Cross asked.

'I'm not sure. Only Brother Dominic used it for the occasional valuable text.'

'Do you know the combination?'

'I have it somewhere.'

He went back to his desk and consulted a ledger. He then came back and opened the safe. There was nothing inside.

7

There had been a seismic change in George Cross's life recently. One he had major reservations about. In fact the whole thing made him quite uncomfortable. It was the re-emergence of his mother in his life. She had left him and his father Raymond when George was five years old. Her turning up in Bristol had, in truth, been a consequence of his own making. Throughout his life he'd always believed that she left them because of him and he wanted to discover if this was indeed true. He knew he had to have been a difficult and puzzling child, as he was equally cognisant now, that he was a difficult and puzzling adult to many. He had a late diagnosis of Asperger's syndrome – or Autism Spectrum Condition, as it was now known. Diagnoses hadn't been made in the UK until the mid-nineties. Up until that point people had just perceived him as odd, antisocial and awkward. People still felt that about him. But they now had a name to put to it. A condition that meant they could understand why he was the way he was. It seemed to give people a small amount of comfort. It was as if they could understand his behaviour now, and to some extent tolerate it. Not all the time, of course. But it was a marked improvement from the way he'd been treated as a teenager and in his first years in the police force.

Cross had also uncovered the truth of his upbringing, which was that Christine had left because his father was in a relationship with another man at work. She couldn't accept it and who could blame her, thought George. She didn't want it to be made public and ruin Raymond and his lover's lives, particularly at their workplace. As George seemed so much more at ease with his father, and Raymond had such a way with him, she thought it best she left George with him. When George had discovered this, he discussed it with his father. Raymond was filled with remorse and regret that he'd never told him the truth. George told him he had no need to be. He himself was just relieved that he'd got to the truth of it after all these years. He was surprised just how relieved he was. Ottey told him this meant it had been bothering him a lot more than he'd known and for a lot longer than he realised.

But there was an unexpected consequence from this discovery which he was still coming to terms with. There was now another person in his tiny social circle. His mother. Because this circle was so small anyway, the introduction of a new member had a huge effect on the balance of it. She now wanted to meet regularly. This discombobulated him. He had his routine. A routine it was fair to say he had developed over time and one he adhered to strictly. He now felt an unwelcome sense of obligation to see her, which made him stressed. Stephen, the priest, had come up with a solution which proved acceptable to them all. Christine would come to one of George's organ practices every month. This suited George perfectly as it didn't actually affect anything in his schedule and, what was more, he wouldn't be on his own with her. Stephen would be there as a chaperone. She had originally wanted to drop in whenever convenient. But George needed specificity and regularity. He didn't want it to be more frequent as these practices were when he could free his mind from work or whatever else was preoccupying him. It was a peaceful time when he could be alone. Stephen described it once as almost being meditative for George. To which he replied that Stephen obviously had no idea how difficult it was to play the organ.

So, the first Thursday of every month was settled on and Christine duly turned up, sat with Stephen and listened to her son play. Tonight, George had come straight from St Eustace's Abbey and was in a contemplative mood. He decided to learn some of Benoit's devotional pieces for the organ and was particularly taken by number 32. It was reflective and soothing and it wasn't long before he'd mastered it. He felt it perfectly encapsulated his current state of mind.

They sat in the parsonage afterwards and drank tea, as had become the new routine. Christine had brought down some cupcakes she'd baked. George had automatically declined the offer of one without even thinking about it. A habit which Ottey told him he needed to change, because he was missing out on things. It was only after Stephen exclaimed his approval for the chocolate offerings that he changed his mind. As he bit cautiously into one Christine explained that she'd made cupcakes because they were individual, and she'd thought that George would prefer that to a cake they had to share.

'What do you think?' Stephen asked.

'It's extremely good. Better than yours,' Cross replied with characteristic candour.

'Oh good. I love baking,' said Christine. 'You'll have to tell me all of your favourite things and I can make them for you.'

'Stephen is actually a very creditable baker,' Cross told her.

'Really? I didn't know that,' Christine replied.

'It's a guilty pleasure. I bake for the congregation,' said the priest.

'That's why he has better numbers than the other parishes. They come for the cake,' Cross told her seriously, as he actually believed it to be true.

'I like to think they come for the sermons,' Stephen said defensively.

'Of course you do. But the truth is more likely to be that they come for a slice of lemon drizzle rather than a passage from the Corinthians,' replied Cross finishing his cupcake off.

'Would you like another?' Christine asked hopefully.

'No.'

'Very well,' she said, disappointed.

'But if you have any to spare, I'll take some home,' Cross went on.

'Of course.'

'Beautiful pieces tonight, George. Were they new? I didn't recognise them,' said Stephen.

'Paul Benoit. Dom Paul Benoit, to be accurate. He was a Benedictine monk who composed as a form of prayer. It was between him and God, he said. He didn't do a single public performance during his life,' Cross replied.

'Really? Why was that?' Stephen asked.

'He was quite shy and sensitive. Not unusual I would've thought in a monk. But he was also well known for being quite awkward socially and had problems relating to others. People perceived him as being difficult and aloof at times.'

Stephen and Christine couldn't help but look at each other. An embarrassed silence filled the room. George finally ended it.

'Sound familiar?' he asked them innocently. They couldn't answer, not knowing which way to go with this. Was he being facetious?

'He was obsessed with organ music, plants and nature. He even set up a small weather station at his monastery, apparently. Died in 1979.'

'Fascinating,' was all Stephen could offer up.

'His assistant wrote in his biography, '*En définitive, Dom Benoît ne fut jamais rien d'autre qu'un enfant... Il avait une âme d'enfant, limpide, naïve et candide*,' George quoted from memory.

'"In the end, Dom Benoît was never anything other than a child... He had a child's soul, pure, naive and innocent",' Christine translated.

'You speak French,' George observed, surprised.

'I do. And Spanish. I studied languages after I left, and became a teacher,' she replied.

'I see. Did you ever remarry?' George asked.

'I did.'

There was a pause which hung heavy in the air. Stephen and

George thinking the same thing but not wanting to ask. In the end she answered without needing to be asked.

'I didn't have any more children.'

'Was that because you couldn't risk having another one like me?' George asked.

'No!' she answered, offended. 'By the time I remarried it was too late. I was too old. And for what it's worth I would've been delighted to have had another child like you, George.'

'Where is your husband now?' George asked, ignoring this.

'In a home. He has dementia,' she replied.

Cross said nothing.

'I'm so sorry, Christine. You never told me that,' said Stephen.

'I was wondering on the way over whether you were working on this awful case with the murdered monk?' said Christine, wanting to move the conversation on.

'I am,' he replied without going any further.

'It's a terrible thing. Who would want to do that to a monk?' she went on. Why did everyone keep asking the wrong question? George thought to himself.

'It doesn't make any sense,' Stephen added.

'Does murder ever make any sense?' asked Christine.

'No, I suppose not. What I'm trying to say is that you can understand the why sometimes, however wrong it might be. There was that killing of a parish priest by a parishioner with mental health problems. But a parish priest by definition is interacting with people all the time. So it's possible to see the how. But a monk who spends his time in seclusion...' said Stephen.

'What do you think, George?' asked his mother.

'It has to be someone he's either been in contact with recently or it's to do with his past,' he replied.

'Have you ruled out a crazed Satanist?' asked Stephen.

'No, I hadn't considered it in the first place. Interesting thought, though. Do you come across them a lot in your line of work?' George asked, perfectly seriously.

'No, but I imagine they exist. The very idea of religion upsets and offends a lot of people.'

'What was his past?' asked Christine.

'We have no idea. His past identity, past life and family are as yet all unknown.'

'Gosh. So where do you begin?' asked Stephen.

'I have to go,' said George, suddenly uncomfortable. He was unsettled by this reminder of the size of the task ahead.

George walked his mother to her car. She turned to kiss him goodbye but he withdrew before she could.

'Thank you for walking me to my car and for playing so beautifully,' she said.

He nodded awkwardly.

'I'll see you next month,' she went on. He perceived this as a valedictory statement so turned away, wheeled his bike for a few yards then got on it.

'His doctor would know,' she said. He turned back to her. 'The monk. Monks get ill, don't they? They have to have a doctor. He'd have his medical history. You could track him down through his NHS number.'

Cross thought about this for a moment, then cycled away without a word.

8

Cross was annoyed when he got into work the next morning. Not just with himself but with everyone else in the unit. Doctors' records. A basic, fundamental line of enquiry at the beginning of an investigation when it came to identifying a victim. How had they missed it? Had they all been taken in by the somehow otherworldly nature of monks? That they didn't need recourse to something as mundane as a GP?

'George, it's a small slip at the beginning of an investigation. It's no big deal,' Ottey tried to reassure him, as they assembled in the open area for a meeting with Carson. But he was in a funk. How could the entire unit have failed to do something so fundamentally basic as checking a victim's health records? People seemed incapable of grasping the importance of such minutiae in a case like this.

'Sorry you've had to come in on Good Friday, but it is what it is. Almost appropriate, you might say,' said Carson, addressing the room.

'Why appropriate?' asked Cross.

Carson was about to answer but thought better of it.

'So, we think we're looking at his former life. Pre-monk existence,' he went on.

'Yes, but it doesn't mean we ignore his recent life as a monk,' said Cross.

'I thought we'd ruled that out.'

'We haven't ruled anything out as such,' said Cross. 'What I am trying to say is we need to look at his monastic life because it is more than likely that something has happened recently which led to his death. Something different. Something out of the ordinary, which hasn't happened before, which is a link to the murder.' He was normally reticent to speak out in meetings but his annoyance that morning spurred him into it.

'Okay…' said Carson in the way that normally meant he didn't understand what had just been said but didn't want to admit to it. 'So, lots of questions. Plan of action, George?'

Cross handed a sheet to Ottey.

'Okay,' she began. 'We need to continue the canvass of the Goblin Combe area. Joggers, dog walkers, anyone who regularly uses the area. George and I will continue talking to the brothers at the abbey. Also, anyone who has interacted with the abbey over the last few months. The road up to the abbey was resurfaced in the last few months. We need to get hold of the contractors. As we all know we should have ascertained which local GP the monks use. I would've thought they probably all go to the same one but let's find out and get hold of Brother Dominic's medical records.' Cross couldn't help shaking his head at this reminder of their basic slip.

'I can do that,' Alice Mackenzie, a young police staffer volunteered quickly. Mackenzie enjoyed her job so much more when working with Cross and Ottey, rather than any other of the detectives. Privately she'd come to think of them as something of a dream team in the MCU.

'Good. Once we have that we can do a deep dive into his past life. Track down any family, previous employers, friends, perhaps. At present we only have a deposition site. Not a crime site. Forensics are still there,' said Carson bringing the meeting to an end.

Cross wanted to talk to the misper team who had been looking into Brother Dominic's disappearance. They had obviously only been working for a couple of days, but to him that meant they were still ahead of the MCU, even if only by forty-eight hours. Ottey arranged a meeting with the head of the team. DI Torquil Scott not only outranked them both, but he was the best friend of DI Johnny Campbell who had recently made an official complaint against Cross. It hadn't been upheld, but it had resulted in Campbell requesting a transfer.

'Don't expect flowers and chocolates from this guy,' Ottey warned him.

'Why would he bring gifts? I don't even know him,' asked Cross.

'He's Campbell's best mate,' Ottey replied, ignoring his response.

Cross was still at a loss as to what she meant. He hadn't done anything wrong to DI Campbell, except showing him up on a murder case. Campbell had quickly dismissed it as a drug overdose and said that there was nothing for the police to investigate. His nose was thoroughly put out of joint when Cross proved the young woman had been murdered.

Scott could easily have been a manager in a local building society or insurance company. He was dressed smartly in a nondescript inexpensive suit, shirt and tie. He had none of the common machismo swagger of some police inspectors. He wore a strong aftershave that came into a room before him, announced itself loudly, then refused to leave. Some detectives liberally applied eau de cologne when they hadn't had time to shower. They just changed their shirts and sprinkled water under their arms. A 'French shower' was how Raymond had once described it to Cross. But Scott looked clean and well presented. He also looked like a nine-to-fiver to Cross.

'Brother Dominic apparently went missing on Friday the thirty-first of March but wasn't reported missing for a further three days on Monday the third of April when we began an investigation,' he said.

'Where did you start?' asked Cross.

There was a momentary pause as if DI Scott felt he'd been

interrupted and wanted Cross to know he didn't like it. He was wasting his time, as it flew straight over Cross's head.

'At the monastery, obviously,' he answered, looking at Ottey, not Cross. 'We interviewed all the monks.'

'Including Brother Thomas?' asked Cross, breaking in again. Scott looked through his notebook, which pleased Cross. It showed the man was interested in being accurate.

'No. I remember him. Bit strange that one,' he said, followed immediately by, 'Sorry,' directed at Cross.

'What for?' Cross asked.

Scott looked at Ottey who, although she was beginning to warm to the man, couldn't help him out.

'Nothing,' replied Scott.

'Any unusual visitors for Brother Dominic in the weeks before he went missing?' Cross went on.

'No, no visitors outside of his normal business. However, they do have two Sunday masses which the public attend. We don't know if he spoke to anyone at any of these. The abbot said he didn't have much to do with the public as he wasn't a parish priest,' replied Scott.

'Did he leave the abbey?' asked Ottey.

'Only for the usual abbey weekly shop. Always at Sainsbury's in Roynon Way, Cheddar.'

'How did he get there?' asked Cross.

'He was driven by his usual volunteer, Ursula Mead.'

'Did she go into the store with him?' asked Cross.

'No. He preferred to go alone,' he replied after consulting his notes again.

'She didn't do a shop of her own at the same time?' asked Ottey with a single mother of two's instinctive sense of efficient time management.

'Not enough room in the car, apparently,' replied Scott.

'Was he in his habit?' asked Cross.

'No, thanks to social media. People started photographing

his trolley and posting it on the internet with comments about what the monks were eating that week. The abbot was unhappy. It was intrusive. So, he told Brother Dominic to wear normal clothes,' replied Scott.

'People really took photographs of his trolley? Unbelievable,' commented Ottey.

'So, he could have been approached by someone in the supermarket?' asked Cross.

'If they knew what he looked like well enough. I mean, not in his usual monk garb. But that also seems unlikely,' said Scott.

'Do you have any idea how he left the abbey the day he went missing? Whether he walked out? Was driven out? Taken by force?' asked Cross.

'We do not. He was last seen at four thirty. He wasn't at vespers that evening. They checked his room to see if he was there. He wasn't. They didn't call the police till they were sure he was missing a few days later,' Scott summed up.

They sat there in silence for a while.

'Look, I'll be honest with you. We came up short on this one.'

'To be fair you only had two days. I wouldn't beat yourself up,' Ottey interjected.

'I know, but these are the ones that really hurt,' Scott said mournfully.

'I can understand that,' said Ottey sympathetically. 'But you didn't take him and kill him, sir.'

'If there's anything we can do, please ask.'

'Oh, I will,' said Cross, unaware that it sounded implicitly critical.

Scott got up to leave.

'Johnny Campbell's a good friend of mine. Best man at my wedding. Having said that, he's always been a little too quick to take the easy option. For what it's worth, you did well to call him out, DS Cross. Might even have done him a favour,' Scott said and left.

9

'D o we have a cause of death?' asked Cross.
He and Ottey were at the mortuary checking in with
the forensic pathologist, Dr Clare Hawkins. They stood with the
body of the monk on the surgical table in between them. Clare
was in the middle of stitching up the large Y incision she'd made
a couple of days before.

'Cause of death is blunt-force trauma to the skull. The blow
was from something with a tortile edge,' Clare began.

'Do you mean twisted like a poker?' asked Ottey quickly
before Cross explained to her what tortile meant. She could see
his obvious disappointment out of the corner of her eye.

'Possibly, but I can't be certain at this stage. I initially thought
cause of death could be hypovolemic shock, he'd lost so much
blood. The extent of broken bones in his body is quite horrifying.
Broken ribs, both legs below the knee, broken cheekbone,
fractured eye socket,' Clare said.

Cross had noticed something.

'May I...' he asked but Clare was already holding out a pair
of latex gloves. He put them on and then looked closely at the
dead man's jawline. He moved the head gently to one side.

'Yes, I noticed that,' said Clare. She then held a small digital
camera close to Dominic's face. An image of the jawline appeared
on a monitor at the end of the surgical table. There was an
indentation and slight pattern in the bruising.

'I thought it might have been a knuckleduster but on closer
inspection it appears to be a large ring. Like a signet ring or

sovereign. There's the outline of another right next to it so whoever did this had a predilection for finger jewellery.'

'Why would someone want to do this to a monk?' Clare's assistant said, almost thinking aloud.

'That is exactly the right question,' said Cross. 'Once you get beyond the natural outrage of this being done to a man of the cloth, it is that very question that is the most relevant and will lead us to his killer.'

This had the unintentional effect of making the assistant quite pleased with herself.

'Or killers,' said Clare.

'A good qualification. Do you have any medical evidence to back it up?'

'I don't. It just would seem to make more sense. What I do know is that there will have been a lot of blood at the crime scene,' Clare answered.

'Which will have been cleared up by now,' Ottey pointed out.

'Yes, but with such a volume there's a chance there will be traces left, however thorough they were,' said Cross. 'And at the moment, other than the probability that wherever it happened was nearer Goblin Combe than Cheddar Gorge, we have nothing to go on.'

Cross and Ottey went back to the deposition site, the only crime scene they had at present. A number of crime scene examiners were still there gathering what evidence they could. They were taking samples of the grass in the surrounding area and the vegetation that had been flattened by Dominic's body. They made notes of the adjacent species of trees, flowers and fauna as well as taking extensive photographs. A footpath ran alongside the ditch in the area of woodland his body had been found. There had been some rain in the area over the last few days. A footprint had been found near the body and a partial tyre impression. Swift was making copious detailed notes in his tiny, neat handwriting. They walked over to him.

'Morning!' he greeted them cheerfully. Ottey often thought his cheery demeanour was at odds with his deliberately curated Goth appearance. All of this was somehow exaggerated because of his height.

'Morning,' Ottey replied for them.

'What have you found?' asked Cross, bypassing any social niceties.

'Well, if you look here you'll notice there are tyre tracks leading into the ditch where the body was located. I think he came from an easterly direction, lost control of the vehicle somehow, which then ended up in the ditch, depositing the body,' Swift informed them. 'Having said that, the tyre tracks lead straight into the ditch.'

'What does that mean?' asked Ottey.

'It opens up the possibility that it was driven straight into the ditch,' said Cross.

'Exactly. Unless the steering failed which is something we won't know till we get hold of the vehicle,' replied Swift.

'This path is too small for a normal-sized vehicle,' Cross commented.

'Yeah, particularly as it seems to have managed a three-point turn to come back this way when they'd got it back out of the ditch. I think from the look of the tyre print and another that has passed over it, it was probably a quad bike pulling a trailer. Pretty much every farm and estate has them these days,' said Swift.

Cross then produced a new Ordnance Survey map from his satchel and begin to unfold it. Swift immediately produced an identical one folded open at the correct part.

'I've ringed various places that I think are in the correct range for someone thinking about disposing of a body,' said Swift.

Ottey couldn't help smiling as Cross looked a little put-out.

'Excellent,' he said, quickly folding his own map back up.

'Do you want to swap?' asked Swift holding his out.

'No, I'd like to look on a clean map and make my own list,' Cross replied.

'But thank you,' Ottey said for him.

Cross and Ottey then wandered down the lane away from Swift and the crime scene. They came to the small parking area where they had parked her car. It was on a road called Cleeve Hill Road. It was small but fairly busy.

'Do you think someone took a quad bike onto the main road with a trailer? It's one sure way of attracting attention,' she commented.

'Unless they did it at night,' Cross replied. 'But I think it more probable it came cross-country.'

'Should we get units out to search the adjoining fields? See if there are more tracks?' she asked.

'Aren't those fields just going to be covered in tracks from dozens of working agricultural vehicles?' he replied. 'Having said that, yes, we should.'

They walked on.

'What are you thinking?' she asked.

'There's always a pattern of logic in these situations which never occurs to people when they're planning them. A logic which either in itself gives them away, or gives them away because they break from it.'

It was these patterns and links that appeared to Cross and no one else, when they'd all been looking at the exact same information, that often cracked a case. It used to infuriate Ottey, and still did many of her colleagues. Cross would often come from left field with an oddly shaped, completely unlikely-looking piece of the jigsaw puzzle that they'd all been staring at for weeks, sometimes months, and finish it with a flourish. She now realised that part of her job, if they were to succeed, was to facilitate his ability to do this whenever she could.

As they turned back to the car Ottey found herself thinking how Goblin Combe would now add itself to the list of local beauty spots, landmarks, rivers, buildings and parks that she would never be able to properly enjoy again. So many that were now forever associated with some dreadful crime. There were places she and the girls had had picnics where the image of a corpse, invariably murdered, would appear before her eyes like an optical floater hogging the centre of her vision and getting in the way of everything she was trying to see. She had taken a decision some time ago that these nightmarish tableaux would be only momentarily depressing. If she couldn't manage that, she would have to give up her job, simple as that. Unless she was promoted, of course. Something she felt she was long overdue and had been hinted at by her superiors. But she'd come to believe that this was just a carrot to keep her working with George. An unnecessary one as it turned out, and truth be told the idea of leaving him to fend with a new partner made her uneasy. But then again, the inevitable salary bump that would come with promotion might lessen the pain.

There were three properties bordering the wooded area where Brother Dominic had been found. None of the names of the owners had flagged anything up. Two of them were farms, the other was a conference centre. But uniform had been sent to interview the owners. Both farms used quad bikes with trailers. Neither of them were damaged and the tyre treads didn't match the casts that Swift had taken from the deposition scene. The farmers were immensely cooperative as neither of them liked the idea of such a murder taking place locally. One of them was a churchgoing Catholic who had actually visited the abbey in the past. He found the idea of a monk being abducted and murdered in this way absolutely abhorrent and incomprehensible. They were completely open to the police officers searching their farmland and any outbuildings they had. One also had a small abattoir. Nothing had been found.

The conference centre didn't have any quad bikes but did

use a few golf trolleys to move luggage and guests. The tyres were completely different from the tracks found at the scene. They too were horrified at the murder, but more from a business point of view rather than a compassionate one. They also were completely open to their land and outbuildings being searched. Again, nothing turned up.

10

Ottey and Cross drove to the monastery after their visit to the mortuary and the crime scene. Cross thought Ottey was angry, as she drove in complete silence. Something he'd noticed she always did when angry. Normally, it had to be said, with him. He was fairly sure, though not entirely certain, that this wasn't the case this morning. He wondered whether it was the extent of the injuries Brother Dominic had suffered before he finally succumbed.

They were greeted at the front door of the abbey house by Father Magnus.

'Detectives, we weren't expecting to see you again so soon. Please follow me,' he continued, leading them into the house. They went into a small room just along from the father abbot's office. 'We thought it might be useful if you had a space you could call your own while you were here. So, we've put a couple of desks into our reading room.'

He opened the door to a small library. The walls were lined with bookshelves filled with an orderly collection of books, mostly religious and spiritual. There were two monks inside.

'This is Brother Jude and Brother Benedict,' said Father Magnus. The two monks nodded as their names were mentioned. Brother Jude was polishing two wooden tables as Brother Benedict wiped down the skirtings. There was a Dyson vacuum cleaner in the corner together with a collection of cleaning utensils and liquids.

'There was no need to go to all this trouble,' said Ottey, touched by their efforts.

'It was no trouble. In fact it gave us an excuse to give the room a good spring clean,' explained Father Magnus.

The two monks left with their cleaning equipment. Father Magnus gave Ottey a sheet of paper.

'A list of the members of our community. I've asked Brother Andrew to look after you. He will sit outside and continue with his studies. If you need anything or anyone, please just ask him and he will see to it.'

'Thank you,' replied Ottey.

Father Magnus remained awkwardly where he was, for a moment. Cross read this discomfort as meaning he had something else to ask or say, but that he was embarrassed to do so. He was fairly sure he knew what the monk was too polite to ask.

'Am I right in thinking that you would prefer my colleague not to stray any further than this room on account of her sex?' he asked.

Father Magnus looked taken aback by the directness of this question, but possibly relieved at the same time.

'While there is no rule as such, and St Benedict would have us welcome all regardless of gender, the enclosure has always been a private one. As we are a male order it might be easier, if you wouldn't mind, for you to stay here. You are welcome to join us in the refectory for lunch, and of course in the church if you wish to pray,' said the monk in a way that implied he was desperate not to cause offence.

'Please don't worry. I completely understand,' Ottey replied.

'Bless you. Right, well I'll leave you to it.'

'Perhaps we could start by talking to you, Father Magnus?' Cross suggested.

Father Magnus thought about this for a moment.

'Yes, of course,' he then replied. 'That would make complete sense. Why don't you get yourselves organised and I'll be back in five minutes.'

Ottey looked around the spotless room.

'You have to admit they're going out of their way to accommodate us,' she said.

'Unless they're going out of their way to confine us,' Cross replied.

'You're such a sceptic.'

'We're not paid to give everyone the benefit of the doubt,' he replied.

'I'm basically the administrator of St Eustace's. If it were a small company, I'd be the general manager, I suppose. I ensure the smooth running of the abbey and our work as a parish church,' Father Magnus began.

'You're a parish priest as well as a monk?' Cross asked.

'I am ordained. Correct.'

'But Brother Dominic was not?' asked Cross.

'Also correct.'

'Was that through choice?' Cross went on.

'I suppose so. He never felt he had the calling. He was more comfortable with just the contemplative life,' replied Father Magnus.

'How would you describe him?' asked Ottey.

Father Magnus laughed quietly, affectionately even. 'Dominic was an extraordinary man. In many ways he became the glue that kept this community together, as well as the oil that enabled it to run smoothly. I always thought he would have made a good diplomat or politician. He was quick to see a problem, find a solution and defuse it.'

'It sounds like he will be sorely missed here,' Ottey commented.

'Oh, so greatly. He was devoted to God but also to his fellow man. Not only to us, his brothers here, but anyone who reached out to us,' said Magnus.

'Explain,' said Cross.

'We sometimes take in waifs and strays, as Dominic called them. But also people come here on retreats or to ponder the possibility of taking vows. Dominic was so good with them. He soon became our guest master, in charge of visitors and managing our guests. He was a consummate listener who had the knack of knowing what to say and when to say it. The father abbot joked that it was a waste him not becoming a priest, because he was such an innately good confessor.'

'Do you have a list of people who have stayed here in the last year?' Cross asked.

'Yes, of course.'

'We'll need to see that,' Cross said.

Father Magnus looked momentarily uncomfortable.

'We'd just need to look at it for what we'd call red flags,' explained Ottey. 'People who have had trouble with the police, or a history of violence, criminal links. We wouldn't trouble anyone on the list without consulting you.'

'I'm sure that would be fine in the circumstances. But there are some people who might prefer their stay with us to remain confidential.'

'For what reason?' asked Cross.

The monk laughed gently. 'I knew you'd ask that as soon as I said it. People with personal problems, perhaps. But we'll let you have the list. The trouble is that the person who knew them all best, was Dominic.' He paused as something occurred to him. 'You don't think it could have been one of our visitors? Who killed him?'

'We can't rule anything out this early,' said Cross, doing nothing to mitigate the horror of this idea for the monk.

'Father,' Ottey began, conscious of the fact that Cross wouldn't approve of the question she was about to ask in these circumstances. He didn't approve of it in most situations, feeling it was as worthless as a television journalist asking someone how they felt after some tragedy had befallen them or their family. 'Can you think of anyone who would want to have done this to Brother Dominic?'

'As someone who lives his life trying to see the best in everyone,

I find it inconceivable that anyone could do this to someone else, Sergeant.'

'Of course,' replied Ottey.

'Father Abbot told me about the beating Brother Dominic suffered. Is it possible whoever did this didn't mean to kill him?' asked Father Magnus.

'It's possible,' replied Ottey.

'God forgive them,' the priest said quietly.

'God may forgive them, Father Magnus, but I for one have no intention of doing so,' said Cross firmly.

When they had finished with Father Magnus and he'd left the room, Cross turned to Ottey.

'Even in a situation like this he tries to find the best in someone who has killed a colleague, a friend,' he observed.

'It's kind of wonderful. Maybe the world would be a better place if there were more people like him,' said Ottey thoughtfully.

'We would almost certainly be out of a job,' replied Cross. 'Which might not be such a bad thing,' he reflected.

The rest of the day was spent interviewing the remaining eight monks. Brother William didn't have much to add to what he'd told Cross during his time in the bookbindery. But Ottey did pick up on his defensiveness.

'I know this might sound a little crass, but do you think there might have been something going on there?' she asked Cross.

'In what sense?' he asked.

'Between William and Dominic.'

'It's possible and might go some way to explain the abbot's latent hostility towards us. Brother William is certainly defensive and was even more so yesterday,' Cross replied.

'Did you ask him directly?'

'No. His attitude alerted me to the possibility that it was too soon. But he's not being entirely open with us. That I'm sure of.'

Some of the order seemed to know Dominic better than others but they all had one thing in common: they all liked him. There didn't seem to be the slightest edge to any of their relationships with him. Not even the smallest, irritating, domestic habit irked them. But both of the detectives felt that something was being held back by all of them. There was a certain qualification to the way they answered questions about their late brother. They were all deeply shocked by his murder. This led to Cross asking each of them whether such an act of violence against a man who had devoted his life to God and prayer didn't in any way make them question their faith. The answer was unanimously in the negative but the conviction with which some of them answered varied a little. There was definitely a spiritual struggle going on within some of them. Cross felt the abbey was filled with self-doubt and confused emotions. Hardly surprising, he thought.

'You're a novice, Brother Andrew,' said Ottey.

'I am.'

'This must be the last thing you were expecting to happen here,' she went on.

'Happen here? He wasn't killed in the abbey, was he? I thought he was found in Goblin Combe,' he asked urgently.

The detectives said nothing.

'Do you think he was killed here?' he asked.

'Do you think it a possibility?' Ottey asked.

'No, of course not.'

'Has it caused you to call into question your vocation?' asked Cross.

'Not my vocation as such.'

'Am I right in thinking your tone implies a "but"?'

The young monk paused as if to say out loud what he was thinking might make it more real.

'It's caused me to question my faith overall,' he finally replied.

'That's understandable.'

'I know, right?' he replied in a vernacular which seemed at odds to his monastic appearance. 'What does God mean by it? Why would God let this happen to a man who has dedicated his life to him? Who has lived like this for years to devote himself to God. It makes no sense.' He looked at Cross.

'Religion makes absolutely no sense at all to me,' Cross replied.

'It's a question I've been asking a lot in the last couple of days,' said Ottey.

'Really?' The monk seemed immediately comforted by realising he wasn't alone in thinking this.

'Absolutely,' she replied.

'I have to confess I'm struggling with it,' he said.

'Surely though, sometimes these things have no meaning. They just happen,' said Ottey.

'Everything we do is an act of God,' the monk asserted.

'Including the killing of Brother Dominic?' asked Cross, to which the novice had no response.

The last interview of a long day was with the oldest member of St Eustace's Benedictine community. Father Wolfson was ninety-seven years old and pushed into the room in a wheelchair by Brother Andrew who still looked a little conflicted. Wolfson's entrance was immediately disarming as he flashed them a smile of ill-fitting but gleaming false teeth and gave them a jolly wave. He had large hearing aids on his ears which were made out of flesh-coloured plastic and looked like they had been discontinued long before either of the police officers had been born. With bright impish eyes and a cleft lip there was something magnetic about his presence. Ottey beamed. Cross just looked a little curious.

'Detectives, how nice to meet you, though unfortunate in the circumstances. Having said that, I'm not sure what other circumstances could have brought us together,' Father Wolfson began.

'How long have you been here in this community, Father?' Ottey asked.

'At St Eustace's? Gosh, over sixty years now. Before that I was at Prinknash Abbey.'

'Near Gloucester,' Cross monksplained, needlessly, to Ottey.

'You must have seen a lot of change in that time,' Ottey continued, ignoring her partner.

'Not really, truth be told. The monastery and life here is much as it was when I joined. Except for the people, of course. All of my contemporaries are in our burial ground now, though.'

'Tell us about Brother Dominic,' said Ottey.

But the old monk just continued with his train of thought. 'I always thought the next space in the graveyard would be mine. But now it will be Dominic's. Which is puzzling and odd. What did you ask?'

'Brother Dominic, what was he like?' Ottey repeated.

Father Wolfson smiled as he thought about his late friend.

'Delightful. Helpful, particularly to me lately. It is hard to think of life without him.'

'Which accords with everything else we've heard about him today. Is there anything you think they might have missed?' asked Cross.

'Anything you think might be relevant?' Ottey clarified.

'It's very difficult to think of anything in a monk's life that could be considered relevant to his brutal murder, Sergeant. The two don't really go together,' the monk replied politely.

'Which leads us to the possibility that it might have had nothing to do with his life as a monk, but something to do with his life before he took vows,' Cross suggested.

'Yes, I've thought about that. Unfortunately, I know nothing of his previous life. None of us do and he was someone who chose not to talk about it if the subject was ever broached.'

'In a way that implied he was keeping something secret?' asked Cross.

'No,' replied the monk. 'Just private.'

'You sound very sure of that.'

'When you get to my age it's easy to see those who don't belong here or are here simply because they have something to hide. We've had our fair share. But he wasn't one of them. No, he just chose to leave that life behind him. Some of us do that. Want a clean break. I understand it because I was like that myself,' Father Wolfson said.

'Apparently he wasn't universally welcome in the community at first,' said Cross.

'What exactly do you mean?'

'Someone voted against him staying in the community,' Cross went on.

'Yes, that's true,' Wolfson concurred.

'Do you know who it was?'

'It was a secret ballot,' Father Wolfson replied.

'People talk. Even monks,' said Cross. 'You might've found out later.'

'There was no need. It was me.'

Cross liked his candour and immediately decided the old monk might not be as cautious as the others in answering their questions. Was it a question of his advanced age? he wondered. The frank view and expression of things observed that often came with age.

'Why?'

'Well, I suppose I would have to say I was wrong in hindsight. I just didn't feel this life was for Dominic at the time. I wasn't sure he was ready, and in many ways he wasn't. But he was something of an enigma. He was one of those monks who, although he'd broken away from his old life and the outside world, never lost the air of someone from the outside. If you know what I'm saying.'

'I don't,' replied Cross.

'He always seemed to have his finger on the pulse of the outside world. Took a keen interest in matters outside of these walls, in a way that most of us don't.'

'Even though he'd cut links with his family and former life?' asked Ottey.

'Yes. An interesting puzzle, don't you think? But in the end I was glad he was here for the money, if nothing else.'

'The money?' said Cross.

'Yes. As you can imagine it's difficult to keep an old place like this going. It's hundreds of years old and things begin to fall apart. I sound like I'm talking about myself, don't I?' he joked.

Ottey laughed encouragingly.

'But when things happen, we never have the money to be able to fix them. So, we normally apply to a charitable foundation to get the work done. It occurred to me when I was preparing myself for this interview that over the last fifteen years or so when we've needed funds anonymous gifts have often miraculously appeared to solve the problem.'

'You don't believe in miracles then?' asked Cross.

'Yes, of course I do.'

'But these gifts started to appear from around the time Brother Dominic joined the order,' Cross said.

'Yes, I think so. I joked about it with him once.'

'And what was his answer?'

'He laughed and said it was a coincidence. Which of course it probably was,' he said with a twinkle in his eye.

Cross looked directly at the old monk, considering what to ask next. The monk picked up on it.

'What is it, Sergeant? You should just ask whatever it is you're thinking of asking. Surely that's the whole point of this exercise.'

'My colleague and I are under the impression that there was more to Brother William's relationship with Brother Dominic than meets the eye,' Cross answered.

Wolfson took a long, wise-looking pause before he answered.

'William was in love with Dominic. It's fair to say it had become something of an issue lately.'

'You're being very forthcoming, which can't be said of all of your colleagues,' Cross observed.

'Because your observation makes me think that the two of you are possibly very good at your job. That being honest with you is probably the best way of finding Dominic's killer.'

'This was an open secret in the abbey?' asked Ottey.

'There are no secrets, open or otherwise, in such a small,

closed community. But it had reached a point where action needed to be taken.'

'What sort of action?' asked Cross.

'The kind of action our order is well practised in. Ignoring the problem and simply moving it somewhere else without addressing the root cause.'

'Which is?' Cross persisted.

'A crisis of calling, plain and simple.'

'You don't sound at all disapproving,' Cross observed.

'I am ninety-seven, Sergeant. One comes to understand over such a lengthy lifespan that disapproval is, more often than not, a pointless exercise. Added to which, I have seen this before. It's hardly surprising. We are but small communities living in close proximity to each other.'

'Who have taken a vow of chastity.'

'Indeed, but if vows were easy to abide by, what would be the point of them?'

'I hadn't considered that up until now,' remarked Cross. 'It makes eminent sense.'

'Had the abbot discussed this with William and Dominic?' asked Ottey.

'He had.'

'And what was his view of the situation?' she asked.

'For that you'd have to ask him.'

'Thank you for your honesty, Father,' she said.

'That strikes me as an odd thing to say to a monk,' said Cross, turning to his colleague. 'As if he'd be anything other than honest.'

'Quite so.' Wolfson laughed. 'But as I'm sure you're well aware from your day job, there are ways of being less honest in life which don't necessarily qualify as dishonesty,' he replied mischievously.

'An excellent distinction,' observed Cross.

There was a pause which the monk took to mean the meeting was at an end.

'I'm going to pray for you both. God bless,' he said with a final cheery flourish.

Then, as if by magic, Brother Andrew appeared unsummoned, and wheeled him out.

'I like him,' Ottey commented.

Father Magnus appeared about ten minutes later.

'Will that be all for today, Sergeants?' he asked, his presence indicating that perhaps it was, as far as the abbey was concerned.

Cross looked down at his list of brothers.

'We haven't seen Brother Thomas yet,' he said.

'Brother Thomas said he spoke with you yesterday,' Father Magnus said politely.

'We'd like to speak with him again, in more detail,' said Cross.

'He told me to say that he'd told you all he had that was useful for you to know and that any further conversations would be meaningless.'

'That's for us to decide,' Cross replied.

'He also asked to remind you that the Father Abbot did tell everyone that these interviews were voluntary,' the monk said with perfect good manners.

'Of course, that's no problem,' Ottey interceded.

'If that's all then, I'll leave you. It's not long before vespers,' he said and withdrew.

Ottey looked at Cross. 'Brother Thomas. Read anything into that?' she asked.

'He probably thinks yesterday was sufficient and that he had nothing to add.'

'Or he's hiding something,' she suggested.

Cross said nothing which meant he either thought it a ridiculous suggestion, and was learning not to keep things to himself, or he thought it was a possibility. She didn't push it.

'Something happened here that led directly or indirectly to Brother Dominic's death. If the reason for his death has something to do with his past life, something happened to alert whoever killed him to his existence within these walls. We need to look for something out of his normal routine. A break in the pattern of his monastic life. Something set in motion a chain of events that led to his murder. Finding out what that was would be a good starting point. We should talk to all the monks again and get them to think back over the last few months to try and remember if something happened with Dominic that was out of the ordinary. A visitor. An event. Something that might seem completely normal that is pertinent,' said Cross.

11

Mackenzie and Swift were now in a quasi-committed relationship. They didn't want anyone to know at work, partly – though they'd never said this out loud and certainly not to each other – because they weren't sure how long it would last, but also because they thought it might look unprofessional. Not that Mackenzie was exactly sure what that meant. In fact they were so convincingly cool with each other at work that she often wondered whether anything was going on between them herself. Perhaps she'd just imagined it all.

If they spent the night together, it was always at Swift's 'bat cave', as she referred to it. This was simply because her bed wasn't anywhere near long enough for his never-ending frame. He had an extra-length bed to fix the problem. They tried staying at hers once, but it was a disaster and never mentioned again. Mackenzie herself was only five feet five inches tall so the height difference between them was quite significant. But as she'd said to one of her friends, the height difference between Swift and most of her friends would've been just as significant. It had several unanticipated disadvantages on her part. Taking photographs together was problematic, selfies were out of the question. Kissing while standing, holding hands, even hugging where she often found herself trapped in one of his armpits. Her neck was starting to ache from staring up at him when they were talking. Aside from these hurdles, they did seem compatible and spent most of their time together, laughing.

He lived in a ground-floor flat in Clifton, right next to Clifton College. He'd bought it, he explained to her, because of the ceiling heights of the rooms in these Victorian mansions. They were high enough for him not to feel they were right on top of him and that he might bash his head at any given moment. He obviously hadn't been thinking of the light the living room benefited from with its high windows, as he'd painted all of the walls black. The darkness of the walls was alleviated by the occasional horror movie poster, mostly vampire-themed. She'd put her foot down with the crime scene photographs that were artfully hung on the walls of the bedroom though. Swift had furnished the room with long black leather curtains and insisted on sleeping with them wide open at night and she'd become fed up with the first thing she saw in the morning being a gruesome nineteen-fifties murder scene.

One positive, on the other hand, was that his flat was fastidiously clean. She would later describe it as 'fanatically' clean. Forensically clean might have been a better description. Swift was an obsessive surface wiper-upper. Normally accompanied with a few short sharp sprays of disinfectant, he was constantly cleaning surfaces, particularly when cooking. 'Cleaning down,' he called it, quoting from one of his favourite TV cooking shows. One of his most annoying habits which she really couldn't tolerate was that everything in the flat had its place. This included her coat, her handbag, her shoes. The trouble was, if the things weren't in their ordained place, he would visibly tense up and get stressed until he was able to put them where they belonged. This began to wind her up.

'I can't relax if I'm forever worrying about where things are supposed to go,' she complained.

'Then just put things where they're supposed to be, or back where you found them, and all will be cool,' he replied.

'No, it's a nightmare, it's not rational,' she pointed out. 'It's like an obsession. No wonder you're so in love with George.'

'What are you talking about?'

'You're exactly like him. You just don't have his excuse. And who, by the way, says my shoes go over there, on the right of the

door but not nearest the door, because that's where yours go?'
she asked.

'I do.'

'Why?'

'Because it makes sense.'

'To who?' she asked.

'Me,' he said, picking up the mug of tea she had literally just
finished and taking it over to the dishwasher.

'Couldn't that have waited? We are actually talking,' she
pointed out.

'We're still talking. It didn't stop us,' he replied.

'I can't do this tonight. In fact, any night. I'm off,' she said,
grabbing her coat and leaving.

Swift walked over to the window and looked up into the night
sky to see if there was a full moon. There wasn't, so, to his mind,
there had to be another reason for her unreasonable behaviour.

She didn't stay over for a while after this, and things had
been frosty with them. This gave her enough time to do a deep
dive into the USB of the abbey computer correspondence Cross
had given her. It was fairly predictable and mundane stuff. A lot
of correspondence with Fred Savage, their contractor, recently,
concerning the road resurfacing and estimates for repairs to the
church ceiling. There were changed completion dates, delays
that were always someone else's fault. Additions to the cost
for unseen problems which Savage then made a big deal out of
absorbing himself and not passing on to the abbey. There was
also correspondence from others about funerals, weddings and
christenings which didn't seem to come under Dominic's purview,
but Father Magnus's. There was an unintentionally amusing
email trail with the local bee association. Dominic had started
a successful queen breeding programme, but some of his queens
had mysteriously gone missing. The association had launched a
'full-scale enquiry' into the matter and enlisted the help of one of
their members who was a retired detective. They had eventually
come up with the culprit and wished to know if Dominic wanted

to involve the police. Needless to say he didn't, but the association made a big song and dance about how the thief had been expelled from their association with a lifetime ban.

There was one email which did attract her attention, however. It was from a Martin Bates who worked for a Patrick Murphy; Sir Patrick Murphy, to give him his full title. In this email Bates was asking Dominic to reconsider a valuation he'd made on a fifteenth-century book of hours Murphy had acquired. Mackenzie inferred from the email that this Murphy was a collector of art and religious artefacts. Bates's email was polite but at the same time unequivocally direct in saying that Dominic had made a mistake, the consequences of which were significant. Although there was no overt threat made to Dominic in the email, there was a definite sense of menace in the way it was written. She made a note of it.

A few nights later she was back at the bat cave. She'd finally relented and accepted Swift's imploring invitation for dinner. He was actually a very good cook. Not exactly spontaneous, he followed a recipe to the letter, almost as if it were a scientific experiment. Which, he had told her once, cooking actually was.

'It's just a tasty, more satisfying form of chemistry,' he'd said.

He always adhered to the exact quantities prescribed by the recipe with a frequent use of his digital measuring scales. There was no room for any estimation or, heaven forfend, improvisation.

Swift had lured her back to the flat by promising to mend his ways and chill about where everything went in his flat. He wanted her to feel comfortable and at home. So, she had decided to immediately test this out on her return. She made a point of mischievously picking up things like books and magazines throughout the evening, and putting them down in different places. All the while making sure that he was watching her as she did so. She picked up a vase of flowers he'd bought for the occasion (his flowers of choice were dark purple tulips, so dark they were almost black) and moved them from the kitchen counter to the table, where they were going to eat.

'Oh, I'm sorry. Did you want them where they were?' she asked innocently.

'No, there is fine,' he replied tensely.

'Shall I put them back?' she offered.

'No, no. All good.'

They had a lovely evening, but as her moving-things-for-the-sake-of-it campaign proceeded she began to feel guilty. She could feel he was uptight underneath his carefully curated exterior of calm.

When she left for work the next morning, he declined to go with her. This wasn't unusual if they were both going to the MCU, as they didn't want to be seen arriving for work together. But this morning he was going to the forensics lab. He also seemed a little on edge. So, she kissed him goodbye and left. She then waited for a little while to execute the last part of her carefully conceived plan. After ten minutes she got back out of her car and went back to the flat. He answered the door – they definitely weren't at the her-having-keys-to-his-flat stage of their relationship yet – and was surprised to see her.

'I forgot my phone,' she said.

'Oh,' he replied as nonchalantly as someone does when caught doing something they knew they shouldn't. She picked up her phone from the bookshelf where she'd left it – it was its designated place so she knew he wouldn't notice it – and looked around at the flat. The flowers were back on the counter, all the magazines back in their correct places and piles, the books too.

'I'm surprised you didn't find it when you were putting all the things back in their rightful, correct and "if they don't go there the building will fall down" places,' she said and left. He leaned against the wall and acknowledged defeat.

12

Unsurprisingly the monks at the monastery were all registered at the same local medical practice. Alice managed to track down the practice manager, and despite the fact that it was Easter Monday, persuade her to let her have Dominic's records as well as his National Health Service number. In truth it hadn't taken much persuasion, so shocked was she at his murder. His real name was Alexander Mount. Mackenzie immediately set about trying to track down his life before he entered the monastery. She began by making a note of all the other GPs he'd been registered with in his life. He was forty-five years old, had been in good health all of his life except for asthma and hay fever. He'd lived in London prior to joining St Eustace's fifteen years before and taking the name Brother Dominic Augustus. The MCU now had his date of birth, National Health number and the various general practices he'd been registered with since birth. He'd been born in Macclesfield and lived there as a child and teenager. He'd been registered at a Cambridge practice from the age of eighteen which would seem to imply he might have gone to university there. He'd then registered with a surgery in Stoke Newington in north London.

Ottey and Mackenzie got hold of Alexander's birth certificate then checked census entries in the Macclesfield area. His father had been a lecturer in a local teacher-training college. His mother was a part-time secretary. He had a younger brother Stephen, but no other siblings. Both parents were deceased, having died at what would now be considered a relatively young age, sixty-eight and seventy-one. It didn't take too long for Mackenzie to find his last known address in Stoke Newington. He'd been there right up until the moment he joined the monastery in 2008. The property had been divided into two flats. Dominic lived on the ground floor. Going back to the 2001 electoral register and comparing it to the 2021 register she discovered that different people lived in the two flats now but the neighbours were still there. She gave them a ring.

'The flat upstairs belonged to a young couple, Serena and Mark. They're married now but have moved. Alex lived below them,' said the next-door neighbour, Derek.

'Do you know what happened to him after he sold the flat?' asked Mackenzie.

'I don't. The first I knew of it was when the removals van arrived. I wasn't as close to him as S & M – that was my nickname for them.'

'So you didn't stay in touch with him?'

'I didn't. S & M might have. They lived next door for another five or six years before they moved, got married and had children.'

'Do you have a forwarding address?'

'Are you kidding? Of course I do. I'm old enough to be their father and yet they still call me a friend. Lovely people.'

With his usual impatient need for progress in any kind on a case, Carson wanted them to set up a Zoom meeting with Serena and Mark, but Ottey and Cross wanted to go to London.

'What is it with you two and your road trips all over the place? Am I missing something here? Is there something going on I should know about?' Carson joked.

Whether it was the obvious inappropriateness of his comment or the sheer absurdity of the idea, the ensuing silence made Ottey's ears pop like she was descending too quickly in a plane. Carson's evident foot-in-mouth foolishness had occurred to him just as quickly as everyone else. As he couldn't think of a suitable rejoinder to save what was left of his face quickly enough, he simply turned on his heel and left the room.

Cross wanted to make the trip because, despite the fact that he struggled to relate to people in life generally, he had learned how to read facial expressions in his typically thorough way. He'd had to do this in a way neurotypical people didn't, as it came to them naturally. For him it was an acquired skill, like a second language. As such he had become something of an expert in it. Ottey herself felt it was important to be there because they were going to inform the couple about the loss of a friend, whether or not they had remained in touch. It was near enough policy to do this kind of thing in person.

Serena Birch and her husband Mark now lived in Crouch End with their three children. The house was detached and double-fronted. It had a long kitchen/informal family living room contained within a vast glass extension at the back of the house leading onto the rear garden. Serena took them into the slightly more grown up, formal living room opposite. Two large sofas faced each other. Contemporary, affordable art covered every inch of the walls. Fresh bright red roses in a vase on the coffee table between the sofas drew the eye deliberately from all the surrounding light furnishings. Serena's clothing was as well thought through and put together as the room.

'What a beautiful home,' Ottey commented as she and Cross sat on one of the sofas. Cross had noticed recently that what started as a routine opening conversational gambit from his partner, when interviewing people in their homes, had become increasingly frequent and accompanied by a thorough examination of her surroundings. He wondered why this was.

'Thank you,' Serena replied.

Mark walked in with cups of tea.

'You said that Alex had dropped out of your lives with almost no warning,' Cross began.

'We didn't even know he'd sold the flat,' Serena replied.

'He managed to sell it off market,' Mark explained.

'Then he just vanished. Said he was going to go away for a while. Wouldn't be in touch and that we weren't to worry,' Serena went on.

'Had he seemed unhappy before he left?' asked Ottey.

'Not in the least.'

'I got the feeling things were a little difficult at work,' said Mark.

'Difficult in what way?' asked Cross.

'Well, it was just before the financial crisis, so I think it was just the same as everyone else. Stress about what was coming,' Mark explained.

'But you're telling us he became a monk?' Serena asked in disbelief. 'He's been in a monastery all this time?'

'Yes,' Ottey replied.

'And now he's dead?' she asked rhetorically. 'It's unbelievable.'

Mark now started laughing. His wife looked suitably shocked. But for Cross and Ottey this wasn't an uncommon reaction in situations like this.

'Mark, what are you doing? How is this in any way the least bit funny?' Serena asked.

'Oh come on, it's classic. Absolutely classic Alex. He always did the unexpected, but this takes enigma to another level.' He stopped suddenly. 'I'm sorry, it's not funny, but I know he'd forgive me for laughing.'

'That's true,' Serena agreed quietly. 'Not about his being dead though.'

'No.'

'What makes you say that? That it's classic Alex?' asked Cross.

'Loads of reasons really,' the young woman answered. 'He was different to us and all of our friends. He saw the best in everyone and every situation. He was also amazingly forgiving.'

'You couldn't have an argument with Alex or pick a fight with him. It was impossible. A discussion, yes, but when it got at all heated, he managed to defuse the situation before it turned nasty,' said Mark.

'He had a weirdly spiritual side to him, looking back on it,' said Serena.

'He was quite soulful,' said Mark.

'Very left wing,' added Serena.

'Which was odd considering his job and where he worked,' said Mark.

'Which was what and where?' asked Cross.

'He was a banker,' said Mark.

'In the City,' added Serena.

'Which bank?' asked Ottey.

'Don't know. He never said, or if he did, I can't remember. Darling?' He turned, asking Serena.

'It was one of the really old ones like Hoare's. Family business. Went bust,' she said.

'Cubitt's. That was the bank's name. Cubitt's,' said Mark.

Cross made a note.

'When did this bank fold?' he asked.

'During the financial crisis, like all the other ones,' she replied.

'Probably couldn't get the government to bail them out,' said Mark.

'That was a disgrace,' Serena said sharply.

'What was?' asked Cross.

'The whole government-bailing-out-the-banks thing. It just enabled them to carry on as if nothing had happened and then, when the upturn happened, behave just as badly as they did before.'

'It doesn't surprise me,' said Mark.

'I don't think it surprised any of us,' Ottey commented.

'Sorry, I was thinking about Alex becoming a monk.'

'He does that. Changes the subject when I get onto what he calls one of my pet rants,' said Serena.

'Never had a girlfriend,' said Mark, thinking out loud.

'Or a boyfriend,' added his wife.

'Or boyfriend. Just didn't seem to interest him.'

'Unless he was fabulously discreet,' she pointed out.

'Nor,' said Cross.

'What?' asked Mark as Ottey raised her eyes.

'Nor a boyfriend. Never had a girlfriend nor a boyfriend,' he said quietly, unable to help himself.

'Don't worry, he has what I call grammatical Tourette's,' said Ottey.

'He was a complex character, Alex. You were never really sure what he was thinking,' Serena went on.

'A difficult read,' added Mark.

'Mark always used to say that silence was the most powerful weapon in Alex's armoury.'

'That's true. He had a wonderful way with silence. He could sit there for hours and not say a word,' agreed Mark.

'But it was much worse when he did it in the middle of a conversation with you. You couldn't help but fill in the gaps and invariably sound stupid.'

'You always felt he was judging you,' Mark commented.

'I did,' she agreed.

'But I don't think he was. He was just a great observer of people and things around him,' he said.

'He was a good listener. People seemed to gravitate towards him with their problems, which he often managed to help with, by saying absolutely nothing,' said Serena. Mark laughed at the truth of this statement. 'They'd ramble on, he'd listen as they explained their issue, laid out all the different angles and points of view, play devil's advocate with themselves, before coming up with the answer without his saying a word.'

'They'd then go away thanking him for his brilliant advice when he had in fact said nothing,' added Mark.

'The monks at the abbey said he was a great listener,' said Ottey.

This made Serena start crying. Mark comforted her. They all sat saying nothing as she gathered herself.

'Who on earth would do this to him? To a monk?' she finally said. That question again. But the way she put it made Cross think. Maybe there was validity in the first part of the question. Who would do this to Alex? That was certainly more relevant than asking who would do it to a monk.

'Is there anyone from the time you knew him, before he entered the monastery, who had an issue with Alex, that might lead to them doing this?' asked Cross.

'No,' Serena answered indignantly.

'He just wasn't the type of person who caused or attracted trouble,' said Mark. 'He was a fixer, a conciliator, a defuser.'

'Who were his friends?' asked Ottey.

'Well, us and our friends really,' answered Serena.

'He did have one friend we met. From uni,' said Mark.

'Can you remember who?' asked Ottey.

They looked at each other as if their faces might hold a clue.

'No, sorry,' said Mark.

'No one at work?' Ottey went on.

'It didn't sound like the kind of environment where you made a lot of friends,' Serena commented.

'Quite the opposite, in fact,' said Mark. 'He gave me the impression they were all at each other's throats, which was part of the reason he wanted to leave.'

'That and the hours,' added Serena.

'Did he actually say that?' asked Cross.

'Oh yes, definitely. The hours made it impossible to make friendships. He worked till all hours. At weekends, and often did all-nighters,' said Mark.

'He was working in their new investment division, I think, so the pressure was on to make it work,' said Serena.

'He told us the only reason we were friends was by geographical accident,' said Mark.

'He lived in the downstairs flat,' explained Serena, forgetting that this was how the police had managed to track them down in the first place.

'So, no friends at work. How about enemies? Any issues at the bank?' asked Cross.

'Like I keep saying, it's difficult to think of Alex having enemies anywhere. He just wasn't like that. He was generally so unprovocative and easy-going,' said Mark.

'But he wasn't particularly happy at work,' Ottey confirmed.

'No,' they both said in unison.

'But I would say it was more *with* his work than *at* his work that he was unhappy, if that distinction makes any sense,' Mark qualified.

'It makes complete sense and is a very good distinction,' Cross said.

'He hated it by the end,' said Serena.

'Well, he hated the City as a whole, is more accurate. He loathed what he saw going on there, which is part of why he left I, suppose,' Mark reflected.

'He hated the investment division. He thought it was designed totally for the benefit of the bank rather than their clients,' said Serena.

'Hardly news,' Ottey commented.

'No, but I think it was the extent of the greed that got to him,' Mark pointed out.

'And the vacuousness of the lives those people were leading,' said Serena.

'They were doing nothing, creating nothing, being of no use to anyone other than themselves by making money for themselves out of their clients' wealth,' Mark said.

'How about family?' Cross asked.

'His mother was alive back then, but his father was dead,' Serena replied.

'He had a younger brother, Stephen,' Mark added.

'We met him once. They were so very alike. Wait a minute, wasn't he going to join a seminary?' Serena said.

'That's right. Obviously runs in the family,' Mark joked.

'I always thought Alex would be a godfather to one of our children,' Serena reflected.

'Really?' her husband asked.

'Yes, I think he would have been a good person to have in their lives. A good influence.'

They talked about Alex for a little longer, but it was mostly the nostalgic musings of a couple who were now faced with the death of an old friend and so had a lingering regret that they hadn't stayed in touch. Despite Cross's obvious desire to leave, Ottey let the couple reminisce until they came to a natural conclusion.

Serena showed them to the door.

'He was a little odd, looking back on it. But good odd, if that makes sense,' she said.

'It doesn't,' replied Cross.

'It was almost as if he didn't belong in this world. Maybe the abbey was the best place for him,' she reflected.

'In the circumstances that bring us to see you, I would have to disagree,' said Cross before turning and walking to the car.

Serena was a bit shocked.

'Ignore him,' said Ottey.

'No, he makes a good point,' Serena replied.

'Oh, he makes a good point. Always does. His problem is knowing when to make them and when not to.'

13

Cross was oblivious to the tension in the MCU when he got into work on Wednesday. This was because he always marched through it head down, to avoid any unnecessary social exchanges of a greeting nature. It meant he didn't see all heads turn towards him as he entered the room that particular morning. What he did know, as he traced his path through to his office, was that the unit had fallen unusually quiet. He glanced up as he approached his office and saw Ottey and Mackenzie exchange a look. He knew this look expressed concern. He took it to mean there had been a development in the case. He walked into his office, took off his backpack, raincoat and various high-vis cycling accessories then sat at his desk waiting to be informed of it. Ottey knocked quietly on the door.

'Come in,' he instructed.

She walked in, followed by Mackenzie.

'I recognise that look,' he said. 'It's the one you use when you're going to give a family a bad piece of news about a relative.'

'Alice has come up with something,' Ottey replied.

'I see.'

'I've found Brother Dominic's brother,' said Mackenzie.

'Good,' he replied.

She pushed a piece of paper across the desk for him to read. He picked it up and did so. He said nothing and his face registered no emotion as he digested the information.

'You need to go and tell him,' said Ottey.

'Yes,' he said. He immediately got up and put on his raincoat.

He was about to grab his bike accessories when he thought of something. He turned to Ottey.

'I think you should come as well. In fact, you should tell him. Experience tells us you will handle it with more emotional finesse than me,' he said.

'Sure.'

'Anything else, Alice?' Cross asked.

'A couple of things but they can wait,' she replied.

They drove in silence to the St Paul's area of Bristol and parked up outside Stephen's church. They walked past the sign which proclaimed the name of the church, the list of services and at the bottom the name of the parish priest. Father Stephen Mount. Cross had walked past this sign hundreds of times over the years when he came to practise the organ. But it hadn't occurred to him in the last few days to put two and two together. Stephen *Mount*. This was essentially a product of his lack of belief in coincidence in their work. After all, what were the chances? Even when Serena and Mark had mentioned that Alexander's younger brother would be going to a seminary, it hadn't occurred to him that his friend, the priest Stephen, could be the victim's brother. He also realised in that moment how little he actually knew about him.

'Both of you!' Stephen said cheerfully as he opened the door to the parsonage. 'What an honour, do come in.'

They followed him into the kitchen.

'Can I offer you some tea?' he asked.

'No thank you, Father,' said Ottey.

Stephen looked at Cross who hadn't said a word and wasn't actually looking at him.

'How can I help?' he asked.

'May we sit down?' asked Ottey.

'Yes, of course. I'm sorry. Where are my manners?'

They sat.

'Stephen, do you have a brother?' Ottey.

'I do,' he replied, smiling.

'Alexander?' she asked, almost willing him to say no.

'That's right. Has something happened? George?' He looked at Cross, appealing for an answer.

But Cross just looked down at the table. He wasn't sure how to react in this situation. He was well aware he'd messed up with a lack of tact so many times in the past, in this exact situation, that he felt it better to say nothing and not risk it. But there was something else affecting him. The fact that the brother of their victim was a friend of his. He simply had no idea what to say or how to react.

'I'm really sorry, Father, but Alexander's body was found last week,' Ottey went on.

'Where?'

'Goblin Combe,' she replied.

'The monk...?' he said, almost as if he should have known.

'That's right. When was the last time you saw him?' Ottey asked.

But Stephen didn't answer. Instead, he got up from the table and filled the kettle. He switched it on and left the room.

'Do you think you should go after him?' Ottey asked Cross.

'Whatever for? He's upset,' Cross replied.

Stephen returned about five minutes later.

'I'm sorry. What were you saying?' he asked Ottey.

'I asked when the last time you saw him was.'

'About fifteen years ago. He just disappeared. I wanted to report him missing, but my mother explained that she knew where he was and there was nothing to worry about. I pushed her and she told me he'd decided to devote himself to God. I found a letter from him in her stuff after she died. He talked about renouncing the world and becoming a Benedictine. He wanted to do it completely, so he could truly turn his face fully to the glory of God which, for him, involved turning away from his family,' Stephen said.

'Did that surprise you?' asked Ottey.

'Um, yes and no. He was always more spiritual, more religious than me when we were growing up. His plan was to go to a seminary. I think that's what first made me think about it. I'd always looked up to him. Hero-worshipped him, truth be told.'

'Cutting off your family, that seems a little extreme,' Ottey commented.

'Turning away, rather than cutting off. No more extreme than my choices, Josie. I've turned my back on the idea of ever having a family which is no more extreme than turning your back on the family you already have. And for such a sacred reason. He had a calling. One he couldn't ignore. I can understand that. Where was he a monk?'

'St Eustace's near Cheddar,' Ottey replied.

'I can't believe he was so near to me,' he said.

'Does that upset you?' she asked.

'No, it makes little difference. But I suppose I'd always assumed he'd gone abroad, like Spain, or Italy, Ireland. To make it easier, maybe,' he reflected.

'For him or you?' asked Ottey.

'Oh, for him. Definitely for him,' the priest replied.

The room went silent. Stephen was well aware that Cross hadn't said anything since he'd arrived.

'Is everything all right, George?' Stephen asked.

'I don't know how to answer that question, because things are so obviously not. You should talk to DS Ottey. That's why she's here,' Cross explained.

'George, why don't you forget for a moment that you're my friend and that you're upset by what's happened to my brother. Concentrate on what you're so obviously good at and treat me like any other victim's sibling. I'm going to make us some tea while you think about that,' said Stephen getting up to boil the kettle.

Cross thought about what he'd said for a moment and then shifted gear mentally and looked up.

'You said your brother wanted to go to a seminary,' he began. 'Why didn't he go? What happened?'

'Well, university happened, I think. He went up to Cambridge to read Divinity and then something changed.'

'Did he discover women?' Cross asked.

'Alex was gay, George. But I think he discovered men there, yes.'

'Was there anyone in particular?' asked Ottey.

'Not that I'm aware of. I always thought it was a crisis of faith that led to him swapping subjects. That maybe studying it academically changed his view of religion. Whatever it was, his eyes were opened up to a whole new world he hadn't seen before, and he liked what he saw. He switched course after a year and read mathematics, which was something he'd always loved,' said Stephen.

'But then he became a banker. That's quite a change of direction,' said Ottey.

'It was,' he replied.

'Did he have a plan? An endgame?' asked Cross.

'No,' laughed Stephen. 'He was never much of a planner. He just went with the flow. He became extraordinarily good at making money. Bought a flat and the obligatory Porsche, upgraded later to a black Ferrari. Spent like money was no object. Holidays, clothes.'

'And then he suddenly stopped,' said Cross.

'Yes.'

'In 2008.'

'Yes.'

Cross thought for a moment then said, 'Was it before the crash of 2008 or after it?'

'Before, but he knew it was coming,' Stephen said.

'Maybe that was why,' offered Ottey.

'I don't think so. He was a star player at the bank. I think he would've come through unscathed.'

'This was Cubitt's?' asked Cross.

'That's right. One of the old family ones. Really exclusive, Alex used to brag. You had to have a lot of money just to open an account there. Founded in the seventeen hundreds. Same family was still running it.'

'So he was making a lot of money, owned a flat—'

'Paid cash,' Stephen interrupted.

'—then suddenly stopped?' Cross asked.

'Did a three sixty on a sixpenny piece, as my mother used to say,' Stephen replied.

'That's one heck of a road to Damascus moment,' Ottey commented.

'Isn't it just?' said Stephen.

'It's nothing of the kind. Something happened. He did something or someone else did something which made him leave,' said Cross, thinking out loud.

'Are you saying he was running away from something? Was hiding?' asked Stephen.

'Not necessarily,' Cross replied.

'He could've just had an epiphany,' Ottey suggested.

'Oh, I'm as sure that is the case as I am equally sure something happened to trigger it. It sounds like he was a logical man. He was a mathematician, after all,' Cross went on.

'Who, by the sound of it, was also quite impulsive. Expensive car, lavish spending,' Ottey added.

'How, or why, he ended up becoming a monk is surely neither here nor there when it comes to his being murdered,' said Stephen.

'That is possible,' Cross conceded. 'But it's just as possible that it might be part of a train of events that led to his death.'

Stephen put the teapot and cups and saucers on the table. Cross leapt up.

'We have no time for this. We need to leave,' he stated baldly.

'We're not going anywhere, George. Sit down,' said Ottey calmly.

'We have to get on, DS Ottey,' he remonstrated.

'Another fifteen minutes won't make any difference. We are not leaving Stephen on his own right now,' Ottey explained.

'Why not? We've told him the news. Now we need to get back to work.'

'You go, I'm staying,' she replied.

'But I haven't got my bike,' Cross protested childishly.

Stephen could see he was becoming quite agitated. 'Josie, go. I'll be fine,' he said.

'Nonsense. Call a taxi, George. I'm going to have my tea and talk to Stephen about his brother,' said Ottey, firmly. 'This is why you asked me to come, remember? Because you don't know how to behave in a situation like this, as you are now amply demonstrating.'

Cross was in a pickle as he realised she had a point. This was precisely the type of situation he'd asked her to come along and ensure didn't happen. But he had a desperate need to go and solve this crime. Now.

'George, why don't you go and play the organ?' Stephen suggested.

'I'm on duty. I can't do that. I have to work.'

'You've told me you often have your best thoughts about your work when playing the organ. That it clears your head,' Stephen pointed out.

'Which basically means you're still working,' Ottey said, which seemed to reassure him.

And so Stephen sat and talked about his brother with Ottey as the sound of Mozart and Bach came through the wall from the church.

'It's like having an unreasonable teenager as a work partner sometimes,' said Ottey.

'He has a good soul.'

As the conversation progressed, so the sense of loss seemed to bear down like a heavy mantel on the shoulders of the priest. Ottey found it strange in these situations, where someone hadn't seen a friend or relative for a lengthy period of time, how the knowledge of their death was still devastating. Maybe in a different way from if they'd still been present in their lives, but still shocking. She wondered if it was tinged with feelings of guilt. Certainly regret, she thought.

When they'd finished their tea, Ottey told Stephen they would probably need to speak to him again about his brother. They walked into the church. Cross saw them in the rear-view mirror he'd attached to the organ, so the organist could see the priest during services, and stopped playing. He thought his friend looked a little older, a little greyer than when they'd arrived. He then reflected how often it was they had this effect on people.

They said their goodbyes and as the two detectives walked down the aisle out of the church, the priest walked up to the altar and knelt before it. Cross thought God had a lot of explaining to do to his bereft friend. As he looked at him kneeling, looking vulnerable and a little shrunken, Cross realised he might not be able to comfort people in this situation, whether he knew them or not – it just wasn't in his ken – but what he unquestionably could do was find out the person responsible for their grief. He wouldn't stop until he'd found this killer and had him put away.

14

George arrived at his father's flat later that night for their regular weekly meal. It was always the same. A Chinese takeaway that George picked up from the same establishment, Xiao Bao's, every week. They often sat in silence as they ate and normally watched the TV quiz show *Countdown* which Raymond had recorded for them. But of late they had spent the entire evening in silence, without the TV on. Which they did again on this particular night. George hadn't noticed anything out of the ordinary. He hadn't picked up that his father seemed out of sorts. Wasn't himself. George just sat there thinking about the case.

When he'd eaten he would wait until his father had finished, clear up their plates and the takeaway containers, then do the washing up. He would wash the plastic containers as well as the plates. Raymond liked to keep them for storing odds and ends in. Like screws, nuts and bolts and other necessary detritus he deemed essential for a satisfactory existence. Raymond had been something of a hoarder in the past, before an intervention by his son. An inveterate collector of basically anything he could see a potential future use for, which was fundamentally anything, plastic containers had been one of the main culprits in his collection. So they had come to an agreement, after the cull of Raymond's hoard a couple of years before, about the keeping of plastic containers. George would wash them every week after dinner. Initially, George proposed that if the cupboard still had the three empty containers from the previous week in it, the new, clean, containers would be put straight into the recycling. But there had been some negotiation about this, as Raymond had pointed out that there might come a time when he needed, say, six, seven or even eight containers, all at the same time. George's approach would mean that he'd only ever have a maximum of three at his disposal. So, they compromised: a stockpile of ten was permitted; anything above that would trigger the recycling. There had been a tricky moment one week, when George realised there were more containers in the cupboard than there should have been, from the week before. It turned out his father had been getting them out of the recycling, once Cross had left and putting them back in the cupboard. This had led to what Cross later described to Ottey as an 'intervention'. He could see that Raymond's hoarding instincts were rising to the surface once again and he had to nip them in the bud. It was an awkward conversation he said, which led her to think, perhaps uncharitably, that weren't most of his conversations with people awkward? She tried to explain that an intervention normally involved more than just the one person intervening, but he wouldn't have it.

There was a reason, on Raymond's part, for this silence during these weekly visits. George was never one to initiate conversation in a social situation such as this. So Raymond normally fulfilled that role when it was just the two of them. But currently Raymond was in something of an emotional downward spiral which he couldn't seem to climb out of. That George's mother Christine had recently re-entered his son's life wasn't a problem for Raymond. If anything, he was glad of it. Glad to have another person in George's tiny social circle, who cared for him and would look out for him. It was the unearthing of the past which had affected Raymond. George's discovery of his mother's real reason for leaving them had rendered Raymond emotionally conflicted. Over the years he'd kept this from George, letting him believe that she'd left for her own reasons, whatever those were. He felt awful guilt about that now. The fact that George had had to find it out for himself, when it would have been a lot easier and certainly more honest just to have told him about it, made it all the worse for Raymond.

He'd always known that George would find out one day. It was in his nature to find things out. Raymond had imagined that when it did happen, he himself would feel an immense sense of relief. Because the truth would finally be out in the open. But it hadn't turned out that way. He'd been left with an appallingly empty feeling. It was as if he'd led his entire life living a lie, both with his son and the memory of his partner Ron. He had failed them both and this left him feeling abjectly remorseful. It was a nauseating realisation which he just didn't seem able to shake off. His silence wasn't out of embarrassment, but he felt he just didn't know what to say to his son at the moment. This was despite the fact that things seemed to have worked out well. His son had accepted it all without a moment's hesitation. What disappointed Raymond, disgusted him almost, was the fact that even when Christine had left it for him to tell George, he still couldn't do it. She'd had the grace not to out him to his son, but leave it for him. However, when George had asked, he'd just shrugged it off. It was the shabby behaviour of a coward and he couldn't move beyond it. When it came down to it, he hadn't had the courage. How much courage exactly was needed? he kept asking himself. But it had left him feeling that he didn't like himself much and certainly had no self-respect.

George had no knowledge that his father was sitting opposite him thinking these things and feeling this way. It also didn't occur to him to tell him that the victim in the case he was working was Stephen's brother. Something Raymond would undoubtedly have liked to know. He just did the washing up and counted the takeaway containers in the cupboard. Six. Well below the 'statutory' limit. He put that night's clean containers in the cupboard and left.

I 5

'Alice? Do you have a moment?' asked Ottey.

Alice walked into Cross's office. Ottey indicated that she should take a seat.

'How was Stephen?' Mackenzie began by asking.

'Obviously a little thrown and upset, but he's fine,' Ottey replied.

'Did he have any thoughts?'

'You'd have to be more specific,' replied Cross.

'About what might have happened?' she replied, regretting this speculative enquiry instantly.

Ottey came to her rescue. 'So, what have you got, Alice?'

'Not a whole heck of a lot. So, guests at the abbey. Not a huge number, four in the last year. Numbers still haven't picked up since Covid. The first was a young man called Dan Summers. A very serious and devout young man thinking of taking solemn vows and becoming a monk. He stayed for a month and came to the conclusion that maybe it wasn't for him. He's now thinking of going into the priesthood instead.

'There was a man in his forties, Jeremy McBride, but he seems to have given a fake name as he's a digital ghost. His marriage was breaking up. He was hitting the bottle and he stayed for what he called a bit of peace and quiet.

'Then there was someone called Robbie Weald. An altar boy as a teenager, he'd been having an extra stressful time at work recently, and wanted to get back in touch with his Catholic faith. He worked with Brother Dominic and the books, as well as the bees, which has led to him getting a couple of hives himself. He's very grateful to Dominic for introducing him to the world of bees.'

'You've spoken with him?' asked Cross.

'Yes, he's still an occasional guest. He liked Dominic a lot and found his counsel a "lifesaver", as he put it. Lastly there's a guy, a young entrepreneur with a successful tech start-up of some sort. To be honest with you, I still haven't a clue what his company does, even though he explained it to me for over an hour. But he's made a shitload of money and took four of his young employees there for a retreat. "To discover their priorities in life." He said he'd asked Dominic for a spiritual boot camp. Dominic was a "cool dude", apparently. The week went so well they were in discussions about offering it as a service to other companies, and make it a money-maker for the abbey. Get a load of this. At the end of the week, they went paintballing and persuaded a very reluctant Dominic to go with them. He really didn't want to, obviously, being a monk et cetera, there was so much wrong with the idea. But here's the killer.' She grimaced at the clumsiness of her choice of words before continuing. 'Dominic won without firing a single shot. Zak – that's the entrepreneur – thought it was the coolest thing ever. "Totally Zen." The single most meaningful thing they'd learned all week. Except that he hadn't worked out what it actually meant yet.'

'So, nothing there?' asked Ottey.

'Well not exactly nothing, but maybe not exactly something,' she replied, eliciting a sigh from Cross. 'Okay, well, a possible red flag. One of Zak's team, called Snip – yes, I know – kept getting high. He became argumentative and aggressive. Zak offered to send him home, but Dominic said it wasn't necessary. Then in the middle of the night he broke into the church, dressed up in one of the priest's robes and started ringing the bell. None of Zak's team got up. It was Dominic who went in and apparently "sorted him out".'

'Sorted him out?' asked Cross.

'Well, no one saw it happen, but that's how Zak described it. Next morning Snip was sporting a black eye when Zak bundled him off in a cab.'

'Dominic hit him?' asked Ottey.

'It would seem so, although he denied it. But Zak said Dominic was smiling when he denied it,' replied Mackenzie, laughing. 'You've got to admire the guy.'

'I imagine Snip got cut from Zak's workforce,' quipped Cross, clearly pleased with himself.

'Oh George, please,' said Ottey which made Mackenzie laugh, adding further insult to Cross's injured pride that his joke hadn't even gleaned a smirk.

'Snip did lose his job,' Mackenzie added.

'Motive for murder?' asked Ottey.

'Torture and murder,' Mackenzie said.

'Hmm. Where does he live?' Ottey asked.

'London.'

'Let's get someone up there to go talk to him,' Ottey finished by saying.

'Anything else?' asked Cross.

'No.'

'Emails?' asked Cross.

'Likewise, nothing. No clues, as far as I can see. There was Queenbeegate. The theft of a few Eustace queens that Dominic was breeding, but I think you know all about that. Peter Mercer was the culprit. But after Dominic forgave him he actually came to help with the bees and has taken over since Dominic's death. They even rescued a swarm from a local school together the week before he died. There was also an email about a valuation Dominic made on an old religious book. But nothing that screamed murder,' she said.

'If you honestly think you're going to solve cases because something screams murder, you're going to be very disappointed,' Cross observed. 'Dig deeper into the book dispute,' he instructed.

'Okay. But that's basically it. I've sent you the contact details for Ursula Mead,' Mackenzie said.

Ottey looked puzzled.

'The volunteer who drove Dominic to the supermarket for the abbey weekly shop,' Cross explained.

16

Ursula Mead was a widow in her mid-seventies, but she looked younger somehow. Her hair was dyed blonde and she exuded a purpose in life, as if she never really had enough time to fit everything into her busy schedule. But behind her eyes there was an immovable sorrow which just hung back and was never really that far away. She lived in a terraced house in a small village outside Cheddar. The front garden had been paved over and there was a middle-of-the-road, mid-range SUV parked on it. The house was filled with photographic reminders of her late husband and her family of children and grandchildren. She welcomed Cross and Ottey into the house. They sat in the garden. It was a classic English cottage garden which she obviously took great pride in and wanted to show off. It was planted with a mix of early flowering spring bulbs and plants. There were narcissi, tulips and hyacinths in ordered pots. She obviously spent a lot of time in the garden which reflected her horticultural prowess and knowledge.

'How long had you been driving Brother Dominic to the weekly abbey shop?' Ottey began.

'Pretty much since he joined the abbey. It was just after my husband died. He was only sixty-two,' she said sadly. 'I needed something to do and it came my way by chance. It was a godsend. Literally, I like to think. Dominic was such good company. He always asked what was going on in my life. Forever asking about the children and the grandchildren.'

'Did he talk to you about his life at all?' asked Cross.

'Oh yes. Of course. I insisted it shouldn't be just one-way

traffic. He told me about things at the abbey, about his book work, the bees. He loved his bees.'

'Did he talk about life before he entered the monastery?' asked Cross.

'No. I did ask. But he didn't seem to want to talk about that. I had the feeling that, for whatever reason, it was something of a closed book. Something he'd left behind,' she said.

'In a sinister kind of way?' asked Ottey.

'Oh no, not at all. He said, in order to devote his life to God completely, he had to look forward and not back.'

'Was he at all defensive or guarded about it?' asked Cross.

She thought seriously about this for a minute.

'Like he had something to hide?' she asked.

'Maybe,' replied Ottey.

'It's funny, I have been thinking about that this week since... No, I don't think so. Do you think it was something from his past? I suppose that would make more sense. Why else would someone want or need to do that to a monk?' she said.

The right question again, but what was interesting, Cross thought, was the use of the word 'need'. Why would someone need to kill him? What end would it serve?

Ursula Mead talked like someone who was making the most of having a willing audience. She was obviously someone who might not speak to people in person for days at a time. Like many lonely people, she often asked a question in a breathless fashion, then answered it herself before anyone else had a chance to. It was a self-deprecating thing to do. As if what she had to say had no real meaning, import, nor could possibly be of any interest to others.

'That's a very good question, Mrs Mead. Very pertinent to the case,' said Cross, causing her to blush with the approbation. Ottey smiled at this. Cross hadn't noticed, nor had he meant to flatter her. 'Did people ever stop to talk to him on these shopping trips?' he went on.

'Not since he stopped wearing his habit. I suppose he was just like another shopper then. But when he was dressed as a monk, they'd stop him all the time. It took him at least half an hour longer to do the shop when he was in his habit.'

'Was he pleased for the opportunity to wear ordinary clothes?' asked Ottey.

'I don't think so. I think he actually missed the interaction, to be honest,' she replied. 'He took pride, if that's the right word when it comes to a monk, in being a monk.'

It also gave him a cloak of anonymity, Cross thought to himself.

'Had you noticed any change in him over the past few months?' he asked. 'Did he seem anxious or worried about anything?'

'He worried about the state of the world, that's for sure. He was concerned about the morality, or lack of, and the quality of the people in charge of the country. He seemed very well informed about the world for someone who led such a deliberately sheltered life.'

'What days did you take Brother Dominic to the supermarket?' Cross asked.

'Every Friday.'

'Always the same supermarket?'

'Always the Cheddar Sainsbury's.'

'So, the last time you took him would be Friday the thirty-first of March?' he went on.

'Yes,' she faltered. 'The day he went missing.'

'Did anything different happen that day?'

'Yes, and I've been meaning to call you. But I wasn't sure who to get in touch with,' she explained, as if she might be in trouble.

'What happened, Mrs Mead?' Ottey asked gently.

'When he came out, a man was following him, arguing. He seemed quite annoyed, angry even.'

'Could you hear what he was saying?'

'No, not really. I wound the window down but I couldn't make it out.'

'What did he look like?'

'In his forties, close-cropped grey hair, trimmed beard, also grey, and I thought he sounded foreign.'

'Where from? What kind of accent?' Ottey asked.

'I'm not sure. Dutch? Norwegian, something like that.'

'Did you ask Brother Dominic about it when he got into the car?' asked Cross.

'Obviously, but he didn't want to talk about it.'

'Did he seem upset?'

'No, actually. I think maybe I was more upset at someone shouting at him than he was,' she replied.

'You felt protective of him. You were obviously very fond of Brother Dominic,' said Ottey.

'Oh, yes. Very much so. It was impossible not to be fond of Dominic...' she said and started to weep. 'Would you excuse me?' She got up and left the room, returning a few moments later with a lever arch file that was bound in leather.

'This is for my shares and pensions. Dominic covered the file with leather, embossed it and put marbled paper inside. Isn't it beautiful? He did the marbling himself. Used all my favourite colours,' she said.

'It's like a work of art,' said Ottey.

'Isn't it?' she replied.

'Why a folder for stocks and shares?' asked Cross.

'Why not?' she responded.

'Well, you go to church, why not a bible? Or a photograph album for your late husband?' asked Cross.

'Oh, I see. I suppose it must look like an odd choice,' she laughed. 'The reason I'm showing it to you is because he helped me after Arthur died. Sorted all my financials out. He even sold and bought some shares for me. He was very good at it, made me a small fortune. Who would've thought, with his being a monk? He could've made a fortune in the City.'

Cross said nothing. He leafed through the files with her financial holdings and dealings. There was just over £250,000 in shares. It had started years before at just over £50,000. Brother

Dominic knew what he was doing when it came to share dealing, it would seem. But then, given his background, this wasn't especially surprising. He came across another account at the back of the file. It was called 'Ursula Mead 02'.

'You have two accounts,' Cross observed.

'Yes,' she replied a little uncertainly.

'And these can be accessed online?' he asked.

'Yes, at quickshare.com.'

Cross reached into his backpack and took out his laptop.

'George?' Ottey asked, hoping to know what he was up to. But he said nothing. He typed the web address for the share company into his browser. The opening page came up. In the username box he typed in UrsulaMead02. He then reached into his pocket for his phone and opened his photos. The last photograph he'd taken was of the post-it note he'd found under the desk in the abbey office. He typed URSM02116ste2011 into the password box and an account immediately opened on the laptop screen. It corresponded with the transactions he'd seen on the last pages of the paper file. There was just over £21,354 in the account. Cross looked up at Ursula.

'Why would Brother Dominic have a password to a shares account in your name, in his office at the abbey, Mrs Mead?' Cross asked.

Ursula didn't answer and looked a little troubled as if she'd made a mistake in showing it to them.

'It seems to me there's nothing illegal in all of this, Ursula. So there's nothing for you to be worried about,' said Ottey.

But the woman still seemed conflicted.

'It was my idea,' she began. 'Dominic had done so well with my shares and pension. My husband, bless him, hadn't left our financial affairs in the rudest of health. I'm not blaming or criticising him. How was he to know he was going to die so suddenly? When I told Dominic, he asked if he could have a look. He then said he could help and I didn't see why not. After a few years he'd basically made my future secure, financially. He was surprisingly good at this stuff, you know, for a monk.'

'What happened then? What was your idea?' asked Cross.

'Well, every now and then the abbey needed money for its upkeep. The boiler broke. The abbey roof needed repair. There was damp. It was so difficult for them. Even though they were a parish church they couldn't countenance appealing to the parishioners for money. They applied for various grants and sometimes the order made money available for them, but it was always a struggle. So I suggested I took a chunk of money from my profits—'

'Twenty thousand pounds?' Cross suggested, looking at the accounts in front of him.

'That's right. It wasn't a gift as such, but a sum that Dominic could manage and invest and then use the profits he made for the abbey,' she continued.

'In the form of anonymous gifts,' Cross said.

'That's right.'

'Wow,' said Ottey.

'You mustn't tell the abbot,' Ursula pleaded.

'Something tells me he might already know,' Cross commented.

'Really?' Ursula replied, immediately unsettled by this.

'Doesn't this mean he broke his vow of poverty?' asked Ottey.

'Well, yes and no. We did discuss it. I argued that it wouldn't be, as it wasn't being done for the purposes of self-enrichment but for the upkeep of the abbey, so he was still abiding by his vows. It's not as if he bought them a widescreen TV or a jacuzzi.'

Ottey laughed. 'I'm sorry, it's just the image of—'

But Cross's look stopped her short.

'Well, that was interesting,' said Ottey as she drove them back to Bristol. 'Interesting but not necessarily relevant.'

'To the case? Probably not,' replied Cross. 'But it might well be something else that made the abbot so reticent.'

'Quite funny when you think about it. A monastic slush fund. I'm beginning to like poor Dominic,' she said.

'You're managing to find quite a lot of unintended humour in this case,' Cross observed. 'A slush fund implies a certain impropriety, which I'm not sure is applicable.'

'True,' she said.

'Do you know the etymology of the term "slush fund"?' he asked her.

'Would it surprise you if I said no?' she asked.

'It wouldn't, because your knowledge of such matters seems quite limited. In fact, general knowledge when it comes to you is something of an oxymoron,' he said.

'Well, don't pick me for your next pub quiz team then,' she said.

'I don't do pub quizzes, as I'm sure you know, but if I did, I certainly wouldn't,' he replied indignantly.

'Why thank you. Now can you just get on with imparting whatever nugget of useless information you have and get it over and done with?' she pleaded.

'Well, if that's your attitude, then no,' he replied pompously.

'Fine,' she said.

'Fine,' he repeated. Not because he or it was, but just because that was what people tended to say in these situations, he'd noticed. So on they drove in a nose-cutting-face-spiting silence for the next five minutes as her curiosity grew at an increasing rate, matched only by his burning desire to tell her.

'All right, go on then, tell me,' she finally relented.

'It's actually a nautical term,' he began with an alacrity which betrayed exactly how impatiently he'd been waiting for her prompt. 'When sailors boiled meat, usually salted, fat or grease would form at the top of the pot. They would skim this off. It was called slush. The officers would then sell the slush to tallow makers and use the proceeds to make small purchases for the ship's crew. So it became known as the slush fund.'

She made no comment.

'Interesting, no?' he said, desperate for her acknowledgement of the truth of this. But he'd annoyed her so it wasn't forthcoming. Despite the fact that she'd found it more interesting than most of his normal 'indispensable' trivia.

17

'A banker who became a Benedictine monk? What are we talking here? A crisis of conscience? Throwing the merchants out of the temple?' said Carson the next day.

'I'm not sure I understand the reference,' said Cross.

'Talk about extremes,' Carson continued, ignoring him, as neither did he. 'I love the idea that he kept his hand in with stocks and shares and made a bit of money on the side for the abbey. I like this guy.'

'It would seem that his time in the City was the anomaly,' said Ottey. 'He'd been very religious and spiritual before he went to university.'

'It's still hard to imagine what he could've done in that time to make someone come after him fifteen years later, torture and kill him,' said Carson. 'More to the point, why now? Why not any time earlier in his time at the monastery?'

No one said anything. Then Cross looked up.

'In that scenario, if it's someone from his past, it would be because, until recently, they didn't know he was there,' he said. 'The question is: how did they find out?'

'Good question,' Carson agreed. 'It's a starting point at least.'

'Sir, you should be aware that George knows the brother of the deceased. Well. Both of us, in fact,' said Ottey.

'Really?'

'He's a priest in St Paul's,' she went on.

'At the church where George gave his recital?' asked Carson.

'Yes.'

'George, I'm so sorry,' said Carson.

'What for?' asked Cross.

'Your friend's loss.'

'Oh, I see. Well, he hadn't been in touch with him for a good few years,' Cross replied.

'Even so, he's still his brother,' insisted Carson. 'Does this make things difficult for you?'

'Why would it?' asked Cross.

'Well in case you're too emotionally close to the case,' said Carson.

No one felt the need to point out the unlikelihood of this scenario, as Cross never got emotionally close to anyone or anything, either at work or in his everyday life.

'Josie, would you pass my condolences on to...' said Carson.

'Father Stephen,' Ottey filled in.

'Yes, and assure him we will do everything in our power to find his brother's killer.'

'Of course.'

'So, George, can I ask you what your current thinking is? How you'd like to proceed?' asked Carson.

'We need to talk to the monastic community again in detail. Did he, or they, do something that drew attention to his being at the abbey? How did he leave the monastery that day? We know he didn't seek permission from the abbot. What made him leave? Did he know the people? Did he leave of his own free will, or was he abducted? The chances are they know something they think is insignificant which could be the key to all of this,' said Cross.

'Well, I think you two should get straight back down there,' said Carson.

'George should go on his own. They're more comfortable with him than me. I'll organise a car,' said Ottey.

Cross and Ottey walked back into the open area. Swift was sitting on the edge of Mackenzie's desk. He stood up as soon as he saw the two detectives approaching.

'Alice, could you arrange for someone to drive DS Cross down to the abbey?' asked Ottey.

'I can do that,' Swift offered, rather too quickly. 'Take him down there, obviously not organise for someone.'

'I think your skills would be better used elsewhere,' said Cross.

'Really? Do we know how Brother Dominic left the abbey on the day he went missing?' Swift asked.

'We do not,' replied Cross.

'Have forensics been there to ascertain whether there's any evidence that might help us ascertain what happened?' he went on.

'It's not a crime scene,' said Alice, laughing.

'You know that for a fact?' Swift asked.

'We do not,' said Cross who was beginning to think such an examination might be useful. Also, he found Swift's SUV very comfortable, and he was more than an adequately skilled driver, in Cross's opinion.

'Then surely, we need to investigate. We're all assuming he left the abbey on the day he went missing. What if he was there the entire time?' Swift asked, knowing full well that 'assumptions' in a case was a dirty word for Cross and playing on it.

'Then why not just leave the body there? Why move it?' asked Ottey.

'That I won't know till I've had a look,' replied Swift. He turned to Cross. 'Please follow me, Sergeant. Your carriage awaits.'

Cross turned on his heel and went into his office.

'Is that a yes or a no?' asked Swift.

'Your guess is as good as mine,' Ottey replied.

Cross then appeared with his backpack, raincoat and walked straight out of the department.

'Well, what are you waiting for?' asked Ottey.

Swift grabbed his black leather saddlebag and ran after Cross.

'Such a fanboy,' said Mackenzie. 'Bit sad really.'

18

On the journey to the monastery Swift asked Cross which areas of the abbey Dominic had worked in. He would search the bookbindery, the office, Dominic's room and the church itself.

'Does it have a crypt?' Swift asked.

'I don't know.'

As they approached the abbey house, with the church visible further up the hill, Swift beamed.

'Oh my god, this place is so cool. Can you imagine living here?'

'Would you like to be a monk?' asked Cross.

'Oh yeah. Who wouldn't want to dress in a hood and habit every day? It takes me ages to decide what to wear in the morning. As a monk, no such first-world problems.'

'What about the religious aspect?' asked Cross while inwardly agreeing with the benefit of not having to choose what to wear. He'd minimised the problem in his own life by basically having the same items of clothing in numbers. This meant that some people at work thought he never changed. When Ottey told him this he explained that he wore clean clothes every day. They just all happened to be the same.

'Might have a slight problem with that,' Swift conceded. 'Come to think about it, I'd also have a problem with sandals. Do they wear socks with their sandals? I bet they do.' He winced at the very thought of it.

'Most of the monks here wear shoes, as far as I've seen,' replied Cross.

Swift got out and stretched his long legs. Cross couldn't help but think that the tall young man dressed entirely in black didn't look at all out of place. He started to walk towards the front door, like a giant black crow, where Brother Andrew was waiting for them.

'This is Dr Michael Swift, one of our forensic investigators. He would like to look around the abbey to ascertain whether he can find any clues as to Brother Dominic's murder,' said Cross, introducing Swift to the father abbot and Father Magnus.

'Of course. Brother Andrew can show you round, unless you'd like to be on your own,' said Father Magnus.

'A guide would be very handy. If that's all right with you?' said Swift. He and the young monk disappeared.

Cross then outlined Dominic's background and name before he entered the monastery.

'A banker?' the abbot exclaimed quietly.

'It explains how he did the accounts so effortlessly,' Father Magnus reflected.

'And make money for various essential things that needed doing round the abbey,' added Cross. This caused both monks' normally pale complexions to blush like guilty schoolboys. 'Why didn't you tell me about Brother William and Brother Dominic?' Cross asked, deliberately taking advantage of their discomfort.

The two monks looked at each other.

'What about them?' asked the abbot.

'The fact that Brother William was in love with Brother Dominic?' Cross went on.

'I'm not sure I'd express it that way,' said the abbot.

'Who told you this?' asked Father Magnus.

'That's neither here nor there.'

'It's actually an internal and private matter,' Father Magnus continued, his kindly demeanour having disappeared momentarily. Cross said nothing but just looked at the pair of them hiding behind their habits. He'd become tired of people declining to give him information during an investigation, on the pretext that it was private.

'You surely don't think he had anything to do with this tragedy?' Magnus finally asked.

'I have no idea. All I know is that it is my job to look at all the circumstances of the victim's life, particularly in the time leading up to his death. Whatever the inconvenience or discomfort of others,' Cross replied.

'We were dealing with the situation,' the abbot said.

'How?'

'It was decided that it was best for Brother William, if he wanted to continue his monastic life, that it would be better done in another of our communities,' Father Magnus explained.

'So, you were just moving the problem on,' Cross observed.

'Not at all. This way would give him the time and room to reconfigure his relationship with God,' said the abbot.

'How did Brother William feel about that?'

'He had taken a vow of obedience, DS Cross. How do you think he felt about it?' asked Father Magnus testily.

'I'm well aware of that. My question is, how did he feel about it?' Cross repeated.

Father Magnus looked at the abbot and then at the ground, deferring the answer to him.

'He was unhappy, of course. He was very happy here and sad that he had allowed this situation to develop rather than seeking counsel before it became irretrievable,' he said.

'It would help going forward if you told me everything, no matter how you think it may look,' said Cross.

'And how does it look to you?' asked Father Magnus.

'You have covered up what I would consider to be a material fact in the circumstances of this case. A case which I am doing my best to solve, whatever obstacles are put in my path, unintentionally or otherwise,' Cross replied.

'You are quite right, and we apologise. Our reluctance was in no way meant to hinder you as we never considered Brother William to have been involved in Brother Dominic's murder,' said the abbot.

'Your apology is accepted,' Cross replied. 'So, Father Magnus, you knew what the password was, when I found it under Brother Dominic's desk?'

'I did,' he replied.

'Another lie. Not the environment I would've expected to encounter mendacity in, unlike others my work takes me to,' said Cross.'

'And yes, we did become aware of Brother Dominic's financial dealings which helped the abbey. We turned a blind eye, for which may God forgive us,' said the abbot. 'So, what now?'

'I would like to go through all the opportunities Brother Dominic had to be in contact with people outside the monastery, however brief or seemingly inconsequential,' Cross replied.

'Have you asked Brother Thomas?' Magnus asked.

'As you know, he was unwilling to speak with me.'

'Yes, well, that notwithstanding, nothing happens here without Brother Thomas's knowledge. He just sits and studies the congregation leaving on a Sunday. You'd be astonished what information he gleans from doing just that,' said the abbot. 'We certainly are.'

'Runs a mile if they approach him though,' added Magnus.

'That's true. But he knows everything about everyone's routine here. Makes it his business to know. I think it gives him comfort,' said the abbot.

'As I said, he seems reluctant to speak with me,' Cross replied.

'I wouldn't take it personally. He's reluctant to speak with anyone,' said Magnus.

'I wasn't taking it personally. It won't surprise you to know that as a policeman most people I encounter are reluctant to talk to me. It's normally because they don't want to tell me something. I was wondering if that was the case with Brother Thomas,' said Cross.

'Would you like me to tell him to speak with you?' asked the abbot.

'No. I'll manage,' Cross replied.

'Your best chance of getting him to talk would be to go down to the vegetable garden this afternoon, and take him a cup of tea,' suggested Magnus.

'Good idea,' agreed the abbot. 'Four thirty on the dot if you want your best chance of success. You're in contact with Dominic's brother, presumably?'

'I am.'

'Would you tell him that he's most welcome to come and pray with us? Celebrate mass with us or just talk, if he'd like?' said the abbot.

'I will.'

'Do you know when you'll be releasing the body?'

'I'll talk to my superior. I can't imagine it'll be much longer,' replied Cross.

'We had assumed we would do the funeral mass and bury him in our graveyard, but it's only right that Father Mount be involved in any such decisions.'

'I'll pass that on,' said Cross.

'Oh, one thing we meant to ask. It's not really important in the grand scheme of things. But you didn't happen to find a phone on Brother Dominic, did you?' asked Father Magnus.

'A phone?' said Cross a little surprised.

'Not one for making calls. It's the phone for answering people at the gate and opening it. We have a spare, but it would be useful to have it back, if possible.'

'Was that one of his jobs? To let people in?' Cross asked.

'We take it in turns. It happened to be his turn that day.'

This interested Cross. Had Dominic let his abductors in?

He spent the rest of the afternoon talking to the other monks to confirm William's whereabouts at the time of Dominic's disappearance and the days following. He made a list of the daily offices, their time and duration and used it as a check list. By all accounts Brother William was present at all of them.

19

Cross walked out of the abbey house and looked out onto the grounds. Despite the private road, or more accurately lane, being only a couple of hundred yards long, there was no sound from the busy main road at the bottom of the hill. All Cross could hear was the rustle of a gentle breeze in the trees and vibrant, loud birdsong. He listened to it for a minute, reflecting how urban the surrounding soundscape was for him where he lived in Bristol. He saw a couple of monks working in the kitchen garden, one of whom was Brother Thomas. It was a well-ordered garden, with row upon row of fresh vegetables. It had to save the community a lot of money in food. Father Magnus had told him that at one time they had thought of diversifying into having some goats and chickens, but decided against it, one of the reasons being that they thought the animals would disrupt the tranquillity of the place. Cross decided not to speak to Brother Thomas at this point and wait till the designated teatime.

He called Swift on his phone.

'Where are you?' he asked.

'I'm in the office building opposite the main gate across from the abbey. I'll explain later,' came the reply.

Cross didn't push him. He turned and looked at the abbey church. Cross was quite partial to a church interior, mainly because of his passion for church organs. He hadn't taken much note of the interior when he and Ottey had gone to Sext. He'd been too busy studying the brothers' faces. He decided to have another look and enjoy a few moments of peace and quiet to think about the case.

The large door creaked open. Cross walked in, closing it behind him. The clunk of the catch echoed round the church. He took a seat. It was cooler inside the church than outside. He felt comfortable in there. No noise, no distractions. Completely still, except for the motes of dust that danced in a diagonal beam of sunlight. It smelled of wood polish and decades of incense.

He surveyed the church and thought about the amount of time the monks spent in there. He liked the idea of their ordered day, regulated identically, every day of the year, by the divine offices, at exactly the same time. He looked at the Stations of the Cross that lined the two side walls. Then he spotted the organ pipes protruding over the altar. He got up to have a look, wondering whether it would be improper to ask the abbot if he could play it. It was hidden behind the altar. A two-manual organ, he recognised the make. It was a Vowles instrument from the nineteenth century. Vowles was a local organ maker based in Bristol. Cross was immediately concerned by the keys on the manuals, which were all uneven, meaning things had to be amiss in the organ cabinet. He was about to give it a closer examination when someone approached him from the nave. It was William.

'Brother William.'

'DS Cross.'

William said nothing more. Cross took this to mean that he'd heard about his conversation with the abbot and Father Magnus, together with the canvas he'd made of the other monks, concerning his whereabouts. Cross knew there was something he should say, then remembered what it was.

'I'm sorry for your loss.'

William didn't reply.

'I have been made aware that you had significant feelings for Brother Dominic. In such circumstances I would imagine you would feel the loss more keenly than the others here,' said Cross, who couldn't help feeling in that moment that Ottey would be proud of him.

'Possibly,' replied the monk tentatively. 'But he wasn't mine to lose. Having said thàt, were he not dead I would have lost him anyway.'

'So I understand. How did you feel about that?'

'Shall we sit?' William said, giving Cross an indication that he wanted to talk.

'Yes.'

They walked back into the nave of the church and sat in the front pew.

'To answer your question; as I saw it, if I wanted to continue with my monastic life, which I did, I would have to move. But by the same token, had I felt my feelings for Dom were an indication that perhaps the monastic calling was not for me, I would've left anyway. So, in essence, feelings didn't really come into it,' Brother William said.

'Had you come to a conclusion and made any decision before he was murdered?' Cross asked.

'Yes. I was going to go to another community and set up another bookbinding workshop there. We were always overrun with work here. It could spread the load. The plan was for Dom to help me set it up and get started,' he replied.

'Wouldn't that have been difficult for you in the circumstances?' asked Cross.

'I don't know. In many ways I think it might have helped me get through it.'

'Was Brother Dominic happy with that plan?' Cross went on.

'As I'm sure you're aware, the feelings I had for him were very much one-way traffic. He was very happy to help solve the situation. He was like that. Always wanting to help.'

'Were you angry with him?'

'No. With myself perhaps, but not him. He did nothing to encourage it. It was just a foolish delusion on my part.'

'What was?'

'That we could have had that sort of relationship here, or anywhere else.'

'You really weren't angry with him?' Cross asked again.

'Angry enough to kill the man I thought I loved?'

'That's an interesting way of putting it. Were you not in love with him?'

'Still working on that one,' he replied with a smile.

'Well in answer to your question, you'd be surprised how often people kill the ones they love. But I should also tell you that it's clear you didn't leave the grounds of the abbey at the relevant times. I therefore have concluded that you didn't kill Brother Dominic,' Cross said.

'Did you ever think I did?'

'I don't work like that. I just investigate. Evidence is generally much more reliable than conjecture.'

Cross's phone vibrated. It was Swift. He looked back at William.

'Was there anything else you think I should know?' he asked. He thought William hesitated before he answered.

'No,' he replied.

Cross wasn't sure he believed him but left the church without another word. There would be further opportunities to talk to him.

They sat in Swift's SUV. Cross wanted to hear what, if anything, Swift had found out before they left. He had grown to like the way the young man worked cases. The way he thought about where he might find evidence. The way he presented that evidence, factually and without any fanfare.

'So, you didn't find anything of forensic interest?' Cross asked.

'I didn't really expect to, to be honest.'

'So, what was the point of your trip?'

'I like to see all locations that are pertinent to the crime.'

'Even if there's no forensic interest?' asked Cross.

'Well, you won't know there isn't until you've had a look, will you? I said I didn't expect to find anything of forensic relevance;

that isn't to say I didn't find something else of relevance,' Swift replied.

Swift had checked Dominic's room in much the same way as Cross had. He'd admired the skill in the leather binding of his bible. He'd examined the bookbindery for any signs of struggle or traces of blood. There weren't any, and as William had pointed out, he had been working alone on the day of Dominic's disappearance. Dominic had been working in the office. Swift checked it. Father Magnus had assured him that he'd been with Dominic for most of the day. He hadn't seen Dominic after he'd made tea for Brother Thomas and Brother Jude in the vegetable garden.

'Do you know what time that was?' Swift had asked the monk.

'Oh yes, he left at four twenty. Brother Thomas likes his routines and has tea at four thirty on the dot,' Father Magnus answered.

'Did Brother Dominic return to the office?'

'No.'

'Were you expecting him to?' asked Swift.

'Not as far as I remember. He was going to see how Brother William was getting on in the bindery,' replied the monk.

Cross turned to Swift in the car.

'Did Brother Dominic go to the bindery after his tea run?' he asked.

'Apparently not. Brother William didn't see him,' Swift replied.

'Which means he went missing between four thirty-five and vespers at six, which he didn't attend,' Cross thought aloud.

'Which is why I was in the office building opposite the main gates. It's a gaming company, quite successful, actually. They made a load of money from a World War One biplane game.' Cross's look of complete disinterest encouraged Swift to quickly get to the point. 'I went there because I was wondering how Dominic had actually left the monastery grounds. I was looking for any CCTV cameras on the buildings opposite the entrance to the monastery, or traffic cameras.'

'Did the building have one?' asked Cross.

'It did. It doesn't cover the entire entrance, but it had enough to confirm what seems to have happened. There's a traffic camera further down the road as well, which we can look into, to maybe give us a complete picture.'

Swift then held up his iPad to show Cross the footage he'd obtained from the gaming company. The camera covered the employee car park at the front of the building. In the top of the frame was the bottom half of the abbey gate which was as far as the camera's range went. At four forty-three, according to the time code, on the day in question, a van was seen pulling up to the gate where it stopped. It was there for eight minutes before the gate opened and what appeared to be the bottom of a monk's habit walked up to the side of the van. The monk was quickly forced into the van.

'I think that's Dominic,' said Swift.

'It certainly fits in with the timings we have. But why didn't he just open the gate remotely with the phone and let them in? The gate's in perfect working order,' Cross observed.

'Presumably because he didn't want them going up to the monastery,' Swift replied.

'Which implies he knew who they were, or at the very least what they wanted,' said Cross.

'Then why not just refuse to open the gates? Why come down?'

'He can't have thought he was in any danger,' replied Cross.

'Thought he could sort it out, whatever it was,' said Swift.

'It also implies that he wasn't surprised by their turning up. He knew what they wanted and wouldn't let them in. Had they been there before?' asked Cross.

They sat there for a few minutes and Swift fell into the trap so many people did with Cross, of filling in the silence. Invariably with bad results.

'Good work, no?' he said, like a schoolboy seeking a teacher's approval.

'What time is it?' asked Cross, checking his wristwatch, which had as usual stopped. It had been a Christmas gift from his father. A watch from the 1950s that Raymond had lovingly but unsuccessfully refurbished.

'Ten past four,' Swift informed him.

'Time to make some tea, said Cross getting out of the car. Swift sat there for a second before realising making tea had to have something to do with the case, rather than just being a desire of Cross's to quench his thirst. This was DS George Cross, after all. So, Swift leapt out of the car and followed Cross back into the monastery.

'Brother Thomas?' said Cross as he approached the monk tilling the soil in between a row of cauliflowers. Thomas was wearing baggy work trousers and a linen top which anywhere outside of this monastery would be classed as a hoodie. It was like a practical, rural interpretation of the monastic habit for outdoor work. Cross had seen other monks wearing them in the grounds of the abbey. Brother Thomas's obvious suspicion was tempered by the sight of a mug of tea in the detective's hand. The sweat on his furrowed brow indicated that thirst would probably outweigh his reluctance to speak to the police officer.

'A cup of tea,' said Cross.

'I can see that,' replied the taciturn Benedictine.

'For you,' said Cross holding it out for him to take.

'What do you want?' he asked directly with no thanks for the tea.

'Why do you think I want something?' asked Cross.

'Why else would you bring me tea?'

'Good point,' Cross replied.

Thomas looked up at Swift looming behind Cross.

'How tall are you?' he asked.

'Six feet eight,' Cross and Swift answered in unison.

'You must have trouble buying clothes,' observed the monk.

'Buying clothes, shoes, fitting into airplane seats, hotel beds...' Swift answered.

'I've never been on a plane,' said Thomas sipping his tea.

'Do you remember the last time you saw Brother Dominic?' asked Cross.

'Of course.'

'Why "of course"? Did something out of the ordinary happen?'

'Yes.'

'What?' asked Cross.

'He went missing,' replied the monk.

Swift couldn't help but smile at this. As soon as he saw that Thomas had spotted this, he hastily adopted the over-serious expression of an admonished child trying to avoid trouble.

'When he brought you your tea, how was he? How did he seem to you? Anything out of the ordinary?' asked Cross. The monk gave this serious consideration.

'He seemed fine,' he finally replied.

'Did you talk?' Cross went on.

'Briefly.'

'Briefly because you were both busy, or briefly because something happened?'

'The gate phone rang,' Thomas said.

'And he answered it? Did you hear what he said?'

'No.'

Cross sensed a little hesitation in this answer. 'What is it?' he asked.

'Nothing.' This reply was so quiet as to be almost inaudible.

Cross didn't say anything. He just looked at the monk and waited patiently.

'You were the last person to see Brother Dominic alive, Brother Thomas. With that, in situations like this, comes a certain responsibility. A responsibility to tell us everything, in case it turns out to be material to the investigation,' Cross said.

'I couldn't hear because he turned away when he realised who it was. I think he was agitated. His tone was different. Then he did something which was very unusual,' the monk confided.

'What was that?' asked Cross.

'He walked away without turning round and saying goodbye. He always said goodbye.'

Cross said nothing. He was oblivious to the fact that the monk seemed upset. Swift stepped forward.

'Thank you, Brother Thomas. It may seem trivial to you, but it could be important,' he said.

'It concerned me at the time as I thought I may have done something wrong and I didn't understand what that was. But now I think whoever was at the gate may have taken him,' said Thomas.

'Did Brother Dominic have any visitors over the last few months?' asked Cross.

'Yes.'

'Do you know who they were?'

'No.'

'Did he often have visitors?'

'No.'

Cross turned and walked away.

'Thank you,' said Swift, trying to make up for Cross's lack of manners. He needn't have bothered though, as Thomas had already gone back to his work and didn't hear him.

20

'I've looked into the story behind the email about the religious book evaluation. It makes interesting reading. There's this guy called Patrick Murphy, Sir Patrick Murphy, a billionaire,' said Mackenzie. She was with Cross and Ottey in his office.

'I know that name,' replied Cross. 'Made his money from online gambling.'

'That's the one. Anyway, he collects religious artefacts and paintings. Really well known for it. Got religion after he married his second wife. Brother Dominic had become something of a world-renowned specialist in those circles and was approached by Murphy's people to evaluate a fifteenth-century illuminated book of hours which was thought to have been commissioned by the Duke of Berry and then belonged to Henry the eighth.'

'Which would have been in the sixteenth century, as his dates were 1509 to 1545,' added Cross pedantically and totally unnecessarily.

She ignored his brief history lesson and showed them a picture on her phone of an elaborately illuminated manuscript. It was highly coloured with ornate black lettering and brightly coloured, hand-painted religious images in red, blue and gilt.

'Wow,' said Ottey.

'The problem was that Dominic declared it to be a fake. An eighteenth-century fake. An exceptionally good one, but a fake all the same. Murphy was furious. He'd paid over twenty million pounds for it and Dominic's valuation put it at about seven hundred and fifty thousand pounds.'

'I can see Murphy being a little upset about that,' said Ottey.

'He tried to get Dominic to reconsider his opinion. But Dominic was adamant he was right. He suggested they get second opinions. Which they did. But they all agreed with Dominic,' Mackenzie explained.

'It got quite acrimonious, with Murphy calling Dominic's expertise into question.'

'Do we think he tried to get Dominic to change his mind by force?' asked Ottey.

'It's possible, isn't it?'

'Find out who gave second opinions and talk to them. Did Murphy do anything to try and sway them?' said Cross.

'Will do. Anyway, the story really gained traction, local press, even an interview with the BBC,' added Mackenzie.

'Television or radio?' asked Cross, showing sudden interest.

'Television.'

'When was this interview broadcast?' asked Cross.

'A few months back,' Mackenzie replied.

'Local or national?' asked Cross.

'No idea.'

The interview in question had been for the BBC local news programme *Points West*. It was based in Broadcasting House in Whiteladies Road, just twenty-five minutes from the MCU. Ottey and Cross had been here many times before on previous cases. They were taken up to the office of the local news editor, Susan Woodward. She was very approachable. Cross detected a north-west lilt in her accent.

'Yes, I remember that interview, particularly in light of what has happened,' she began.

'Why particularly in light of what's happened?' asked Cross.

'Well, because the poor man has been murdered, that's all.'

'What was the interview about?' asked Cross.

'Brother Dominic had questioned the authenticity of Murphy's book of hours. You can imagine it didn't go down very well with the collector. Things became quite heated – at least on the collector's side. Brother Dominic said he was just trying to protect Murphy, who in his opinion had been defrauded. Murphy refused to accept Dominic's opinion, but it unfortunately became something of a cause célèbre in those circles. He started to challenge Dominic's expertise, so we gave them both a chance to come and discuss it.'

'Was Murphy interviewed as well?' asked Cross.

'No, he sent a spokesman.'

'Can you remember his name?'

'Not offhand but I can find it for you.'

'So, this was just a local news item?'

'Initially yes, but it gained quite a lot of traction. The Benedictine monk against the billionaire was the tackiest version of it. It was then picked up by *Newsnight*. They asked Dominic to go on the show but he refused. He didn't like the attention it was attracting. But they used our interview, so it was broadcast nationwide.'

'What kind of attention?' asked Cross.

'Well any, I think. It went against the grain for his way of life, being a Benedictine monk. I think he ended up regretting doing the interview in the first place.'

'Did he stay in touch?'

'No. He just wanted to draw a line under it. But it just wouldn't go away. He felt it was getting out of hand.'

'What did you make of Brother Dominic?' Ottey asked.

'I liked him. He wasn't how I imagined a Benedictine monk would be.'

'In what way?'

'I don't know. Now that I've said it, I'm not at all sure I had an idea of what a monk would be, before I met him. But he was very comfortable in his own skin, in a modern kind of a way. Very confident, quite outgoing. He seemed, what's the right word? Quite worldly for a monk.'

'That's an interesting observation,' said Cross.

'There was one odd thing though, now I think about it. It didn't seem odd at the time but now with what's happened... He was very concerned we didn't mention the name or location of the abbey. He didn't want St Eustace's referred to in his name caption. Maintaining their privacy, perhaps.'

'Or not wanting anyone to know where he could be found,' said Cross.

'Oh my god, you don't think this had anything to do with his death, do you?' she asked.

Cross didn't answer.

'It can't have, surely. Why would anyone want to kill him because of a book valuation?' she went on.

'Unless they didn't mean to kill him and they were just trying to persuade him to change his mind and went too far,' replied Ottey.

Cross was now fairly confident that Dominic's appearance on the local TV news would prove to be relevant. It appeared to be the only change in his pattern of behaviour, the only irregular or unusual thing that had happened to the monk over the past twelve months. It had been broadcast nationally. Someone had to have seen the interview and recognised him. Either that or he'd been killed by someone with an interest in the value of that text. But he knew Carson would jump on Murphy as the obvious lead, to the exclusion of everything else.

21

'A billionaire who's made his fortune from gambling, who by all accounts is used to getting his own way, was in the middle of a rancorous dispute with our victim which was costing him upwards of twenty million pounds and you don't think he's a suspect?' Carson asked Cross, looking around the room of detectives with a smirk of disbelief.

'What accounts?' Cross asked.

'I beg your pardon?' said Carson.

'What accounts have told you he is used to getting his own way?' Cross explained.

'I don't know. I think I read it somewhere,' replied Carson, flustered.

'Can you remember? It's just that we haven't seen them and they could come in very useful,' said Cross, in all seriousness.

'Set up a meeting with Murphy,' Carson instructed, trying to bring an end to Cross's awkward questions.

'It's proving difficult,' replied Ottey.

'Well if the BBC can get hold of him, I'm sure it's not beyond our capabilities.'

'They couldn't. He wasn't interviewed. It was his spokesman, a Martin Bates,' Ottey replied.

'Well fix up a meeting with him then,' said Carson.

Cross was looking thoughtful, something which Carson now knew better than to ignore.

'What is it, George?' he asked.

'I think that Murphy is an obvious lead which needs following up. He is at present the only individual we have knowledge of, who wanted something from Brother Dominic. It's possible he tried to persuade him to change his mind about the book of hours and went too far,' replied Cross.

'But? I sense a "but" here,' replied Carson.

'But I think the television interview with Brother Dominic cannot be discounted. It's so out of the normal pattern of things for the victim that it could well be significant. It could have alerted the killer to Dominic's whereabouts,' said Cross.

'Murphy already knew his whereabouts. What difference does the interview make in the scheme of things?' asked Carson.

'In the scheme of things whereby you have readily jumped as being the solution to this case? Absolutely nothing. But in the scenario where the killer is not Patrick Murphy but someone else completely, I would suggest it makes a considerable difference,' Cross pointed out.

'Sir,' Carson replied.

'I don't understand,' said Cross.

'You get a lot of leeway in this office, George, but don't make the mistake of forgetting our respective ranks here. You will address me as "sir",' Carson said before leaving the room with as much dignity as he was able to muster.

Cross was unsurprised by the speed and lack of thought with which everyone hurtled down the Murphy lead at the behest of their leader DCI Carson and at the expense of everything else the following week. They seemed to have forgotten that they now had an identity for Brother Dominic prior to his entering St Eustace's. He worked in the City for a bank that crashed. It was the only other thing they currently knew about his previous life. It had to be looked into at the same time and with as much effort as they were devoting to Murphy. He instructed Mackenzie to research Cubitt's bank.

She already knew the bank had gone under in the 2008 crash. But other than that, she knew very little. She quickly found a surprising amount of information on the internet. It was going to take some time to sift through it all though. It would also take a while to present it to Cross in the ordered and logical way that he liked. So, the 'digital detective', as Michael Swift affectionately called her, set about her task with relish. As she started looking, something told her – could she call it her instinct, she wondered, after only a couple of years on the job? Anyway, whatever it was – told her she might be onto something.

She dug deep into the workings of financial institutions in the City of which she knew precious little. Specifically banks and in particular Cubitt's bank. The more she got drawn into the convoluted ways the City worked and made money, the more appalled and shocked she was. She quickly came to the conclusion that it was one of the most dysfunctional worlds she had ever read about. The left hand rarely knew what the right hand was doing in these giant institutions. The superiors were completely oblivious to what was going on below them.

She was in Swift's flat working late one night, when he came home.

'Do you know anything about the 2008 financial crisis and the subprime mortgage scandal?' she asked him straight out.

'Hi,' he replied, but got no response. He put his bag down and went over to the fridge, got out a bottle of white wine, which he proceeded to open, then pour into two glasses. 'I made a decision early in life not to look at big issues politics and economics until I had propagated my first pubic hair. However when that occurred and I was in possession of a full groin area hedge, I found myself to be totally disinterested.'

'Remind me not to introduce you to my parents,' she said.

'Really? I didn't even know that was on the cards.'

'It isn't, idiot. I remember my folks being incandescent at the time. I never understood it. But bloody hell it's plain and simple criminality,' she went on.

'Despite my declared lack of interest, why do I get the feeling you're going to tell me anyway?'

'It might have a bearing on the case and if George was to bring it up in a meeting, wouldn't you want to show him you knew about it?' she asked, knowing full well this was a closer.

'I'm all ears,' he said quickly, sitting down and handing her a glass of wine.

'Michael, I'm working,' she protested indignantly. He withdrew the glass immediately and started to pour its contents into his. 'Hey!' she exclaimed, grabbing the glass and taking a large swig. 'So back in 2008 the banks in the US exploited people who couldn't actually afford mortgages by offering absurdly low interest rates fixed for a couple of years.'

'That was nice of them,' he commented.

'Will you listen? They then raised the rates to a level where the borrower couldn't repay and they defaulted.'

'Well, that's not right.'

'It gets worse. Before it happened, their mortgage was pooled with others into something called mortgage bonds, by their own banks, who then traded in them, earning new vast amounts of commission.'

'Even though they knew they'd default?' he asked.

'Exactly. These bonds had been invented by the very institutions that had given them the mortgages in the first place, so they could sell them off and make even more money for doing precisely nothing except dealing in other people's misfortunes.'

'Are you sure about this?'

'Yes! They were monetising misery and it not only seemed to be perfectly legal, but these people were making billions annually from it. They were inventing profit where it had no right to exist and in actuality didn't. Hence the crash, and hundreds of thousands of reclaimed homes and homeless people.'

'Okay, so that's appalling, but what has it got to do with the case?' he asked, which threw her a bit.

'It's the economic background you need to know about in order to understand what happened to Cubitt's bank.'

He looked a little blank at this.

'The bank Alex worked for.'

'Ah,' he said.

She went on to explain that at the turn of the millennium Cubitt's was one of a dwindling number of small exclusive private banks still functioning in London. Like its main competitor Hoare's, it had been established in the late 1600s. The founder was one Samuel Cubitt. Its main branch had still been in the original grand building on Fleet Street. Customers had written about how its interior hadn't changed much. It still had a small dining room for the most important of its clients and a wine cellar which would have been the envy of many a private London club. The bank only dealt with private, wealthy clients. You had to be known to three other Cubitt's clients and have assets of at least five million pounds to open an account there. You also had to maintain a balance of a hundred thousand pounds in your current account at all times.

Before its collapse, Julian Cubitt was the tenth-generation head of the bank. The board had for years been populated by members of the Cubitt family. But the family line had shrunk, thanks to two world wars, a sexist attitude to female members of the banking family joining the board, and an unfair amount of personal tragedy for one family, it seemed to Mackenzie. Only two members of the family then represented the Cubitts in the bank. Julian and his son Nicholas. They had a controlling interest in the bank and were pretty much the sole owners.

From what she could see, Julian Cubitt, Nicholas's father, had a reputation as a trustworthy, quiet and considered businessman. A solid, safe, pair of hands. Quite old-fashioned in his approach, this seemed to be entirely in keeping for the running of such an old and traditional institution. This was borne out by the photographs of them at the time. Julian was conservatively dressed in corporate suits. Nick was a lot flashier than his father with a long mane of hair that proclaimed a self-confidence and regard. There were even articles about his style in various magazines at the time. Mackenzie felt the strong arm of a stylist and publicist at work for the young man; odd for a banker. When he joined the bank, its priorities seemed to change. In various profile pieces he talked about their need to look forward for the bank to survive. They could no longer continue to do business as if they were still living in the seventeenth century. It needed to broaden its base, modernise and not hold onto the old ways just for the sake of it. His answer to this was for the bank to move into investment banking. So, with a great fanfare in the City trades and the financial pages of the major broadsheets, the investment wing of Cubitt's bank was opened in 2002. It was billed as a significant departure for such an old bank. Nicholas went on a big recruitment drive to get the best people to work for him.

This was the start of the downfall of Cubitt's bank.

22

Sir Patrick Murphy's headquarters were based in Hammersmith, west London. Cross wanted to speak to the man himself, but knew it would be quicker initially to speak to Murphy's spokesman Martin Bates. After all, that was his job. Literally. A Zoom meeting was arranged for the next day, Tuesday, which saved them a long drive up the M4 and back. He would need to see Murphy in person at some point, but experience told him this wasn't going to be easy to set up.

Martin Bates was everything you'd expect from a man who was the face of a large multimillion-pound corporation. Well spoken, he had a military bearing about him in his choice of clothes and their immaculate presentation. Cross thought that retired military officers were so used to wearing uniform that they'd developed an unofficial uniform for retirement, as a kind of comfort blanket when they left the services. This generally took the form of a blue blazer, sharp shirt with a stiff collar, cufflinks and a tie of regimental stripes which looked like it had been impressively knotted by their personal batman. Bates was all smiles and eagerness to help, although he had no idea how he could. He had the easy deflecting charm of a politician, which in his case had doubtless come from years of batting back questions about the morality of a company making so much money from gambling. Everyone knew the house or the bookie were always the winners. Cross thought online gambling was the most insidious exploitation of people, especially the vulnerable and the poor, desperately trying to find a way out of their situation. People with a gambling habit were easy prey for these companies. The temptation was just too great for them. Gambling was made to seem so innocuous and easy. All you needed was a smartphone and a credit card. This made the reality of betting and losing money seem theoretical and not at all real. Until credit card limits were reached and debts mounted with interest.

Bates stared out of Ottey's computer screen in the MCU with the Hammersmith flyover in the background of his spacious corner office. He was obviously valued by Murphy. Bates had an open, disarming expression as the two officers appeared on his desktop computer.

'Thank you for taking this meeting,' Ottey began.

'Of course. As soon as I saw it was the Avon and Somerset police, I assumed it had to be about poor Dominic,' he replied mournfully.

'Why would you assume that?' asked Cross.

'Because I suppose he's been at the forefront of my mind since the news of his death broke. It's so shocking. Who would do that to a monk? A man of the cloth? It's unbelievable.'

'A man of the cloth indeed, but also a thorn in the side of your employer,' Cross observed.

'I wouldn't go that far,' Bates replied.

'Really?' said Cross.

'No, Brother Dominic expressed his opinion when asked to do a valuation for Sir Patrick. He'd done several for us before, successfully, but this one was questionable at the very least.'

'If his opinion was questionable, then why ask him in the first place?' said Ottey.

'Because he's a renowned expert in this field.'

The two police officers let the obvious contradiction just hang in the air.

'But in this instance, he was mistaken,' he went on.

'In your opinion,' Cross qualified.

'In our opinion, yes.'

'Are you an expert in old ecclesiastical works, Mr Bates?' Cross asked.

'No, of course not.'

'And Sir Patrick?'

'No, but he's a well-known and respected collector.'

'It seems to me more likely that your opinions in the matter were more questionable than those of the expert monk,' Cross pointed out.

'They are not just ours. We've had other opinions,' said Bates.

'And what did they conclude?' asked Ottey.

'It's an ongoing process,' came the reply.

'One thing maybe you could help me with. Why was Dominic's opinion of such concern to Murphy?' Cross asked, having grown tired of using the man's title.

'Well, to begin with, it decimated the value of a twenty-million-pound investment,' answered Bates.

'If it's a fake why not sue the auction house who brokered the sale?' asked Ottey.

'It was a private sale,' Bates answered quickly.

'And you don't sue that kind of seller,' Cross inferred.

Bates's silence seemed to confirm this.

'It also called into question Sir Patrick's taste and the value of the rest of his collection. His reputation as a collector,' Bates went on.

'I understand the problem with the devaluation, but as for his reputation, why is that so important?' asked Ottey.

'Our insurers have now insisted on a complete revaluation of the collection, which is not only enormously inconvenient but, for a better word, quite humiliating for someone of his standing.'

'I don't know much about this field, probably less even than you,' Cross said as a matter of fact, not as a way of scoring points. 'But when you did that interview with Brother Dominic on the BBC, he came across very authoritatively. He had very specific questions regarding the provenance of the book and some technical observations about the ink and the material. Whereas you simply reasserted, several times it had to be said, that such valuations are a complex field, no matter what question was put to you. It was like listening to a cabinet minister refusing to answer a relevant, awkward question on the *Today* programme, by just repeating whatever message he or she had been briefed to give. I often find myself thinking, why do they actually bother to come on the show at all? It's infuriating for the listener and insulting, don't you think, DS Ottey?'

'It is a complex field,' Bates retorted.

'There you are, at it again,' said Cross.

'Perhaps we could cut to the chase, detectives. I do have quite a full day,' Bates replied, his well-rehearsed PR veneer hastily cast aside. His tone had shifted, making Cross think they might be getting somewhere. 'What exactly do you want?'

'Were you in touch with Brother Dominic after the interview?' asked Cross.

'We exchanged a few emails, but that was it,' said Bates.

'Did you ever visit him at the abbey?' Cross asked without looking up from where he was making the note.

'No.'

Cross now looked at Bates. This was where a Zoom meeting was less effective than an in-person meeting. Cross was looking directly at Bates, but of course to Bates he appeared to be looking to one side. Cross was well aware how effective his silent stares could be in an interview. Less so here.

'Did you have any further contact with him other than the emails?' asked Cross.

'I did not.'

'Why not?'

'It would have been pointless. His mind was quite made up.'

'Did he realise the ramifications of his opinion for your employer?'

'He did and expressed his sorrow for it,' said Bates as if proving a point.

'Did you see him again before his death?' asked Cross.

'No, I did not.'

23

Ottey gave Cross and Mackenzie a lift to Dominic's funeral. It was one of those early spring days where rain felt inevitable. A grey sky with constantly moving clouds which threatened rain, then suddenly changed density and flew by innocuously. Stephen had decided the right and proper place for his brother's service was St Eustace's. As they drove through the abbey gates which had been left open for the day, they were surprised to see cars parked to one side of the lane extending as far as they could see. Ottey pulled over and the three of them walked. The narrow road was flanked by cars all the way up the hill. The area outside the abbey house was filled, as was the large turning circle outside the abbey church.

'It's beautiful,' Mackenzie commented. 'Just how I imagined it. Maybe a little smaller.'

There were a couple of vans, one a passenger van, the other Fred Savage's building van parked in the circle. No sign of a hearse as Dominic's open coffin had been in the church for a couple of days. The monks had continued their daily offices around him, as if he were still part of the community. They had taken it in turns to sit in vigil with the coffin over the two days so that their brother was never alone.

As indicated by the number of cars, the turnout for the Benedictine monk was huge. Cross had somehow imagined that it would be just the three of them, the monks and Stephen. But there had to be over a hundred people there. The small church was packed to the gills.

'Who's that woman looking at you, George?' asked Ottey. It was Christine, who had found a seat at the back of the church. Cross turned round. She gave him a small, discreet wave.

'What is she doing here?' he asked.

'Well, I don't know. Who is she?' Ottey repeated.

'My mother,' said Cross turning back and looking over at his father Raymond, who had also made the trip. Cross's immediate instinct was to leave. But at that point four priests walked onto the altar. Father Abbot Anselm and Father Magnus, together with another monk who had come from Prinknash. Leading them was Stephen, who seemed to be the main celebrant. It was a solemn Catholic funeral mass with a lesson from the bible read by Brother William. There was communion for those who wanted it. Ottey was quite taken by the Gregorian chant. It was beautifully sung with such simplicity and purity. The ranks of the Cheddar monks had been swelled by a group of monks from Prinknash Abbey who knew Brother Dominic. Their voices rose as one to the vaulted ceiling, which then distributed the sound into every corner of the church like a divine Dolby surround sound system. Ottey found this, together with the incense, quite intoxicating. It was markedly different from the services at her local Pentecostal church which were almost raucous by comparison, a riot of colour, clapping and swaying, singing at full pelt. She'd been brought up in the church by her mother who was still a member of the choir. Ottey had also sung in it, right up until the time she joined the police when she no longer had the time. The community was very small and predominantly of Jamaican descent. Sundays had become something of a police surgery for her with congregants seeking advice, mostly, it had to be said, 'for a friend'. She enjoyed this and saw it as her own unofficial form of outreach.

There was no sermon and no eulogy, but what really preoccupied Cross was the fact that there was no organ accompaniment for the hymns. Father Magnus explained to those who weren't their regular congregation, that the organ was out of commission. He asked the congregation to let the monks begin each hymn and then join in.

Finally, the monks sang the Gregorian requiem chant of *Libera me Domine*. The church bell sounded mournfully throughout this part of the service. Mackenzie found herself transported to another time, another world. Stephen led the priests to the front of the now closed coffin, where they all turned and bowed. Holy water was sprinkled on it. The monks left their stalls and pulled their hoods over their heads in unison. Six of them took hold of the rope handles on the sides of the coffin and lifted it up to waist height. They then processed, singing the Gregorian chant, behind the crucifer carrying a tall silver crucifix, and the four priests. The church bell continued to toll. Ottey thought the monks' serene expressions and reverent singing somehow made the process of death just a normal part of life. But then again, they clearly believed that their brother had gone to a better place. A place he had prepared himself all his life to go on to.

The congregation followed the slow procession as they carried Dominic to the side of the church where their burial ground was. It was no bigger than an allotment. There were several small, plain, identical crosses with just the name of the late monk followed by the initials OSB on them. The congregation instinctively held back as if to give this family of monks some privacy, and watched from a respectable distance. The monks laid their brother gently to rest.

As the interment took place, the rain that had threatened to come all morning arrived in a deluge. People who had come prepared opened their umbrellas. Cross took a small fold-up umbrella from his backpack and opened it over his head. After a couple of seconds, he realised that Ottey and Mackenzie didn't have umbrellas and were getting wet. They showed no inclination to find shelter. This presented him with a conundrum. He couldn't offer only one of them protection from the rain under his umbrella, as the other would be put out. There was no reason for him to give them the umbrella. Why should he suffer when he was the only one to have had the foresight to have brought one? Then he remembered that the mackintosh he was wearing, a relatively new one, had a hood hidden in the collar. He turned to Ottey, holding out the umbrella.

'Here,' he said.

'Are you sure?' she replied.

'You're both getting wet,' he said, then pulled the hood out of its secret hiding place and over his head.

Ottey looked at the hooded figure now standing next to her. 'Very appropriate,' she said, turning back to the hooded monks at the graveside. They stood, heads bowed as they prayed, oblivious of the rain as it ran down their hoods, dropped onto their noses and fell to the ground.

As soon as the burial was completed, the rain suddenly stopped. The monks left the graveyard and stood in small groups outside the church, their hoods now back on their shoulders, their arms folded underneath their habits. Some of the congregation left, others stood around talking. There was to be no funeral tea which Cross thought probably disappointed some of them. He saw Father Magnus introducing Ursula Mead to Father Stephen. He would doubtless want to talk to her at some point about his brother, whom she had seen a lot more of than him over the last fifteen years.

'Oh, this should be interesting. George?' said Ottey who had quietly appeared at his side.

'What?' he replied, turning to see Father Stephen now introducing Cross's mother Christine to his father Raymond. A sense of panic suddenly overwhelmed Cross and he bolted down the side of the church to the side door and sought refuge inside. Ottey watched him go and thought he was probably best left alone for the time being.

Cross sat in the front pew. Beads of sweat prickled above his forehead. He realised he was hyperventilating. This often happened when something took him by surprise socially or there was something in his life he had no control of. He couldn't work out what he was upset about. Was he upset for his father? His mother? She must have known Raymond would be there. His father would have been sideswiped. But it wasn't this, he realised. He knew at some point his mother and father might meet again. He had no problem with that. It was none of his business. But for some reason he knew he wanted no part of it. Why? It was a complication that he had no time for. A change, an upheaval that wasn't welcome. Cross compartmentalised areas of his life which he liked to keep separate, like his food. He had his work, his organ playing and his father. This was sufficient for him. He found it difficult enough when work started to merge with his personal life with Ottey and Mackenzie meeting and taking an interest in his father.

He would have to work this out, but he was saved from this emotional upheaval when he noticed the organ pipes behind the altar and went to investigate why exactly it was out of commission. Cross had had his suspicions that something was possibly wrong with the organ the first time he saw it, and noticed that the keys on the manuals were uneven. This probably meant that it was a tracker organ and that the trackers were out. These were thin lengths of wood that linked the key with the valve. When a key was pressed the wooden tracker pulled open a valve in the corresponding pipe above to let the air out and create the note. He found a door behind the organ and went into the old bellows room where the air for the organ was generated. Originally it would have had a manually operated bellows like a blacksmith's, but this one had been updated at some point and was electrically operated. Cross was horrified to see cleaning equipment piled up on the air reservoir. The leather corners were broken which meant they had to leak air. It obviously couldn't be used in this condition; it simply wouldn't play properly. At the back of the organ chamber was a ladder leading to a small door. Cross climbed up and opened it. The pipes inside were all covered in dirt and dust. Large pieces of plaster were lodged between the pipes. He looked up and saw that part of the ceiling directly above the organ had fallen down.

Cross heard voices in the church below. He looked down through the organ pipes and saw the four priests walking down the aisle, talking quietly. They each genuflected in front of the altar then disappeared from his view. He climbed out of the organ chamber and down the stepladder, being careful not to knock any of the organ's tracker action. He assumed the priests had gone into the sacristy to disrobe. He knocked on the door and went in.

'Your organ is in need of repair,' Cross announced.

'As is your mackintosh,' replied Father Magnus.

Cross looked down at his raincoat, which was covered in filth and cobwebs from the organ cabinet, and saw that it had been torn. He looked back at the abbot.

'Yes,' the abbot sighed. 'It is indeed. There was a partial ceiling collapse above it, which is also in need of repair.'

'I'm assuming you don't have the funds to fix it?' said Cross.

'Well, in point of fact we've just secured some money to repair the ceiling, which is more urgent and dangerous, but not the organ, alas,' replied the abbot.

'Then I shall repair it for you,' said Cross, who suddenly felt it was inappropriate for him to be in a room with priests disrobing. Despite the fact they were all wearing cassocks. Cross looked at Stephen. He urgently wanted to ask him about his mother and father. Not just what had been said, but why he had seen the need to introduce them. He wasn't sure how to broach it, particularly in front of the other priests. Stephen sensed this immediately.

'Why don't we talk about it the day after tomorrow, George?' he intuited. 'You will be coming to practise?'

'That's Thursday,' Cross stated.

'It is.'

'Then I will be,' he said and left.

The father abbot turned to Stephen. 'Am I right in thinking George intends repairing the organ himself, or will he get someone else to do it?' he asked.

'No. He'll repair it himself. He's very accomplished. It's how we know each other.'

'Oh, I thought he might be a member of your congregation,' the abbot replied.

'Gosh, no. George is a very committed non-believer. But he looks after the organ at my church,' said Stephen.

'I see. A man of myriad talents.'

'Indeed.'

As Cross got to the main door of the church he stopped before going outside and phoned Ottey.

'George, everything okay?' she asked.

'Are they still there?' he asked.

'Who?'

'My parents,' he replied irritably.

'No.'

He cut off the call, opened the door and went back outside, looking around anxiously.

'Are you sure she's gone?' he asked Ottey.

'Absolutely. She gave Raymond a lift back to Bristol,' she replied.

'She *what*?'

He was genuinely concerned by this idea.

Serena Birch and Mark, her husband, Brother Dominic's friends from London, walked over to them together with another man in his forties. Serena had been crying and was obviously still very upset.

'This whole thing is so surreal,' she began by saying. 'Not just that he's dead, but seeing all the monks and this setting, the abbey, it just feels so odd when you see the reality of it.'

'That he actually was a monk all this time, living with this community,' Mark explained.

'I'm still getting my head round the fact that he was actually murdered,' said the man with them. He was well dressed in a black suit, white shirt and black tie, with close-cropped hair.

'Oh, I'm sorry. This is Andrew. Andrew Beresford, one of Alex's oldest friends from Cambridge and then the City,' said Mark.

'The one we told you about in London?' Serena clarified.

'Ah yes. The one whose name you couldn't remember,' Cross pointed out unhelpfully.

'DS Ottey and Cross,' said Ottey.

'Are you absolutely certain he was murdered?' Beresford asked in disbelief.

'I'm afraid there's no question about it,' answered Ottey.

'When was the last time you saw him?' asked Cross.

'Not for years. Ten, fifteen years? Certainly not since before he became a monk.'

'Did you become aware where he was through all the media coverage?' asked Cross.

'Yes. Actually, the first time I saw him was on the local news. I wasn't sure at first, but it was definitely him. I couldn't believe it.'

'Was that about the book of hours?' asked Cross.

'Yes, that was it.'

'Did you get in touch with him? Come and see him?' asked Cross.

'Well no. I didn't know where he was. I suppose I could maybe have worked it out by process of elimination. I don't know how many abbeys there are in the *Points West* area, to be honest. I was just amazed it was him.'

'Where do you live now, Mr Beresford?' asked Ottey.

'Just outside Bath,' he replied.

'Oh good. We'd like to talk to you and today probably isn't the right day. This is my card. Could I have your contact details?' asked Ottey.

'Of course,' he replied, fishing in his pocket for his wallet and producing a business card for her.

'Mr Beresford—' she began.

'Andrew,' he corrected her.

'Andrew. Do you have any idea who might have wished Alex harm?' she asked.

'None at all,' he replied.

'You say that with a surprising amount of certainty, Mr Beresford,' observed Cross.

'The only surprising thing here for me is that one of my friends has actually been murdered. The whole idea is preposterous to me.'

'That's a fair point,' replied Cross. 'What is it you do these days?'

'I'm a financial adviser.'

'Are you two driving back to London?' Ottey asked Serena and Mark, in an everyday conversational way which Cross knew signalled she wanted his conversation to end. He saw William talking to another mourner. The monk beckoned him over. Cross duly obliged.

'DS Cross, I wanted to introduce you to Snip. He was—'

'I know who he is,' Cross interrupted. 'I'm surprised at your presence here.'

'I get that. So am I, if I'm honest. I just felt I had to come,' the young man replied. He was very thin, his suit hanging off him, as if he'd either recently lost a lot of weight, or borrowed it in haste from a friend.

'Why?' Cross went on.

'In the end Dominic had a huge impact on my life.'

'You lost your job because of him,' Cross pointed out.

'I lost my job because of my behaviour. It had nothing to do with Brother Dominic. However, more importantly, because of that I got sober. I figured out that if I could behave in such a way that a Benedictine monk was driven to punch my lights out, I must've hit rock bottom.'

'I see,' said Cross.

'And this is Robbie Weald. Robbie has been a frequent guest of ours. He helps in the bookbindery and with the bees. He had many conversations with Brother Dominic who, as you know, was guest master here at the abbey.'

'DS Cross,' said the man holding out his hand. He withdrew it shortly afterwards, when he realised it wasn't going to be shaken. He was quite short. His head was shaven completely bald. He had a thick beard but a pasty, almost unhealthy-looking pale complexion. 'Sorry to meet you in these circumstances,' he went on.

'In my experience people are generally sorry to meet the police in any circumstances,' replied Cross.

The man laughed politely as did William. Mackenzie walked over and silently stood at the edge of the group.

'It feels strange to say this, and I certainly don't want to waste your time. I wouldn't normally have thought anything about it. But now that Dominic has been murdered in such a brutal way... What am I talking about? The fact that he's been murdered at all, full stop, has made me wonder whether it might be relevant. But I'll let you be the judge of that. Brother William tells me you're aware of the book of hours controversy,' Robbie said.

'Correct,' replied Cross.

'Have you actually seen it?'

'I have not.'

'It's a beautiful thing, but unfortunately for Sir Patrick Murphy not *the* beautiful thing he thought when he spent a fortune on it.'

'Dominic was deeply upset when he reached the conclusion that the book was a fake. He was upset for Sir Patrick whom he'd come to know quite well over the years,' added Snip.

'You also spoke to him about it?' asked Cross.

'Yes. We all did.'

'But after Dominic made it clear he wouldn't change his opinion, Murphy and his associates' behaviour, became worrying,' Robbie said.

'In what way?' asked Cross.

'Well, in truth, it wasn't so much Murphy as his consigliere who behaved with real malice,' Robbie continued.

'Martin Bates?' Mackenzie suggested.

'That's him. He came to the abbey himself on a number of occasions, attempting to persuade Dominic he'd made a mistake and should rectify it.'

'This was after the television interview?' Cross clarified.

'That's right.'

'Are you sure?' Cross asked.

'Of course. Why do you ask?'

'Because he assured me, he hadn't made any contact with Brother Dominic after the interview,' replied Cross.

'Well, he did, and more often than not, in person. He became increasingly aggressive, threatening Brother Dominic, pretty much.'

'Did Brother Dominic talk to the police?' asked Cross who was unaware of any such reports. But that didn't mean they didn't exist.

'No. It's not the Benedictine way, after all,' Robbie replied, looking at William for approval. 'Of course, I wish I'd done so myself. But I never imagined this would happen. I'm absolutely racked with guilt.'

'And as I keep telling him, there's absolutely no need,' said William. 'This whole thing was completely unexpected. What is more, we don't actually know that Sir Patrick Murphy is responsible for this. Let us not forget that he's a man of profound faith and Christian belief.'

'I don't see many other potential suspects, Brother William,' Robbie said.

'Is there anything else you think I should know?' Cross asked the two men.

'Well, Brother Dominic thought there was something distinctly fishy about the provenance of the book,' said Robbie.

'How, exactly?' asked Cross.

'He told Murphy he should return the book to the seller and demand his money back. If he wasn't willing to repay him, he should sue. Brother Dominic volunteered to appear as an expert witness. But this was impossible, apparently. I don't know the details, but the seller was not entirely respectable and what you might call legitimate.'

'Then why buy it from him in the first place?' asked Cross. 'Surely this kind of thing was an obvious risk.'

'Because of the allure of the piece. Had it been genuine it would have been the crowning jewel of his collection. A simple case of greed and ambition,' said William. But his attention seemed to be distracted by Andrew Beresford walking to his car. Cross also noticed Beresford looking quickly away from William when he became aware of Cross looking at him.

'She seemed very nice, your mum,' said Ottey as she drove Cross and Mackenzie back to Bristol.

'Your *mother* was there?' asked Mackenzie with a familiarity that irritated Cross. 'No way,' she said, which annoyed him even more.

'And his father,' Ottey added.

'Oh, I know. I had a chat with Raymond. Was it me or is he not himself?' she asked.

'Hardly surprising in the circumstances,' said Cross.

'I thought so too the last time the girls and I popped over for tea. We'd baked a cake and took it over,' Ottey replied.

'When was that, exactly?' asked Cross.

'Last weekend. Saturday afternoon.'

'He didn't mention it to me.'

'Well, there you are. He's definitely not himself. There's nothing wrong medically, is there?'

'He's absolutely fine,' Cross insisted.

'George...' Ottey began, before thinking better of it.

'What?' he asked.

'I'm not sure you'd notice if your dad was a bit down. Let's be honest,' she said.

He would've objected to this had he not known it was the truth.

24

Cross was one of the most open-minded officers in the MCU when it came to an investigation. He now decided to investigate Sir Patrick Murphy's background and history. Their victim had been in a dispute with a powerful businessman. Despite his belief that the TV interview was central to all of this and couldn't be ignored, Robbie Weald and Snip's information definitely needed investigation. But unlike his colleagues he never pursued one line of enquiry to the exclusion of others.

Murphy was the youngest of six children, and he grew up in the north of England, in Liverpool, after his parents had come over from Ireland. A happy childhood it would seem, with a problematic but loving father and a worn-out mother, both now deceased. Cross detected a constant need for Murphy to prove himself throughout his life. He hadn't gone to university but had trained as an accountant. His career had been middling, it was said. He worked at a large national firm for just under a decade after qualifying. According to him he wasn't particularly ambitious and certainly didn't make any waves at the firm.

'A high-flier I certainly wasn't,' he said in one interview. 'More of a glider taking advantage of the occasional opportunistic thermal to keep afloat when necessary.'

The galvanising event in young Patrick Murphy's life had been being made redundant in his late twenties.

'It gave me a huge urge to prove myself,' he'd said in another interview.

He set out to work on what he'd felt for a long time had been a hole in the market – the betting market, to be precise. He had foreseen the possibility of betting online and saw huge potential growth. This was twenty years earlier, when the technological development of the smartphone was still in its infancy. But he was sure that in time it could revolutionise betting. He felt ease and convenience for people, as well as reinventing the way bets were placed, could tap into a huge, as yet unexploited market. This ease would come when people could place a variety of bets with just a touch of a button on their phone. No need to type in credit card details or email addresses. He was way ahead of his time, but sure he was onto a winner.

He not only changed what you could bet on, like an individual player scoring in a certain part of the game, but also when you could cash out your bet. This was crucial. You could do this early if it was a spread bet, which was tempting. But all the more tempting were the rewards the app offered up if you didn't. If you held out, you could possibly win much more. This was where Murphy ended up making a lot of his money. By people not cashing out when they should and then losing their whole stake. It was tough and slow initially, but as technology caught up with his vision, Murphy became enormously successful. His company became a leading gambling brand in the country. He had his own executive box at Anfield, from which he'd watch advertisements for his company flashing round the electronic pitchside advertising hoardings. The sixth son of a working-class Liverpool family had done good.

The more successful and richer he became, the more remote and unavailable the previously media-friendly billionaire became. This was, it seemed, partly to avoid answering awkward questions about some of the methods his company employed. Specifically, when it came to collecting unpaid debts. People defaulting, unable to pay their debts, hadn't been part of the original business plan. He became increasingly frustrated with conventional methods of debt collection and started resorting to more direct and brutal methods of recovery. Bailiffs were replaced by gangs of debt collectors who looked like they'd been recruited from outside the gates of prisons all over the country. Dressed completely in black with menacingly cropped hair and Doc Marten boots, they would have blended in perfectly at a fascist rally. They rapidly became a fear-inducing law unto themselves, recovering debts in any way they saw fit. Breaking into people's homes, taking electronic goods and any money they could find. Illegally towing cars. They made private wheel clampers look like the AA. It became a national scandal, particularly when it transpired that the police had absolutely no interest in curbing their activities. One thing became increasingly clear to Cross: Murphy was not averse to using coercion and threats to get his way. This man was no stranger to violence.

Things had changed though, about a decade earlier, around the time of his second marriage, when he found religion. Murphy suddenly announced that he wanted to protect the people who couldn't afford to gamble and got themselves into trouble. It seemed to be counter-intuitive. But he started to set limits on people's online gambling accounts with his company. He was trying to bring the 'defaulting culture' to an end. He said he didn't want people gambling with money they simply didn't have. This seemed to be socially responsible but when Cross had a closer look he realised what this actually meant was that he didn't want them betting if they couldn't pay their losses. He had no qualms if the money was owed to credit card companies, or other payday loan companies, as long as he was paid. It had nothing to do with his self-proclaimed desire to stop people gambling with money they didn't actually have.

Murphy's PR machine portrayed him as a man with a huge social conscience – this, despite how he actually made his money. Murphy himself claimed to have had a Damascene moment when he met his second wife, a practising Catholic, and had converted to Catholicism himself. He wanted to enhance people's lives and yes, that did include having the occasional harmless flutter, as he himself had described gambling. He didn't want to exploit them. A different truth emerged from several ex-employees. It was that he had realised his unique brand of violence was damaging the business badly. Murphy had originally been okay with people writing about his violent methods of debt collection – he saw it as a 'nuclear deterrent'. It discouraged people from messing with him. But now people were increasingly betting with his growing number of competitors. He wasn't just losing customers; he was haemorrhaging them. Something had to change.

On balance, Cross reflected that Murphy was exactly the kind of man to kidnap and beat someone to death to protect his interests, man of the cloth or not. It was while he was going through all the publicity and press about Murphy that Cross came upon a recent picture of the man himself. He was standing beside a brand new private jet. His private jet. Cross made a note of the tail number and made a phone call.

25

Cross was surprised to discover that getting to St Eustace's that weekend under his own steam was much harder than he thought. At over twenty miles it was too far and too tricky a journey to cycle. It was even longer to get there with a mix of cycling, train and bus. At least two hours. As he wasn't going on police work, he couldn't use a police vehicle. There was only one thing for it. To fork out for a cab. He had stated his intention of repairing the organ to the abbot and he wasn't going to let a forty quid cab fare get in his way. Weekends were really the only free time he had, so no time like the present to get going. He put a spare set of clothes in his backpack, as he imagined he was going to get quite dirty in the process, and called a taxi.

Brother Benedict was surprised to see the police officer at the weekend and thought he must be on police business. He could be forgiven for having assumed this as Cross's choice of weekend clothing, even when it came to the refurbishment of a defunct organ, was exactly the same as he wore during the week at work – jacket, V-neck sweater, shirt and tie, corduroy trousers.

'DS Cross, welcome. Who are you here to see today?' the monk asked politely.

'No one. I just need the keys to the church.'

'I see. Well, Fred and his gang are up there this morning. So, it's open.'

This was annoying to Cross. He'd assumed he'd be working on his own, in welcome peace and quiet. Brother Benedict smiled as Cross turned away without saying anything. He had no idea why Cross wanted to get into the church and was bemused by the man's lack of any social grace. He watched as Cross walked up the hill, with his vintage canvas plumbing bag in his hand. In it were his organ tools, another find from his father's eBay obsession. Raymond had found the tools and bag being sold by a retiring organ technician, as the seller liked to refer to himself. The tools had belonged to this man's father, who in turn had acquired them second-hand himself. It meant that they had to be at least a hundred years old. Cross liked this sense of history about them. He enjoyed thinking about all the instruments that had been tuned and maintained with them over the years.

As he walked into the church, he saw that two large scaffolding towers had been erected either side of the altar, adjacent to the organ, with a platform suspended between them. Two builders were standing on the platform working on the ceiling above. They were scraping away the flaking plaster. Most of it fell onto the platform below. But, to Cross's horror, large chunks fell directly into the organ pipes below.

'Stop!' he shrieked in a voice he didn't actually recognise as his own. 'What do you think you're doing?'

The men on the platform didn't reply but another appeared from behind the altar. He was a burly brute with hands the size of a goalkeeper's gloves.

'What does it look like, mate?' he asked.

'The plaster is falling directly into the organ pipes,' said Cross.

'Is it?' the man asked. He walked down the aisle and looked up. 'Peter, you bloody idiot! Where's the tarp?'

'The what?' answered one of the men on the platform above.

'The tarpaulin you were supposed to put over the organ?' the man in the nave asked.

'You said not to bother in the end, as the organ don't work,' came the reply.

'I said no such thing. Get the bloody tarp.' The man turned to Cross. 'A misunderstanding. You're that copper, aren't you?'

'I don't know, am I? I am a policeman but whether I am the policeman you're referring to, I have no idea,' Cross replied.

'Fred Savage, builder. I would shake your hand but they're filthy. How can I help?'

'Well, putting up that tarpaulin would be a start, before you cause any more damage,' said Cross.

'I was talking about the case. I assume you're here to talk about Brother Dominic,' said Savage.

'I'm here to do no such thing. I'm here to repair the organ.'

'You what?' asked the bemused builder.

'I'm here to fix the organ in the same way you are here to repair the ceiling,' Cross replied and walked down the aisle towards the altar. Then he stopped and turned.

'Mr Savage, there is one thing you could do for me. Give me permission to go up on to the platform, so I can look down into the larger pipes,' he said.

'Of course. Help yourself.'

'Good. Also, do you have a hard hat I can borrow?' asked Cross.

Savage looked at him, trying to figure out whether he was taking the piss. None of his men were wearing hard hats.

'If I'm to work under your men it would make sense, bearing in mind how carefree they seem to be when it comes to falling plaster, to have some protection for my head. I'm actually quite surprised none of you are wearing them. Who is your health and safety officer?' Cross asked, probably sounding a little more officious than he meant to.

'I am,' replied Savage, who was rapidly beginning to regret his decision to come in that weekend.

Five minutes later Cross was on top of the platform with the two builders after ensuring what the total safe load of the platform was. They were all now wearing bright yellow hard hats with *Savage* emblazoned on them. Cross shone a torch down the large principal pipes and made a note of which ones seemed to have debris at the bottom of them. Strictly speaking he could have just left the debris there, as it wouldn't really affect the sound. But he wanted to be thorough. He then press-ganged the two men to help lift five of the principal pipes up a few inches, so he could get the errant plaster out and quickly put the pipes back in place.

When they'd done this Cross realised he needed to give the entire chamber a clean inside before he started with the individual pipes. He marched back down to the abbey house and knocked on the abbot's office door.

'Come in, DS Cross,' said the abbot from within.

Cross came into the room.

'How did you know it was me?' he asked.

'The monks here tend to be a little more temperate and gentle when it comes to knocking on doors. More in keeping with asking the occupant's permission to enter the room, rather than announcing one's presence,' the abbot replied quietly, as if to emphasise his point.

'I see. You have a vacuum cleaner. I saw a Dyson in the library when it was cleaned for myself and DS Ottey. I need it,' said Cross.

'Of course. It's very good of you to come and repair the organ for us,' replied the abbot.

'On the contrary, it's completely selfish. I enjoy it.'

'Would you like one of the brothers to assist you?'

Cross thought about this for a moment.

'I'll need Brother William to come and help at a later stage. The leather corners and folds on the air reservoir have perished so need replacing. I think he could apply his bookbinding skills to that task,' he replied.

'Very well, but what about general less skilled work? Would another pair of hands help?' asked the abbot.

'Yes. Brother Thomas would be a good choice,' said Cross.

'Really?' replied the abbot, unable to disguise his surprise. 'Very well, I shall send him up. Will you join us for lunch afterwards? It's simply bread and soup today. Brother Jude's bread has to be tasted. It is quite a marvel.'

'I won't,' said Cross. The idea of eating lunch at the same table as other people horrified him.

'You won't be bothered, I can assure you. We eat in complete silence with a brief reading during the beginning of the lunch. You won't even know anyone else is there. It is one of my favourite times of the day. Food in silence. I have a sense that might also appeal to you, DS Cross.'

Cross hadn't thought to bring anything for lunch and what the abbot was describing seemed to him to be, in all probability, quite acceptable.

'I will.'

Thomas appeared a little later with the Dyson vacuum in a wheelbarrow together with a variety of attachments. He also brought a couple of long feather dusters.

'What are those?' asked Cross.

'Feather dusters on long handles,' replied Thomas.

'Why have you brought them?'

'Father Abbot said you wanted to clean out the pipes. I didn't see you carrying any when you arrived this morning.'

'Good thinking,' replied Cross.

He thought Thomas looked uncomfortable and suspicious, though. His clean-shaven face, dark grey from the thick black beard lurking below the epidermis, and a pronounced monobrow didn't help. Cross was sure that were it not for his vow of obedience the taciturn monk would be anywhere else but with him.

They set to work in silence. Cross had noticed that the builders were quiet as they went about their work. He wondered whether this was their being respectful of working in a church, or whether it was the presence of a monk below them. He was slightly concerned by the monk's refusal to wear the proffered hard hat. But Thomas said were he to be hit by a piece of descending plaster, it would be God's will.

They spent a couple of hours cleaning the chamber around the pipes, sweeping and vacuuming up decades of dust and dirt. They took a break when the bell sounded for Sext. Brother Thomas joined the other monks in the choir stalls of the church.

Cross stopped working as they prayed. When they finished they left silently, Thomas with them. Cross realised it was time for lunch. So he followed them down to the refectory in the abbey house.

The monks stood at their allocated places. The abbot then indicated a vacant place at the end of one of the two tables for Cross. He was pleased to see how much space there was between each monk. It was as if these men had been practising social distancing for some time. Father Magnus said grace in Latin and they all sat. There were jugs of water on the tables. The monk next to him poured a glass for Cross.

'Thank you,' said Cross. The monk smiled and put his finger to his lips. Ottey would have laughed out loud at this, thought Cross. She was forever reminding him of the social niceties of life, such as 'please' and 'thank you', and here he was being gently reprimanded for doing just that.

He was offered bread from a basket. After the reading was over, they continued to eat. At such a distance from each other and in silence, they might as well have been on their own. It occurred to Cross that this was designed in a way to let them continue their contemplation. He thoroughly enjoyed lunch in these conditions, even though he was with other people. The main revelation, however, was Brother Jude's bread. The abbot hadn't been exaggerating. It was possibly some of the lightest, flavoursome bread Cross had ever eaten. The soup was a simple vegetable soup made with produce from the kitchen garden. It was extraordinarily fresh, the vegetables – carrots, potatoes, onions, broccoli, among others – perfectly cooked and all beautifully seasoned. These monks may have eaten simply, but they ate well. Cross felt replenished and invigorated as he and Thomas walked silently back to the church.

That afternoon they set about the mammoth task of cleaning all the pipes. This was fairly straightforward with the easily accessible small pipes. They removed them one by one and cleaned them with pipe cleaners then replaced them. But as they got deeper into the chamber it was obvious they would have to take all the pipes out as a job lot, including those they'd already cleaned. Cross was annoyed that he hadn't worked this out a couple of hours ago. He had, though, brought sticky labels and Sharpie pens so he could label each pipe and their location, before taking them out and laying them on the altar floor. He was about to start when Thomas stopped him.

'Why are you doing that?' he asked.

'So, we know where they belong. It'll save time in the long run,' Cross replied.

'No need. Just take them out. I'll remember,' said the monk confidently.

'That won't work, I can assure you.'

'I have a photographic memory. It'll work and save more time in the long run,' Thomas assured him.

The risk of him getting it wrong, and the extra work that would entail, was far outweighed in Cross's mind by his curiosity of seeing if the monk could actually do it. They took out all the pipes on that side of the organ and laid them out. They then started to clean them one by one. It took a further couple of hours. Cross was sure that the monk hadn't taken into account the amount of time between them removing them and then putting them back. He had to have forgotten where they all went.

'Right, now we, or rather you, have to put them all back,' Cross said as a challenge.

Thomas climbed up the small ladder back into the organ. He then asked for each pipe in turn and automatically put them into the correct place.

'Impressive,' said Cross.

'I know,' replied Thomas.

They made excellent progress for the rest of the afternoon, Thomas's photographic memory making the whole process so much easier. They stopped when it came to vespers. But they had managed to clean at least a quarter of the pipes.

'Will you have supper with us?' asked Father Magnus.

Cross thought for a moment.

'No,' he replied.

'May I ask why?' the priest enquired softly.

'I prefer each constituent of my meal on separate plates. I don't like them to touch. It's a characteristic of my autism but people tend not to like it, on the whole,' replied Cross.

'Supper is a self-service operation. You can have as much or as little on as many or as few plates as you wish,' replied the priest with a smile. So, Cross joined them.

Later, after another successfully relaxed meal in the company of the monks, Cross sought out the abbot and told him he was leaving and would return first thing in the morning.

'Why don't you stay the night with us? We have a guest room. It's actually en suite so completely private. Basic, but perfectly comfortable,' added the abbot.

Cross thought about this, weighing up the pros and cons of the suggestion. He looked very serious as he came to his conclusion.

'That would certainly make sense and save on two taxi fares,' Cross replied.

'I'll get Brother Andrew to show you to the room. Will I see you at Compline?'

'You won't.'

'Very well. Good night and God bless.'

As the abbot walked away Cross was suddenly suffused with an odd sense of nostalgic familiarity. He then remembered something he hadn't had cause to think about for years. It was his mother bending over his bed to kiss him goodnight and saying those words. So, he had to have been under five. He went to sleep that night strangely at peace with himself. Content and relaxed after a good day's work that had nothing to do with murder and death.

26

Ottey and her mother, Cherish, were washing up after supper that night when there was a sudden scream from the girls' bedroom down the corridor. This was followed by raised voices in a dispute of world-ending proportions. Ottey went to the kitchen door and shouted.

'Whatever it is, it stops now!'

A silence followed. Ottey's word was obviously law in this household.

'Impressive. You never shut up when I yelled at you like that,' said Cherish.

'I know. Sorry about that,' Ottey replied.

'Everything all right?'

'Yeah, just tired.'

'Work?'

'Yep.'

'That man, he exhausts you,' Cherish commented.

'Who? My boss?'

'No, George.'

'He does not. He's fine. Leave poor old George alone,' Ottey protested, but she wondered whether there was just an element of truth in it. Probably not. In many ways he made her work life much easier, he was that good.

'That poor monk. I've been praying for you,' said Cherish.

'Thanks, no wonder we're making such good progress.'

Cherish was about to object when another deafening scream careered through the small flat, bouncing off the walls. Ottey was back at the kitchen door.

'Clara! Sitting room, now!' she yelled. This was followed by a loud groan of indignant injustice and the slamming of a bedroom door.

'It's time you moved, sweetie. Clara's too old to be sharing a bedroom with her sister,' said Cherish.

'I know,' Ottey agreed.

'Then stop putting it off and get on with it.'

'I'm not. I'm busy at work.'

'And do you see that changing any time soon? No,' she said, answering her own question. 'So you might as well get on with it now because you're always going to be busy. Unless you want to stay here for the rest of your working life.'

'It's easy for you to say.'

'And it's easy for you to do nothing. You want to get yourself that promotion. More money and less work, I'd bet.'

Ottey said nothing but her mother was right, to an extent. There was certainly more money and more control of your hours with a higher rank.

'Ideally, I'd like a house. But I don't know if I can afford it.'

'Well, you won't know if you don't look, honey.'

That night she lay in bed wondering about what her mother had said. She remembered Det. Supt Heather Matthews talking to her about promotion the previous year. Maybe now was the time to push instead of just sitting back and waiting to see what happened.

27

At five forty-five the next morning Cross heard a monk knocking on the doors of the other monks, waking them up gently with a soft Latin supplication. Sleepy, muffled Latin responses came back from inside all of the rooms. There was no knock on Cross's door. But he decided to get up anyway. He wanted to observe a full day in the life of a monk. He sat in the church as the monks sang lauds. As someone who liked his routine there was something satisfying to Cross at starting the day in the same way every day. He liked the continuity, the predictability of it. He found it calming and almost soothing.

As he was walking into the refectory Father Magnus came up to him with a pile of wrapped clothing.

'The monks were talking last night about how filthy your clothes had been getting, working on the organ. So, we thought you might like to have these. It's what we use when doing manual labour. Very comfortable and practical. Also keeps your clothes clean.'

Cross took them to his room. There were dark blue canvas trousers and a hooded top. He wasn't sure it was necessary but then imagined what Ottey might say to him in these circumstances. He decided to wear the clothing as he thought that's what she'd advise because the monks had been so considerate. To all intents and purposes, he now looked like one of them.

After breakfast he and Thomas set about their task in an efficient, contented silence. They made good progress and took a break mid-morning sitting outside in the sunshine.

As if by some sort of telepathic communication Brother

William arrived with a tray of tea and biscuits. He was helped by Snip. The presence of a teapot and strainer lifted Cross's spirits. William and Snip sat with them.

'Snip is giving me a hand in the bookbindery,' said William who still seemed a little subdued and quiet.

'We met at the funeral,' said Snip.

'We did,' Cross said. 'And here you are again.'

'How is the work progressing?' William asked.

'Very well,' replied Cross.

'Are you enjoying it, Brother Thomas?' William inquired.

'It's quite satisfying, but I am concerned about neglecting the lawn,' Thomas replied.

'I'm sure it'll survive for a couple of days. If you'd like, though, I could help DS Cross and you could go back to the lawn,' William said.

'Do you have an eidetic memory?' Thomas asked.

'I do not,' William answered with a smile that suggested to Cross this was a frequently used question in Thomas's vocal armoury.

'Then I think not,' said Thomas.

'There is something you could help with, though,' said Cross. 'I'll show you after we've had our tea.'

'Excellent.'

Cross was glad of William's presence. There was something he wanted to ask Brother Thomas. He thought the presence of another monk might set him at ease. Given the fact that Brother Thomas had refused to come to the interview with him and Ottey, he was sure that something was troubling him. That he did indeed have something to add. Cross thought he hadn't told them for fear of his being at fault, in some way to blame for what had happened. He had obviously felt this about witnessing Brother Dominic's conversation on the gate phone, but Cross wondered whether there was more. He often felt this himself, that he was at fault for things when he wasn't. It was a product of never really being sure how he was coming over to people.

'Brother Thomas's memory is quite something,' he began by saying to William.

'Oh yes. Nothing happens here without Brother Thomas knowing. He has all our birthdays memorised. Saints' feast days, anniversaries of the parishioners who come on Sundays,' William replied.

'What kind of anniversaries?' Cross asked.

'Husbands' and wives' deaths, wedding anniversaries, birthdays,' William replied.

'Not all of them, surely?' asked Cross. 'There must be some parishioners whose details he doesn't know.'

'I know them all,' Thomas suddenly said. 'You can test me if you like,' he said with almost childish defensiveness.

'So, if any strangers come on a Sunday, you would know?' Cross asked.

'Of course,' Thomas replied.

'The same for any visitors to the abbey?' Cross asked.

'Brother Thomas makes it his business to know everything that happens here,' said William with the tiniest air of irritation, Cross thought. It was possible Brother Thomas had been aware of Brother William's feelings for Brother Dominic before anyone else at the abbey. Perhaps Brother William still resented it.

'Did Dominic have any visitors at the weekends?' asked Cross. He thought that if anyone involved in his death had visited him at the abbey, a visit at a weekend with the church full of people would be the easiest way to go unnoticed.

'It's difficult to say whether they were visitors or new congregants,' replied Thomas.

'So, there was someone?' said Cross. 'Someone you weren't familiar with?'

'Yes.'

'Who were they?'

'I don't know their names,' replied Thomas.

'You didn't ask Brother Dominic?'

Thomas seemed horrified by this idea. 'It was none of my business,' he replied.

'How many people were there?'

'Two.'

'At the same time or on different occasions?' Cross asked.

'Two at the same time, then each returned individually,' said Thomas.

'Male or female?' asked Cross.

'Both men.'

Cross got out his phone and pulled up a press photograph of Patrick Murphy with Bates at his side.

'Are these them?' he asked Thomas.

'Yes.'

Snip leaned over to have a look.

'Is that Patrick Murphy?' he asked.

'It is,' replied Cross.

Snip nodded knowingly, then said, 'You know about his past, right? Murphy's? All this ethical gambling is bullshit – sorry, Brother William. He's just a Scouse thug dressed in a fancy suit.'

'People can change,' William suggested.

'Then why was Dominic so disturbed by the whole situation and by him?' Snip asked.

William reflected on this for a moment then conceded, 'He was definitely preoccupied by it.'

'Was he frightened?' asked Cross.

'He was really upset by it. Not so much frightened, as alarmed at the change in Murphy. It was like he was suddenly dealing with an entirely different person.'

'But murder? Over a book? It seems extreme,' said William.

'It wasn't about a book, Brother William. It was about twenty million pounds. People have killed for a good deal less,' said Snip.

'Murder is always extreme, Brother William, and he has a point. People have killed for a good deal less,' said Cross.

'And it's not always intentional,' Snip added.

'What makes you say that?' asked Cross.

'Well let's say it was Murphy, or more likely someone employed by him. I read that Brother Dominic was badly beaten,' Snip continued.

Cross noticed how William winced at the thought of this. Thomas was looking away, as if he didn't want any part of the conversation.

'What if the idea was to persuade him to change his mind, thereby saving Murphy millions? Brother Dominic refused and they just went a bit too far? It's not as if they were going to benefit from his death, were they?'

'Indeed. Which begs the question, who would benefit from the death of a Benedictine monk?' asked Cross.

'A good question, Sergeant. The fact is, though, that this Murphy bloke was like a changed man after Brother Dominic told him about the book,' Snip added.

'Disappointment manifests itself in many different ways,' William pointed out.

'Now this is why I could never be a monk,' Snip joked. 'Always seeing the best in people.'

'I too have observed that in the brothers,' agreed Cross.

'And that's why you could never be a monk either, Sergeant. Your job is the polar opposite. Always looking for the worst in people,' said Snip.

'I disagree. I don't go looking for the worst in people. I go looking for the truth and sometimes that leads me to see the worst in them,' replied Cross.

'A fine distinction and well put,' William commented.

28

'How was your weekend? Ottey asked Cross as they made tea in the office kitchen on Monday morning.

'Fine,' came the response.

'That's exactly how my daughters answer the same question about school,' said Ottey. 'And just as useful. How was Raymond?'

'I didn't see him.'

'Why not? I thought you saw him every Wednesday night and Sunday,' asked Ottey.

'I wasn't here.'

'Really? All weekend?'

'Yes.'

'Well, where were you?' she asked, getting irritated by the unintentionally teasing responses of her partner.

'At St Eustace's,' he replied.

'Seriously?'

She hated it when he did this. Went off on his own, following a lead during an investigation.

'Why didn't you let me know?' she asked.

'Why should I? Do I ask what you're up to at weekends?'

'No, but that's because you are incapable of normal conversation. Are we really going to have to have this discussion again?'

'I have no idea, as I have no idea which particular discussion you're referring to,' he said.

'Why were you there?'

'I was repairing the organ,' he replied.

'Oh,' she said.

'I stayed the night on Saturday as the taxi fare there was unexpectedly expensive.'

'I could've driven you down, or Mackenzie,' she protested.

'It was the weekend.'

'So? Did you fix it?'

'No,' he replied indignantly. 'It's a far more complex task than you realise.'

'Are you going back next weekend?' she asked.

'I am.'

'Well, we'll take you,' she said purposefully.

'We?'

'Yes. I'll take the kids to the gorge. And before you say anything, I'm going to ask Raymond to come along too, as you'll be abandoning him for a second weekend in a row,' she said, expecting an objection. But secretly Cross was pleased. He had been thinking of asking his father down to the abbey to check out the electric blower of the organ, so this could work out well.

Andrew Beresford, Brother Dominic's university friend, now lived near Bath in a small Georgian country house on a hill overlooking the city. He must've done well out of his work in the financial sector, Cross thought, as they drove up the gravelled drive. He had been working more from home than at the office since the pandemic, he'd told Ottey on the phone. The grounds surrounding the house were beautifully maintained with a showing of spring flowers. The interior was a classic contemporary take on country house chic. Andrew was unsurprisingly around the same age as Brother Dominic. He was bald and wearing a crisp white T-shirt, jeans and a fashionable grey cardigan. He had a look of considered intelligence about him which was topped off with an expensive-looking pair of spectacles.

'You have a beautiful home,' commented Ottey as she sank

into a pair of impossibly large sofas in the living room, wondering what she had to do to live in a place like this. Cross looked at her. She definitely had property on her mind.

'Thank you. Well, it's my husband mostly. He's a theatre set designer by profession, an obsessive amateur gardener and homemaker by nature. My only contribution is the occasional hour of forced labour. He says I'm so reluctant I look like someone doing community service,' he replied nervously. 'All I need is a high viz jacket to complete the look.'

'So, Alexander Mount,' Ottey began.

'Alex. Yes. I can't believe it. Any of it really. Except maybe his being a monk. He was reading Divinity when I met him, after all. So, in a way that is the least bit surprising to me about all of this really. But murder?' he replied.

'I'm so sorry for your loss!' Cross blurted out with alarmingly inappropriate volume, and with all the sincerity of someone reading from a cue card. He said it with such force that Andrew almost jumped. Cross looked over at Ottey for some supportive approbation, but she was too startled to oblige.

'It's so strange feeling this way, when you haven't seen the person who's gone, for such a long period of time,' Andrew continued.

'What way?' asked Cross. He was always interested and trying to learn about people's emotional reactions to things.

'So... bereft,' he began. 'So upset. I just can't stop thinking about him. From the moment I get up. Even though I'd neither seen nor heard from him in years. And he was so near. All this time just down the road. I don't know why, but it seems to make it all the worse. I wish I'd known. I could've seen him.'

'No one knew, not even his brother Stephen,' said Ottey.

'Oh, Stephen,' he said warmly in the way people do of someone they're fond of but haven't thought about in a while. 'It was nice to see him at the funeral.'

'How did you first meet?' asked Cross.

'Auditioning for a play at the ADC in Cambridge,' he replied.

'What's the ADC?' asked Cross.

'The Amateur Dramatic Club of the uni, but everyone just calls it the ADC.'

'Did you get the part?' Cross went on.

'I didn't. He did, of course.'

'Why of course?'

'Because he was so damned good at everything. Right down to being such a great person,' he said, laughing quietly.

'Were you good friends?' asked Ottey.

'Yes, we were,' he said thoughtfully and looked at the floor.

'Were you in love with him, Mr Beresford?' Cross asked out of nowhere.

Andrew laughed again. A warm affectionate laugh. 'I was. For a bit. A sort of classic, unrequited love. He used to tease me about it mercilessly, after I told him.'

'That seems a little unkind,' Ottey commented.

'Oh no, not at all. It wasn't meant unkindly and I didn't take it that way. If anything, it made it all so much easier,' he replied.

'Did you sleep with him?' Cross asked. Beresford paused at the intimate nature of the question.

'I did. We did. But nothing developed, despite my desperate persistence,' he replied, laughing self-deprecatingly. He seemed to be laughing quite a lot, Cross thought. Often just a sign of nerves but, more often than not, because they were concealing something.

'So, you were friends, for how long?' asked Cross.

'Well, throughout university and then after, in London. We went on holiday together. Did loads of stuff when work let us.'

'Was he reading Divinity when you first met?' asked Cross.

'He was. For the first year, then he changed to Maths.'

'What were you reading?' asked Cross.

'Physics.'

'So how did you end up in the City?'

'I just followed my friend, truth be told. I hadn't got a clue what to do. He was brilliant. Helped me with the applications, the interviews, even trained me in all kinds of reasoning tests. I would never have got into HSBC with him, without him,' he said.

'Why did he change degree?' asked Ottey.

'I don't know. A crisis of faith, he called it. I thought he was just testing the waters. He'd always talked about going into a seminary but I think he wanted to find out about life first. And he went about it full on. Did everything to the absolute limit.'

'Did he have any relationships at Cambridge?' asked Cross.

'No. None. The occasional fling, but he just didn't seem interested. It was almost as if he didn't have time to fit it in,' Andrew replied.

'So, you both went into the City,' Ottey prompted him.

'Yes, as I said, HSBC. But he soared. I was just happy plodding along in comparison. The boy was a star and he soon got noticed. He was a brilliant mathematician. But his great skill lay in research. He could forecast trends, analyse companies. He was astonishing.'

'Did you live together?' asked Cross.

'We shared a flat,' Andrew replied, making the distinction.

'For how long?'

'A couple of years until we were able to buy. Then we lived separately but not too far away from each other in Stoke Newington. I was also in a relationship with someone by then,' said Andrew.

'Your husband?' asked Ottey.

'No. Someone else.'

'Why did Alexander leave HSBC for Cubitt's?' asked Cross.

'Well, it was the opportunity of a lifetime. Nick Cubitt really wanted him. He wooed him for months, before their investment wing was even set up. They wanted him so badly he could almost dictate his terms. It was insane. Everyone was talking about it,' said Andrew laughing in delight at the memory.

'So, he left for the money?' asked Cross.

'No, it wasn't just that. It was a huge opportunity – the gig of the decade. How often do you get the chance to go in on something like that at the outset and build it from the ground up?' Andrew asked.

'Did you talk about it?' asked Ottey.

'Oh absolutely. Initially he loved it. Thought it was terrific. It was crazy hours but he revelled in it all. Particularly when it started to do so phenomenally well.'

'How did it succeed so quickly?' asked Cross.

'Well, unsurprisingly Cubitt's had several high-net-worth individuals who banked with them. But it was the institutions where some of those individuals had positions of power that Nick focused on. He was a great salesman and traded off the good name of Cubitt's. The main selling point was being at the front end of the recoupment queue. It's a huge advantage financially and was too tempting for many. Within twelve months he was managing over two hundred million pounds of other people's money. It then became a feeding frenzy as other institutions begged to be part of the fund. The two things you have to remember about the majority of people in the City is that they're greedy, and they don't have a clue what's going on around them. Ignorance is one of the biggest currencies traded in there.'

'How did it then fail so quickly when it had such a promising start?' asked Cross.

'Nick may have been a great salesman, but he was no trader. He was also dreadful when it came to man-management. Basically, he'd recruited really well. He had the best people in the City working for him. Right up at the top of the tree was Alex, now earning an absolute fortune with his salary, commission and absurd bonuses. But Alex said it rapidly became a toxic place to work. Nick was one of those people who find it impossible to give anyone any credit. He truly believed it was all about him,' said Andrew.

'Is that why Alex left?' asked Ottey.

'Do you not know anything about the collapse of Cubitt's? I thought that was why you were here,' replied Andrew.

'We don't know as much as we probably should,' replied Cross looking at Ottey. She had insisted on coming to interview Andrew before Cross thought they were ready.

'No problem. It's probably easier if I just tell you. Nick really did start to believe that the success of the fund was all down to him. He'd set it up, after all. Raised the money and recruited the right people. He should've been happy with that. But he needed people to think it was all down to him. More and more people started to leave, it just wasn't a great work environment. Then instead of replacing them he started dealing himself. But he wasn't willing to do the work or run the numbers. You have to do the research, which was what Alex devoted hours of his waking day to and why he excelled. Nick traded on hunches. He fed off the rush when it went well, and it increased his appetite for it. But he was basically gambling with his clients' money. Then he started to lose vast amounts. Unmanageable amounts. He tried to hide these losses by creating fake offsetting. He made it look like everything was okay.

'Alex knew something was up as the returns were waning for some incomprehensible reason and the figures didn't make any sense. Then he realised that was exactly it. *The figures actually didn't make any sense.* He started digging and found that when new investors joined the fund, they were given quick returns by Nick raiding other investors' pots. It was like a Ponzi scheme. Nick couldn't disguise the massive losses for much longer. He then made the mistake of raiding Alex's clients' accounts to make everything appear to balance. This was too much for Alex. For weeks he stayed up late, sometimes through the night, while Nick was at the opera or treating clients to lavish meals at three-Michelin-starred restaurants, until he uncovered the horrific reality of the situation. Nick had lost billions of pounds. Alex knew it was irretrievable, not just for Nick but also the three hundred and fifty-year-old bank.

'Alex went to Julian the head of the bank out of loyalty, to tell him what was going on. But he wouldn't listen. Instead, he begged Alex not to do anything. It would be the end of Nick's career and, if what he was saying was true, could end up with Nick in prison. In that moment Alex knew Julian was fully aware of the extent of the problem and simply wasn't going to do anything about it. He thought it was strange that Nick was Alex's first thought and overriding priority. He tried to explain to Julian that if he didn't do anything it could be the end of the bank in the prevailing economic climate, not just Nick's career. Julian obviously thought the idea of the bank collapsing was absurd. But he perceived it as a threat and Alex suddenly saw a different side to the normally equable man. He was furious, shouting at Alex, threatening him that if he told anyone it would have serious consequences for him. He'd never work in the City again. But I have the feeling Alex just wanted out at that point. He'd had enough of it all and it didn't sit well with who he was. He then went to Nick and pleaded with him to come clean. Nick's main concern seemed to be whether his father now knew any of this. When Alex told him he'd already been to see Julian, Nick completely lost it. He fired Alex on the spot and had him escorted off the premises. Which was pointless and stupid.

'Alex was an honourable man according to his clients. These were major institutions run by powerful people. They demanded an immediate investigation by the bank. When Julian tried to placate them and with the majority of his board resigning, the clients went to the police. Nick had lost over five billion pounds. Not even Alex could figure out how the sum was so astronomical. A classic case of city ineptitude fuelled by sheer greed,' said Andrew, finally finished.

'And the bank collapsed,' said Ottey.

'Hundreds of ordinary cash clients started withdrawing their money. It was like a modern run on a bank. All their private accounts were closed within a matter of weeks. It folded. There was no way back and with the financial crisis looming it was game over. Nick went to trial. Alex was called as an anonymous witness. Mr C, they called him, to maintain his anonymity so it wouldn't prejudice his chances of further employment.'

'That explains why Alice didn't find it,' Ottey said to Cross.

'He was questioned about the initial success and about Nick but then they dived into the false accounting which was incredibly complex,' Andrew continued. 'They went through each transaction with him as he'd uncovered them. He was in the witness box for over three days. Nick was sentenced to seven years in prison and Alex disappeared,' said Andrew.

'Did Nick blame Alex?' asked Cross.

'Oh absolutely. The thing about Nick is that he was one of those vindictive children of privilege who are entitled and spoiled to such an extent they don't know how to behave and can't take any responsibility for their actions. Haven't a clue. Nothing was ever Nick Cubitt's fault.'

'Do you know where he is now?' asked Cross.

'No. He obviously couldn't go back into the City. He lost everything: his job, his future, his marriage,' said Andrew.

'Is Julian Cubitt still alive?' Ottey asked.

'I believe so. Father and son are still estranged. You don't think Nick could actually have anything to do with this, do you? And why now, after all this time?' Andrew asked. It was a good question reflected Cross.

The interview came to an end and Andrew showed them out. Ottey reflected that the entrance hall alone was bigger than her kitchen at home. As they reached the front door a car pulled up. It was a Volvo estate which had bits of wood and building detritus in the back. It looked like it could have belonged to a builder. A man got out. There was something impeccably put together about his appearance. Also in his forties, he had a clipped grey beard and hair. He looked like someone who worked out in a gym regularly and was as well manicured as the gardens of their home.

'Ah, this is my husband, Hans,' said Andrew cheerfully. 'Hans, this is DS Cross and DS Ottey. They're investigating poor Dominic's murder.'

Both Cross and Ottey had heard this kind of slow and specific introduction of them, several times before in their work. It was generally when a person wanted someone to know, without question, that they were police and so they should be careful, on their guard.

'Hi, and how exactly do they think you can help?' he asked in an accent which wasn't English.

'They're just after background,' Andrew replied.

'Visiting all his exes, are they?' Hans replied testily.

'Your accent, where are you from?' asked Cross.

'Denmark.'

'Mr Beresford—' Cross went on.

'My husband,' Hans interrupted.

'Indeed, your husband tells us you're a theatre designer.'

'That's correct,' he replied. There was something quite rigid and uptight about the way he held himself.

'Where do you work?' Cross asked.

'All over the place. I'm freelance.'

'Do you have a base?'

'I do,' he replied, not particularly helpfully.

'And where is that?' Cross continued, oblivious to the growing hostility.

'Why so many questions?'

'It's my job. To ask questions when conducting a murder investigation,' replied Cross.

'Cheddar,' Hans replied.

Cross let the answer sit there for a moment.

'Near the abbey? Brother Dominic's abbey?'

'Apparently.'

'Have you ever been there?'

'I have not.'

'Do you know the big Sainsbury's outside Cheddar?' Cross

asked. Ottey wasn't sure where this was going, but said nothing and left him to it. Hans paused a moment before answering.

'I do, it's quite near my studio actually.'

'Do you ever go there. To shop?' Cross asked.

'What's this all about?' asked Andrew.

'I do. Sometimes for the weekly shop. Other times to get something for lunch,' said Hans.

Cross nodded as he thought this through.

'Hans, what's going on?' asked Andrew urgently. Cross turned to him.

'Why did you tell us you hadn't seen, or been in contact with Brother Dominic since 2008?' he asked, suddenly redirecting the questioning.

'What do you mean?' asked Andrew, defensively.

'If I'm right, Hans had an argument with Brother Dominic on Friday the thirty-first of March, the day he went missing,' Cross announced.

'Can you prove that?' asked Hans.

'We have a witness, but an interesting question nevertheless. It's normally used by people who have something to hide when they've been accused of a crime. A defensive stance, if you like,' Cross commented.

'How long had you been back in contact with Brother Dominic, Andrew?' asked Ottey, now up to speed.

'About a year,' Andrew admitted.

'How were you alerted to his whereabouts?' asked Cross.

'I saw him on a local news programme. Then I did a little research and found the abbey. It wasn't difficult,' he replied.

'Why?' asked Cross.

'Good question,' added Hans pointedly.

'Hans,' Andrew pleaded.

'It was because he still loved him,' Hans said.

'Completely untrue. I don't know. I was intrigued and I felt this huge pang. I mean he was living as a monk. It was a shock and I wanted to check in on him.'

'What happened when you found him?' asked Cross.

'He was actually quite pleased. He then came and visited us occasionally. Stayed a couple of weekends.'

'And how did you feel about that?' Cross asked Hans. Andrew answered before his husband had a chance.

'Completely irrationally. He didn't want him here and made it quite clear. Not one of his finest moments,' Andrew replied.

'Why was that?' Cross asked.

'You'd have to ask him,' replied Andrew.

'He obviously still had feelings for him,' Hans replied tersely.

'Not in the way you think,' Andrew replied wearily. They'd clearly danced around this topic endlessly.

'Was that why you had an argument with him at the supermarket?' asked Cross.

'Of course it was. Which is why this is the first I've heard of it. He was jealous. Absurdly jealous with no good reason or cause,' Andrew continued.

'I was not jealous,' Hans replied.

'Then you find another word for it. Your English is good enough. If it wasn't jealousy, what was it?' Andrew asked. Hans didn't reply and the two police officers didn't step in to fill the gap, implying that he should continue. 'I'd said I wouldn't see Dom again, because it made my husband so unhappy,' he said, putting a meaningful emphasis on the word 'husband' as if still making a point about his personal loyalties. 'I wasn't particularly happy as nothing was going on and it was nice to see an old friend. So Dom started coming to the house when Hans wasn't there. It was so good to see him. He was such a spiritual man. I really felt Hans would have benefited from getting to know him, but there we are. Anyway, recently Dom had started having a personal issue at the abbey.'

'Brother William,' suggested Ottey.

'Exactly,' replied Andrew. 'He wanted to discuss it with someone else who wasn't a monk. I'm the only friend he had in the outside world. The only gay friend, what's more. His visits had become a little more frequent, then just before he died, William followed him here.'

'Why?' asked Ottey.

'He was desperate, poor boy. He thought he could have a more honest and frank talk with Dom outside of the abbey.'

'So, Brother William wasn't over it?' asked Ottey. 'Surely by this time he must've been told the order thought the best course of action was to move him.'

'I think it was his last chance to convince Dom. They stayed for hours. We lost track of time. It was so emotional. William left, then Dom a little after. But Hans saw him leaving as he got home.'

'Did you talk to him?'

'No. He didn't see me,' Hans replied.

'We had a terrible argument, though. I tried to explain. The man Hans was jealous about was here to discuss this personal crisis. But he just couldn't see it that way. Did you really see him at Sainsbury's that day, Hans?'

'I did,' he replied.

'You had an argument,' said Cross.

'I was angry. I just asked him to stay away, that's all,' said Hans. Cross thought for a moment.

'Why didn't you tell us any of this? It doesn't make any sense. You hadn't done anything wrong and your friend was dead. Didn't it occur to you that it could have been relevant to our enquiry?' asked Cross eventually.

'How could it be relevant?' asked Andrew.

'Brother William was in love with Brother Dominic. You yourself have said he was desperate,' Cross said.

'You don't think William…?' asked Andrew.

'It doesn't matter what I think. You should have said something. Why didn't you?' asked Cross.

There was a pause.

'I have a criminal record,' said Hans. 'Assault. Long time ago. He was protecting me.'

'Well, that should tell you something,' Ottey observed pointedly for Hans's benefit.

'Where were you the night of March the thirty-first?' Cross asked.

'We were in Chichester staying with friends. We went to the theatre,' Hans replied. 'I have the tickets somewhere. I keep them because I can put them against tax.'

29

Cross's train of thought was interrupted on Wednesday morning, which irritated him. It came in the form of a text from his father. Raymond was averse to texting and only did so in cases of emergency. He also knew that his son didn't like being disturbed at work as it was an unwelcome distraction. This meant the arrival of a text worried Cross initially and then when he'd read it, thoroughly discombobulated him. Cross was due to go round for their usual weekly Chinese meal together that night. Raymond's text, however, informed him that they would have a guest. Christine. Cross's mother. He then listed her choice of dinner from the takeaway menu. This sent Cross into a tailspin. Not because he thought she'd over-ordered for one person – which by the way he did – but because Wednesday was their night when he and his father ate together. Alone. He hated change. It unsettled him in a way that people just didn't understand. Except for his father. He understood. So why had he done this? Or had it been at his mother's instigation? Probably not, as how would she actually know that they always ate together on a Wednesday?

Ottey could tell immediately that something was wrong with her partner. But when she asked, he refused to talk about it. His refusal came over as completely childish. In truth it wasn't just that he thought it was none of her business, but he thought talking about personal matters on police time was unprofessional. She knew him well enough to know that if his current mood had been brought about by something at work, he would have been more brusquely businesslike and rude. She then remembered what day it was and thought it might have something to do with Raymond.

'Are you seeing your dad tonight?' she began by asking.

'It's Wednesday,' he replied, as if this made the answer obvious.

'Has something happened?'

Cross was silent and went about gathering up his bicycle accessories to leave.

'It might help to talk about it,' she insisted. But he was halfway across the office. Then she had an inspired thought. Cross didn't have many people in his life so narrowing down the possibilities wasn't too difficult.

'He's invited your mother round for dinner, hasn't he?'

This stopped Cross in his tracks. He turned to face her with an expression of pained indignation. Mackenzie looked up from her computer.

'I wish you would stop talking to my father behind my back,' he said.

'I didn't.'

'Then how could you possibly know?' he asked.

'Because some suspects are easier to read than others, George,' she said smiling.

He turned on his heel and left.

'So, what do you make of that?' Ottey asked Mackenzie.

'I'm not sure. But it made me think I might take tomorrow off,' she replied.

Even Xiao Bao, the owner of the takeaway, knew something was up when after many years the order for that night was suddenly different.

'Having company tonight, George?' he asked. 'Or are you guys just really hungry?'

George scowled and paid without saying anything. Xiao Bao smiled as his favourite and most regular, literally, customer left with his order.

When he arrived at his father's flat, George deposited his bike in the hall as usual, on the newspaper Marina had left for him, knowing he'd be round that evening. He knew his mother was already there as he'd seen her car parked in the road outside. This wasn't particularly difficult as he'd made a note of the make, model, colour and registration number when he'd first seen it some months before. If anyone had asked him why he'd done this he probably wouldn't have been able to provide a cogent answer, beyond the fact that he felt he should.

He took the food into the kitchen. His parents – the plural of this struck him as an alien concept as soon as he thought it – were not in the living room. He heard their voices coming from the spare room at the back of the flat which housed Raymond's latest project. His ever-expanding and improving model railway. Mounted on vast swathes of plaster of Paris mountains and lakes, with stations, signal boxes and small people, there was a gap in the middle where his mother and father were standing. They were laughing like children who then suddenly stopped when an adult walked into the room.

'Hello, son,' said Raymond.

'Hello, George,' said his mother.

He really wanted to ask them both what they thought they were up to, but it seemed pointless. His mother was there. There was nothing he could do about it. They were drinking bright red cocktails from tumblers, with ice and a large slice of lemon. They were aided in this endeavour by garish red and white striped straws. The kind that had folds in them enabling them to bend. The entire effect was topped off by a cocktail umbrella each.

'Negronis,' announced Raymond. One of his latest hobbies was to look up cocktail recipes and make them. The fact that George was teetotal by no means put him off. It just meant that his search extended to exotic alcohol-free concoctions, most of which tasted distinctly medicinal. Mocktails, he reliably informed George.

'Christine's never had one before,' Raymond continued.

'Well, she probably shouldn't be having one at all as she's driving,' George found himself saying.

'I'm just having one and Raymond made it weak, so there's no need to be concerned,' his mother assured him.

'I'm not in the least bit concerned. Merely making a point. The food will be getting cold,' he replied, leaving the room.

They sat at the dining table to eat. George reflected how satisfying, well a relief really, that the table was actually visible, let alone available for use these days. In the past it had always been covered in magazines, books and pieces of electronics that Raymond was fixing. He did repairs mainly for the neighbours, which made him very popular in the community, it had to be said. The tidiness and general cleanliness were thanks to his new cleaner, Marina, who amazingly had got the measure of Raymond and managed to keep him in check.

Their dinner was accompanied by the unusual sound of conversation. George and his father normally ate in complete silence, but thanks to Christine's presence there seemed to be plenty to talk about. Well, for her and Raymond. George just sat there eating, not speaking, and found himself longing for the peace and quiet of the refectory at St Eustace's Abbey. The conversation centred around him, which he found pleasing at times and infuriating at others. Raymond told her about George's growing up after she'd left. His problems at school, fitting in. Then his problems when he first joined the police force, with the amount of bullying and abuse he suffered on account of his condition.

'They weren't to know,' said Raymond. 'But even so it was pretty inexcusable. I was amazed he stuck it out, to be honest with you.'

'I stuck it out, as you put it, because it was clear to me that it would be no different wherever I was, whatever work environment I was in,' retorted George.

Had George looked up more often from his egg fried rice he might have (there was no guarantee as he didn't know his mother well enough yet to be able to read her expressions), noticed her concern as Raymond unflinchingly relayed to her some of the indignities George was subjected to at the beginning of his career – outright name-calling, officers talking to him in a slow loud manner, implying he was stupid, hiding his uniform and at its worst, urinating in his helmet. He would also have seen the obvious pride in her as she learned of his success as a detective with the highest conviction rate in the Avon and Somerset police. There was a surprising warmth between Raymond and Christine – surprising bearing in mind his father's behaviour to her in the past – and a familiarity they seemed to slip into with ease, as if the few years they had spent together and produced George had left an indelible mark on their emotional inner selves.

'How is Stephen's brother's case progressing?' she asked.

'Oh, he doesn't like talking about his work,' Raymond said with protective authority.

'But this is different. Father Stephen is his friend,' Christine pointed out.

'We are making some progress. I hope things will pick up pace this week, as more facts emerge,' George replied.

'He will be pleased,' Christine continued. 'He says he hasn't seen much of you recently.'

'I've been busy,' replied George, unsuccessfully trying not to sound defensive.

'He thinks you're avoiding him,' she went on.

'That's because he is,' replied Raymond. 'I imagine he finds it awkward when slow progress is being made and the case involves a friend's relative. Isn't that so, son?'

'It is difficult for the relatives when it feels as though nothing is happening. They don't see how hard everyone is working behind the scenes. It's awkward, all the more so when a victim's relative is known to you. Stephen has forgone the opportunity to have a family liaison officer working with him, who would normally field all his worries or concerns,' replied George.

'Why did he do that then? Maybe he thought it wasn't necessary because he knew you,' suggested Raymond.

'He didn't want to use up scarce police resources when they could be used elsewhere by people who really needed them,' George explained.

'Typical of him,' Raymond commented.

'I think you should call in on him and see how he's doing,' said Christine.

George was taken aback at receiving what was tantamount to a parental instruction, from such an unfamiliar source, and was about to say something, but managed to stop himself. After dinner he washed the plates and takeaway containers while explaining his system to Christine.

He walked his mother to her car, wheeling his bike alongside them. She didn't offer him a kiss this time, as he opened the door for her to get in.

'Good night, George,' she said.

'Good night, Christine,' he replied. He watched as she drove off, then cycled home. As he pedalled the familiar route back to his flat a strange realisation suddenly dawned on him. Despite his reticence, he'd actually enjoyed the evening. He also had to admit how much he'd liked being the centre of attention for these two people. It was something he hadn't experienced in his life before and it wasn't completely intolerable.

30

Ottey and Cross were on their way to London the next morning, which he assumed meant he wouldn't be back in time to go to Stephen's church and practise the organ. He was relieved in a sense because he knew Stephen would have a number of questions for him about the case which he wouldn't be able to answer, and would doubtless want to discuss Christine. They were driving to RAF Northolt on the A40 just west of London. Cross had got hold of the flight plan for Murphy's plane the day before, using the tail number in the photograph he'd come across. It was heading for Northolt from Waterford airport in Ireland and had two passengers on board. It was landing at 11.40.

They arrived at the private jet centre lounge and were then escorted to a series of aircraft hangars next door. A large Rolls Royce was already parked outside the hangar. It was one of those enormous ones that looked like it would take at least two gallons of petrol just to park it. Absurdly ostentatious, with suicide doors, it shouted 'LOOK AT ME!' at the same time as yelling 'STAY WELL AWAY.' It had the number plate *PM36*.

'Looks like he's definitely on board,' said Ottey as she saw the car.

Just after 11.40 a Cessna Citation Latitude landed and then taxied towards the hangar. After a few minutes the front door opened and steps automatically lowered themselves to the tarmac. Martin Bates appeared and disembarked. He walked breezily towards them, as if expecting them, with a smile designed to disarm at a hundred yards.

'Detectives, how nice to meet you in person. What can I do for you?' he opened with.

'You? Nothing,' Ottey replied. Bates looked at them for a moment. 'If you're about to tell us your boss isn't on that plane, don't bother. We've seen the flight manifest,' she went on.

'I wouldn't insult your intelligence, Sergeant Ottey. Why don't you follow us to the office?' Bates suggested.

'I don't think so. We've driven far enough for one day,' said Cross.

Bates looked at his watch. 'Very well. Follow me,' he said and walked back to the plane. The two detectives followed. 'We've just been visiting Sir Patrick's stud in Ireland. Up early to see the gallops. Quite something, those thoroughbred horses. Really impressive, like living muscular statues.'

The interior of the aircraft was much smaller than Cross had imagined the cabin of a private jet would be. Unsurprisingly, he hadn't been on one before. All wooden veneer and light-coloured leather, he thought you could possibly get quite claustrophobic in it when flying. But then again, flying wasn't something he did very often, through choice.

A sullen figure sat at the back of the plane. He looked up at the two police officers with a practised disdain. He had the air of someone who instinctively didn't enjoy life. He was sitting in one of four seats around a small table. Cross and Ottey waited for an invitation to sit. None was forthcoming. Bates finally said, 'Please sit.'

Ottey sat on a seat across the aisle from the table. Cross plonked himself in the seat directly opposite Murphy, knocking the man's legs in the process and forcing him to move across slightly. He then examined the seat he was sitting in carefully.

'Very comfortable,' Cross began. 'Not as comfortable as the Roller though, I should imagine.'

He looked out of the window at the car waiting for Murphy.

'I mean that car's built for luxurious comfort, isn't it? It's basically four armchairs on an army tank chassis, with all the trimmings.'

'Can I get you something to drink?' asked Bates, trying to bring these observations to a close.

'We're good, thanks,' said Ottey.

'Do they recline like normal aeroplane seats?' asked Cross, now warming to his theme. There was no response. Cross saw a door at the end of the fuselage. 'What's in there? It's not a bedroom, is it?' he asked with a tinge of disbelief. He turned to Ottey. 'I bet it's a bedroom, DS Ottey. What's it like sleeping in a bed on a plane?' he asked Murphy. 'I think I'd find that a bit disconcerting. Having said that, probably no more disconcerting than sleeping in a motorhome when it's travelling. Except for the fact that you're thousands of feet up in the air, of course.'

Ottey loved Cross when he was like this. It was like watching a comedian on a riff. It was also when her colleague was at his most dangerous, she'd come to learn.

'If you could just get to the point of your visit, we'd appreciate it. We have quite a full day,' said Bates.

'Mind you,' continued Cross, as if completely oblivious to what had just been said. 'I'm surprised you'd have a bed in here. It's not as if this is a long range jet, is it? Not a Rolls Royce of the private jet world, more of a Vauxhall Corsa, wouldn't you say?'

'Raymond would love this,' Ottey commented, joining in.

'Oh, he would,' agreed Cross enthusiastically. 'My father, Raymond, is a retired aeronautical engineer,' he explained.

Still nothing from Murphy, but silence never put Cross off in these situations. More often than not he just used it to his advantage.

'I wouldn't complain, though. Seems one of the main advantages of a private plane, even a budget one like this, is no queues. I hate queues. Do you hate queues, Mr Murphy?' Cross said, deliberately not using Murphy's title. 'The very idea of queues anywhere horrifies me, but in airports? It makes me just not want to fly. Well, that and a few other problems I have with the whole concept of being in a small tin tube, thousands of feet in the air, riveted to a jet engine, piloted by a complete stranger who might have all kinds of personal issues affecting him on the day. But queues seem so unnecessary to me. Take airports for example. They're basically doing the same thing every day, with roughly the same schedule, same number of staff, check-in desks, X-ray machines. Very little change from one day to another, so you'd think maybe they could sort it out. Possibly it's like Madame Tussauds, though. They eliminated the queues and the visitors were unhappy. They wanted to queue for an hour on a congested Marylebone Road. They liked the anticipation. Do you think that's it?'

Cross came across as slightly stupid and naive at times like this. Someone who liked the sound of his own voice. None of this was true, of course. He did it not only to unsettle his interlocutor, but also to lull them into a sense of having the upper hand. As was the case here. He then noticed the coat of arms embossed on the seat behind Murphy's head. 'Is that your coat of arms?' he asked, sounding impressed. He turned round to see the same coat of arms was on his seat as well. He ran his fingers over it. 'Did you have them commissioned specially? Of course you did. When you got your knighthood. I bet that was fun going to the college of arms. Can you imagine?' he asked Ottey before carrying on. 'I bet you have the original artwork framed on the wall behind your office desk, don't you? Is it in watercolour? What odds would you give me on that? On my being right? Would you give me odds? Could I place a bet on that? You allow people to make bets on anything, don't you?' he asked enthusiastically.

'You've seen a photograph of me at my desk in the press,' Murphy replied quietly. The first thing he'd actually said.

'Do you know what? I actually haven't. It's just with the racehorses, the fancy cars – there must be more of them, probably in a garage somewhere the size of an aircraft hangar, all in concours condition – the private jet. There's a certain clichéd inevitability about it that only comes from being an extremely wealthy, insecure man. Is that what you are, Patrick Murphy? Extremely insecure?' Cross asked.

'What is it you want, Sergeant Cross?' Murphy asked with strained politeness.

'Are you a religious man, Mr Murphy?' asked Cross.

'As it happens, I am.'

'Irish Catholic?'

'My grandparents were all Irish, as were my parents. I'm Irish but I was brought up in England. I converted to Catholicism before I married my wife.'

'Second wife,' Cross added for the sake of accuracy.

'Correct.'

'Your father was a plumber,' Cross continued.

'He was.'

'And yet here we are. Look at all of this,' he said, indicating the jet. 'He died before you made your fortune.' Murphy chose not to respond to this. 'Tell me, is it true your father's love of a bet – well, that's putting it mildly, the fact that your mother would have to go to his place of employment every week to get his wage packet off him before he drank and gambled it away would indicate a significant problem. A right old Andy Capp you called him once – was it his willingness to throw his money away, time and time again, that encouraged you to go into the betting industry? Can we call it an industry? Can we even call it a business? I don't know.' He addressed this question to Ottey. 'That's what a lot of financial journalists have written as your story. Odd sort of parental inspiration.'

'It's nonsense. I made my money from online gambling. I saw an opportunity to encourage people to bet responsibly,' Murphy began.

'You sound like a health warning on a bottle of wine,' Cross commented.

'I imposed limits on people's accounts, automatic shut-outs when they got to a certain limit. I created an ethical betting platform which would prevent people like my mother having to grab their partner's wages before they frittered it away,' said Murphy with a fluency that implied it was a point he'd made several thousand times.

'Ethical? There you go again using words that I would never associate with gambling. I'm going to have to rethink all of this. I just had no idea there was such a thing as the ethical exploitation of people,' said Cross.

'I'm getting tired of this conversation,' replied Murphy wearily.

'Is that because it's one you have to have on a regular basis? To justify creating so much wealth based on the weakness and misery of others? How do you square gambling with your religious beliefs?'

'I provide a service. A legitimate, transparent business, subject to strict regulation.'

'It's still morally ambiguous,' Cross pointed out.

'That is your opinion.'

'But there was nothing ambiguous about the way you used to collect unpaid debts,' Cross went on.

Murphy's eyes narrowed as he debated whether to answer this. He decided against.

'You used teams of thugs, basically, to threaten people, beat them, steal from them, terrorise them. Is that a fair statement?' Cross asked.

'We all learn from our mistakes, Sergeant,' Murphy said.

'Is that so? To my mind, though, it simply demonstrates the fact that you're willing to go to any lengths to protect your interests. You were willing to beat your money out of people, Mr Murphy.'

'It was a long time ago and was regrettable.'

'Regrettable?'

'It was a mistake,' said Murphy trying to draw a line under it.

'Brother Dominic,' Cross stated.

'At last, we come to the point,' Murphy sighed.

'Another mistake?' asked Cross.

'He was just wrong about a book I acquired. The mistake was his,' Murphy replied.

'A spectacularly expensive book,' Cross pointed out.

'Indeed.'

'Until Brother Dominic's valuation made it significantly less expensive,' Cross commented.

'It did.'

'Tell me, I'm curious. Is it the fact that it's not from the fifteenth century but was made in the eighteenth century, or that it didn't belong to the Duke of Berry or Henry the eighth, as it was designed to make people believe, that makes it so much less valuable?' Cross asked.

Murphy didn't answer.

'Is that why he's dead?' asked Cross.

'Brother Dominic's death—' Murphy began.

'Murder,' Cross corrected him.

'—murder, is tragic and incomprehensible. As I said, I am a religious man. I'm a regular churchgoer. I go to confession so that I can take communion. I am a benefactor to various Catholic charities. As such, murder accords neither with my beliefs, nor the way I choose to lead my life,' Murphy said very calmly, as if sure this should put any doubts to rest.

'What about a beating which goes too far? We've established your track record when it comes to beating people who owe you money. What if this was a beating which accidentally resulted in murder?' asked Cross.

'Sir Patrick has recently been made a papal knight,' added Bates as if this had to contradict what Cross had just said.

'A papal knight as well?' asked a seemingly impressed Cross. 'Would I be right in thinking that, not far away from the framed coat of arms on your wall, is a photograph of you and the Pope?' Cross was like a fan talking to their favourite pop star on an afternoon radio phone in.

'You've definitely seen a photograph of my office,' said Murphy with the first hint of a smile.

'I most definitely have not. I should've placed that bet. I can just see that you're concerned, worried even, about your status in a way that a man of your wealth and standing shouldn't be. Brother Dominic challenged your status as a leading collector of religious artefacts,' said Cross seriously.

'He did, yes. Did it hurt? Yes,' replied the businessman.

'Because you'd made a mistake?' said Cross.

'No. I didn't and still don't believe I did,' Murphy replied.

'Where were you on March the thirty-first?' Cross asked.

'I have absolutely no idea. But if you check with my office, they will be able to give you the information,' said Murphy.

'We'll need your whereabouts on that date as well,' Ottey said to Bates.

'Of course,' he replied.

'Did you have any further contact with Brother Dominic?' Cross then asked him.

'As I think I said in our initial conversation, we exchanged a few emails, yes,' Bates replied.

'Did you ever see him again? At the abbey perhaps?' Cross went on.

'I did not.'

'Did either of you visit Brother Dominic at St Eustace's Abbey after September of last year?' he asked.

'DS Cross, I have just answered that question,' said Bates.

'Sunday November the sixth of last year, to be exact,' Cross went on, ignoring him and consulting his file. He looked back up. 'You were seen at the abbey, Mr Bates.'

There was a pause as Bates constructed his response.

'Oh right, yes. That would be the organ recital, if I'm not mistaken,' said Bates.

'Why didn't you tell us this before?'

'You asked whether I'd been to the abbey to see Dominic. I hadn't. As I said, this was an organ recital. There's one on the first Sunday of every month.'

'Are you interested in church organ music, Mr Bates?' Cross asked.

'I am, as it happens.'

'No organ recitals nearer to home?' asked Cross.

'I have no idea.'

'Organ recitals on instruments that are actually in working order?' asked Cross.

'I don't know what you mean.'

'The organ at St Eustace's hasn't been functioning for almost ten months,' Cross said.

'Um, well, I wasn't aware of that,' came the awkward reply.

'Evidently,' said Cross. 'Monday December the twelfth. Tuesday February the seventh. Thursday March the sixteenth,' he listed. Bates said nothing while trying to give the impression that these dates were meaningless to him. But he just succeeded in looking uncomfortable.

'You visited Dominic on the first two of those dates,' said Ottey. 'Have you forgotten, or are you lying for some reason?'

This direct approach immediately made the suave corporate affairs suit become defensive.

'I must've forgotten. Why would I lie?'

'That is a good question, Mr Bates. Why indeed?' said Cross. 'Why were you there?'

'I was trying to persuade Brother Dominic to see reason,' Bates replied.

'How exactly was he being unreasonable? By not acquiescing to your employer's will? A Benedictine monk who has given an honest opinion about something, when asked to do so. With no axe to grind. No agenda. Perhaps Sir Patrick is unused to encountering such integrity in his chosen line of business,' suggested Cross.

Bates just gazed back at Cross as if he wasn't going to grace such a statement with any comment.

'Persuade him how?' asked Ottey. 'Money?'

Bates shifted uncomfortably in his seat which seemed to affirm this to Cross.

'That's pretty low, wouldn't you say, DS Ottey? Trying to bribe a monk. What on earth made you think that could possibly work, Mr Bates?' said Cross.

'When that was refused, then what?' asked Ottey.

'Did you threaten him?' asked Cross.

'No! Look, I can see where this is going,' said Bates. 'If you are suggesting that we had a hand in any way in Dominic's tragic death you are barking up the wrong tree. It's a completely outrageous idea and I think it might be better if you concluded this conversation with our lawyers.'

Neither of the police officers replied. Cross turned his attention to the man opposite him.

'March the sixteenth, Sir Patrick,' he stated.

'I flew down in my helicopter to see Brother Dominic,' Murphy answered, causing Bates to look at him, surprised.

'Did you land at the abbey?' asked Cross.

'I did not. I wouldn't dream of it. We landed nearby.'

'What was the purpose of your visit? To try and succeed where Mr Bates had failed?'

'Not in the least. I was there to surrender. To make my peace with him. To drop the whole thing. It may be difficult for you to understand, but I came to realise I had never met anyone like Dominic in my life. Such simple integrity. I began to feel there had to be a reason we'd met, a divine purpose if you like. I wanted him to be a part of my life. As a spiritual presence, a confessor if you will,' said Murphy.

'His response?' asked Ottey.

'Was as you would expect from a Benedictine. He agreed, but then obviously...' He faltered as if he couldn't go on.

'If that's a fabrication, Sir Patrick, full marks for creativity. It's certainly not one I've come across,' said Ottey with such boldness it was obvious she didn't believe him.

'You have both lied to the police. I wonder what your spiritual advisor would have said about that? Lying in the course of an investigation into his murder,' Cross began. Murphy looked down at the table. 'We now consider you both to be persons of interest in this case. Please do not leave the country without informing us. You might want to consider bringing in lawyers for our next conversation.'

'I have in-house counsel,' Murphy replied.

'I would advise you to think about criminal lawyers in this instance,' said Cross.

'Thank you for that advice, Sergeant, but I have no intention of hiding behind a lawyer. Neither of us have anything to hide.'

'Your lying to us would seem to contradict that,' said Cross.

'Agreed. A mistake. If you need to speak with us again, please don't hesitate to get in touch.'

'If you are interviewed under caution, Mr Murphy, I really would advise retaining lawyers with criminal experience,' Cross reiterated.

Sir Patrick Murphy now sat up in his seat and leant forward on the table in between him and Cross as if to emphasise the truth of what he was about to say.

'DS Cross, I had nothing to do with Brother Dominic's murder. From the gruesome details I've read in the papers, it seems he was essentially beaten to death. No doubt you think this was me trying to persuade him to change his mind about the book of hours. But it was not. I'm not a criminal. I'm a straightforward Catholic businessman who works in an area you obviously disapprove of. Don't let your low opinion of how I make my money cloud your judgement or characterise me as someone who would commit such a heinous crime. I am a deeply religious man. I wouldn't subject anyone, let alone a Benedictine monk, to this kind of barbarity, and let alone for his opinion on a piece in my collection, however wrong.'

'You are no stranger to barbarity, Mr Murphy, papal knight or not,' Cross said and started to leave.

'We'll be in touch with your office to confirm your whereabouts on March thirty-first,' said Ottey, getting up herself.

'You should know that Sir Patrick has actually made a contribution to the abbey. He has paid for the church ceiling to be repaired,' said Bates.

'Ah,' replied Cross, turning at the door, as if this was of interest. 'Yes, Fred Savage is doing the work. Like you, another man trying to buy his way into heaven,' said Cross and he left.

They arrived back in Bristol in good time for Cross to get in his organ practice. But having made his mind up earlier that he wouldn't be back in time, he decided to go to the office instead and avoid Stephen.

31

Both of Murphy's and Bates's alibis checked out on the dates that Brother Dominic had gone missing and the days that the police thought he was still alive.

'It doesn't mean they're not involved. They can't be ruled out,' Carson said at the daily meeting the next morning. 'It's highly unlikely they would have been anywhere near the abduction. If they were trying to beat Brother Dominic into changing his mind, they'd've paid people to do it.'

'But why now? If it's them, why now?' asked Cross.

'How do you mean?' asked Carson.

'The book of hours dispute had been going on for over ten months. What made them do this now, if they did it?'

'I don't know. Maybe Murphy had just had enough,' replied Carson.

'I agree with George. The timing of the television interview, being so close to the date of the murder. It has to be a factor. It can't just be a coincidence,' said Ottey.

'You're not suggesting we rule Murphy out just because of the interview?' said Carson.

'She's not suggesting anything of the sort,' said Cross stepping in. 'She's merely pointing out what we've said before. That this TV interview has something to do with all of this.'

'Why?' asked Carson.

'Because it's the only thing vaguely out of the ordinary to have happened recently in this monk's very ordinary, monastic existence,' Cross pointed out.

'I thought you didn't theorise, George,' replied Carson.

'I am not theorising. I'm merely stating my opinion that logic surely dictates the interview cannot just be coincidental. No one had known where Alexander Mount was for fifteen years. Not even his brother. He then does a local TV interview which attracts some media attention along the billionaire-versus-the-monk lines. It's broadcast nationally on *Newsnight* and a short time later the monk is killed. You cannot rule out the possibility that it alerted someone to his whereabouts,' Cross surmised.

The meeting ended shortly after.

One thing about the case was still preoccupying Cross and the whole team. They didn't have a crime scene. This was crucial not just for the forensic evidence it might hold, but also vital for them to be able to put together the narrative of the case. He'd studied the deposition site photographs over and over again, but nothing was forthcoming. Finally, he went back to the Ordnance Survey map of the area which he pored over inch by inch with a magnifying glass. It was then that he saw it: a line of broken green dashes. This signified a public footpath. It ran from the wood across one of the farms and alongside part of the conference centre land. If you followed it a few miles north, it came to and crossed a small country estate. So this was, in effect, linked to the wood, but had been ignored thus far as they'd been concentrating on the land that actually bordered it. It could so easily have been missed. In fact, up until this point it had been. The estate was owned by a Rosemary Tate, but it was its history that grabbed Cross's attention. He texted Ottey. She looked up from her desk and frowned. Why did he always do this? Why couldn't he just open his door and ask her to step into his office?

He pointed to the map.

'See this?' he asked.

'What am I looking at?'

'It's an Ordnance Survey map of the area around the deposition site,' he answered.

'I know that, you numpty. What am I looking at specifically?'

He'd obviously found something material to the case. She knew this because he always wanted her to tease it out of him. It was his little game, reflecting how pleased he was with himself. She'd found it really irritating at first, until she realised it was just his way of asking for approbation, which at times it appeared he really needed. Where was the harm in that? she'd asked herself. Who was she to deny it to him? So now, she always played along.

'Easily missed. See the green line of dashes, here?' he said.

'Yes.'

'It's a public footpath going over one of the farms, alongside the conference centre, through another property and onto this private estate,' he said.

'Right...'

'It doesn't border the wood which is why I didn't notice it before. But it is linked by the path.'

'So, what is it? The estate?' she asked.

'It's an early eighteenth-century stately home owned by a Rosemary Tate,' he said meaningfully.

'Is that supposed to mean something to me?' she'd asked.

'It is not. Rosemary Tate has been the owner of the estate since 2010.'

'Okay, so now you're getting interesting. Who owned it before then?'

'It had been in the previous family for over three hundred years. It was originally built by one Samuel Cubitt,' he said.

'As in the bank,' she said.

'As in the bank,' he confirmed.

'So old man Cubitt had to sell the family home when the bank collapsed?' she thought out loud.

'He didn't have to. Rosemary Tate is his wife. Tate is her maiden name.'

32

That weekend Ottey picked Cross up at his flat early on the Saturday morning. He wasn't particularly looking forward to it, as she was also bringing his father and her two girls to go to Cheddar Gorge and caves. This meant he'd doubtless have to sit in the back seat squashed up with the two children. He was equally sure they'd be eating crisps. The sound of people eating crisps, invariably with their mouths open shooting fragments at whomever they were talking to, was unbearable to Cross. It was like people scraping their fingernails down a blackboard. It was going to be forty-five minutes of hell for him. But when the car pulled up, there was only Raymond in the front seat.

'Where are the girls?' he asked suspiciously, thinking they must be in some corner shop stocking up on incredibly noisy things to eat, with the sole purpose of annoying him.

'They had some social engagements I'd forgotten about, so they're with my mother. The gorge and caves will have to wait,' she replied.

'So why are you here? Why didn't you just cancel?' he asked, still on the pavement.

'I'm here to drive you to St Eustace's and save you a cab fare. Would you just get in? A "thank you" wouldn't go amiss,' she said.

'And what about him?' asked Cross as he finally got into the back seat.

'Him? Your father, you mean? He was looking forward to getting out of the flat for the day and I didn't want to disappoint him. So, he's coming to see the abbey. He's very curious about it.'

Cross grunted. Something he did when he knew some sort of verbal acknowledgement was required, but he didn't know exactly which one to use.

As they drove south Raymond reeled off a history of the abbey, which he'd researched. Cross was actually interested and it passed the journey very pleasantly until Ottey burst the bubble.

'I understand you met Christine, George's mother, at the funeral,' she asked Raymond.

'I did, and then had her round for dinner,' he replied quite cheerfully.

Cross was furious, but helpless. There was nothing he could do about this gross invasion of his privacy.

'Really? How was it?' Ottey went on.

'It was nice to see her,' Raymond said.

'Will you be seeing her again?' she persisted.

What did she think she was doing?

'I think so. We have each other's phone numbers. So perhaps. I know George sees her once a month.'

'I never told you that,' said Cross.

'Of course you didn't. Stephen told me,' Raymond replied sanguinely.

'I didn't know you were seeing her on a regular basis,' said Ottey.

'Well, that's surprising as everyone else seems to know,' said Cross tetchily.

'You should be flattered we all take an interest. How was she, Raymond?'

'She seemed glad to see me, if I'm honest. I was a little surprised as I thought if I ever saw her again, she'd be angry.'

'But she wasn't,' Ottey said.

'I think Father Stephen might have had something to do with that. You know, prepared the ground,' replied Raymond.

'Oh, I'm sure of it,' she replied.

'He's a wonderful man. I'm so sorry this has happened to him. I do hope you'll get to the bottom of it. But even in this situation he seems to always be thinking about others rather than himself,' Raymond reflected.

'Raymond, can I ask you a personal question?' Ottey asked.

'No,' answered Cross from the back. 'I'd rather you didn't.'

'Weren't you at all angry, seeing the woman who abandoned you with a small child all those years ago?' Ottey persisted.

'Yes and no,' Raymond replied quietly.

'Just tell me to mind my own business,' she continued.

'Mind your own business,' said Cross, as instructed. Raymond and Ottey ignored him in the way parents often ignore an irritating child who asks how far it is to their destination every five minutes.

'It's complicated,' Raymond replied. 'I'm assuming George hasn't filled you in on what happened back then.'

'What do you think?' she said.

'I think that's very tactful of him,' Raymond replied.

'Thank you!' said the voice in the back, sounding like he was proving a point.

'Put it this way. Christine was in no way to blame for what happened back then. It was entirely my fault. What I was angry about was the way she decided to opt out of our lives completely. I thought that was wrong and I still feel it was regrettable. She missed out on so much. Particularly with our son.'

There was that pronoun again. Our. Cross was so unused to this. Throughout his life Raymond had referred to him as 'his' son. 'Our' was completely alien to him in this context. It made him feel like he was someone else completely.

'But now you can put that right,' said Ottey.

'DS Ottey, please don't put words into my father's mouth,' Cross protested.

'I think so, yes,' replied Raymond. 'We both made mistakes when we were young, and I don't see any reason to prolong those now that we're older and wiser.'

'I think that's lovely. Don't you, George?' said Ottey.

'I stand by your initial observation,' replied Cross.

'Which was what? Remind me.'

'That it's none of your business.'

Ottey and Raymond shared an affectionate smile which Cross couldn't see from the rear of the car.

33

The trees that bordered the lane to the abbey were in fuller bud and leaf than they were just a couple of weeks before. This seemed to make it feel even more secluded. Father Magnus greeted them at the door.

'Josie, how nice to see you again. George, welcome.'

'Father Magnus,' replied Ottey. 'This is George's father, Raymond.'

'How do you do, Raymond?' said the priest.

'Well, thank you. Hello, Father.'

'Gosh, we are blessed with visitors today. Brother Thomas has already taken your colleagues up to the church,' the priest continued.

'What colleagues?' asked Cross.

'Alice and Michael,' Magnus replied.

'Who?' asked Cross.

'Mackenzie and Swift, George. Come on, you can do better than that,' said Ottey.

'Can I leave you to find your own way?' asked Magnus.

'Of course,' replied Ottey.

'Why are you here?' was the closest thing to a greeting that Mackenzie and Swift were going to get that morning.

'Good morning, George,' replied Mackenzie. 'How was your journey?'

He was about to answer when it occurred to him that there

was every possibility she was being sarcastic. So, he just looked at Swift.

'We thought we could help,' he said. 'Works outing. Think of it as a team-building exercise.'

'What is he talking about?' Cross asked Mackenzie.

'We thought there must be some manual labour, requiring no brains or ability, that we might be able to do,' she said.

Cross realised there was no way out of this situation, which to his mind was tantamount to an ambush. He just had to adapt to it, which he did with his usual lack of grace. He took them all into the room behind the organ which housed the blower and air reservoirs. This was where the air flow was generated for the organ. There was an electric rotary fan which was the blower for the two reservoirs. One of these collected the air from the blower and topped up the other reservoir when necessary. This was the one that supplied the air to the organ itself. Cross pointed to the other tank which had a concertina-like lid. They were linked by a large duct across the ceiling.

'When the organist presses a key it opens a pallet, which is like a valve, and this reservoir provides the air to make the sound. There are weights on top to regulate the pressure and make the flow regular,' Cross told them.

'Why?' asked Swift.

'Because if it's not regular it would make the note waver like a tremolo. This makes it constant.'

'Brilliant. The man knows his organs,' Swift joked.

Raymond walked over to look at the blower on the wall. It was encased in a metal box.

'May I?' he asked his son, indicating the power switch.

'Yes.'

Raymond flicked the switch, the fan ground into action. A cacophony of wheezes and clunks filled the room. It sounded like an asthmatic learner driver changing gears without using the clutch. He quickly switched it off.

'I can sort that out,' he said.

'I was hoping you could,' replied Cross. He turned to Mackenzie and Swift. 'It would be helpful if you could remove everything except for the weights off the top of the reservoir. I imagine you can reach without the need of a ladder?' he said to Swift.

He turned to Thomas and William who had now arrived.

'Can we find anywhere for all this cleaning equipment? It has no place in here,' he said.

'Of course. Brother Thomas, could you see to it?' William asked politely. Thomas immediately went off to look.

'I was wondering if we could use your skills with leather?' Cross then asked William. He showed him that the folds on top of the reservoir were made from leather. 'Some of these have perished and are letting the air out. Could you fix them?'

William had a closer look.

'Well, I could patch them up, but I think they would last longer if I just replaced them completely,' he said.

'Yes, that would be better. I can help you attach them whenever you're ready.'

William left to get his tools. Cross turned to Ottey as if she were waiting to be assigned a task. She read the situation quickly and said before he had a chance to speak, 'Oh, don't worry about me. I have plenty to do. Not here, just to be clear. Sorry, but there's no way I'm wasting free childcare on organ restoration. I'm also going to see a few houses.'

'Why?'

'Just window shopping.'

'I didn't know you were having a problem with your windows,' Cross said.

'I'm not,' she replied, laughing despite herself. 'I'll pick you up at six?'

'I'll be staying the night,' Cross replied.

'Really? You really are starting to feel right at home here, aren't you, George? You'll be wearing a novice's habit before we know it,' she replied.

'Oh, how cool would that be?' Swift interjected before Cross was able to give expression to his indignation.

'We can give Raymond a lift home,' volunteered Mackenzie.

'Excellent. Enjoy yourselves. Bye, Raymond,' she said. But he said nothing, already lost to the world, removing the metal casing round the rotary fan.

Cross and Thomas carried on with the remaining two ranks in the organ chamber. Having learnt their lesson the previous week, they removed all the pipes at the same time and cleaned them before replacing them. Great progress was made in the reservoir room. The rotary fan was now in pieces and spread across the floor. Mackenzie and Swift had cleared out the cleaning stuff and other detritus which seemed to have gathered in there magnetically, and set about cleaning decades of dust and dirt from the equipment, walls and floor. They stopped for Sext when all the monks appeared and sang the midday office. Mackenzie took lunch orders. She was going to drive into town and get them all something to eat.

'No need,' said Thomas as the side door opened and Father Magnus appeared.

'We've prepared you a light repast,' he said. 'Just soup and bread with some apple juice from our own apples.'

Jude and Benedict were wheeling a wheelbarrow containing a small pot and some bowls.

'I hope this'll suffice,' said Jude.

Mackenzie was really touched by their thoughtfulness as they poured out the soup and juice and handed out slices of sourdough. The monks then left them to eat in peace.

'Oh my,' exclaimed Swift. 'This bread!'

'It's miraculous,' agreed Raymond.

'Literally, perhaps,' added Mackenzie.

Cross took his bowl off to the steps of the side entrance to the church. Not just for the comfort it afforded him but so he could eat in private.

They all relaxed after they'd eaten.

'It's so peaceful here,' commented Mackenzie.

'I love it,' said Swift, who then started identifying birds from their birdsong. 'That's a sedge warbler. The jerky-sounding one. It's like a nature reserve here. I could happily live like this.'

'You, live like a monk?' Mackenzie asked him teasingly.

'Well, when you put it like that, then no. Obviously,' he replied.

'You'd miss all the blood and gore,' she added.

'That's true,' he agreed.

'What about you, George? Any appeal?' Raymond asked his son.

'Its routine, predictability. The simplicity and repetitive nature of their life is very appealing. But for me it's all based on a fallacious premise, so pointless,' he replied reflectively.

'DS Ottey thinks it's like a home from home for you,' said Mackenzie, immediately regretting it.

'Why?' Cross asked.

'Do you think monks have worries?' Swift asked, quickly changing the subject, in the hope of earning points with Mackenzie.

'Oh, I'm sure they do. They may be different to ours, but everyone has worries, don't they?' asked Raymond.

'But they've got such a cool stress-free vibe about them. I love the way they fold their arms under their habits. It's a perfect, sartorial way of being enigmatic. It makes it look like they're being permanently thoughtful. As if they're in a different dimension,' said Swift as Thomas strode up towards them purposefully. His feet moving rapidly under the hem of his habit like a duck's legs underwater, he looked neither enigmatic nor other-dimensional. He walked past them and into the church without a word.

'I suppose that's our cue to go back to work,' Raymond observed.

'We'll clear up the plates and glasses,' said Mackenzie.

★

By the end of the afternoon the rotary fan was operating almost silently. Raymond looked very pleased with the outcome. It had been a very satisfying day.

'I enjoyed that. Thanks for asking me,' he said to Cross.

'I didn't. You were supposed to be going to the caves,' Cross replied.

'But I knew you were going to ask. That's why I brought my tools,' said his father.

Cross couldn't dispute this because it was completely true. It also reminded him that the one person in the world he could never fool was his father. Although that number seemed to be growing, he'd noticed with increasing alarm.

Mackenzie and Swift took Raymond home. As Swift drove them away from the abbey Mackenzie looked back and saw Cross and Brother Thomas walking into the abbey house, hoods up, without a word.

'Oh my God, he's gone native,' she said to Swift.

Joking aside, it had seemed almost the perfect environment for her boss. She'd noticed how relaxed he seemed throughout the day and how he and Thomas had said no more than three words to each other but seemed to be working telepathically. Ideal for George Cross.

Ottey had spent an interesting but frustrating day house hunting. The truth was that she found the whole process overwhelming. Partly because she was worried with not having the time to do it properly. But also because she was always terrified of making decisions in her private life. This was odd considering how decisive she was at work. She looked at several houses and rejected most of them, but two stood out as being ideal, in theory. The fact that she'd found them on day one of her search made her instinctively suspicious. Both were perfect and had one thing in common. They were way outside her budget. One of them could be discounted immediately because, although its location was ideal, it had a self-contained flat which she didn't need. The thought of taking it on and renting it out was immediately discounted. She didn't have time in her life to be a landlady as well as everything else.

That night her mother was over for supper, having brought the girls home, and she showed her the two properties.

'They're both lovely,' Cherish commented.

'I know,' said Ottey. 'Which just makes the whole situation worse.'

'Are you really sure you can't afford it?'

'I could if I did a load of extra overtime maybe, but then I'd see the girls even less than I do now.'

'You could always rent this out,' Cherish suggested, pointing to the self-contained flat.

'I've thought about that, but I can't deal with the hassle of having a tenant,' Ottey replied.

'True,' agreed Cherish.

The next morning Ottey took Clara and Debbie to Sunday worship at their regular Pentecostal church. She always found it an uplifting experience, a tonic to her working week. That day, though, she was in something of a fug about the houses she'd found. She watched her mother singing in the choir and remembered the absurd idea she'd had in the middle of the night, when she found herself unable to sleep. She felt guilty about it now. It was inherently selfish, her only justification for entertaining it at all being the desperation of her situation with the girls living on top of each other. Maybe she should sell up and rent somewhere for the time being. But she knew this was just a way of procrastinating and putting off any decision. People were talking about a downturn in the market. It would be just her luck, though, for the opposite to happen, leaving her high and dry.

After the service she sat in the church hall next door, having coffee with her mother, while Clara and Debbie volunteered manning the refreshment stall.

'I've been thinking about what we talked about last night,' Cherish began.

'We talked about a lot of things,' her daughter replied.

'About the houses. The solution is staring us right in the face. I sell my place, we buy the house, the one with the self-contained flat, together and I move in there.' Thereby articulating the very same idea Ottey had pondered during the night.

'No, I couldn't ask you to do that,' Ottey replied with as much conviction as she could muster.

'Why not? It's perfect. You get the house you want. I still have my independence. Let's face it, I spend so much time round at yours looking after the girls I might as well live with you,' Cherish continued.

'That's not fair,' protested Ottey.

'Maybe not, but we both know it's true. It'll be a lot more convenient for me.'

'Are you sure?' asked Ottey.

'Totally. You had me at "self-contained".'

34

By the end of the next day all the ranks of pipes had been cleaned and replaced in the abbey church. The organ chamber was now spotless. The reservoir still needed new leather folds, but the blower was as good as new. Cross would have to adjust some of the trackers so that the keyboard was even. But on the whole, he was immensely satisfied. Ottey had texted him to say that she would pick him up at the end of the day, which was convenient, if unexpected. Cross was invited to wait for her in the abbot's office with the abbot and Father Magnus.

'How is the case progressing, George?' the abbot asked.

'It's beginning to take shape, I think,' Cross replied.

'That's interesting, you make it sound like you're writing a play or a story,' Father Magnus said. Cross thought for a minute.

'Every crime, in this case, murder, has a narrative. There are many contributing factors that go into that narrative, but they don't come to you in a sequential order. My job is to work out which ones are relevant and where they fit into that narrative. So in a sense your analogy is correct. With the added qualification that the narrative I'm working on isn't fiction. It's fact,' Cross answered.

'We say prayers for you and Josie every day, George,' said the abbot.

Cross was unsure how to respond to this, as he felt it was a pointless exercise. But he said nothing. This was his default way of not causing any offence. But he did have another question for them. While working on the organ that day it had occurred to him that they hadn't considered what had happened to all of

Alexander Mount's money when he entered the abbey. He was obviously immensely well off at the time he became a monk. So where was it?

'When Brother Dominic arrived at the abbey, did he bring anything with him?' Cross asked.

'People arrive here with nothing, and they leave with nothing, George,' said Father Magnus. 'Why do you ask?'

'It's my job. At times it's like shaking a fruit tree which has already been harvested or picked, one last time, to see if any fruit you might have missed, drops,' replied Cross.

'I see,' replied the abbot. 'We'll ask Father Wolfson. He was in charge of any gifts the abbey received. Money, mostly. But we kept track of everything, so in the unlikely event Dominic brought anything with him, he would know.'

'What else do you get given other than money?' Cross went on.

'Candlesticks,' they answered together and laughed.

'Alcohol from the parishioners when they come back from holiday. We have a cupboard full of it,' said the abbot.

'We call it the duty-free cupboard,' added Magnus. 'We have quite a collection of spirits and what you might call an eclectic array of obscure liqueurs from around the world.'

'The Scandinavian ones are like firewater,' said the abbot.

'Which should of course make Father Abbot feel right at home. To be fair I think that's why they buy it for him,' said Magnus.

'It's filled to bursting after the summer holidays,' said the abbot smiling to himself.

Cross's phone vibrated. It was Ottey who had arrived and was outside.

The journey that Cross had been dreading the day before now confronted him. Ottey had taken the girls and Raymond to the Cheddar gorge and caves. Cross was treated to a full account of their day by the girls, punctuated by the noise of incessant crisp crunching for the entire journey back to Bristol. While one spoke the other ate and then the roles were reversed which meant there was no let-up for Cross, who was squashed in the back seat with them. They informed him of all the interesting facts and statistics that Raymond had told them throughout the day, sometimes with such enthusiasm that, to Cross's horror, partly chewed pieces of crisps did indeed fly in his direction. The same interesting facts and statistics Raymond had told him on their trips in the white Ford Cortina with red leather seats, some forty years before. Cross was about to say something to this effect when Ottey gave him a pre-emptive glance in her rear-view mirror. He clamped his mouth shut tight and suffered in a well of noble silence. The peace and tranquillity of the abbey suddenly seemed a million miles away.

35

Carson had insisted that Ottey and Cross put together a progress report on the case. Unlike Ottey, Cross was always happy to do this. It gave him an opportunity to go over everything methodically and see whether a picture was forming. He also suspected that it was the result of pressure from upstairs. Ottey just viewed it as Carson flexing his rank and it annoyed her. This annoyance was sent off the charts the next morning when they came into the unit and found Carson writing condensed bullet points from their own report on a whiteboard, with the intention of then presenting it to them, and the unit, as if it were new to them all.

'So, I think it's useful if we try and figure out where we are at this precise moment in the monk case,' said Carson.

'About two minutes away from losing my shit,' said Ottey just loud enough to elicit a smirk from Mackenzie.

Carson looked over in their direction like a teacher realising that trouble was brewing in a familiar part of the classroom and deciding that if he took them on now, it would inevitably be a downward slope. So he ignored her and carried on. After ten minutes of mind-losingly crass statements like, 'so, we have a dead monk in a ditch', he finally asked Cross, of all people, to take over and finish up. Why did he always do this? He had to know by now, that Cross wouldn't address the entire team. And so –

'No,' he replied.

'Okay,' said Carson, as if this blunt refusal being accepted was simply a part of his man-management strategy, that mere mortals weren't aware of. 'Josie?'

'What?' She wasn't going to make it easy for him.

'Next steps?' he asked.

'Our main point of interest at the moment is obviously the van but we're still waiting on Catherine for a registration number. Dominic was also involved in a dispute about the value of a fifteenth-century book of hours owned by the betting billionaire, Sir Patrick Murphy. Both he and his consigliere, Martin Bates, have alibis throughout the time of Dominic's disappearance.' Ottey read from Cross's notes, not only because they were thorough, but also because his handwriting was more legible than her own.

'We do know that both Murphy and Bates visited Dominic at the abbey, after the interview, despite denying having been in any contact with him, when asked,' Ottey added.

'Which is obviously suspicious. What were they doing there?' Carson asked.

'Trying to get him to change his mind,' said Ottey.

'When he refused maybe they tried to persuade him in other ways,' said Carson as if no one in the room had had the same thought during the investigation.

'Perhaps,' Ottey conceded graciously. 'So now we come to the latest bit of information we have about Dominic's previous life. He worked as an investment banker in the City, at an old bank called Cubitt's. It folded after Alex discovered a major fraud being perpetrated by the son of the chairman, Nick Cubitt. Nicholas spent seven years at Her Majesty's pleasure for his trouble,' Ottey concluded.

'What has that to do with our man?' asked Carson.

'Alex was the star witness for the prosecution,' she replied.

'Anonymous star witness!' asserted Mackenzie from the back of the room, reminding them again why she hadn't been able to come up with this information.

'So, he has motive,' said Carson.

'For what? Exactly?' asked Cross.

'Oh, come on, George, isn't it obvious? Revenge.'

'Then why the beating?'

'I don't know. Because he was angry?' Carson suggested.

Cross made no reply. He got up and walked over to his office.

'Do you have a better suggestion?' asked Carson.

'Of course,' said Cross as he opened his office door, about to disappear inside.

'Well, what is it?'

'What about the money?' Cross asked and went into his office.

'Josie, care to elaborate?' asked Carson.

'George feels the one thing none of us has asked or considered as yet is what happened to Alexander Mount's money? He'd earned a fortune. His deal at Cubitt's was incredibly rich. He was minted when he left. Where is it? His commissions, bonuses, the money from the sale of his flat, his Ferrari?' she said. 'Is that what Dominic's killer was after?'

'He had a Ferrari?' said Carson, who seemed more impressed by this than by the point she was making.

36

As well as researching Cubitt's bank Mackenzie had busied herself building up profiles of the family from social media and the internet. Julian Cubitt had pretty much retired from public life. He had been approaching retirement, or probably elevation to emeritus chairman, when the debacle occurred. He'd given no interviews after the bank's collapse, but it was widely reported how he'd worked tirelessly to find employment in other banks for all his staff. Apparently, according to financial commentators at the time, he'd demonstrated a deep sense of social responsibility, rare in the financial world. He did this, despite the blame for the demise of the bank being laid firmly at his son's door. Rosemary Tate was from an ordinary middle-class family. She had been married and divorced with no children. She had worked as a masseuse, occasionally on cruise ships, which was where she'd met her future husband. She claimed in one of the two interviews Mackenzie managed to find that she was, at heart, a frustrated designer. She was grateful that she'd found a place to channel that talent, with Coxton Hall and its gardens. She and her husband had also set up a small charitable foundation, but on the whole managed to exist well and truly under the radar. Photographs of her when she was younger showed a striking woman with a thick mane of black hair and matching, determined black eyes.

Coxton Hall had an ornate pair of black and gold entrance gates off a country lane. The gates looked like they'd had a new lick of paint recently. Cross wondered whether this meant the place was still generally well maintained. He and Ottey drove down the long drive whose curves occasionally gave way to views of the private estate. The gardens had originally been landscaped by Capability Brown. The grounds had a lake with rolling hills and beautifully planted trees. Sheep grazed; ducks and swans populated the lake. The presence of several impressive oak trees announced how old this estate was. They pulled up at the front door of a large stately home which was built in a variety of architectural styles over the centuries as various Cubitt generations extended the property and left their mark. There was an orangery to one side of the building, and a small private chapel set in its own grounds some way off the main house.

A woman in her late sixties greeted them at the door. This was Rosemary Tate, Julian Cubitt's second wife. His previous wife had died at a relatively early age of cancer. Tate still had thick luxuriant hair flowing over her shoulders. She had let it grey and so it had quite a dramatic and startling effect, which oddly seemed to make her look younger than she was.

'Detectives, how can I help?' she began.

'We'd actually like to speak with your husband if that's okay?' Ottey replied politely.

'Of course. Why don't you come through to the kitchen?'

They walked through a huge hall with a grand staircase at the back of it. The floor was black and white square tiles and made Cross feel that he was walking across a giant chessboard. The walls were painted yellow. There were a couple of Stubbs equine paintings on the walls. Portraits of various generations of the Cubitt family adorned the stairs. The kitchen was modern and relatively newly renovated. So modern that it looked like a kitchen showroom had just been transplanted into the house. There was a double-fronted Aga oven in a bold racing green enamel along one wall. It had the air of being owned by someone who liked cooking. Various well used and seasoned pans hung from a rack above the island in the middle of the room. A door was open, revealing a walk-in larder whose shelves were filled to the gills with home-made preserves and jam, sealed with small pieces of gingham cloth held on by elastic bands. Ottey found herself looking at things like an American tourist in a National Trust property.

A few minutes later, Julian Cubitt came into the kitchen followed by a woman in her sixties. A good decade or so older than his wife, Julian greeted them with a beaming smile. He had wispy white hair that seemed to cling desperately onto his head like a small animal terrified of falling off. He had baggy green corduroy trousers that were held up by wide blue braces adorned with white polka dots. The cords of his trousers were so thick he could easily have lost hundreds of pounds' worth of loose change in them. He wore a flannel Viyella shirt with a paisley cravat, disguising a baggy neck that wouldn't have looked out of place on an adult iguana. He had a protuberant purple bottom lip which seemed to clash with his pale complexion. Half-moon spectacles were perched on the end of his aquiline nose. A pair of discreet hearing aids completed the look. He walked with the aid of a stick.

'Hello,' he said as if genuinely pleased to see them. 'Julian Cubitt.' He grasped for the back of a chair and sat down with an ungainly thump. His voice was a little faint, not hoarse, just faded by age.

'Charlotte, why don't you make our guests some refreshment?' he began by saying.

'I don't think they'll be here long enough for tea,' she replied with a polite smile.

'An interesting observation,' said Cross, 'as you presumably have no idea of the purpose of our visit, which questions your ability to predict the length of our stay.' But he thought she had an admirable sense of defensiveness on behalf of her employers, which was interesting. She was about to answer him when Rosemary pre-empted her.

'That'll be all, thank you, Charlotte,' she said, perhaps wanting to put an end to it.

The woman, presumably the housekeeper thought Cross, now left.

'For some reason Charlotte isn't very fond of the police,' Rosemary explained.

'I have yet to discover anyone who is,' Cross replied.

'Good point,' laughed Julian.

'Are you aware of the recent discovery of a murdered Benedictine monk in Goblin Combe?' Cross asked.

'Of course we are. Dreadful business,' replied Cubitt. 'Who on earth would want to do that to a monk? It beggars belief.'

'That's what we're trying to figure out,' said Ottey.

'Well, I'm not sure how we can help,' interjected Cubitt's wife.

'Alexander Mount,' Cross announced.

Cubitt thought for a moment. 'Yes.'

'Does the name mean anything to you?' Cross asked.

The old man laughed quietly. 'Of course it does. I may be old, but I haven't completely lost it,' he said.

'What's he got to do with this?' asked Rosemary. 'Is he a suspect?'

'No, quite the opposite. Brother Dominic, the murdered monk, was in fact Alexander Mount,' Cross informed them.

'Gosh,' Julian said. 'Are you certain?'

'A hundred per cent,' answered Ottey.

'How extraordinary. He became a monk? Who would've thought?' Cubitt said to his wife.

'You find that more interesting than the fact that he was murdered?' asked Cross.

'No, sorry. That was thoughtless,' Cubitt apologised.

'So, you remember him?' asked Cross.

'Well of course.'

'Why?'

'Why do you think?' snapped Rosemary. 'He brought down the family bank.'

'He did no such thing. Nicholas brought down the bank.

Alexander bears absolutely no responsibility for that,' Cubitt contradicted her.

'If it hadn't been for him—' she started.

'It would've been someone else,' the old man interrupted.

'So, you harboured no grudge against Mount then?' asked Cross.

'No, of course not,' Cubitt replied. 'Oh,' he said, glancing up. 'I see. You're here because you think I might've had something to do with this?'

'Oh that's ridiculous, Julian. Of course they don't. Do you?' Rosemary asked.

'When was the last time you saw Nicholas, your son?' Cross asked, ignoring the question.

'We're well aware of the fact that he's Julian's son,' replied Rosemary tartly.

'Julian's son?' Cross commented.

'I'm his stepmother, obviously.'

'When was the last time you saw him?' Cross persisted.

Cubitt now looked quite uncomfortable. Quietly pained.

'We aren't in touch,' he said quietly.

'Not at all?'

'No.'

'They're completely estranged. After what happened... it wasn't just what he'd done, but the fact that he brazenly took no responsibility for it,' said Rosemary.

'Rosemary...' her husband cautioned.

'Nothing is ever that boy's fault,' Rosemary continued.

'Boy?' commented Cross. 'He's in his mid-forties.'

'He behaves like a spoilt teenager. He looked around for people to blame. He killed off a well-established, successful, centuries old, business in under twelve months,' she said. 'Even when he was convicted, when the evidence of his malfeasance was staring him and everyone in the world in the face, he tried to claim the conviction was unfair. Julian tolerated it for a while but then he couldn't take it any more. People lost millions.

People Julian had been in business for years with. In the end he had to cut him off.'

'Financially?' Cross asked.

'Financially, emotionally. There is no contact,' she replied.

'When was the last time you saw him?' Cross asked. Cubitt seemed reluctant to answer. He looked at the table in silence.

'Not since the trial,' she said.

'What about his children?' asked Ottey.

At this the old man smiled fondly.

'Oh, we see them. Sarah, their mother, has been very good at staying in touch,' he said.

'That would be Nicholas's wife?' Ottey clarified.

'Ex-wife,' Rosemary corrected her.

'Two of the grandchildren have gone into the City, can you believe?' Cubitt said proudly.

'Must be in the genes,' replied Ottey.

'Sarah was keen for them to know their grandfather—'

'And step-grandfather,' interrupted the old man.

Rosemary smiled at his thoughtfulness. 'She didn't see why the sins of the father should be visited on the children. We're very fond of them,' she added.

'How are relations between the children and their father?' asked Cross.

'Very poor,' she replied. 'Again, mostly his fault. Sarah tried to make good the relationship when they were younger, but now they're grown up they can obviously make their own decisions. Nicholas made virtually no effort when he got out of prison. He was too busy feeling sorry for himself and casting around for someone to blame.'

There was a momentary pause.

'Was that everything?' Rosemary concluded.

'We'd like to have a look around the property,' Cross answered.

'Of course,' answered Cubitt who was then immediately countermanded by his younger wife.

'Actually no, that won't be possible.'

'Why?' asked Cross.

'Because this is private property,' she replied.

'And this is a murder enquiry,' Cross pointed out.

'That may be the case, but it has nothing to do with us,' she insisted.

'It would be extremely helpful,' said Ottey, trying to lower the temperature.

'Why?' she asked.

'As part of our investigation.'

'Well, as I've just said, I can't see why you'd think that unfortunate man's murder has anything to do with us.'

'We currently have no idea what to think,' said Cross. 'But the fact is that the victim was known to you and his body was found in this locality.'

'Then you'll have to get a warrant,' she replied coldly.

Neither Cross nor Ottey responded to this. They showed neither disappointment or interest.

'Would you say she seemed angrier about the collapse of the bank than him?' Cross asked as they walked to the car.

'Maybe, but she married him after the bank's collapse, which is interesting,' she replied.

'Why is that interesting?'

'Well, with the bank gone she presumably married him for love,' she replied.

'Hmm,' responded Cross.

'What does that mean?'

'It's an indication of reflection. In this case not a positive one.'

'What are you thinking?' she said, failing to rise as she knew that wasn't his intention.

'He may have lost the bank, but he's still a wealthy man,' Cross replied, looking around them.

As they were about to drive off, Charlotte, the housekeeper, appeared round the corner wheeling an old-fashioned bicycle with a wicker basket on the front of it. Cross called over.

'Charlotte?'

'Yes,' she replied and stopped.

'Do you mind if we have a talk?' He noticed her look back at the house nervously.

'I'm a bit busy,' she replied.

'It'll only take a minute.'

'All right then. I suppose so,' she replied.

'What's your surname, Charlotte?'

'Hoskins.'

'Is that Mrs, Ms or Miss?'

'Mrs. I'm just taking my husband his lunch,' she replied, pointing at the basket in which there was a plate covered with a dishcloth. 'Cold cuts.'

'Shall we walk?' he suggested.

'Where to?'

'Well, wherever your husband is.'

'Why would you want to see him?' she asked.

'I don't. It's merely that you said you were taking him his lunch.'

'Oh, I see.'

'Do you live on the estate?' Cross asked.

'Yes, we have one of the cottages.'

'And how long have you worked for the family?'

'All my adult life really.'

'Does your husband work for them too?'

'Used to. That's how we met. He's mostly retired now but he does help out when needed.'

'Have you always been the housekeeper?' asked Cross.

'No, they didn't have one when Dorothy was alive.'

'Dorothy was Julian's first wife?'

'That's right. She died.'

'So, what did you do then?'

'I was Nicholas's nanny.'

'From what age?'

'From birth.'

'They had no other children.'

'No, she had a couple of miscarriages. Poor thing. Nicholas was, is, an only child.'

'Didn't I read that he went away at an early age to school?'

'Yes. They sent him away at seven, poor thing. I'm not sure Dorothy was ever in favour of it but he went to the same school as all his ancestors at the same age. He went on to Eton in the end.'

'And what did you do then?'

'They kept me on. They've, Julian, has been very good to us.'

'What were your duties then?'

'Helping round the house, then looking after Nicky when he came home for the holidays. Julian was always in London on business, and Dorothy was often with him. She knew all the bank's clients. She said being the wife of a banker was a bit like being an ambassador's wife. So, it was often just me and Nicky at the house,' she explained.

'Are you still close to him?'

This question seemed to make her a little guarded.

'Are you in touch with him?' Cross pushed, but she looked like she really didn't want to answer the question. His enquiring gaze remained fixed to her, though. 'I know his father's out of contact with him. After all that happened with the bank and his going to prison,' Cross continued. 'But it sounds to me like you almost brought him up yourself. More so than his actual parents.'

'I did,' she replied instinctively.

'It must be upsetting seeing their relationship at such a low point.'

'Oh, it is. But it was never the same after Rosemary showed up.'

'In what way?'

'She blames Nick for everything that happened. The collapse of the bank, the loss of the family business.'

'But isn't that actually what did happen?' Cross asked.

'Have you spoken to Nick?'

'I have not.'

'Then you don't have the whole story.'

'I see.'

'Julian's disowned the poor boy. But it's broken his heart. Rosemary gets everything. Nick, nothing. She does everything she can to keep a distance between him and his father,' she went on.

'Do you know why we're here, Mrs Hoskins?'

'No. I have no idea.'

'Did you hear about the Benedictine monk being murdered?' Cross asked.

'In Goblin Combe? Yes, I did. It's awful. But what's that got to do with us?' she asked.

'We're talking to all the people in neighbouring properties.'

'I see.'

They arrived at a cottage in a small cluster of agricultural buildings.

'This is me,' she said.

'Have you heard from Nick recently?' Cross asked again. He noticed her immediate hesitation.

'Why are you asking about Nick?' she asked. Cross didn't say anything but just waited for a reply. 'Not for a while,' she said finally.

'How long exactly is a while?'

'Not since my birthday. He always remembers my birthday. Sends flowers. He's so good like that,' she said affectionately.

'When is your birthday?' Cross asked.

'November the twenty-seventh.'

'Does Mr Cubitt know you're in touch?' Cross pressed.

'Yes.'

'Mrs Cubitt?' asked Cross.

'Of course not. Goodbye.'

Cross watched her wheeling her bike up to the front door of the cottage. There was a limestone lintel above the door into which was carved a goose with its goslings and a sign to the side which said 'Weald Cottage'. A man appeared behind a net curtain in one of the front windows and looked at Cross in such a blatant and obvious way that he must've felt he couldn't be seen from the outside. He watched Cross leave with an expression that was familiar to the detective – suspicious interest. Cross walked away from the building past an open barn where various agricultural machinery, some of it ancient, was stored, as well as a couple of other vehicles under tarpaulins.

37

The van Swift had discovered on CCTV snatching Brother Dominic at the abbey gates, had, after days of scanning, been spotted on various local traffic cameras. It had been a painstaking, time-consuming process as they had no full image of the van. It had been like piecing together a large jigsaw puzzle with various vital pieces missing. Having found it, it had taken even longer to find an image clear enough to identify the van. But Catherine, the CCTV officer, with her usual diligence and refusal to be beaten, finally had a registration number. It had taken almost two weeks, but they had it. Its registered owner lived just outside Frome. It felt like they had a break in the case at last. Cross and Ottey drove out to the address. It was on a housing estate just outside the town. Uniformly and unimaginatively boxlike, the houses were all made from limestone, or more probably faux limestone, without a trace of individuality. If the stone was meant to give it an aged, elegant feel, it had failed spectacularly. The name of the van owner was Jeff Evans. As they drove up to the house they saw the van parked in plain sight in the drive.

A scowl the width of the front door, wearing a pink tracksuit, welcomed them. The woman was in her mid-thirties. One look at her told Ottey the outfit was obviously for leisure, as the closest she came to any form of exercise was probably leaning forward to get the TV remote. She was wearing copiously applied make-up and had such long white fake nails it made it quite difficult for her to hold the door open. She'd also had so much filler in her face that she could have kept a biro on her top lip while she did her sudoku. She took one look at them and asked, 'Jehovah's witnesses?'

'Police officers,' said Ottey holding up her warrant card.

'Not sure which is worse,' the woman replied. 'Have you come about the van?'

'We have,' said Ottey.

'Well, you're a bit bloody late. It's back, as you can see. No thanks to you lot,' the woman said.

'I don't understand,' replied Ottey.

A skinny man appeared behind the woman.

'It's the police,' the woman said without turning round. 'About the van.'

'It's back,' he said.

'I know that. I've told them.'

'Are you saying it was stolen?' asked Ottey.

'Well, isn't that why you're here?' the woman asked.

'Can we come inside?' Ottey said, much to Cross's dismay as the woman's sickly and overpowering perfume, which had been liberally applied, was in danger of making him sneeze. The woman hesitated; Cross willed her to say no, while at the same time wondering whether her reluctance was just evidence of a habitual dislike of the police, or whether they had something to hide.

'Sure.'

They sat around the kitchen table. The house was garishly decorated, with plastic covers on the sofa suite, but at least it was clean and tidy.

'Are you Jeff Evans?' Ottey began.

'I am.'

'And you are?'

'His wife. Dolores.'

'So, when was the van stolen?' Ottey asked.

'Last week,' Dolores replied.

'Did you report it stolen?'

'Well, obviously. Why else would you be here?'

Cross checked his notes. 'No such report was made,' he said, without looking up. Dolores turned to Jeff.

'I thought you said you'd reported it,' she said.

'I said I was going to,' he replied.

'But?' she asked.

'It came back,' he replied.

'What do you mean, it came back?' Ottey asked.

'Here. Outside. It came back, so what was the point in reporting it stolen?' he asked.

'Where was it stolen from?' asked Ottey.

'Go on then,' Dolores said. 'Tell them. Tell them how they got the keys. Tell them how many times I told you not to do it.'

'They were in the hall. On the radiator cover,' he said quietly.

'They use a bamboo pole or a fishing rod with a magnet on the end. Stick it through the letter box and see what they come up with. He knew. He just paid no bloody attention,' said Dolores.

'Why nick a van?' asked Ottey.

'Oh, they didn't want the van. Bloke next door owns a Porsche. Always parking it outside, not that I mind. If people think we have a Porsche I don't have a problem with that. They obviously thought he lived here and in the end the van was better than nothing. Probably just took it for a spin,' Dolores explained.

'And then they brought it back here? To the house?' asked Ottey.

'Yep,' replied Jeff. 'Just a bit of fun, I guess. Bloody annoying, but that was it.'

'No,' interrupted Dolores giving her husband a look. 'They left it down the road. Anyway, he's buying a steering lock now and not leaving his keys in the hall.'

'We'll be needing to take the van away,' said Cross.

'What for?' asked Dolores.

'Forensic examination,' he replied.

'Oh, don't be soft. You'll never catch the little buggers. Haven't you got better things to do?' Dolores asked.

'Why do you need to examine it?' asked Jeff, nervously.

Ottey wasn't going to answer but Cross jumped in.

'It's part of a murder enquiry. The van was used to kidnap and murder someone. A Benedictine monk. Perhaps you've read about it in the local paper?'

A silence followed. 'They beat him to death in my van?' asked Jeff without thinking.

'Shut up, Jeff,' Dolores snapped.

'Who's "they"?' Ottey asked.

'Well, obviously the bastards who nicked it,' he said quickly.

'I hope you catch them. I read about that poor monk,' Dolores began. 'It's a disgrace what they did to that holy man.'

Cross felt this was being directed particularly at her husband. There had been an increased tension between the two of them, ever since the murder had been mentioned.

Cross and Ottey waited outside for the forensics team to come with the low-loader, to make sure the van wasn't tampered with. Cross was in need of some fresh air after the onslaught of Dolores's perfume. He stood quite close to the front door, but to one side so he couldn't be seen from within. After a brief pause Dolores could be heard shouting at her husband. Cross listened but couldn't make out exactly what was being said but it was clearly as a result of their visit.

38

Jeff Evans looked terrified, plain and simple. Whether this was because he'd been brought into the MCU for questioning, or because his wife had also, despite vociferous objections, been brought in and he was thinking about the inevitable consequences when he next saw her, was anyone's guess. Cross thought the wife card was definitely one to be played though. That's why he'd brought her in. Chances were they wouldn't have to interview her at all. Her mere presence might be enough to get Evans to tell them the truth. He and Ottey sat opposite Evans in the interview room. Cross placed a blank A4 pad in front of him. He adjusted it so it was equidistant from the edges of the table. Evans observed this nervously. He had a duty solicitor with him, as he'd been cautioned.

'Why do you think you're here today, Mr Evans?' Ottey began.

'I don't know. I haven't done anything wrong,' he replied.

'Well, let's start with that statement,' said Cross. 'It's a good starting point because we know for a fact that you have done something wrong. You lied to the police.'

'About what?'

'The van. Your van, used in the commission of a kidnapping and murder,' said Cross.

'Nothing to do with me. I didn't kidnap no one,' Evans protested.

'Well, double negative aside, why don't you have a look at this,' said Cross. Ottey then pushed a frame grab from the CCTV footage across the table. The driver could be seen, wearing a baseball cap, but it was completely blurred. Evans snorted with derisive relief.

'That could be anyone,' he said.

'Precisely, which of course means it could be you,' said Cross.

'But it isn't. You'll see that when you get a better picture,' he said with a confidence that told Cross maybe he wasn't driving the van after all. Evans knew that when the image was enhanced it would show that it wasn't him. So, Cross changed tack.

'Unless of course we can't. In which case we'd say that, on balance, with it being your van, it's you at the wheel. With a good prosecuting lawyer and an emotive case involving the death of a monk, that may well be enough for a jury to convict,' said Cross.

'Convict me of what?' Evans asked.

'Kidnap and murder.'

Evans looked immediately less confident.

'The van was nicked,' he protested.

'Oh, come on, Jeff,' said Ottey jumping in. 'Do you know how many vehicle thefts we know about where the vehicle is returned to the registered owner, rather than driven to the bottom of a lake or burned to a crisp? Precisely none.'

'Because, like me, if they're returned, they don't get reported, do they? That's my point,' Evans insisted.

'Where were you the afternoon of March the thirty-first?' asked Cross.

'No clue.'

'It was the day you claim the van went missing,' Ottey explained.

'Probably at home with Dolores watching one of her bloody antiques shows,' Evans said.

'She likes those shows, does she?' asked Cross.

'Bloody loves them.'

'How long do you think she's going to stick with the stolen story, Mr Evans?' asked Cross.

'It's not a bloody story.'

'When we tell her that if she doesn't tell us the truth, she could be an accessory to murder?'

Evans looked like he might be about to vomit.

'I think she'll tell us the truth. That you took the van, she didn't know where, and the next thing she knows, the police have come round asking about a kidnapping. But here's the problem with that version. She had to have known where you'd taken the van, because you'd both come up with the van being stolen story. Which would definitely make her an accessory. Long sentence, accessory to murder. Do you know what it is, DS Ottey?'

'Not offhand, but I can find out,' she replied.

'It's time to tell us what happened, Mr Evans. Who asked you to go to the monastery and take the monk and who was with you?'

'No comment.'

Dolores Evans had calmed down a little since her arrival but unlike her husband she hadn't been cautioned and so didn't have a lawyer.

'Mrs Evans, you should know that your husband is being interviewed under caution,' said Ottey. There was no reply.

'You're an intelligent woman,' Cross began.

'Bullshit, pull the other one,' she replied.

'Well, I know you're smart enough not to take the blame for something you didn't do,' Cross went on. She didn't reply.

'Can you account for your husband's whereabouts on the afternoon of March the thirty-first?' asked Ottey.

'Was that the day the van was nicked?' she asked.

'It's the day you say it was nicked, yes,' said Ottey.

'We were in. He didn't have a job that day,' replied Dolores.

'This is his work as a man and a van,' Ottey asked.

'That's right.'

'Okay, so you're providing each other with an alibi,' Ottey commented.

'I'm not providing him with anything. I'm just telling you what happened,' she snapped.

'Dolores, your husband is facing charges of abduction and murder here,' Ottey informed her.

'What?'

'It's extremely serious,' Ottey told her.

'The fact that you are also perpetuating the lie about the van being stolen makes you an accessory. To murder,' added Cross.

'Fuck that,' she said, as the reality of the situation dawned on her.

'Was Jeff driving the van that afternoon?' Cross asked.

She thought for a moment.

'No,' she replied.

'Why did you have to think? I thought you said it was stolen. Why was that even a question you had to answer, if it had been stolen?' asked Cross.

'Do I need a lawyer?' she asked.

'Has she been arrested or cautioned?' Cross asked Ottey, in such a way that it sounded like he actually didn't know this himself.

'No,' Ottey replied.

'I can understand your confusion though, because it must have been quite difficult to hear anything under the volley of abuse you apparently directed at the officers who brought you here. But you have not,' Cross concluded.

Dolores looked like she wasn't entirely sure what Cross had just said.

'Look, Mrs Evans,' he continued. 'A monk has been abducted in your husband's van and subsequently murdered. I don't think for a moment you were involved in this.'

'Good, because I wasn't,' she said.

'But you need to tell us the truth about the van.'

'No comment.'

*

Cross put the CCTV image back on the table in front of Jeff Evans.

'Is that you, Mr Evans?' he asked as if it were for the first time.

'I've already told you. No,' came the reply.

'Very well,' said Cross turning to Ottey and getting up to leave the room.

'Jeff Evans, we are going to charge you with the kidnap and murder of—'

'Wait a minute. Wait a minute. Stop, stop…' he said, laughing at the sheer absurdity of the idea but panicking at the same time.

Ottey stopped. Cross turned at the door.

'It wasn't me. I swear. All right, I did lie about the van. I lent it to a mate, but I didn't know what he was going to use it for. Honest,' he pleaded.

'What mate?' asked Ottey.

'I can't tell you that. He'll kill me,' he said desperately.

'Not if he's inside,' replied Ottey.

'You don't know him. He'll find a bloody way. I'm telling you.'

'Why did you lend it to him?' Cross asked.

'Because he's not the type of bloke you say no to,' Evans replied.

'What did he want it for?'

'I don't know. He didn't say.'

'You didn't ask?'

'No.'

'You weren't in the least bit curious?' asked Ottey.

'No.'

'You don't strike me as the kind of woman who's frightened of much, if anything at all, Mrs Evans,' Cross reflected.

'I'm not.'

'You don't brook any nonsense,' he went on.

'That's right.'

'Are you frightened of whoever your husband lent his van to?' Cross asked.

Dolores took a second as she tried to process whether this was a new piece of information, or a trick on the part of the detective opposite her.

'Jeff has told us the van wasn't stolen and that he lent it to a mate,' explained Ottey.

'But he seems a little reluctant to tell us who. Because he's terrified, he says,' added Cross.

'It's not a crime to lend someone a van if you're unaware it's going to be used in the commission of a crime, Dolores,' said Ottey.

'Did either of you know what the van was going to be used for, Mrs Evans?' Cross asked.

'Of course we didn't. Do you think we're bloody stupid? Do you think his cousin just pitched up and said, "I need to borrow your van to bump off a monk," and we just said, "Oh, sure, no trouble. Just make sure you fill up the tank before you give it back?"' she said.

'His cousin?' asked Cross.

Dolores took a second to register her slip and figure out what to do next. She obviously came to the conclusion that there was no turning back.

'Frankie, Frankie Davis. He lives in Cardiff. He's always been trouble. In and out of prison. Jeff is scared shitless of him. But I don't care. I'm not going to swing for something I didn't do. We didn't do. My Jeff had nothing to do with this. You have to believe me,' she said with a sudden pleading tone entering her voice.

'In the same way you wanted us to believe the van had been stolen?' asked Cross. 'Why did you lie about that?'

'Because we knew Frankie was probably up to something wrong,' she replied.

'So you knew it would be used for something illegal?' asked Cross.

'He comes up all the way from Cardiff, unannounced, and demands to use Jeff's van? We hadn't heard from him in months. Of course it was dodgy. But if we'd known what he was really up to, do you think we'd accessorise that?' she said.

It wasn't her mangling of the English language that caused Ottey to hide a smile behind her hand, but the look of complete confusion on Cross's face as he tried to work out what had just been said.

From their usual vantage point, the back stairs of the building, Cross and Ottey watched Jeff and Dolores walk through the car park. Dolores practically chased her husband to the patrol car that was taking them home. She was hitting his head, kicking him, swinging her handbag at him, while screaming unintelligible abuse. It got so bad that the officer driving them home had to step in and restrain her.

'Why have you let them go?' Carson asked in disbelief.

'He's been released on police bail,' said Ottey.

'When we first told them about the murder they were genuinely shocked. They had no idea what the van had been used for,' Cross told him.

'How do you know he wasn't driving the van?' Carson went on.

'Because of his obvious relief when we told him we had CCTV footage of the driver which we were going to enhance. He knew it wasn't him. So the clearer the better, as far as he was concerned,' said Cross.

'What if you're wrong?'

'We're not,' said Cross emphatically.

'How can you be so sure?'

'The hiding she gave him in the car park, for one thing. If

uniform hadn't been so quick, she'd be downstairs right now being charged with assault,' said Ottey.

'It was our only lead,' Carson protested pathetically.

'It still is and now we have a name – Frankie Davis,' said Cross.

'Well don't just sit here. Go find him,' Carson instructed them unnecessarily and without even knowing who Davis was and what link, if any, he had to the case.

39

It was a really early start the next morning. They were going to arrest Frankie Davis at 6, which meant a 4 a.m. briefing in Cardiff. South Wales Police were going to make the arrest together with Cross and Ottey. As Davis was considered to be a dangerous individual a tactical team was going to be used. After the briefing they all assembled on a run-down council estate. Cross wondered whether it had ever been a good place to live. Built in the nineteen sixties, the estate consisted of small, terraced houses. Constructed in dark red brick, they had white wooden panels underneath the ground-floor windows. The paint was now flaking like the promise with which this estate had been originally conceived. Some residents had built porches over their front door. Whether this was to add a bit of self-important individuality to them or for practicality, it was hard to tell. Bedrooms had sheets hung across them instead of curtains, or bin liners, pages of newspapers and the occasional Welsh flag.

The tactical team thumped on the door and yelled, 'POLICE!' They waited a minute, then smashed it open and charged in with more shouts of 'POLICE!' Ottey actually liked donning a stab vest and charging in behind a tactical team whenever she got the chance. She wanted to see the fear and surprise in the suspect's eyes. She also wanted their first encounter with her to be an intimidating one. Cross hated the noise and chaos of it all. The truth was he found all the commotion of these vocal charges into a suspect's house more startling than they did. So these days he tended to hang back in the car, doors locked, of course, and sit it out till the tactical team withdrew and the drama was over.

When the team entered the house, they were greeted with a fetid atmosphere of un-emptied ashtrays, stale alcohol, unwashed laundry, foul body odour, rising damp and curry. A nausea-inducing cocktail at any time, let alone first thing in the morning. Wallpaper was coming off the walls, black damp climbing up from the floor. Things were written and drawn on the bare plaster which would've been more suited to a derelict public lavatory. The living room was littered with half-drunk bottles of spirits and crushed cans of lager. A large, round ashtray was in the middle of a coffee table, overflowing with cigarette butts disintegrating in a pool of spilt lager. A couple of empty airport duty-free carrier bags were on the dining table with the remains of an Indian takeaway.

When Cross ventured in, Frankie Davis was getting dressed in his bedroom, having been read his rights by Ottey. In the kitchen below, his father was screaming obscenities at the Welsh officers. Davis junior was a thin, rodent-faced man whose skin was pockmarked like a map of lunar craters. He'd obviously had terrible acne at some point in his life. His complexion was residually red from the profuse blood supply that had been needed to fuel such volcanic boils and his skin was oily with unpleasantly large blackheads clinging to the side of his nostrils like barnacles on the hull of a beached boat.

He was taken to Bristol in a custody van. Ottey and Cross followed. The only things they had removed from the house were a couple of mobile phones. When Davis was booked in, Cross noticed the large sovereign coin rings on his fingers. They left white tan lines when he took them off and the custody sergeant bagged them. Cross asked for them to be sent immediately to Swift in forensics. They waited for a duty solicitor to become free and then started the interview. Davis looked on suspiciously as Cross went through his pre-interview routine at the desk, with his careful placing of his folder.

'Have you been offered a drink?' Ottey asked.

'Nope,' replied Davis.

'Tea? Coffee?' she asked.

'Tea, milk, four sugars,' he said, making Cross grimace. Why bother with the tea at all? he thought.

'Aspirin?' Ottey asked.

'What for?'

'Fine. I won't be offering again,' she said.

'All right. Yes, I will then.'

'Mr Davis, where were you on March the thirty-first of this year?' Cross asked.

'I have no bloody idea, mate.'

'None at all?'

'I can't remember specific dates like that,' Davis replied.

'Why's that?' Cross asked.

'Because I'm unemployed. One day is just like another. I was either at home, at the bookie's or in the pub.'

'You still go to a bookie?' Cross asked, interested by this.

'Where else am I supposed to place a bet? The doctor's surgery?' Davis asked.

'If you could get an appointment,' Cross observed.

'That's true!' Davis laughed.

'You don't bet online? I thought everyone bet online these days,' said Cross.

'And there lies the path to ruin, mate. I'm not that stupid.'

'Can you explain what you mean by that?'

'I only bet with what I have in my hand. Not what I don't. Not what I might have. Online betting's for mugs. They make you think it's all a bit of fun and no money's involved. I like to see the cash,' Davis explained.

'Your winnings, I take it, you mean by that?'

'Winnings or losses. I need to see it counted by the cashier. I like to know what I'm losing or winning for real. Online's like betting with pretend money, like monopoly money. Only it's not. Wait till the bloody credit card bill comes in,' he said, looking at his solicitor knowingly.

'So, you live off benefits?' asked Cross.

There was a pause. Cross wondered whether Davis was trying to work out whether it was a trick question.

'What if I do?' Davis asked defensively.

'You've just been on holiday. Portugal, is that right?' Cross went on, looking at his notes which included Davis's credit card statements.

'What's that supposed to mean? I'm not allowed to go on holidays because I'm on the social?'

'It was just a question,' said Cross.

'Don't piss about, mate. Why don't you just tell me why I'm here and get on with it?'

'Did my colleague not tell you when she arrested and cautioned you?'

'Wasn't listening, mate. I was half asleep.'

'You're here on suspicion of kidnap and murder. You must've taken that in,' said Cross.

'Oh yeah. Who? That's what I wanted to ask. Who am I supposed to have kidnapped and murdered?' Davis asked.

'Brother Dominic of St Eustace's Abbey,' Cross answered.

'What? Well, that's just bloody stupid,' Davis laughed. 'A monk? Why would I kidnap a monk?'

'That's a very good question and one to which you are currently the only one with the answer,' Cross said and stared at the man. 'Where were you on March the thirty-first?'

'Already answered that question, mate. I don't know,' said Davis getting a little testy.

'Do you own a car?' asked Cross.

'Yes.'

'A VW Passat?'

'Yes.'

'Is this the registration of that vehicle?'

Cross pushed an A4 piece of paper with a blown-up photo of a car licence plate on it. Davis looked up, but said nothing.

'This photograph comes from an ANPR camera at a petrol station in Applegreen Farleigh,' Cross continued.

'Never heard of it.'

'It's on the A36 just south of Bath and was taken at twelve thirty on the thirty-first of March. Here, you can see from the time and date stamp. See?' Cross pointed out helpfully. 'What were you doing there?'

'Who says it's me? Who says I was driving it?' Davis challenged him.

'Well, we do, in point of fact,' said Cross, who then showed him some CCTV footage of the station forecourt. Davis could plainly be seen filling the car up and then walking over to the kiosk. He said nothing.

'What were you doing there?' Cross asked.

Davis thought for a moment then said, 'I was on the way to the coast.'

'Where, exactly?'

'Bournemouth.'

Cross wrote this down diligently, even though he knew it was a lie. Partly because he wanted to make a record of it, but also because he wanted Davis to think, even if only for a moment, that he might believe what he was telling them. This might mean he would begin to think they had less on him than he'd feared.

'What was the purpose of the visit?'

'I was having a few days off,' replied Davis.

'Off?' Cross said. 'From what? You don't work.'

'I just needed a break. I'm allowed a break, aren't I?' he asked, turning to his solicitor as if for help.

'The thing about these little lies you've started telling, these tiny fibs if you like, told during a police interview, is that they seem innocuous at the time, but then they mount up and once they mount up they gain a momentum of their own. Which means you're eventually forced into conceding the truth. You have no choice. Juries, they don't like that kind of momentum. They tend to think it was unavoidable and that you've brought it upon yourself. Any vestige of sympathy for you, or indeed any attempts to see any given situation from your point of view, just evaporates.'

Cross paused and looked at Davis. He then went back to his folder, giving the impression that he had forgotten exactly where he was in the interview. He eventually found his place again and looked up.

'You have a cousin who lives in Frome,' Cross went on. He turned to the solicitor. 'I detect a north-eastern accent in your voice, Mr Antcliff. I'm thinking Sunderland or Middlesbrough, but I can't be entirely sure. But just in case your knowledge of local geography is a little sketchy, Frome is just off the A36 in between Bath and, if you're going in that direction, certainly on the way to Bournemouth.'

He turned back to Davis.

'Jeff Evans.'

'No comment,' said Davis.

'I didn't ask a question, Mr Davis. But I will now. Did you visit your cousin that afternoon? Maybe on your way to Bournemouth?'

'No comment.'

'Specifically, to borrow his van.'

'No comment.'

'Before you answer the next question, perhaps you should take a moment and ask yourself how we know. Did you borrow your cousin's van on March the thirty-first?'

'No comment.'

'The other thing you might want to consider is that it's quite clear that Jeff Evans is far more frightened, terrified even, of his wife Dolores, than he is of you. Which might be why he told us that you borrowed his van on March the thirty-first.'

Cross then looked at Ottey. She addressed the solicitor.

'Kidnap and murder, Mr Antcliff, both serious charges. You might want to remind your client of the benefits of cooperating at this stage of the enquiry. Why don't we take a break?' she suggested.

★

'He asked a very good question in there,' began Carson in the MCU kitchen. 'Which was why? Why would he kidnap and murder a monk from Somerset?'

'He does have form,' said Ottey.

'For kidnap and murder?' asked Carson, who already knew the answer.

'No, obviously not. But he has done a few stretches,' she replied.

'Who's going through his sheet?' he asked.

'Mackenzie,' she replied.

'Okay. So apart from that, would it be any use to look for links between Davis and Murphy or Cubitt?' Carson asked.

'Mackenzie is already on it,' Ottey replied.

'My client concedes that he did borrow his cousin's van on March the thirty-first,' the solicitor said at the start of the next interview session.

'Concedes?' asked Cross. 'Since when did telling the truth amount to a concession, Mr Antcliff?'

'What is this, an English lesson? I was driving the van, okay?' spat Davis.

Cross wondered whether the inevitability of his situation was beginning to dawn on him, making him irritable.

'You admit to driving your cousin Jeff Evans's van on March the thirty-first?' asked Cross.

'Isn't that what I just said?'

'Just answer the question, Mr Davis,' his solicitor advised quietly but firmly.

'I was driving the van on the thirty-first, yes.'

'Of March,' Cross persisted.

'Yes.'

'Why did you need to use his van?'

'I had a job to do.'

'In Somerset?'

'Yes.'

'What was that job?' Cross went on.

'Moving some stuff for a mate.'

'What stuff?'

'Building materials.'

'So, he's a builder?'

'Who?'

'This mate.'

'Yeah.'

'So, he must have his own van or truck, surely.'

Davis said nothing.

'What's his name, this mate?' Cross asked, pen poised in anticipation of an answer.

'No comment.'

'Who was with you?' Cross asked.

'No one, I was on my own,' replied Davis.

Cross duly wrote this down.

'Why do you write it down when you don't believe me?' Davis couldn't help asking.

'What makes you think I don't believe you? The truth?' asked Cross. Davis said nothing. 'Perhaps we should look at what happens when you go into the garage shop, to pay for your fuel.'

Ottey held up her iPad for Davis and his solicitor to see. It was a continuation of the footage from the forecourt CCTV which they'd seen previously. As Frankie disappeared into the shop another man got out of the passenger side of the Passat and emptied some rubbish into one of the bins.

'That's your brother, Luke, isn't it?' Cross asked.

'Prat.'

'Your brother or me, Mr Davis?' Cross asked, perfectly seriously.

'No comment.'

'Well, we'll soon be able to ask him ourselves, as he's already been picked up from his girlfriend Bryony's flat by our South Wales colleagues,' said Cross, letting this detail sink in. 'Perhaps he'll be able to tell us why you abducted Brother Dominic. Or rather, who had you do it. It would look better for you in court if you told us first though. So I'd take advantage of that if I were you. Why did you abduct Brother Dominic?'

'No comment.'

'Let's take this one step at a time, then it'll be easier for a jury to decide exactly how uncooperative you've been during this enquiry,' said Cross. 'Are you denying that you abducted Brother Dominic?'

'No comment.'

'Maybe this will help. We have footage of the van at the monastery. Your cousin's van. Footage of Brother Dominic being forced into the back of the van and you at the wheel as the van drives away. The thing that doesn't add up for me at the moment is the very question you asked us when we began this interview. Why kidnap a monk?' Cross asked.

'No comment.'

'Did someone pay you to do it?'

'No comment.'

'But if they'd paid you, why wouldn't you just tell us?'

'No comment.'

'Are you afraid of them, perhaps? Are they frightening people?' asked Cross.

Davis sniggered before he answered, 'No comment.'

'So, they're obviously not, I'd infer from that, which leaves me with one other possibility. The promise of payment. Quite a sum for you, I should imagine. Otherwise, again, why not just tell us who it was?'

Cross stopped at this point and looked as if he was thinking really hard.

'I think Mr Davis might benefit from a break. Take a little time to contemplate the facts as we now know them. That he's admitted to borrowing his cousin's van. His brother was with him on the journey and in all probability the kidnap. We have footage of the kidnap and Mr Davis driving the van away with the monk inside. A kidnap, I might add, that ended up with the murder of Brother Dominic. What do you think, DS Ottey?' Cross asked his colleague.

'I'm sure Mr Antcliff would appreciate some time with his other clients in custody who are happy to be more cooperative than Mr Davis. Although I'm not sure any of them are in on suspicion of murder,' she replied.

Luke Davis was very unlike his brother. For one thing he was a large man in his early thirties, the size of a prop forward – unsurprising as this was the position he played for his local rugby club. He had a thick beard. His front two teeth were missing and had been replaced by an ill-fitting bridge whose two false teeth were much brighter than his natural ones. This together with the fact that his gums above were receding quicker than a Morecambe Bay tide, gave away the fact that they were artificial. Unlike his older brother he was quite shy and quietly spoken. It was clear he was keen to speak to the police as soon as Cross and Ottey sat down opposite him.

'Frankie, he just asked me to help him with a job over the bridge. Made it sound like furniture or something,' he began.

'Mr Davis, you are aware that you're speaking under caution. You were cautioned when the police picked you up at your girlfriend's,' said Cross.

'Yes, I was.'

'And you realise that the charges are kidnap and murder?' Cross went on.

'Course I do. Why do you think my hands are shaking?' replied Luke.

Ottey liked this about her partner. He never took advantage of a situation like this. He wanted to make sure that everything was legitimate and that procedure had been correctly followed so that everything would stand up in court. But it wasn't just that. He had an inherent need for things to be fair.

'So, you're saying you had no idea of your brother's intention to kidnap Brother Dominic?' asked Cross.

'Of course I didn't.'

'When did you realise?'

'When we got to the gate and Frankie told me to put the monk in the back of the van.'

'And did you?' asked Cross.

'I was confused.'

'I'm going to stop this, if you don't mind. I think I need to speak with my client further,' said the solicitor who was a little taken aback by his new client's apparent willingness to speak.

Cross was disappointed as he expected a chorus of 'no comments' would now follow on from the solicitor's intervention. He decided to turn his attention back to Frankie.

'You're quite different to your brother,' Cross began.

Frankie said nothing, suspecting this was a trap. Cross knew he was also wondering what his brother had said to them.

'He's quite talkative. Quite helpful,' Cross said.

Davis smirked. His solicitor had probably talked to Luke's, and he knew that the interview had been shut down.

'Said he wasn't aware the job you asked him to go on was to kidnap a Benedictine monk. You told him it was moving some furniture, which is odd as you told us it was to move some building supplies. So which was it?'

'No comment.'

'Well whichever, it doesn't matter. Either way, Luke was shocked when you arrived at the monastery and told him to put the monk in the back of the van.'

Cross looked at Davis. There was no response. He turned to the lawyer.

'Your client's brother has told us that your client and he kidnapped the monk. So that's now confirmed. Can we discuss that?' Cross asked.

Frankie turned to his solicitor who leaned over and whispered in his ear.

'Maybe,' said Frankie.

'Where did you take Brother Dominic?' Cross asked.

'I don't remember.'

'It was only a few weeks ago. I find that hard to believe,' said Cross.

'I was given a postcode. We took him there.'

'Who gave you this postcode?' asked Cross.

'No comment.'

'What was the postcode?'

'I've no bloody idea, mate.'

'So, you're given a postcode. Was that an instruction as to where you should take Dominic?'

'No, it was a point of outstanding natural beauty.'

'Really?' asked Cross, surprised.

'Did you take the monk to this postcode?' asked Ottey.

'Yes.'

'Then what happened?' she continued.

'We left him there,' Frankie replied.

'Left him how?' Cross asked.

'Tied to a chair.'

'So, you were in a building?' Cross asked.

'No, mate, we were in the middle of a bloody field.'

'What kind of a field?' Cross asked.

'What? Are you serious?'

'Perfectly. What kind of field? A meadow? One with crops?' asked Cross, pen poised for the answer.

Frankie's solicitor looked at Ottey who said nothing, but just stared back blankly.

'Are you stupid?' asked Frankie, beginning to get agitated.

'You said the monk was tied to a chair in a field. Why does

my asking you what kind of field make me in any way stupid?'
Cross asked.

'Because it obviously wasn't a field, you fucking idiot,' spat
Davis.

'It wasn't a field,' said Cross slowly, in time with his writing it
down. 'So if it wasn't in a field, where was this chair?'

'It was in a cottage.'

'Whose cottage?'

'I don't bloody know.'

'Was the cottage locked?'

'Yes.'

'So how did you gain access?'

'There was a key under a pot.'

Again, Cross made a note before looking up.

'Who told you where the key was?' he asked.

'No comment.'

'Were you paid to abduct the monk?' Cross asked.

'I've already answered that.'

Cross frowned as if trying to remember, then checked his
notes, going back a few pages in the pad.

'You said, "no comment",' Cross told him.

'Like I said. I've already answered that question.'

Cross stared at him for a few moments and thought about
this.

'I would argue that an answer would have furnished me with
the information I'd requested. I think "no comment" qualifies
as a response, not an answer. Wouldn't you agree?' he said,
addressing this question to the solicitor who, like many in their
first encounter with DS George Cross, was beginning to wonder
what they were dealing with here, and it was starting to concern
him.

'Who asked you to do this? Abduct Brother Dominic from
St Eustace's abbey on the thirty-first of March this year?' Cross
asked, as if he hadn't asked it before.

'No comment.'

Cross duly made a note of this then got up and left.

'Is there something wrong with him? Is he stupid or something?' asked Davis.

Ottey got up.

'You'd save yourself a lot of time, not only in this room, but also in the amount of time the judge gives you when he or she convicts, which they will, by answering my colleague's questions when he puts them to you. What you're charged with is still up to you. Currently it's looking like kidnap and murder. Doesn't get much more serious than that. You might want to think about that. A word of advice, though. Thinking DS Cross is stupid is a mistake many have made in your situation and have come to bitterly regret. I wouldn't make the same mistake if I were you. Either of you,' she said, directing this final word to the solicitor before leaving the room.

40

Cross and Ottey took the decision, much against Carson's better judgement, to leave the Davis brothers in their cells overnight. Cross was of the opinion that it might soften the brothers up and hopefully bring the interviews to a swift conclusion.

'When was the last time you spoke with Stephen?' Ottey asked Cross as they were making tea in the office kitchen.

'Not since our notification visit,' Cross replied, secretly willing the kettle to boil so he could leave quickly and avoid the incoming flak which he suspected was coming in his direction imminently.

'Seriously? Have you called him?'

'I have not.'

'Right, let's go over there now,' she said.

'I'm making tea,' he said, pointing out the inconvenience of such an idea.

'All right, when you've had your tea.'

'What for?'

'Well, aside from the fact that he's a friend who's lost a close relative, we need to interview him as the brother of the deceased in our current murder investigation,' she pointed out.

'It's actually a good day to go,' added Cross.

'Tuesday? Why?' she asked.

'He bakes on a Tuesday.'

Cross winced as he reflected on this exchange alone in his office a few minutes later, waiting while his tea steeped in the pot. Of course they should interview Stephen. He felt a pang of guilt that perhaps he wasn't doing his job quite as well as he should. In the course of events of any normal case he would've been around already to interview Stephen, maybe more than once. But he wasn't thinking straight. This had nothing to do with the fact that Stephen was a friend and Cross being too close to someone in the case to be objective. It was because of Stephen putting Christine and Frank together at Brother Dominic's funeral and the priest's inevitable desire to discuss it. He castigated himself for being so infantilely unprofessional.

Mackenzie then came into the kitchen.

'I think I may have something. A link between Nick Cubitt and Frankie Davis. They spent a year together in the same prison. Wormwood Scrubs. When I called the governor's office, they told me they'd actually shared a cell for four months,' she said.

Cross said nothing.

'This is great work, Alice,' said Ottey. 'George?'

'Oh yes. Well done,' he replied. Which was as good as it ever got with him, so Mackenzie was relatively pleased.

Stephen was up to his wrists in flour, which had also found its way across his apron and into his hair. The kitchen in the parsonage smelled of freshly baked cakes. It was like a small production line in a cottage baking industry. Cakes were cooling on racks. Others were already stored in Tupperware boxes. What had started as a way of rewarding his regular congregants on Sunday after a service, with a cup of tea and a slice of cake, had expanded exponentially. His parish committee had pointed out, as delicately as possible, that they could monetise the priest's baking skills for the benefit of the church. Like St Eustace's they always needed money for something gone wrong. A successful local tearoom, which was run by one of Stephen's regular parishioners, had asked for three cakes a week, an order which he gladly fulfilled. This was followed by a new coffee shop asking the same, and a local provision shop. People at the church then started asking for cakes for birthdays and anniversaries. So it was becoming quite a business, so much so that 'Father Kipling' as he'd become known, was thinking he might have to bring it to an end before he got in trouble with the Catholic church. He had two women helping him, Pamela and Margaret. He told them to have a break and so they left.

The two police officers sat opposite the priest. He'd just made a fresh pot of tea and poured them all a cup. He noticed Cross staring at a bowl in which they'd made a chocolate filling for a couple of cakes. The detective looked about eight years old as he gazed longingly at the remnants smeared around the glass bowl.

'Would you like to lick the bowl?' asked Stephen.

'Certainly not,' Cross answered, affronted that his professionalism should be challenged in this way.

Ottey smiled affectionately with just a tinge of sadness that Cross would never really understand how fond of him people were, and how many friends he actually had.

'How are you doing, Father?' asked Ottey.

'I'm fine, I suppose. It's odd how grief hits you even when it comes to someone you haven't seen in a long while,' Stephen replied.

'But you have your faith,' said Cross.

'My faith is indeed a way of tempering my grief at a time of loss, in that I believe I will see him again. That doesn't mean to say I won't miss him in this world,' Stephen replied.

'Even though, as you say, you hadn't seen him in well over a decade, you'll still miss him?' asked Cross. He wasn't trying in any way to be argumentative. He was genuinely interested, however insensitively it came across.

'I'll miss knowing he was somewhere in the world, yes. He was my brother. It was a subconscious comfort to know he was around in the world serving the Lord as am I.'

'Ah, I understand,' replied Cross.

'How is the investigation going?' Stephen then asked.

'It's progressing, if slowly,' replied Ottey.

'I imagine it's all the more difficult with his being a monk,' Stephen suggested.

'When things like that make an investigation difficult, they often in turn narrow the parameters in which to look. So, conversely, the more difficult it appears at first hand, the easier it might seem on closer examination, as the possibilities become fewer,' said Cross.

'That's interesting. I read in the local press this week that Alex, sorry Dominic, had been involved in something of a spat with Sir Patrick Murphy,' Stephen said.

'That's right, though I think the spat was more on the side of Murphy,' said Ottey.

'A big noise in the Catholic church,' said Stephen.

'Do I sense disapproval?' asked Cross.

'He made his fortune in online gambling which is something a parish priest is always going to have an issue with.'

'Why is that?' asked Cross, who suspected he already knew the answer.

'Because it often causes problems within my community. But he does seem to be a man of genuine faith,' added Stephen.

'We have spoken to him, and he remains a person of interest,' said Ottey.

Stephen noticed Cross staring at the glass mixing bowl again. He sensed Stephen looking at him and immediately looked elsewhere with an exaggerated determination and focus.

'George, please,' said Stephen, indicating the bowl. Cross looked at Ottey.

'Well, if it is only going to be washed up it makes sense,' he said before taking the bowl and starting to wipe it out with his finger. 'Do I detect some dark chocolate in here?' he asked Stephen, like a serious connoisseur at a wine tasting.

'Very good. Colombian, 70 per cent,' replied Stephen, laughing.

As they were leaving the priest sifted through the Tupperware containers on the side, opening the lids to check what was inside.

He found the one he wanted and handed it to Ottey. He showed her the contents. A perfectly round chocolate cake with an indulgent thick chocolate icing.

'For the girls,' said Stephen.

'Are you sure?' she asked, taking it.

'Of course,' he replied.

'Technically speaking you are accepting a gift while on duty, DS Ottey, and will have to log it as such,' said Cross.

'And how is that any different from my gift to you of the remnants of the chocolate filling, DS Cross?' Stephen asked. Cross thought for a moment.

'The gift is in fact for her daughters, no?' Cross asked, perfectly seriously, trying to find a legitimate way round this problem.

'Correct,' replied Stephen.

'Then I think it's fair to say that she is not accepting a gift in her capacity as a detective sergeant, but as a mother. In which case there is no conflict here,' Cross said and gave the bowl one final exuberant wipe with his finger as if to prove his point.

'You would have made a good lawyer,' said Stephen.

Cross looked at him, surprised.

'I would've made an excellent lawyer,' he replied and left the kitchen.

41

L uke Davis was keen to speak to them the next morning. He wasn't going to rely on repeated 'no comment' responses, apparently. They interviewed him before his brother, as they thought what he had to say might prove useful when it came to interviewing Frankie. Luke had that look of numb shock Cross had seen before. It was usually written large across the face of someone who had been involved in something, either unknowingly or having been compelled to do so. The seriousness of the situation, which obviously they hadn't prepared for, slowly dawns on them with a chest-tightening realisation.

'My client has been nothing but cooperative and would like to continue to be so,' Luke's lawyer stated.

'Good,' replied Cross.

'But I would ask that his cooperation is relayed to the CPS prior to charging my client. We accept that a charge may be inevitable in the circumstances, even though he was inadvertently and unwillingly involved in this crime.'

'Duly noted,' replied Cross. 'Unfortunately, one fact that can't be ignored in all of this is that, by his own admission, he did put Brother Dominic in the van. Now I'm no lawyer, but I would venture that might constitute kidnap. What the CPS charge your client with and the sentence a judge may deem appropriate will, I'm sure, reflect the circumstances of the kidnap. His brother corroborates the fact that your client had no prior knowledge of the purpose of the trip, so this, together with his cooperation, will obviously have some impact. But we do have one more question.

What happened after you put Dominic in the van? Where did your brother drive you to?'

'To a house,' Luke replied.

'What kind of house?'

'Like a cottage.'

'Can you describe it?'

'I didn't go in.'

'From the outside then,' said Cross.

'It was like a country cottage. On its own.'

'How did you reach it?'

'It was down a long private track. Wasn't a road or anything.'

'How big was it?' asked Ottey.

'Not very big. The road was overgrown. Brambles and stuff scratched the van as we drove down it. There was a cattle grid, I remember. But that was it.'

'Nothing else?' said Ottey.

Luke thought for a moment.

'It looked very run-down. Like no one lived there. Everything was overgrown. The windows were filthy. Roof slates were missing.'

'Is that it?' asked Cross.

Luke thought again, as if trying to give the impression that he really was doing his best.

'There was a cow. A cow, I think it was, carved in the stone above the door.'

Cross made a note of this.

'What happened then?' asked Cross.

'Frankie told me to help him with the monk. I said no. He started swearing at me. But I wouldn't go. So he got the monk out of the van by himself and took him into the cottage.'

'What did you do?'

'Stayed in the van.'

'How long were you there for?'

'I don't know.'

'You don't have a watch?' Cross asked.

'I fell asleep.'

'For how long?'

'I don't know, but it was dark when I woke up.'

'So that would be after eight?'

'If you say so.'

'What happened when you woke up?' asked Cross.

'I woke up because Frankie came back to the van.'

'What did he say?'

'Nothing.'

'Did you ask him what had happened?' asked Cross.

'Yeah. He told me to shut up.'

'Did you notice anything about him? Anything at all strange?' asked Cross.

For the first time Luke looked like he wasn't sure whether he should answer the question.

'His hand. His hand on the gear stick. It had blood on it. Like he'd hit someone.'

Cross didn't react to this in any way but just wrote it down.

'And then? What did you do?' he went on.

'We left.'

'Did you ask him what had just happened?'

'No.'

'Why not?'

'Because I didn't want to know. Didn't want any part, not that that's done me any good,' he said, looking at his solicitor.

'So you left the monk in the cottage?' asked Cross.

'Yes.'

'Didn't that worry you?'

'What are you talking about? The whole bloody thing worried me. But there was another car. Must've come when I was asleep. It wasn't there when we arrived.'

'What kind of car?'

'I don't know. It was dark. Some sort of SUV.'

★

'What happened to your hand? When you were in the cottage?' Cross asked Frankie Davis when they sat across from each other in the interview room again.

'Nothing.'

'Luke said it was red and bloody. Like you'd hit someone,' said Cross.

'Well, he's wrong. I didn't.'

'Then why was your fist red?' Cross persisted.

'Who said it was?' Frankie asked.

'I just informed you of that. Your brother,' replied Cross patiently.

'It was dark, so I'm not sure how he could've seen that.'

Cross looked at him for a moment then turned to Ottey. She pushed a small plastic evidence bag across the table for Davis to see.

'Recognise these?' she asked.

'Are they my rings?'

'They are. Your sovereign rings.'

She then produced a close-up of Dominic's jaw with the marks made by the rings clearly visible.

'This is a photograph of the victim's jaw. As you can see you very much left your mark on the deceased,' Ottey pointed out.

'That could be anyone's ring.'

'In the circumstances it seems unlikely. But you might have a point. However, I think the DNA that we've managed to pull from one of your rings will match our victim.'

Davis looked surprised.

'Oh, I know. You've washed your hands, had showers. Doubtless thought no traces would be left. Oops,' she finished.

'I'd like to speak with my client,' said the lawyer quickly before this went any further.

'My client acknowledges that he did strike the victim,' Frankie's lawyer began.

'How many times?' asked Cross.

'A good few,' volunteered Davis.

'Why did you hit him?' asked Ottey.

'No comment.'

'Were you angry?'

'No comment.'

'Did you want him to tell you something?'

'No comment.'

'Did someone tell you to do it?'

'No comment.'

'Someone you were with?' Ottey persisted.

'No comment.'

'You broke the man's jaw, Frankie. You must've hit him pretty hard,' said Ottey.

This fact seemed to rattle Davis.

'Your brother told us there was another vehicle which arrived after you took the victim into the cottage. Who was driving that vehicle?' she continued.

'No comment.'

'Does the name Cubitt mean anything to you?' asked Cross. 'Nicholas Cubitt?'

'No.'

'Are you sure about that?' Cross continued as he removed a sheet from his folder.

Davis declined to comment.

'You were in Wormwood Scrubs in 2012 for eleven months. Do you recall that?' Cross asked.

'Obviously.'

Cross pushed a list across the table. Two names had been highlighted.

'Nicholas Cubitt was also an inmate of that prison at the same time,' he said.

'So?'

'So, you still maintain no knowledge of the name?'

'There are over a thousand inmates in that prison,' replied Davis.

'All right, enough of this,' said Ottey jumping in. 'Frankly I prefer a "no comment" to this bullshit. You shared a cell with Nicholas Cubitt for over four months. So cut the crap.'

'Oh, you mean Nick. Yeah, I remember him.'

'Have you heard from him recently?' Ottey continued. Cross sat back, happy for her to.

'Nope.'

'We have a warrant for his phone records and we already have yours. Do you want to reconsider your answer?'

His solicitor whispered into Davis's ear.

'He did call a couple of times recently, yes.'

'What for?'

'Just a catch-up.'

'Had you stayed in touch with him since your time in the Scrubs?' asked Ottey.

'Occasionally, yes.'

'What did you talk about in your cell?' asked Cross.

'Are you serious?'

'Perfectly.'

'It was years ago.'

'Let me be more specific. What did you learn about Cubitt's bank and why he was in prison?'

'His bank ran into trouble, and he took the fall, is all I know.'

'That's certainly an interesting interpretation of events, and one which fits with what we know about him. Was he angry about it?' Cross continued.

'Course he was. Lost everything.'

'Angry enough to want revenge?'

'No idea, mate.'

'Are you aware of Brother Dominic's identity before he took his monastic name?'

Davis seemed to hesitate at this point. Was it, Cross thought, because he was becoming aware of how much evidence they might have? That they were no longer flailing about trying to figure out why an unemployed ex-convict should want to kidnap a Benedictine monk?

'No comment.'

'I think it might benefit you if you moved on from the "no comment" stage of this interview, Mr Davis. Let's look at the situation you currently find yourself in. You admit that you kidnapped and assaulted Brother Dominic, who subsequently succumbed to his injuries. You maintain that no one asked or paid you to do this. That there was no one else at this cottage. This means you and you alone are guilty of his murder. What other conclusion can we be expected to reach if you continue in this way?' said Cross.

'I told you. He was alive when I left him.'

'That's irrelevant, Mr Davis. He died and apparently you were on your own.'

'I didn't kill him.'

'Then who did, Mr Davis? Who did?' Cross turned to the solicitor. 'This strategy of yours for your client has reached the point of diminishing returns. I suggest you have a rethink before it's too late.'

An extension was then applied for and granted, for the custody of both brothers.

First thing Thursday morning Frankie Davis finally folded. His lawyer had obviously advised him that with all the mounting evidence there was no point in holding back. Davis had probably concluded that the way things were going the chances of getting his payday from Nick Cubitt were becoming slenderer by the hour.

'It was Nick,' he began.

'What was?' asked Ottey.

'Who told us to grab the monk.'

'Why?'

'Money. He said this monk had worked for him and was the reason his family's bank had collapsed. He said this bloke had ruined him,' Frankie went on.

'Explain what you mean by money?' asked Cross.

'He said this bloke had made a fortune in the city off the back of Nick. He'd disappeared with millions. Nick now knew where he was and wanted his money. He wanted me to grab him then we'd find out where the money was. He promised me half a bar.'

'Half a bar? Would you explain exactly what that means for the tape?' said Cross.

'Five hundred grand. Half a million,' replied Davis.

'So, what exactly happened?'

'We took him to the cottage. Luke was freaking out by now. He stayed in the van. I took the... bloke—'

'The monk,' interrupted Ottey. 'Why can't you say that?'

'I took him inside and did a number on him. He told me what I wanted after about half an hour.'

'Told you what?' asked Cross.

'He'd bought a painting with his money. It was at the abbey.'

'Then what?' asked Cross.

'I heard someone coming and I ducked out the back.'

'Did you see who it was?'

'Wasn't interested. Didn't want to see, didn't want to be seen. We had what we wanted. Job done.'

'Who was "we"?' asked Cross.

'Nick, obviously.'

'Was he the driver of the other car?'

'I have no idea. Maybe. I didn't look and anyway, he said he was in London,' Davis replied. But Cross was thinking that didn't mean to say he actually was. Was Davis covering up for Nick? Had he seen him and was denying it?

Detectives in London had tried to arrest Nicholas Cubitt but there was no sign of him nor his car at his flat. He wasn't at his office either. This made Cross immediately suspicious. How did he know? Had he been tipped off? Only two people knew: Julian and Rosemary Cubitt. They knew the old man hadn't been entirely honest about the extent of his contact with his son. Then it occurred to him that there was a third, Charlotte. It was more likely to have been her, as she still had a soft spot for Nicholas and was still in contact. Cross was surprised by the address of Nicholas's offices. They were in the heart of Mayfair. Maybe things weren't so bad for his business or maybe it was just an indication that there were some vestiges of his old life that he just couldn't get rid of. It was near the ostentatious Mayfair house in which his ill-fated investment fund had been installed. He had wanted to be in the thick of it with all the other major funds and players in Mayfair with their memberships of Annabel's. It transpired, though, that 'offices' plural was something of an exaggeration. There was only the one office, and it was tiny with room just for his and his secretary's desk. It turned out she only worked part-time, three days a week, and had no idea where her boss was. He was supposed to have been on a site visit in Essex that morning and hadn't shown up.

They froze all of Nick Cubitt's bank accounts and credit cards, then alerted all airports and ports in case he tried to leave the country. A press release also made his arrest warrant public. There was nowhere for him to hide.

42

Cross had asked Mackenzie to examine the grounds of Coxton Hall on the Ordnance Survey map for other buildings. The GPS in the van was no use. They looked through Davis's map apps on his phone but couldn't find a local postcode in the history. She also did a land registry search for nearby properties. It transpired that the Cubitt family owned several properties in the nearby area. Three of them on the estate grounds and another four in the surrounding countryside. Two of the houses on the estate were currently occupied but there seemed to be one which was quite isolated towards the south end of the estate. It had been unoccupied for some years. It was a few hundred yards off a track which petered out before it reached the property. This was enough for them to get a search warrant, which they executed the next day.

Cross and Ottey followed Swift's SUV down a tarmac country lane which eventually became a rutted mud path with two deep tyre channels. In the middle was a strip of overgrown grass. The hedgerows on either side were exactly as Luke Davis had described. Overgrown and stretching across the lane, they scraped along the side of Ottey's car with a high-pitched squeal. They travelled over a cattle grid, just as Luke had remembered. In August and September, it would be a fabulous place to come and pick blackberries. Beyond the hedgerows there were acres of farmland. It was owned by Cubitt, but leased to a local farmer. Cross was interested to see that the farmer had built in margins of wild meadow flowers and uncultivated land. He was obviously interested in encouraging biodiversity. The cottage was at the end of the lane which went no further. There was a rusty iron gate lying at a drunken angle against the hedge, more discarded than opened.

Swift pulled up before he reached the gate and they parked behind him. He obviously didn't want them to add all of their tyre tracks to the ones on the ground in front of the house.

It was incredibly peaceful. Other than an orchestra of birdsong in full swing and the occasional rustle of leaves in the trees, it was completely quiet. The windows of the cottage were intact, but filthy. The entire building had been untouched by anything other than the elements for however long it had been abandoned. It was so far off the beaten track that vandals and thieves hadn't managed to find it. Slate tiles that were missing from the roof lay in smashed piles at the foot of the walls. Moss clung to the tiles that remained in place. A buddleia was growing out of the chimney stack. From the size of the thing, it had been there for some years.

They walked round the edge of the parking area at the front of the cottage. There was a carving of a pig above the front door in a limestone brick.

'A pig, not a cow,' commented Ottey.

'Possibly goes some way to confirming that Luke stayed in the car,' observed Cross who was looking for a key under any nearby pot. There was none.

'I'll go round the back and see if anything's open,' said Swift, promptly disappearing.

'So, this is definitely part of the estate?' asked Ottey as she looked at the decrepit state of the building.

'It is,' confirmed Cross.

'Why is it in this condition then? All the other properties are let to tenants,' she said.

A Land Rover Defender arrived noisily and at speed, crunching the loose ground as it braked behind Ottey's car. A purposeful-looking Rosemary Tate strode towards them.

'She's really stylish this woman, even in wellies, don't you think?' asked Ottey.

'I think she's pretty quick, if nothing else,' replied Cross.

'What's going on? This is private property and I have no recollection of granting you permission to be here,' she proclaimed as she neared them.

'This is a warrant,' said Cross holding it up. 'Which means we have no need of your nor anyone else's permission.'

'How did you know we were here?' asked Ottey.

But she ignored her and stretched out her hand for the warrant. She looked at it briefly before handing it straight back. Cross often wondered whether people actually read search warrants when they demanded them. They seemed to read them awfully quickly. Did they even know what they were looking for in order to judge their authenticity? Or even know what a genuine one actually looked like?

'So, what exactly is going on?' she then asked.

'As yet we have no idea,' said Cross. 'But we should do soon enough.'

Swift then reappeared round the corner. Tate looked up at him, alarmed.

'Who is this?' she demanded.

'Dr Michael Swift, our forensic investigator,' Cross informed her.

'Would you all mind retreating behind the vehicles?' said Swift pointing to their cars. 'This is now a crime scene.'

What?' exclaimed Rosemary.

'Mrs Cubitt, you'll need to sit in your vehicle while we speak to our colleague,' said Cross.

She was temporarily lost for words and did not remonstrate with him. Ottey took her gently by the arm.

'Why don't I take you back to the car and I'll answer any questions you have, that I'm able to,' she said, guiding the distraught woman away.

'Something definitely happened in there. Do you want to

come back when I've had a closer look, or do you want to suit up with me and come inside?' Swift asked Cross. The resultant expression of disdain was just long enough for Swift to instantly regret what he'd said. He actually swore at himself, but before he could apologise, Cross was off on one.

'Tell me, what do you think the purpose of my being here this morning is, exactly? Why was my presence required? Simply to confirm that this was the correct address? To help DS Ottey navigate her way here, perhaps? Or simply to accompany her as she led you to the cottage safely? When a simple entry of the appropriate postcode into your car's navigation system would've achieved exactly the same result without the need of my presence?' Cross asked him without a hint of sarcasm.

'I was actually thinking the very same thing at the very moment I opened my mouth and uttered my banal enquiry. Let's go to the car,' he said.

Cross followed, not imagining for a moment that his young colleague was actually congratulating himself for having witnessed, no, been the actual subject of, one of Cross's legendary dressing-downs. He couldn't wait to tell Mackenzie when he got home.

They suited up in brand new white paper suits and hoods, then headed back to the house. They went in through the back door, which gave Cross a chance to look at the garden to the back of the building. It looked like it had once had a great deal of care, planning and thought given to it. The remains of a herbaceous border was now a jungle of twisted, mostly dead plants, while ferns and hostas seemed to have weathered such hostile neglect. The back of the house was entirely covered in a rampant wisteria which threatened, Triffid-like, to swallow the building in one gulp. What was once a lawn was now a four-foot high meadow with flowers floating above the top of it. There was something rather beautiful about it, Cross thought. How nature had reclaimed it for itself.

They went in through the back door. Swift strategically laid out small plastic platforms for them to walk across. The air was fusty, having been entombed in there for years with the added iron-like tang of blood, which often accompanied a violent crime scene. The dirt on the windows, and closed curtains on others, made the interior dark and quite sinister. Peering through the gloom it appeared that the place was ordered, but abandoned. Swift led Cross into the kitchen. Again, the place was completely tidy and ordered. There were recent dried stains on the floor.

'Blood?' Cross asked.

'Yes. You can see how the chair was placed there. The blood formed a pattern around it,' replied Swift. 'I'll request a team to come down and help, but it's going to take a couple of days to gather evidence. Minimum.'

'A confirmation that it's our victim's blood would be extremely useful,' replied Cross.

'Sure.'

Cross felt it was better for Swift and his team to continue their work undisturbed. He went upstairs and looked at the three bedrooms. Two of them seemed to be children's bedrooms, but were empty of any possessions. The main bedroom's wardrobe was open. In it were a couple of men's suits, their shoulders covered in thick dust. All men's clothing, Cross noted. No women's items. The bathroom had dusty bottles of shampoo and shower gel.

He took off the forensic suit outside and threw it into the back of Ottey's car. He would dispose of it later. He walked over to Rosemary's SUV.

'We need to speak to you and your husband again,' he told her.

'Why? What's happened?' she asked.

'It's unconfirmed as yet, but the indications are clear. Brother Dominic was murdered in this building,' Cross replied undramatically.

The woman went white and held onto the armrest in between the front seats as if it might stop her toppling over.

'Shall I drive you back to your house, Mrs Cubitt?' asked Ottey.

'Yes please.'

Ottey and she got out of the car to change places. Ottey gave her keys to Cross.

'Can you bring my car round to the house, George?' she said.

'I can,' he replied, slightly anxious at the prospect, and trying his best to conceal the ever-growing terror that was enveloping him. He could drive. He just chose not to and it was something he normally had much success in avoiding.

He arrived at the house a full five minutes after Ottey, having endured a slow, white-knuckle drive back. While the odometer never went over seven miles an hour, the terrified concentration had made Cross break out into a sweat. He walked into the kitchen looking like he'd just been the recipient of some truly terrible news. His face was pale and clammy. Ottey couldn't help but smile at the same time as reprimanding herself for being so uncharitably amused.

Julian Cubitt sat still for a good few minutes after Cross told him the grisly news that someone had recently been murdered on his estate. They sat in the kitchen, Cross, Ottey and the Cubitt couple, as Charlotte made tea and coffee.

'Why is the cottage in such a state of disrepair?' Cross began.

'It belonged to Nicholas. That is to say, he had use of it until… until he went to prison,' Rosemary began.

'Rosemary,' Julian muttered pathetically.

'Enough, Julian. We need to be as helpful as we can here. This is obviously another nightmare situation of that boy's making, and I will not have us drawn into it.'

'No one has said it was him,' her husband pleaded.

'They don't have to,' she replied.

'Do you know it was him?' he asked her. 'For a fact?'

'You know I don't.'

'Well then, don't jump to conclusions,' he chided her.

'I'm not. I was merely answering the sergeant's question about the cottage. It was Nicholas and his family's. Not officially, but they spent a lot of time there when they weren't in London. Sarah and the kids eventually stopped going there. We didn't ask them to, but it was what she wanted and who could blame her?' she said. 'No one's been in it since.'

'Except to turn off the electricity and services,' said Julian.

'Yes, except for that.'

'Why not renovate it and let it out like the other properties on the estate?' asked Ottey.

'A good question,' said Rosemary looking at her husband. 'Julian can't bring himself to do it for some reason, known only to him.'

'When was the last time you had any contact with your son?' asked Cross.

'Like I told you before. Not since he was convicted and went to prison,' she replied for her husband. 'But to be fair to him and for the sake of full disclosure he has tried to call Julian a few times. On his birthday. At Christmas. But Jules wouldn't take the calls, and so in the end he just gave up.'

'Where were you both on March the thirty-first of this year?' Cross asked.

'I'm pretty sure we would've been here. We don't go out anywhere much these days. Poor Rosemary has suffered the fate of all younger wives, where they become carers for the old crock who once promised never to get old,' he said.

'Did you notice anything going on at the cottage?' Cross went on.

'You mean a monk being murdered inside?' asked Rosemary, still upset. 'I'm sorry.'

'You were there pretty promptly after we arrived this morning,' Cross pointed out.

'That's only because Adam, the farmer who rents the fields, saw your car coming and called me,' she replied.

'Does he often do that?'

'No. No one's been down there for years. He just happened to be working in that field when you arrived.'

'Sergeant,' interrupted the old man, 'may I ask exactly what it is you think has happened here?'

'I don't know exactly. But we do know that Brother Dominic, aka Alexander Mount, was abducted by someone who claims to have done it at the behest of your son, Nicholas,' replied Cross. 'That he left Brother Dominic at a country cottage on March the thirty-first when he was still alive. A few days later his body was found in this locality.'

'The body of Alexander Mount, who you know to be the whistleblower who brought down the family bank, just to be completely clear. The man who destroyed a three-hundred-year-old business,' Ottey elucidated.

'Oh, dear God,' the old man muttered to no one in particular. 'What will happen now? With Nicholas?'

'We have a warrant for his arrest which the Met is attempting to carry out for us. He'll then be transported down to Bristol for questioning,' Cross explained.

'Do you have any means of contacting Nicholas?' asked Ottey.

'No, we don't have his current contact details,' answered Rosemary.

Ten minutes later, she showed them to the door, leaving the shrunken figure of her husband staring at the kitchen table.

'I don't know if he'll survive this,' she said.

'You'd be amazed what people can get through,' replied Ottey.

'The bank business about did for him. He had a coronary. Do you really think Nicky could have done this?' she asked.

'It certainly looks that way.'

'But why? What on earth for?'

'That is the key question,' Cross observed.

43

Swift had stayed in the cottage well into the night. This was when he was in his element. Now he knew this was the scene of the crime, it was his domain. No one else's. He was in charge. Things went the way he wanted. His real satisfaction came not from the obvious evidence, such as the blood on the floor and the duct tape that had been used to secure the victim to the chair, but from the evidence invisible to the naked eye which he uncovered, and which could often be crucial to the conviction of a perpetrator. Forensics had moved on and become so much more sophisticated, even in his short career. What he enjoyed most, though, was not just the collection of the evidence, but being able to present it in context. The evidence produced a narrative, if followed correctly. He'd learned this from his study of historic crime photographs. As well as the ones on the walls of his flat, he had an extensive collection. The best of these photographers, Rodolphe Archibald Reiss, managed to contain a story in the way they shot a scene. The victim's body and the environment it was found in all had things to say. This was how he approached investigating a scene. Everything in it was a potential witness to what had occurred. So nothing, absolutely nothing, could be overlooked. He was a little like his idol George Cross in this respect. What he found gave him a clear view of what had happened and how. But it would take him a few days to put it all together, and present to Cross in a way that he hoped would impress.

So, there was not much they could do now but wait for Swift's findings and Nick Cubitt to be located.

*

Swift worked through the weekend, so Mackenzie took the opportunity to catch up with some old university friends. Her relationship with Swift was at that nascent stage, where their friends had been excluded temporarily and not been introduced to them as a couple, either because they were completely wrapped up in the novelty of the relationship, or through fear of it not lasting and looking foolish to their mates. Either way, it meant that she hadn't seen her regular circle of friends for some time. So this seemed like a good opportunity.

Ottey owed her children some mummy time, even though this particular weekend it seemed to consist entirely of her functioning as a private taxi service for the two of them. There were parties, a sleepover and a couple of sporting fixtures to be fitted in. She also took her mother to view the house with the self-contained flat they were interested in.

Cross devoted his time to his new labour of love, the organ at St Eustace's. The chamber was now clear of debris and dirt, the pipes restored, the blower running efficiently and silently. Brother William had promised to have the new leather folds for the reservoir ready by the end of the week, the installation of which was the next job at hand. He had been going to organise a taxi down to the abbey, where he was going to stay the night again, when he got a call on his mobile. It was from Ursula Mead, whom he'd spoken to a couple of Sundays before, after mass, as he was waiting to get back to work on the organ. She, like everyone else, was eager to find out how the case was progressing. She was surprised to see the detective there and touched when she discovered that he was fixing the organ.

'Oh, we have missed it these last few months,' she said. 'It will be lovely to have it working again and I know that Peter will be thrilled.'

Peter turned out to be the abbey organist who played at Sunday services, weddings and funerals. It hadn't occurred to

Cross that such a person existed, but of course it made sense, as none of the monks themselves could play. He was now curious as to why Peter hadn't visited him while he worked on the organ.

'He's in hospital,' Ursula informed him. 'Lung cancer. Never smoked. Can you believe it? Thankfully it's one of those they can just get in and take out. So, the prognosis is good. Strange how it happened as soon as the organ was out of commission though. You can't help but feel the hand of God in there somewhere, can you?'

Cross decided to treat this as a rhetorical question and so didn't furnish her with an answer or opinion.

Ursula had called Cross to offer to pick him up and drive him to the abbey. She was insistent and wouldn't take no for an answer. He was giving up his entire weekend to work on the organ. What was a couple of hours to her? The easiest thing to do in the end was say yes.

'Something's been troubling me since I was told about who Dominic was before he entered the abbey,' she began, almost before they'd made the first turning off his road, which brought to an abrupt halt Cross's, perhaps naive, hope that it might be a quiet journey down to Somerset. 'His working in the City obviously made complete sense to me when I thought about what wonders he'd achieved with my little pension pot. From what I've read, and I'm sorry but curiosity got the better of me, he was obviously a success in banking and made a lot of money.'

'And you're wondering what happened to that money?' Cross asked.

'Yes. I was trying to work out why someone would do this to a Benedictine monk. I read about the downfall of that bank but he hadn't done anything wrong. Then I read about an anonymous whistle-blower who was a witness at Nicholas Cubitt's trial. Cubitt's—' She was about to explain.

'Yes, I'm aware who he is,' interrupted Cross.

'So my question is, was Brother Dominic the whistle-blower

and if he was, did someone want revenge? Is that what you think this is all about?' she asked.

'It's a very perceptive question, Mrs Mead, but I can't possibly comment,' he replied.

'Well, I do have an alternative theory, if that would interest you?' she continued.

'As you've gone out of your way to give me a lift to the abbey, the least I can do is listen to it,' he replied.

'True, it would be a little churlish of you to refuse, but I somehow think such considerations are not at the top of your priority list,' she retorted.

'If I had such a thing,' he replied.

'Well, anyway, you never know, you might find it useful,' she said brightly.

'That, I doubt,' he couldn't help but reply.

'Money doesn't just disappear, does it?' she went on, ignoring him. 'My question is, where is Dominic's? He could've given it away. Did he give it to his relatives, perhaps? It would've made more sense to have given it to the abbey or the Benedictine order, but I know that didn't happen.'

'How?'

'Well, I asked, obviously. So, I think the money's still around somewhere. The question is where?'

'And what conclusion have you reached?' Cross asked.

'I haven't. After all, you're the detective.'

Ursula dropped Cross off at the abbey and informed him that she would drive him home the next day. He couldn't say he was looking forward to another forty minutes in the company of Miss Marple.

44

'Come!' Brother William instructed Cross from the confines of the bookbindery. Cross walked in. William was busy working on a small volume on his workbench.

'Good morning, Sergeant.'

Cross made no answer as he agreed with this statement. He moved further into the workshop to get a closer view of what the young monk was up to.

'It's a collection of someone's mother's cookery recipes which we've bound. Anne, that's the customer, wants to give it to her daughter who apparently loves to cook,' William told him.

'A kind of culinary heirloom,' Cross volunteered.

'Yes, that's right,' William answered.

'Isn't leather a little impractical for a kitchen?' Cross asked, pointing at the red cover.

'It's artificial leather. A sort of vinyl, I think. Here,' he said, handing Cross a piece.

'So it is.'

He then looked a little more closely at what William was up to. He'd cut a small panel out of the cardboard cover and placed a lock of hair in it. He then replaced the cardboard and sealed it up. He saw Cross looking intently, not wanting to interrupt his concentration, as he carefully attached a piece of marbled lining paper over the top of it. It was completely invisible.

'It's a lock of the grandmother's hair. Anne wants her to be a part of the book. Her daughter will always be in touch with her grandmother whenever she cooks from the book, even though she doesn't know it,' he said.

'The daughter won't know?'

'No. It's Anne's secret. Her private memorial, if you like.'

'Do people often do this?' asked Cross.

'Occasionally, but not often. Some people like to use them as personal time capsules. A surprise if anyone ever came across them. Some put in letters about themselves.'

Cross heard a noise coming from the back room.

'Is there someone else here?' he asked.

'Yes. Just Robbie,' replied William.

The man in question then appeared with two mugs of tea.

'Sergeant. I didn't hear you come in. Can I make you a cup of tea?'

'No,' came the reply.

'Robbie's on another weekend retreat with us. Bit like you.'

'Except that I'm not on a retreat. I'm merely fixing the organ,' Cross corrected him.

'True, well, Robbie's here for the good of his soul and is a handy source of free labour for me. He can help us with the organ.'

They took the leather folds and corners up to the church and spent the rest of the morning repairing the reservoir. By mid-afternoon, having been interrupted only by a blissfully silent and delicious light lunch, they'd finished. Cross realised he was going to miss the food at the abbey. It was simple but so fresh, like nothing he'd eaten anywhere else. It was all about the produce from their garden. They sat on the steps of the side door to the church, Brother William and Robbie drinking more tea. Cross was drinking some of their fresh apple juice. He'd become obsessed with it and drank it at every available opportunity.

'Why do you come here?' Cross asked Robbie.

'Um,' he said, thinking out loud. 'Well, this is only my second actual stay. But I like the tranquillity, the peace it affords me. It's like a spiritual cleanse.'

'Are you religious?' Cross went on.

'Of course. Are you not?'

'No,' replied Cross.

'I think in another life I could have been a monk,' Robbie said.

'Why not this one?' asked Cross.

'I don't know. Good question. Too much to leave behind, perhaps. Mind you, having said that, now I think about it, there isn't that much to give up,' said Robbie.

'Do you get many people around Robbie's age taking solemn vows?' Cross asked William.

'One or two. Yes,' he replied.

'What appeals to you about the monastic life exactly, Robbie?' asked Cross.

'It's just so far removed from the modern world and all its problems. I like the order of it. The same routine every day. The offices of day at exactly the same time. The silence at meals. I get the sense you like order too,' he replied.

'I like order and I like the order of things here. I'm not so enthusiastic about that order being imposed on me by others. I like my own sense of order. But I can see the attraction,' said Cross.

'Do you have family?' asked Robbie.

'I do,' Cross replied.

'Consisting of?'

'My father... and more recently my mother.'

'That sounds intriguing,' said Robbie trying to encourage him to elaborate.

'It is.'

'Well, are you going to share it with us?' asked Robbie.

'I am not.'

There was an awkward pause which William thought it incumbent on him, as host, to fill.

'Do you have family, Robbie?' he asked.

'I do,' he said sorrowfully. 'But I messed it up. Big time. Now they're just a source of aching regret.'

'Are your parents still alive?'

'My father is. My mother died decades ago.'

'And you're not close to your father?'

'You could say that. We don't speak. Well, none of my family speak to me is the truth of it. Not my father, my ex-wife, my children.'

'Your children? That must be painful,' observed William.

Robbie nodded in a way that indicated that while he agreed with the expressed sentiment, this conversation was now at an end.

They turned towards the abbey house as they heard Brother Jude call out to Cross. The monk was pushing Father Wolfson in his wheelchair up the path towards them.

'Detective Sergeant Cross!' the old monk hailed him cheerfully, his dentures bobbing up and down with enthusiasm.

'Father Wolfson,' Cross replied.

'It's so wonderful you've taken all this time to restore our organ. We have missed it so.'

'It was an entirely selfish act,' Cross replied.

'Nonsense. That might well be what you're telling yourself but we both know it's entirely untrue. How much more is there to be done?'

'Well, Brother William has just repaired the reservoir, so everything is now airtight. Tomorrow I'll fix the trackers, but I think the organ can do with regulating,' Cross replied.

'What is that exactly?'

'The organ needs tuning, but its tonal quality will also need calibrating. It would be a good opportunity to get its speech, sustained tone and volume tailored to the acoustic characteristics of the church. It's a skill I'm lacking in, but I know some people who will come and do it.'

'Presumably for a fee?' the old monk asked.

'I'll see what can be done,' Cross replied. He intended paying for this himself but didn't want it to be an issue. From a selfish point of view, he'd never seen anyone regulate an organ before, so at least he'd get that experience out of it.

'You asked the father abbot and Father Magnus if Brother Dominic had brought anything with him when he entered the abbey. I couldn't think of anything at first but then I remembered that he did bring a small Victorian painting of the Virgin Mary,' said Father Wolfson.

'I see,' replied Cross, waiting for more.

'We hung it in the church.'

'Is it a valuable piece?'

'No, not really. We had it valued for insurance purposes, like everything else in the church. I looked it up and it was valued at between five and seven hundred pounds,' the monk replied.

'I see. Where is it? I'd like to have a look at it,' said Cross.

'Well, that's the odd thing, George. It's gone. It appears to be missing.'

'Do you know when it went missing?' asked Cross.

'No. It wasn't till I remembered his bringing it that I thought to have another look. But if you follow us you'll see it's no longer there.'

They went into the church.

Father Wolfson indicated a space on the wall by the lectern. There was the faintest of outlines where a picture must have been hanging for some time. The nail it had hung from was still in the wall.

Cross was staying the night at the abbey. After dinner the monks tended to gather in the sitting room for an hour's recreation where they would talk and read. Cross joined them and asked them if they could recall the last time they had noticed Brother Dominic's Victorian painting.

'I dust the Stations of the Cross and other paintings in the church on the last Monday of every month,' said Brother Jude. I dusted that painting on Monday the twenty-seventh, I think it was.'

'Four days before Brother Dominic went missing,' Cross realised out loud.

'Yes indeed,' Jude replied sadly.

*

'Do you think the painting has something to do with Dominic?' said a voice behind him as he was walking to his guest room later. It was Robbie.

'I don't know. It does seem a bit of coincidence,' replied Cross.

'Well, it either puts paid to my theory of Murphy being the killer or, it's exactly that. Just a coincidence,' said Robbie.

'There haven't been any thefts from the abbey in over fifty years. So why now?' said Cross.

'Good point,' conceded Robbie, shaking his head. 'I find this all so upsetting. I can't believe it's happened.'

To Cross's way of thinking, the missing painting had to be relevant. But why a painting of such little worth by an obscure Victorian painter should be, he was unsure. But now it was missing, and they had a window of time in which this could have happened, to examine. There were several opportunities, the most obvious being when the abbey gates were left open. This was on Sundays for the parish services. He ruled out the Sundays he'd been there working on the organ, as he'd gone straight back into the church immediately after the service ended, thereby denying anyone an opportunity to slip in and steal it. He narrowed it down to the Sunday after Dominic had gone missing, which was Palm Sunday. There'd also been a multiple christening of five babies from different families that day. The congregation was boosted by family members and godparents. People always took dozens of photographs on occasions like this so he would action Mackenzie when he got back to work to liaise with the abbey and see if people would send in all their photographs and videos for them to study.

The next day before he left, he signed the abbey guest book again. He flicked through the pages at all the names and saw Robbie's signature. Robbie Weald.

He realised he'd seen that name recently.

45

Cross, Ottey and Mackenzie went over to see Swift in his office – which he insisted on calling his lab – first thing Monday morning. He'd pulled a couple of all-nighters and looked like a vampire from an independent horror movie, whose budget was so low all the actors were doing their own make-up. The venetian blinds were, as always, closed, as if to keep sunlight from getting in and killing him. Cross had never been to the office before, unlike the others. He was taken aback by the sheer number of small plastic comic book superhero figurines which not only populated the shelves, but were also suspended mid-flight from the ceiling. But the object that actually stopped him in his tracks was a large stuffed black crow glowering down on them from a corner of the room, its large wings outstretched, as if about to swoop down on them all. Its cold black eyes stared challengingly at anyone who dared enter the room.

Cross took one look at the crow and turned to Swift.

'Yes, it is a Michael Ribble original. I paid full price. I didn't use my position as a forensic investigator to influence him in any way. Ribble was also no longer a person of interest in the Frampton case when I commissioned him,' said Swift.

He was referring to the taxidermist in Portsmouth who had briefly been a person of interest in a previous case. Swift had been unprofessionally entranced by the taxidermist's studio when they'd paid him a visit, in Cross's opinion.

Cross made no comment. Ottey and Mackenzie had both seen the crow before and didn't have the heart to tell Cross that Swift had given the bird a name. George. He'd probably find out in good time, and they hoped not to be around when he did.

'So, the headlines are – the cottage on the Coxton Hall estate is definitely the site of Brother Dominic's murder scene. It took place in the kitchen. He was secured to a wooden chair with duct tape attached to his wrists and ankles. A roll of duct tape which matches the tape used was found in the kitchen. The chair Dominic was secured to is also identical to three others found in the cottage. There is significant blood on the floor of the kitchen. It is Dominic's. After he was tortured, the chair Dominic was secured to was dragged to the back door. The lack of blood leading to the door suggests this was done post mortem. He was loaded onto the trailer and driven off.'

'Murder weapon?' asked Cross.

'By that do you mean the implement that delivered the fatal blow to the head?'

'I do.'

'As yet unfound at the scene.'

'We should do a fingertip search in the surrounding area,' suggested Ottey. 'Extend it to the deposition site. The accident implies that probably wasn't the intended location, doesn't it?'

'Good question,' replied Cross. 'Alice, can you have a look at the map again and see where that quad bike might have been on the way to? It can't have been far as it was avoiding main roads.'

They were all called in to a meeting with Carson when Cross received a message that someone was waiting to talk to him in reception. When he saw who it was, he chose to go down to reception rather than obey the summons to Carson's office. Sir Patrick Murphy and his aide de camp Martin Bates were sitting there, like a couple of guilty schoolboys outside the headmaster's office. He walked up to them.

'Sergeant,' Murphy began.

'You wished to see me?' Cross replied.

'Could we perhaps go somewhere more private?' asked Bates.

Cross checked to see if the Voluntary Assistance suite was free, and then took the two men up to it. As Ottey wasn't with him, he checked his notebook once they got there, for some guidance. He found it, then looked up and said, almost reading out loud, 'Would you like something to drink?'

Thankfully they declined. They sat.

'We're here because we read that Nicholas Cubitt is now wanted in connection with Brother Dominic's murder. Although how that makes sense is still a mystery to me,' began Murphy.

Cross said nothing.

'You've asked for any information that people might think is relevant to the case and Martin has something I believe to be exactly that. Martin?' Murphy finished.

'Many years ago, before it collapsed, I worked for Cubitt's bank. I was in their marketing department,' Bates began.

'Did you know Alex Mount?' asked Cross.

'No, he was after my time.'

'But you know the name,' Cross observed.

'Of course.'

'It's how we met,' explained Murphy. 'Cubitt's. I banked there for years before it went belly up.'

'I know I should've mentioned this before, it just didn't occur to me. Or maybe it was out of a sense of misguided loyalty. I don't know. But I didn't make the link, I'm afraid. Why would I?' he began. 'Nick Cubitt approached me after the television interview with Brother Dominic was broadcast on *Newsnight*.'

'What did he want?' asked Cross.

'He wanted to know where the abbey Dominic lived in, was,' Bates replied.

'And did you tell him?'

'I'd worked for his father for years,' Bates insisted.

'Did you tell him?' Cross repeated.

'I didn't see any harm in it.'

'Even though Dominic had told you at the time of the interview that his location was to be kept confidential?'

'I was unaware of that stipulation, or else I would obviously have abided by it.'

'Did you ask Cubitt why he wanted the information?' Cross went on.

'It wasn't a long conversation.'

'So, you told him?' asked Cross.

'Yes, and obviously I now deeply regret that as it seems to have been part of this tragic narrative.'

'There is no "seems" about it, Mr Bates. Without that information it is unlikely that Brother Dominic would be dead. Did you have any further communication with him?' Cross asked.

'I did not.'

'Anything else I should know?' Cross asked.

'No.'

As Cross showed them out, Murphy turned to him.

'Thank you for your time,' he said. 'I'm obviously deeply upset about this whole business. If I hadn't challenged Brother Dominic's opinion in the first place, perhaps none of it would've happened.'

Cross saw no need to offer his agreement to this sentiment.

'Father Magnus tells me you've been restoring the organ at the abbey,' Murphy went on.

'I have,' replied Cross.

'That's very commendable of you.'

'It's a purely self-interested venture.'

'I doubt that somehow. I just wanted to say that if there's anything you need help with, just let me know.'

Cross thought for a moment.

'Actually, now that you mention it, do you know what regulating an organ means?' Cross began.

46

That night Cross decided to pay Stephen a visit. It had been on his mind for a while. Specifically, after Ottey had commented that as a friend he should look in on him and see how he was faring. The concept of Stephen being his 'friend' was something that Cross was still juggling in his mind. He preferred his life to be without complication of any kind, particularly of the social relationship ilk. This meant that he'd never really had any friends, and now that he apparently did, he wasn't entirely sure how to deal with it. This apparent obligation to pay Stephen a social visit in order to determine how he was coping in the aftermath of his brother's murder was exactly the sort of decision that had to be made based on various emotional factors and instincts, that he normally shied away from. It was the very reason he'd avoided entertaining the idea of social relationships his entire life.

'It's not Thursday,' observed Stephen as he opened the door to the parsonage.

'Agreed. It is Monday,' replied the detective.

'Come in, come in,' said the priest ushering him in without touching him. 'Has something happened?'

'With regard to what?' asked Cross.

'The case.'

'Oh, I see. There is some progress, yes. We've issued a warrant for the arrest of a former work colleague of your brother's.'

'Oh, all right. Good. I think. Do you need to ask me something?'

'No,' replied Cross.

'Then why are you here?'

'I'm not entirely sure. Josie told me to come.'

'Ah, right. Well in that case, I'm fine, thank you.'

'I didn't ask. Was I supposed to?' said Cross.

'I think so.'

'Duly noted,' said Cross who then noticed that the kitchen table was covered with letters, old photographs and books, which Stephen was obviously sorting through.

'This is all I have of my brother. Not a lot. But hardly surprising, really. What is surprising, though, is how pleasant it is going through it all. Sad, obviously, but tinged with happiness. Remembering how we used to be.'

'Were you close?'

'When young, yes. But not as adults,' Stephen replied.

'I find that part of this a little curious,' Cross replied. 'That his devotion to God robbed you of your relationship with him.'

'I don't see it that way.'

'Why should a life devoted to God deny that same life to others?' asked Cross. 'Particularly his family.'

'God chooses different paths for us all, George. Alex worshipped God to the exclusion of everything and everyone else, including me, in the knowledge that we would be reunited in the glory of God at a later date,' replied Stephen.

'Belief,' corrected Cross.

'I beg your pardon?'

'Your belief, not knowledge. If it was knowledge there would be no need of faith. Isn't faith one of the load-bearing pillars of religion?' Cross went on.

'You are, of course, completely right.'

'It must be some comfort to know—' Cross began.

'Believe,' corrected Stephen.

'Well, there you are. I'm now doing it myself. Your very presence is indoctrinating me. What I meant to say was that it must be some comfort to believe that you will get to see him again, make up for lost time,' said Cross.

'I suppose so. The truth is, though, I'm finding very little comfort in any of this, George.'

'Perfectly understandable. When you think about it why would a god to whom you've both devoted your lives let this happen to one of you? After such a life of devotion?' Cross continued.

'What I'm finding disconcerting is that if Alex hadn't been murdered, it's quite possible I would've gone to my grave not knowing what had happened to him, where he was, what he was doing. His murder brought him back into my life.'

Cross was thinking about this while he was handling Dominic's leather-bound bible which he'd picked up from the table. The leather was incredibly supple, he was thinking. It was beautifully made.

'He was immensely talented,' Cross said.

'Wasn't he?' Stephen answered with obvious fraternal pride. 'I'm so glad to have that bible. It's a strange feeling to think of the many hours he held it in his hand, either at prayer or just reading.'

'Another comfort,' said Cross.

'I think so, yes.'

Cross then noticed something. He was looking at the marbled paper on the inside cover of the bible. He flicked through to the end and looked at the paper in the back. They seemed identical, as presumably they had been taken from the same single sheet. But as Cross looked closer, he noticed small differences.

'Do these pages look the same to you? The front and back inside covers?' he asked Stephen, passing him the bible. Stephen looked carefully.

'No. They're different. Ever so slightly. But they're definitely different,' Stephen observed.

'I need to borrow this,' Cross said, taking the bible back from Stephen and getting up.

'Of course, why?'

But Cross had already turned on his heels and left.

47

Cross had always been a light sleeper. It didn't take much to wake him. So when his phone vibrated early next morning with a text he was immediately alert. He assumed it was work. No one else would get in touch with him this early. Certainly not if they knew him well. He was surprised to see that it was Stephen asking him to ring him urgently. He gave himself a couple of seconds to fully come round then called.

'George. It's the church. We've been burgled.'

Cross and Ottey arrived there just after seven. It was a wet morning with the kind of persistent drizzle that seemed innocuous until you realised big drops had accumulated on your chin and were trickling down the neck of your shirt.

'I wouldn't normally have bothered you, George. But what with Alexander's murder, I don't know, maybe my imagination got the better of me,' said the agitated priest as soon as they arrived.

'Is anything missing?' asked Cross.

'Nothing from the church or sacristy. But they went through the vestment drawers.'

'What makes you say "they"?' asked Cross.

'No reason. He, she, they, whatever. The office has been ransacked but I don't know if anything has been taken.'

The office was a mess, the contents of the drawers thrown all over the floor.

'They found the petty cash, only about a hundred quid, but they left it. I'm not really sure there's anything to steal. To be honest with you the most expensive thing here is probably the lead on the roof,' said Stephen.

'And that's still there?' asked Cross.

'I haven't actually looked. But I'm sure I would've heard if anyone had been up there.'

'Has there been anyone new to your Sunday services?' asked Ottey.

'Not that I've noticed. No.'

'Any strangers just popped in recently or knocked at the parsonage door?' she went on.

'Not recently.'

'The funeral,' Cross began. 'Did you talk to anyone there?'

'Several people, yes.'

'Anyone strike you as odd? A little strange in their approach?'

'I don't think so, no. Gosh, I'm not really being any help, am I?'

Back at the MCU Alice had been looking for Cross and nabbed him as soon as he came in. She had, as he'd asked, managed to get hold of a lot of the congregation's photographs from the Palm Sunday christenings. In two of them a man was seen, as bold as brass, walking through them with the painting under his arm. His face could be made out partially in one of them.

'Recognise him?' Mackenzie asked.

'No,' replied Ottey.

'We need to go to the abbey now,' said Cross picking up Brother Dominic's bible as he got up to leave.

'Well, he obviously did,' said Ottey following him.

'I would ask you what's going on, but I've learned from experience that it's so much more fun just to watch,' Ottey said to Cross in the car.

'"So much more fun?" There you go again. This is a murder investigation, DS Ottey. I fail to see the fun in any of this,' Cross replied.

She smiled as she knew perfectly well that he also didn't want to tell her what he was up to as he too preferred to let it play out and show it. It was his way of having fun. He just didn't know it. They arrived at the abbey thirty minutes later. Parked and walked over to the bookbindery. William and Robbie were working inside.

'Good morning, Sergeants,' said William.

He saw the bible in Cross's hand.

'One of our bibles?' he asked.

'Brother Dominic's, in fact. I'd like your opinion on something. About the marbling on the inside covers,' replied Cross.

'Of course,' replied William taking the bible.

'Brother Dominic covered all of the monks' bibles here at the abbey. So beautiful,' William informed Robbie, who then walked over to him to look at it.

William examined the marbled paper inside the front and back covers of the bible then looked up.

'They're definitely different. Quite hard to see. But they are.'

'Exactly what I thought. The question is why? Why wouldn't he have used the same paper for both covers?' Cross asked.

'I have no idea,' replied the monk.

'Examine the back cover more closely,' Cross instructed him. 'Run your fingers over it.'

William did so. He looked away from the book as if by not seeing it his sense of touch would be greater.

'There's something in it,' he replied.

'I thought so too, which is why I brought it to you. As you know the bible has been given to Brother Dominic's brother, so I don't want to cause any unnecessary damage. Given your expertise I thought it better for you to find out what's concealed in there.'

'Of course,' replied the monk, who reached for a scalpel.

'If you could put these on,' said Cross, holding out a pair of latex gloves.

William put them on. He then delicately tried to peel the paper back without success.

'I can't preserve the paper. Perhaps it's best I just get it off and then replace both the front and back with new marbled paper,' William offered.

'I think Stephen would appreciate that,' said Ottey.

So, William became bolder in his approach and cut the paper away. It revealed a shallow panel cut out of the book's cover which was packed with what looked like tissue paper. He held the book out for Cross.

'You have the gloves on, Brother William,' Cross pointed out.

'Of course.'

He removed the tissue to find a folded-up piece of paper below. He pulled it out and unfolded it. It was an A4 printed sheet with a signature and official stamp on it. William read it.

'It appears to be a bill of sale for a painting,' he said.

'Presumably not a Victorian painting of the Virgin Mary, but something of similar dimensions,' said Cross, who already knew the answer. Ottey was astonished. How on earth had he come up with this one? She was beginning to feel maybe she should keep a diary of these moments. Become a Watson to his Holmes.

'It's for a small Lucien Freud oil,' said William.

'Date of sale?'

'Twenty-seventh of June 2008.'

'And the purchase price?' Cross asked.

'Five million, seven hundred and fifty thousand pounds,' William said slowly as if trying to ensure while reading it out that he was reading it correctly.

'Made out to?'

'Alexander Mount.'

'Gosh. What do you think that would be worth now, DS Ottey?' Cross asked.

'I have no idea. But I'm guessing we now know what Alexander did with his money,' she replied.

'What do you think, Nick?' asked Cross. But Robbie had slipped out quietly. Seemingly unconcerned, Cross turned back to the monk and produced an evidence bag which he held out in front of the monk. William dropped the bill of sale into it. Cross sealed it correctly then produced another for the bible.

'Nick?' said Ottey, in case she'd misheard.

'Nicholas Cubitt, yes,' replied Cross.

'Okay, two questions. How did you know that was him, and why have we just let a prime suspect go?' Ottey asked.

'He used the name of Charlotte Hoskins's cottage as his fake surname, Weald, which could have been a coincidence, but I doubted it. Then I recognised him in the photographs Alice unearthed.'

William looked completely at sea with this turn of events.

'Who is Nicholas Cubitt?' he asked.

'Long story, but I'm afraid we need to go,' replied Ottey.

'But you just called him a prime suspect. Does that mean all this time—'

But Cross interrupted him by taking the evidence bag with the bible in it from him.

'It seems he duped us all, Brother William. Don't feel badly about it,' said Ottey.

'Shouldn't I fix it first?' William asked, indicating the book.

'It's evidence now. That'll have to wait till after the trial,' Cross informed him.

'But I'll bring it back for you to fix before it goes back to Father Stephen,' Ottey assured him.

They walked out towards her car as a black Range Rover Evoque sped down the lane and out of the abbey. Robbie was at the wheel.

'Shit, did you get the licence plate?' she asked.

'No,' he replied casually and marched off towards the abbey house.

'Oh, okay. Don't worry I'll just wait in the car,' Ottey said to herself, not for the first time.

Thomas was tending his lawn. He was standing in the middle of it and looking down at a section, perplexed. Cross arrived in the courtyard and stood to one side. He knew better than to trespass on the lawn without permission.

'Everything all right, Brother Thomas?' Cross asked, reading the consternation on the monk's features.

He summoned the detective onto the lawn unceremoniously then pointed at a patch of grass.

'Stellaria media,' he said solemnly. 'Common chickweed, the devil's work.'

Cross saw he was pointing to the tiniest little weed in the perfect lawn.

Thomas produced a penknife from his leather toolbelt and knelt down. Then, with all the care and precision of a neurosurgeon faced with a brain beneath an open skull, he began to cut into the ground around the sides of the offending weed. He lifted a square inch of lawn from the ground and carefully extracted the weed and root from it. Satisfied he'd excised the whole thing, he replaced the small square piece of turf back into the lawn. Cross bent down and took a closer look. You couldn't see where the repair had been made.

'Perfect,' he commented.

'Yes,' agreed the monk.

'Brother Thomas, I have a question for you. The guest Robbie – do you know the registration number of his car?'

'LT20 YJT,' came the immediate reply. 'Something off about that one,' he commented as Cross walked away and smiled.

'George, what is going on? What are we doing?' Ottey asked wearily when he got into the car.

Instead of answering her Cross pulled out his mobile phone and called Mackenzie. He put her on speaker.

'I need you to check a licence plate number for me,' he said.

Normally these kinds of requests were issued over the radio. Cross didn't like to do this as he said that the radio channels should be kept open and free for urgent police business, which of course this was. They were in actual fact in pursuit of a car. Ottey had her own theory about this idiosyncratic reluctance. She thought that speaking over the radio for him was like speaking in public. Something he didn't like to do.

'A black Range Rover Evoque?' Mackenzie checked before giving him the name.

'Correct.'

'Okay, well, that car is registered to Nicholas Cubitt. Why are you asking?'

Cross cut off the phone without providing her with an answer.

'So, Robbie is actually Nicholas Cubitt. I got that much. But why didn't we just arrest him?' Ottey asked.

'Because he still has the painting and our best chance of recovering it and catching him red-handed was to let him go. I'm fairly confident the attraction of a possibly ten-million-plus painting is too much to resist, and that he'll let his guard down.'

'So, Brother Dominic hid the painting in another painting?'

'Yes, bought it with his fortune before entering the abbey. That's where he put all his money,' Cross explained.

'Saving for a rainy day, perhaps?'

'Who knows, but it crosses my mind that Stephen is now a very rich young priest,' he commented.

'Oh my God,' she said at the thought of this.

48

'H e's been hiding in plain sight all this time?' spluttered Carson in disbelief.

'So, it would seem, sir,' replied Ottey.

'So, what now? Why did you let him go?' asked Carson.

'It's our best chance of getting the painting back. His being caught with the painting in his possession is good for court. We need you to call the Surrey police and get an unmarked car to sit outside this antiques shop in Dorking. They paid six hundred pounds into Nick's account ten days ago. Sir,' he said with great emphasis.

Nick Cubitt was duly picked up by Surrey police the next day, Wednesday, walking out of the said antiques shop with the painting under his arm.

The following morning, while they were waiting for the arrival of Nicholas Cubitt at the MCU, they obtained a search warrant for Coxton Hall. There was still one piece of evidence missing and Cross was fairly sure he knew where they'd find it. When he and Ottey arrived at the estate, there was a slight delay in the gate opening after they'd pressed the entry button. When they pulled up at the front of the main house Julian Cubitt came out.

'Sorry about the delay letting you in. I'm having trouble with that bloody gate,' he began by saying.

'No problem,' replied Ottey.

'How can I help?' he asked.

'We have a search warrant for the estate, Mr Cubitt.'

'Really?'

'It's just routine,' she fibbed. 'We've searched all the properties in the area. It's your turn now, I'm afraid. We shouldn't be too long.'

'Is it completely necessary?'

'I'm afraid so,' Ottey replied, then walked away with Cross.

They passed a walled kitchen garden and a formal garden comprising of small paths between an ornate pattern of tightly clipped box hedging, until they came to Charlotte Hoskins's cottage. They knocked on the door, which was answered by a large burly man dressed in outdoor working clothes. He had a ruddy complexion from working outside and such enormously bushy eyebrows that it was immediately obvious he didn't tend to them as frequently as he did the topiary in the garden.

'Mr Hoskins?' asked Ottey.

'Neil, yeah,' he replied.

'Would you mind if we looked in the barn?' Ottey asked, indicating the barn next to the cottage.

'Who are you?' he asked.

'Sorry. Police,' she replied as both she and Cross held up their warrant cards.

'Have you asked Mr Cubitt?'

'We have. But we also have a search warrant,' she informed him.

'All right then,' he said and led them round to the barn.

It had a vaguely agricultural smell of dried hay crossed with engine oil. Cross went up to a large vehicle covered with a tarpaulin, next to a vehicle which he could see was an old Jaguar XJ6 raised up on bricks.

'What's under here?' he asked.

Instead of answering Hoskins pulled the tarp off. Cross noticed he had huge hands. They had to be at least a third bigger than his. They were rough and cracked from a life of working outside. Under the tarp was a beautiful vintage Rolls Royce. It was two tone in colour, black and maroon.

'A nineteen forties' Rolls Royce Wraith. It was Mr Cubitt's father's,' said Hoskins.

'Does he still drive it?' asked Cross.

'Not so much. It was used for both his weddings. Nick's too. I take it out every couple of months. Don't know why he keeps it really,' Hoskins said.

There was another covered up vehicle in the far corner of the barn. Cross went over and took the cover off himself. It was a quad bike with a trailer attached to the back of it. Cross examined it. The keys were in the ignition.

'Do you always keep the keys in the ignition like this?' he asked.

'Yep. It's not as if anyone is going to steal it and it saves me time having to find them,' replied Hoskins.

'Why was it covered with a tarp?'

'No idea. Hadn't noticed to be honest,' Neil replied.

Cross had a closer look at the right side of the quad. There was a large dent and deep scratches on the paintwork.

'Is this damage recent?' he asked.

'Could be. It's always getting bashed about.'

'Does anyone else have use of it?'

'Couple of the lads.'

'It's quite a lot of damage. Must've had quite a bang.'

'Possibly, yeah,' replied Hoskins who didn't seem bothered, as if it were nothing out of the ordinary.

'None of the lads told you about an accident?' asked Cross.

'Fat chance,' laughed Hoskins. 'If it works, they'll just get back on it. Like I said, it's always getting beat up.'

Ottey came over and had a closer look. The damage looked consistent with sliding into and spilling over into a ditch. There was a mechanical winch built into the back of the trailer.

'Shall I call for a low-loader?' she said.

'Yes,' replied Cross.

'What's going on?' asked Hoskins.

'We need to take the bike and trailer away with us,' replied Ottey.

Before Hoskins could ask why, his wife, Charlotte, appeared.

'What's happening?' she asked.

'They want to take the quad bike,' replied her husband.

'Why?' she asked.

'Is it always kept here?' asked Cross, ignoring her.

'Yes,' replied Hoskins.

'Do you recall it being used on the night of March the thirty-first?' Cross asked.

Hoskins and his wife looked at each other then back at Cross and Ottey.

'No,' they replied in unison.

'Would you have heard it if it was?'

'Not necessarily, no,' said Hoskins.

'Charlotte, I want you to think about my next question very carefully before you answer it. Have you seen Nicholas Cubitt recently, here on the estate?'

'No,' she said immediately.

'Mr Hoskins?' asked Cross turning to him.

'No.'

'Neither of you saw him on March the thirty-first of this year?'

'No,' they replied.

'Mr Hoskins, did you lend Nicholas Cubitt the quad bike that night?' Cross probed.

'No,' Hoskins insisted. 'He's not been on the estate for donkey's years.'

'He came once,' said Charlotte. 'Just after he got out of prison. Came to see his father. Mr Cubitt hadn't been to see his son once in prison. Can you imagine?'

'Why did he come when he got out?' asked Ottey.

'Well, he wanted a reconciliation, didn't he? But she soon put a stop to that,' said Charlotte.

'By "she", do you mean Rosemary?' asked Ottey.

'I think Julian was willing. But she wasn't,' Charlotte continued.

'Well why should she be?' asked her husband. 'When he pops his clogs she gets the lot.'

'Did you see him that day? When he came to see his father?' asked Cross.

'Yes, he came over. He was so distressed. He loved this place. I used to visit him in prison, and he always asked after his father. Julian knew I was going, and used to ask after him. But only if she wasn't in earshot, mind. Nick came over because he wanted one last look at the cottage. He used to spend a lot of time here when he was young and helped Neil in the kitchen garden,' she said sadly.

'He loved doing that,' agreed Hoskins. 'But he's not been back since.'

The low-loader arrived and took the quad and trailer away. Cross and Ottey walked back to their car. Julian Cubitt and his wife appeared at the front door.

'Neil tells us you've taken the quad bike away,' said Rosemary.

'Yes,' replied Cross.

'May I ask why?' she went on.

'Yes,' replied Cross.

'Are you trying to be funny?' she said.

'No,' came the reply.

The woman thought for a moment.

'Wait a minute. Are you saying Nick has been here, on the estate?' she asked.

'Who said anything about Nicholas?' Cross asked.

'No one, I just assumed,' she replied.

Cross and Ottey got back into the car and followed the low-loader.

49

Cross organised his files neatly and perfectly equidistant from the edges of the interview table. Only then did he look up at Nick Cubitt and his solicitor.

'So, Robbie. I'm sorry, Nick. It might take me a little getting used to as I've been calling you Robbie these past few weeks. You look very different to the photographs we had. Very different, but I think you knew that. Otherwise you wouldn't have stayed around so long.'

'Well, prison will do that to you,' Cubitt replied.

'I knew someone at school called Paul who later became an actor,' Cross continued. 'He had to change his name to John. When I saw him years later, I just couldn't get used to it. Kept calling him Paul, but he didn't seem to mind. How did you know Brother Dominic Augustus, Nick?'

'I met him at St Eustace's Abbey while on retreat,' he replied.

'Ever met him before?' Cross asked.

'No.'

'Why did you choose St Eustace's, out of interest?' Cross went on.

'I just came across it on the internet when I was looking for places to go on retreat. I liked the look of it,' Nick replied.

Cross looked at him. He was deciding which path to take in this interview. Obviously, he wasn't going to produce all their evidence to Cubitt and charge him. He wanted to help the prosecution case as much as he could in this room. Construct a narrative that could be used convincingly in court. Paint a picture of Nick Cubitt as well as provide the evidence.

'We all, with the possible exception of your lawyer, know that's not true,' he said.

Cubitt made no response.

'All right, let's move on to what we know is irrefutable. The painting. The Victorian religious painting of the Virgin Mary. Why did you steal the painting from the abbey?' Cross asked.

'I didn't.'

'But you were arrested with it in your possession,' Cross pointed out.

'That doesn't mean I stole it.'

'That's true. So why don't you tell me how it came to be in your possession?'

'It was a gift.'

'A gift from whom?' asked Cross.

'Brother Dominic.'

'Oh, I see. Did you tell anyone it was a gift before you took it from the church?'

'I did not.'

'Why was that?'

'I don't know,' replied Cubitt. 'It didn't seem necessary.'

'All right, let's work on the basis that that is the truth. Why did you sell it?' asked Cross.

'For the money, obviously. I'm not big on religious art.'

'Did you need the money?' asked Cross.

'Not particularly.'

'Why did Dominic give you the painting? Did he give you any reason?' asked Cross.

'He wanted it to be a memento, if you like, of my time at the abbey.'

'Which you promptly sold.'

'It reminded me of the terrible thing that had happened to him. I didn't want to have it around anymore. It upset me,' replied Cubitt.

'I can understand that, or could understand it, were it not for the fact that you didn't remove it from the abbey till after his death,' Cross pointed out.

'It was a confusing time.'

'Of course. Why did you return to the antique shop to get it back yesterday?'

'I changed my mind.'

'Did that have anything to do with the Lucien Freud bill of sale we found concealed in Dominic's bible?'

'It did not.'

'It didn't occur to you that possibly a piece of art worth several millions was hidden behind the religious painting you had sold for six hundred pounds?'

'It did not.'

'How was your time in prison?' Cross asked, suddenly changing the direction of the interview.

'How do you think?'

'I have no idea. My experience goes no further than a few hours now and then in an interview room within a prison,' replied Cross.

'Well, I wouldn't recommend it,' came the terse reply.

'Are you resentful about your time there?' asked Cross.

'I don't understand the question.'

'How do you feel about the sentence you received? Do you feel it was justified?'

'I do not.'

'I thought that might be the case. Even though you committed serious fraud?' asked Cross.

'That's one way of looking at it,' replied Cubitt.

'Well obviously it was the way the court looked at it. How do you see it?'

'I was in the middle of a process far too complex for even a judge and jury to understand, let alone a detective sergeant of the Avon and Somerset police,' Cubitt replied witheringly.

'Indulge us,' said Ottey.

'I was managing millions of pounds across several currencies in an array of different financial instruments. That involves movements up and down, and in basic terms you have to balance the books,' Cubitt replied.

'Balance the books? You took money from people's client accounts without authorisation and moved it simply to cover your enormous losses,' Cross pointed out. 'Is that what you mean by balancing the books?'

'My client was tried for this and served time. What exactly has this got to do with the arrest today?' asked the lawyer.

'Frankie Davis,' Cross stated.

'What about him?' asked Cubitt.

'Do you know him?'

'Obviously.'

'How?'

'We shared a cell for a while when I was inside.'

'Is he ever in contact with you?'

'No.'

Cross took a sheet out from his file.

'I have a copy of your mobile phone records here. Would you like to reconsider your answer?'

'He was in touch quite recently, now I think about it.'

'Why?'

'He wanted help. Getting a job.'

'And he thought you could help? What, by giving him a job?'

'Either giving him one or putting him in touch with someone who needed labour.'

'What is your business these days?' asked Cross.

'Property development.'

'Were you able to help Davis? Furnish him with a job?' asked Cross.

'I was not in this instance, no.'

Cross made diligent notes every time a question was unanswered which gave the interview an uneven tempo. A deliberate ploy on Cross's part. He found it often made the interviewee impatient and anxious.

'Had you given him work at any instance in the past?'

'No.'

'And you didn't this time?'

'No.'

'So why did he persist in calling you?' asked Cross.

'He's very persistent.'

Cross looked at Cubitt, deciding whether he was attempting to be humorous. He couldn't tell.

'Except that it wasn't him who initiated contact was it? It was actually you. He didn't call you looking for a job at all.'

Cubitt didn't react.

'Where were you on the thirty-first of March this year?' Cross went on.

'I have no idea. I'd have to check. You could ask my secretary. She'd know.'

'Mandy? We already have. She's not very happy at the moment.'

'Is that right?'

'Yes, apparently you haven't been around much the last few months. Keep disappearing. She also hasn't been paid in three months. Bit of an odd way to treat someone you seem to be intimate with,' Cross observed.

'Fluctuations of business. I have a small cash-flow problem at present.'

'Presumably a smaller one than you had at Cubitt's bank,' Cross commented. 'Do you not deal in stocks and shares? Not have your own little portfolio for a rainy day?'

'I do not.'

'Well, I suppose that's unsurprising really,' observed Cross looking directly across the table. If he was trying to get a rise out of his suspect, he didn't succeed. 'Trading wasn't exactly in your skillset as an investment banker. Not something you excelled at. Something, in fact, you failed at spectacularly to your own cost and that of your family. After all, that's why you got into trouble in the first place and is why you're sitting opposite us today.'

Cubitt made no response.

'You don't have an alibi for the thirty-first of March, according to your unpaid secretary,' Cross informed him.

'So?'

'So that is the date of the abduction and murder of Brother Dominic.'

'And what exactly has that got to do with me?'

'Well, that's hopefully what we're here to ascertain,' Cross replied.

'Can I ask a question?' said Ottey, jumping in at the appointed cue. Cubitt turned slowly towards her. 'What's it like to destroy a successful family business that's been around for over three hundred years, in less than eighteen months?'

'That strikes me as completely irrelevant,' said Cubitt's lawyer.

'What you think is relevant or irrelevant is neither here nor there,' she replied. 'How is your relationship with your father?'

'There is no relationship,' replied Cubitt, shifting his weight slightly in his chair.

'That must be difficult. Presumably you were close at one time. As his only son and heir,' she said.

'To an extent. He's quite old-fashioned. Edwardian even. Not given to displays of affection,' Cubitt replied.

'In better times you had use of a cottage on your father's estate.'

'I did.'

'But not anymore.'

'No.'

'You used to go down there with your children,' she said.

'That's correct.'

'Did Charlotte help with them? The children?' she asked.

'Charlotte? On occasion, yes, if our nanny was on holiday.'

'You were close to Charlotte. Are you still?'

'We're in touch, yes. She was like a second mother to me.'

'That's exactly how she put it. Have you been down to the cottage recently?' Ottey went on.

'I have not.'

'Beautiful estate, Coxton Hall. You must have looked forward to inheriting it. But not any more. That mistake you made in the City really was so costly in the end. That must haunt you,' she observed.

'I've moved on,' he asserted.

'Really? Are sure about that? I'm not sure I'd be able to be so sanguine. Especially if I believed, as you seem to, that I'd done nothing wrong. Even though your actions did bring down a bank.'

'I didn't bring down the bank,' he answered testily.

'It still annoys you that people like me think you did though, doesn't it? Do you hold anyone else responsible?' she went on.

He didn't answer.

'According to our research, your robbing-Peter-to-pay-Paul scheme was exposed by one of your own traders when you made the mistake of raiding his client accounts to disguise your losses. And we're talking hundreds of millions of pounds here, not petty cash. Money which didn't belong to you. Didn't belong to the bank. But unlike you, this trader had a sense of responsibility to his clients.'

'Does that sound familiar?' asked Cross. 'His name was Alexander Mount.'

Cubitt said nothing, so Cross turned to the lawyer.

'Alexander Mount was a big star in the City, brilliant mathematician. The Lionel Messi of city traders and a must-have for your clients' investment vehicle. And your client got him. Offered him the most extraordinary deal to lure him away from HSBC. Huge signing-on bonus, performance bonuses, and that's before his eye-watering salary and commissions. But he was worth it, wasn't he, Mr Cubitt? Initially, at least.'

'Again, I have to ask why this is relevant?' persisted the lawyer.

'Well, Alexander Mount withdrew from the City after the implosion of Cubitt's. But he was very much the secret whistle-blower who had drawn attention to this, in the end, catastrophic fraud. He withdrew from the City and pretty much from view. He entered St Eustace's Abbey and took the monastic name Brother Dominic Augustus.'

Nothing was said but the lawyer struggled to conceal his surprise.

'Tea?' Cross suggested brightly as if he was hosting a very polite bridge party in Clifton.

50

When they reconvened in the interview room, Cross went through his file slowly, until he found his place in his prepared interview structure.

'Let's go back to why you were actually at the abbey in the first place,' Cross began.

'My client has already answered that question,' said the lawyer.

'And I'm giving him the chance to reconsider his answer,' replied Cross.

'I was there for a retreat,' replied Cubitt.

Cross looked at him as if to give him yet another chance to answer differently. He didn't.

'So, it must've come as quite a shock when you discovered Alexander Mount was there as a monk,' Cross said.

'I didn't recognise him at first,' said Cubitt.

'What happened when you did? Did you tell him who you were?'

'I didn't have to.'

'You were there under a false name,' Cross pointed out.

'A lot of people do that. It's a question of privacy. I also happen to have a criminal record, which not everyone is always understanding about.'

'Did he recognise you?' Cross asked.

'Immediately.'

'What was his reaction?'

'He was surprised, but I think quite pleased.'

'Did he ask why you were there under a different name?'

'He did not. I think he knew why.'

'Did he know why you were there?'

'After I told him, yes.'

'And what reason did you give?'

'The truth, of course. I'd been unable to settle after getting out of prison. I had lost my family. I was lost and needed time to reflect and some spiritual succour.'

'Did he believe you?'

'Why shouldn't he? It was the truth.'

'Why did you go back so often?'

'Because I found all of those things there. Brother Dominic took me under his wing. I found it irresistible. He was such an extraordinary man.'

'I don't think that's why you were there at all. I think you were there because you resented him and you wanted to confront him,' said Ottey.

'You can theorise as much as you like. The fact is, it was a coincidence,' Cubitt replied.

'My colleague may theorise, as you put it, but I don't. I only deal with the facts as they are put in front of me. I should also tell you that in my experience of these situations, coincidences always turn out to be the exact opposite. The fact here is that you became aware of Brother Dominic's location through his interview on *Newsnight* which alerted you to the fact that he was now a monk. The man you believe had ruined your life then disappeared was now on the screen right in front of you,' Cross said.

'That's not true. Again, a theory,' replied Cubitt confidently.

'The problem you had, though,' said Cross, ignoring him, 'was you had no idea where he was. Brother Dominic had been very insistent on the location of the abbey and its name not being mentioned in the interview. But that didn't matter to you, because you knew the other individual in that interview. Martin Bates. He had worked for your father in the marketing department of Cubitt's.'

Cubitt said nothing.

'He thought he recognised the monk but couldn't place him. It was annoying him. He just couldn't help trying to work out where he'd known him. Then you called him and put him out of his misery. Brother Dominic was in fact Alexander Mount. You then asked him where Dominic's abbey was, and he told you. Thinking nothing of it. He had no idea what you were going to do with that information. What rational person would?' Cross asked.

Cubitt didn't respond.

'Are you going to deny that's what happened? That that was how you knew where Alexander Mount was?' asked Ottey. 'It's just that we have a signed witness statement from Bates, and a quick look at your phone records tells us that you did call him. From your mobile.'

His lawyer leant over and whispered in his ear. Cubitt thought for a moment then turned back to the police officers.

'Yes. That's how I found out where Mount was,' he said.

'So, why did you go to St Eustace's Abbey?' asked Cross. 'You obviously weren't there for a retreat.'

'I went to see Alexander Mount.'

'Why?'

'I was just curious, I suppose.'

'About what?' asked Cross.

'How life had worked out. I couldn't believe he'd ended up in a monastery. I wondered if I was in some way responsible. I think I also went looking for forgiveness. Reconciliation,' Cubitt replied.

'Reconciliation of what?' asked Cross.

'The two of us.'

'You spent quite a few weekends at the retreat and a fair amount of time with Brother Dominic, by all accounts. What did you talk about?' Cross asked.

'All sorts of things. Prison. He was interested in how I dealt with that. What it was like. He was sorry I'd ended up there.'

'Was he sorry about what happened to the bank?' Cross went on.

This seemed to give Nicholas Cubitt pause for thought.

'He was sorry in as much as he had great respect for my father,' Cubitt said.

'But no regrets or sorrow about you?' Cross pushed.

'He was a very spiritually generous person. I think his sorrow encompassed what happened to me.'

'It's interesting. There you go again,' said Cross. 'You talk about "what happened" to you. You can't, won't, accept that you brought it all on yourself.'

'You don't understand,' Cubitt replied.

'No one understands according to you, Mr Cubitt,' said Cross.

'I mean about city finance,' Cubitt continued.

'From what I've read neither do you. You brought down a three-hundred-year-old bank,' Ottey pointed out. 'Pretty much single-handedly.'

'That kind of thing, what my colleague has just said, absolutely enrages you, doesn't it, Mr Cubitt?' asked Cross. 'But no one enrages you quite as much as Alexander Mount. The architect of your misfortune. Do they?'

'No comment.'

'Tell me something. Back in 2008 when Alexander discovered how badly wrong things were going, did you ask him for time? Time to put it right?' asked Cross.

'Of course I did.'

'And he wouldn't give it to you?'

'No.'

'That must have infuriated you. Because you knew how to fix it, didn't you?'

'Yes.'

'But he wouldn't let you and you knew what the consequences would be. The collapse of the bank and possibly prison for you. But it didn't have to be that way, did it? If only he'd given you the time.'

Cubitt said nothing.

'That's what you want to believe. That's what you've believed for years. That was the injustice inflicted on you by Alexander Mount. Except that wasn't true. He knew you had deluded yourself, in the way you continue to delude yourself still. That you hadn't really done any wrong and that it could be fixed. But he was a man who had earned his reputation in the City. Not someone who'd been given his position and the custody of millions of pounds of other people's money as a birthright. He knew numbers in a way you could never understand, and he saw that the position was irretrievable. There was a hole of billions of pounds from which the bank would never recover.'

'He didn't have to do what he did,' replied Cubitt visibly tensing up at the injustice of it all.

'What did he do?'

'He went to the clients.'

'To tell them you'd lost their money. Of course he did, or else he would have been complicit in your fraud.'

'Had I had the time I could've sorted it,' Cubitt maintained.

'As you have quite rightly pointed out, I'm no expert in financial matters. But from all the several articles I've read, written by well-respected financial analysts and academics about the fall of Cubitt's, I haven't come across one who would agree with you. You created an irretrievable situation from which there was no escape.'

Cubitt made no response.

'Your father. He's disinherited you. Is that right?'

'Correct.'

'That must've hurt. What will happen to Coxton Hall after his death?' Cross pushed.

'I have no idea. I assume it will go to Rosemary.'

'Have you tried to reconcile with your father?' Cross asked.

Cubitt thought about this for a moment. Cross wondered whether he was deciding to answer. Whether it was a private matter.

'Several times.'

'Why?'

'He's my father.'

'Were you successful?' Cross asked.

'Have you spoken to him?' Cubitt asked in return.

'Of course.'

'Was Rosemary present?'

'She was.'

'Then you will only have half the story. I'm his only son. To be out of contact with me was eventually too much for him. As he got older, had a few health scares, his attitude changed. He finally reached out. We spoke. We're now in touch. In fact we had lunch together in London at the end of last year.'

'Presumably Rosemary is unaware of this,' said Ottey.

'What do you think?'

'She doesn't know,' said Cross.

'She is unaware, yes. He lives in constant fear of that woman. It's awful,' Cubitt replied, with the first bit of emotion he'd shown in the interview.

'Has he forgiven you?' Cross asked.

'For what?'

'The downfall of the bank. The destruction of three hundred years of family history,' Cross said.

'There's nothing to forgive, Sergeant. You probably don't know as much about the facts of the collapse of Cubitt's as you should,' Cubitt replied pompously. 'My father can see that now, which says a lot about his character. His life was ruined at a point when he could reasonably have looked forward to a happy retirement, having done his job as best he could. Not see everything crumble round his ears end in disgrace and leave him with a tarnished reputation.'

'And in your view that was Alexander Mount's fault?' asked Cross.

'That man cost me everything. I lost everything because of him. My family, my career, my father. All of it gone. I live in a rented flat, for God's sake. I don't even own the roof over my head,' Cubitt protested.

'What's the worst part of it?' asked Cross.

'There is no worst part. I wish I could make it up to all of them but I don't see how I can,' Cubitt responded mournfully.

'Is that why you went to the abbey? To confront Mount?' asked Cross.

'I don't know.'

'Oh, but you do, Mr Cubitt. You know exactly why you were there and what you wanted,' said Cross.

'Oh yes? And why was that?'

'Money.'

'What money?'

'Alexander Mount's money.'

'What are you talking about? He was a monk.'

'Exactly. He had become a monk. But you knew for a fact he'd made a small fortune before he entered the abbey, and you began to wonder what had happened to it all. He owned a flat in London outright. Had a Ferrari. But there wasn't much else he could've spent his money on. Not with the hours he put in. He had to have a fortune stashed away somewhere. His only living relative was his brother, a priest, who certainly hadn't been given Alexander's fortune. So where was it? That's what you wanted to find out from Dominic, wasn't it?'

'No comment.'

'As you've told us, you don't own any property, your car is a lease. Your company has shown an operating loss for the last couple of years according to Companies House. Your only employee, your secretary, hasn't been paid in months. You saw Alexander Mount on the TV and you thought, "He's a monk? He owes me." Where's all his cash?' Cross concluded by saying.

'No comment.'

'That's what you were after, wasn't it? That's what you told Frankie Davis, wasn't it?' asked Cross.

A look of resigned defeat passed over Cubitt's face.

'You should know he's been arrested and charged with kidnap and possibly accessory to murder, or indeed murder,' said Ottey.

'He told us you called him and asked him to abduct Brother Dominic from the abbey and take him to a cottage. An abandoned, overgrown cottage on your father's estate. The one you had use of when you were still in contact with your father. The cottage was the scene of Brother Dominic's beating and consequent death. Davis was initially reluctant to speak and was quite uncooperative. But the possibility of being charged with murder seemed to make him a little more loquacious. The reason for his holding out as long as he did wasn't out of any sense of loyalty. People like him are rarely loyal, in my experience. He was holding out for the possibility of a large payday, which you had promised him. Telling him who Brother Dominic was, and how he'd ripped you off millions of pounds when you both worked in the city. That he was the reason the bank collapsed, and it was payback time. You persuaded your gullible cellmate that he was righting a wrong. You promised him a six-figure sum if he simply abducted the monk and found out where the money was. Nicholas Cubitt, did you ask Frankie Davis to abduct Brother Dominic Augustus from St Eustace's abbey on March the thirty-first?' Cross ended by asking.

'No comment.'

'You couldn't get it out of him at the abbey, so you had him grabbed and attempted to beat it out of him,' Ottey clarified.

'No comment.'

'But Davis got the information out of him. Dominic had bought a painting. You then went to the cottage but, unfortunately, killed him before he was able to tell you that the really valuable painting was hidden underneath the Victorian Virgin Mary. Is that not the case?'

'I'd like to speak with my lawyer.'

51

'My client admits involvement in the abduction of Brother Dominic Augustus on March the thirty-first. That he instructed Frankie Davis to take him to a cottage on his estranged father's estate, with the purpose of eliciting information from him about his wealth. He wasn't aware of the methods Davis intended to employ. My client also wasn't there. He received the information about the painting from Davis and that was the end of his involvement,' said Cubitt's lawyer reading from a sheet of paper.

'Do you really expect us to believe that?' asked Ottey.

'It's entirely up to you what you believe,' replied the lawyer.

'If that's the case, when did you become aware of Brother Dominic's death?' Cross asked Cubitt.

'I heard about it on the news just like everyone else,' Cubitt replied.

'How did you react?'

'I was shocked.'

Cross thought for a moment.

'What was the plan? After Davis had got what you wanted. What was he supposed to do with the victim?' Cross went on.

'Take him back to the abbey and leave him there.'

'Wouldn't he then be able to implicate you?'

'I wasn't there. I wasn't involved.'

'Oh, come on. Do you really think he wouldn't put two and two together?' asked Ottey. 'Seems like a completely flawed plan to me. You meant for him to be killed.'

'I did not.'

'Did you ask Davis if he'd taken Dominic back to the abbey?' asked Cross.

'I did not. I assumed that's what had happened,' replied Cubitt.

'What did you do when you found out the monk was dead?' Cross went on.

'Nothing.'

'You didn't call Davis and ask him what had happened? Why Dominic was dead?'

'What good would that have done me? Why would I make contact with him? It would only link me to him,' replied Cubitt.

His lawyer put his hand on his arm, leant over and whispered something in his ear.

'So, what exactly do you think happened?' asked Cross. Again, he noticed, Cubitt paused for thought.

'You should ask Davis,' Cubitt replied.

'We already have. He says that Dominic was alive when he left him.'

Cubitt said nothing.

'Before you then arrived,' Cross added.

'How did you know the cottage was unoccupied?' asked Ottey.

'I'm still in touch with Charlotte. She lets me know what's going on at home.'

'You still call it home?' Cross observed.

'What else am I supposed to call it?'

'Davis told us that he didn't leave Dominic on his own. Someone else was there,' Cross went on.

'Who?' Cubitt asked.

'He won't say,' Cross answered.

'There was another car,' said Ottey. 'His brother, Luke Davis, had fallen asleep. When he woke up there was another car there and the driver of that car was still in the cottage when they left.'

Cubitt said nothing.

'Here's what I think happened,' Ottey went on. 'Davis beats the info out of Dominic and then left you with him. I don't believe he didn't see the other driver. It was you. But you wanted more. After everything this man had done to you, you were so angry. Seven years in prison, left with nothing when you came out. It all got too much for you. There he was, right in front of you. These things happen so quickly. In an instant. One blow to the head and it's all over. They're dead. You didn't mean it. But it's done. Is that what happened, Nick?'

'No comment.'

'Mr Cubitt, you should know that we retrieved a quad bike and trailer from your father's estate,' Cross informed him.

Cubitt said nothing. 'We've found blood on the floor of the trailer. It's currently being analysed. But we're fairly confident it will be a match to Brother Dominic.'

Silence.

'There was also damage to one side of the bike that seems consistent with its sliding down into a ditch. Our forensic geologists are currently analysing the mud on the side of the bike and comparing it with samples taken from the ditch where Dominic's body was found. It always amazes me how much evidence can be gleaned from flora and fauna and soil. Forensic analysis has become so advanced and detailed,' observed Cross.

'The evidence is stacking up against you, Nick. Why don't you just tell us what happened?' said Ottey.

'I did not kill that man,' Cubitt said slowly and emphatically.

And that was all he had to offer for the rest of the interview. Hour after hour of 'no comment' was all they got out of him.

The CPS felt they had enough to charge him with murder and kidnap. He was remanded in custody and charged. The case was closed. Carson congratulated them all on a good result.

'Even now Cubitt can't take responsibility for his actions,' Ottey commented at the end of the day.

'He's probably rewritten the narrative again and convinced himself that it was someone else's fault,' added Mackenzie.

52

The team went to the pub to celebrate the conclusion of the case. It was a Thursday, so Cross went to his usual organ practice at Stephen's church. Even if it hadn't been a Thursday he still wouldn't have gone to the pub. He never did. He found it too noisy and on occasions like this, way too rambunctious. His mother would be at the church tonight. He couldn't believe another month had passed. He'd been so wrapped up in the case and the fixing of St Eustace's organ he hadn't noticed time sweeping by.

He let himself into the church and put his bike just inside the door. His way of celebrating the satisfactory end to the case that night would be to play an uplifting piece. He'd chosen Jehan Alain's *Litanies*. He put the sheet music out, set his stops and began to play. For the next hour he stopped and started as he tried to learn the piece. He became completely lost in the music. Thoughts of the Brother Dominic case, something which would normally occupy his thoughts for weeks after its conclusion, drifted out of his consciousness. He was in his place, the organ loft at Stephen's church, which at times like this seemed to be the safest and most enjoyable place for him to be in, in the world.

At the end of the hour, he was satisfied with the progress he'd made. The fact that there was more to learn and finesse made him very content. It meant he had something to look forward to next week. He walked down into the nave of the church and found Stephen there, alone.

'Have I got my weeks wrong? Shouldn't my mother be here?' he asked.

'Yes, but she thought she wouldn't come this week,' Stephen replied.

'Oh, very well. Goodnight,' replied Cross and started to make his way down the aisle to his bike. No thought of asking why she wasn't there or indeed, more importantly, perhaps, how Stephen was feeling, not just about the successful conclusion of the case involving his brother's murder, but also about how he might be dealing with his loss.

'Why don't you stay for a cup of tea and some cake?' said Stephen.

Cross stopped.

'What kind of cake?'

'A rather spectacular lemon drizzle cake, even if I say so myself,' replied Stephen who had already turned and was walking towards the side door, confident that Cross would follow. His lemon drizzle cake was pretty famous.

When he walked into Stephen's kitchen Cross noticed the cake was already centre table on a doily and cake stand. There were two cups of tea set out. He rarely stayed for tea or even a chat after his Thursday practices, unless his mother was there. Something about the situation – his mother's absence, Stephen's expectation he would stay for tea – suddenly struck him as being both orchestrated and premeditated.

'What do you want?' he asked as he sat down warily, as if he wasn't sure whether he was going to have to make a bolt for the door at any given moment.

'Why should I want anything?' Stephen asked innocently.

'My mother's unexplained absence from her regular monthly visit, together with your preparations for tea and cake in the obvious certain knowledge that I would be staying after practice, would suggest you want something,' Cross replied.

'Which of course is why you're a detective.'

'It has nothing to do with why I'm a detective. I attended Hendon, spent years in uniform before graduating to CID. That is why I'm a detective.'

'I thought we'd talk about, or rather I'd give you the chance to talk about, how you feel with your mother being more present in your life,' said Stephen.

'I have no feelings about it, one way or the other,' Cross replied.

'We both know that's not true.'

'In point of fact only I can know that. You can merely surmise,' said Cross, taking his first bite out of the lemon drizzle. It was sublime. Certainly worth ten minutes of his time, while Stephen tried to engage him in this emotional twaddle.

'You've seemed quite discombobulated since Christine reappeared,' Stephen pointed out.

'Well, I think that's hardly surprising, bearing in mind you kept springing her on me unannounced,' Cross protested.

'That's true. But you still seemed a little put-out after that.'

'I'm not one for change, as we both know. I find it quite difficult and disconcerting. It takes me a little while to adjust. I'm in that period of adjustment at the moment.'

'You don't like change and yet it was you who reached out to Christine after forty years.'

'I did. I had some – misguided in light of what later transpired had happened – notion that I needed to demonstrate to her that everything had worked out for me and Raymond. I can also see, now, that I didn't think it through entirely,' Cross agreed.

'Do you regret it?'

Cross thought for a moment.

'I don't regret it as such. I just didn't consider the possibility that, from that moment on, she would want to be a part of my life and see more of me.'

'And how do you feel about that now?' asked Stephen.

'What I feel is neither here nor there. She wishes to see me, and we've made arrangements so that she can do that. I have no objections to it.'

'Do you want to see her?'

'I don't think I can answer that yet.'

'Okay.'

Stephen now decided to change tack in a way that he knew could possibly bring the conversation to an abrupt conclusion.

'What do you think about the circumstances which led to her leaving you?' he asked.

'I think she was in a difficult situation. Impossible even. I can't and certainly don't blame her for that decision.'

'And what about Raymond?'

'That, I confess, is quite complicated. When it comes to life, I don't like complicated. I don't deal with it well. Which is ironic as I seem to thrive on complications at work, in other people's lives, in investigations. Interpreting and unravelling those complications gives me a great deal of satisfaction. It's also something I appear to excel at,' said Cross, not realising that out of anyone else's mouth, this would've come across as fantastically arrogant. Somehow with him it was different. 'Complications in my own life are something else entirely,' he finished by saying.

'Why?' Stephen probed.

'Because I seem incapable of making sense of them when it comes to anything that affects me. I don't react to them or seem capable of viewing them clearly, like neurotypical people. I have to make on-the-spot calculations about how to respond and experience tells us that more often than not I get it wrong. Sometimes terribly wrong.'

'Can you explain?' Stephen asked.

'Take the situation with my mother and father. My father is one of the only people in the world who comes anywhere near to understanding how I am. He tolerates things other people view as objectionable or offensive in the way I behave and speak. At times when other people are upset by me he understands what I'm trying to do. He understands how difficult it is for me sometimes to communicate effectively with people in certain situations. But when I see him with my mother now, I find it complicated. I find myself wondering whether he, and by implication I, behaved badly to her. But I don't know the answer to that yet. I find myself imagining what her life must've been like because of what happened.'

'Wouldn't it be easier just to ask her?'

'Well, it's very personal and possibly intrusive,' Cross pointed out.

'She's your mother.'

Cross thought for a moment. He really wanted to articulate what he was about to say as best as he could, with as little chance of it being misinterpreted as possible.

'When I look at them now, I see memories of a terrible time together in their lives, at the centre of which is me. Whatever they say, my being the way I was as a child, the way I am, had to have had a bearing on her decision to leave,' Cross explained.

'I think that is possibly true,' Stephen agreed.

'So, in effect I am responsible for the great sadness in their lives.'

'This is where we disagree. Your parents' marriage was an impossible situation because your father was in love with another man. He was incredibly brave to acknowledge it at the time. She was equally brave and immaculately behaved in a situation which was more about the times they lived in, than each other. But the decision they made ensured that they could go on and try to live fulfilled lives. Such a mature decision in two so young. They know now, and acknowledge the fact that, however terrible it was at the time, they both made the right one,' said Stephen.

'Do you think?'

'I know.'

'How can you know?'

'Because I speak to them, George.'

'I think my father feels terrible about keeping the truth from me for so long. Letting me believe she abandoned us,' said Cross quietly.

'Which was his way of protecting you. As a father he would do anything to do that, even if it meant not telling you the truth about who he was, what Ron was to him. Imagine the sacrifice that took for him. All because he's your father. That's what a lot of fathers do, George.'

Cross considered this for a moment. But in truth it actually made him think about the Brother Dominic case, and Julian Cubitt. Had he missed something there?

'You should talk to him about it,' said Stephen.

'We did. Or at least I think we did,' replied Cross, coming back to the present briefly.

They sat there for a while in silence as Cross thought about his father.

'I think it's probably best left alone. All of it,' he said finally.

'Why?'

'Because that's how I cope best. That's how I deal with things.'

'By not dealing with them at all? That's just idiotic,' said Stephen.

Cross looked genuinely shocked by this statement.

'Can we just look at the current situation? Forget about the past,' Stephen continued.

'Isn't that exactly what I just said?' asked Cross, confused.

'I don't mean like that. I mean stick a pin in it.'

'Stick a pin in what?' asked Cross, getting more confused by the second.

'Your mother likes to see you every month. She loves to hear you play the organ. She thinks it's wonderful you taught yourself how to play. She loves to hear and read about your work in the local paper. She's thrilled you love her cupcakes,' Stephen began.

'I wouldn't go that far. I did express an admiration for them, admittedly. I think "love" is going a little too far,' said Cross.

'I don't need to tell you about Raymond,' Stephen continued, ignoring him. 'You know him better than anyone. Does he have regrets about the way he dealt with the situation with your mother? Yes. He's awash with guilt. But he's actually been really pleased to see her after all these years and she, it turns out, is just as pleased to see him.'

'But why? After all that happened?' asked Cross.

'It's so simple. But you really don't see it, do you, George? It's because they, together, made you and that's something they're inestimably proud of. Something no one can take away from them. Not even you, George, old thing.'

When Cross left that night, he was thinking about his father and what he'd done to protect his son. This led to him wondering how far Julian Cubitt might go as a father to protect Nick.

53

The sight of Cross in his office, door closed, with a determined look of concentration on his face, was not a welcome one to any member of the team, the morning after lengthy alcohol-fuelled celebrations in a public house to mark the successful conclusion of a case. The murder team noted it as one, with dread. This was because it could only mean one thing: Cross was reviewing the investigation. He always did this before he prepared his files for court. It drove everyone mad as more often than not he'd find something amiss, and more often than not it would seem to them a completely irrelevant detail which made no difference to the outcome of the case. But it was wrong. A mistake, no matter how small, he would insist on putting it right.

He would spend hours, sometimes days, going through every detail of the case they had just closed in minutiae. The leads that had been pursued as well as those not. The interview transcripts of all the suspects and witnesses. Witness statements. The coroner's report. His notebook. He would construct a new timeline of the crime and make sure there were no inconsistencies. Check the call records of everyone connected to the case. Even when most of the team in the MCU were convinced it was a clear open and shut case, as with Nicholas Cubitt, they would all be in a state of heightened expectation of more work or just plain awkward questions about why protocols weren't adhered to, or things, to his mind, not done properly. For the most part they tended to be small things that just needed straightening out for court. But every now and then he would come up with something none of them had noticed, something that perplexed him and brought the whole investigation into question for him. Some of his discoveries were so seemingly mundane that people made the mistake of trying to get him to just ignore them and sweep them under the carpet. After all, they did have their man or woman. The problem was that once he'd found an inconsistency, he just wouldn't let go until it had been resolved. He did this even if it meant reopening a closed investigation, inevitably in the face of stern opposition from Carson or higher above. But now and then he came across something that, despite its first appearance as something innocuous, called the entire case into question. The successful conclusion of Brother Dominic's murder had seemed a slam dunk to most of the murder team, despite Cubitt's continuing insistence that he was innocent.

Ottey knew better than to interrupt Cross when he was like this. He would come to her if he found something. She was also fairly sure he wouldn't find anything in this case. It had all slotted into place quite nicely. She wasn't sure Nicholas Cubitt meant to kill Dominic. But he had. Her confidence was somewhat short-lived as later that morning she saw Cross stand bolt upright, as if something on his desk had given him an electric shock. He stood there staring at the desk as if he couldn't believe what he was looking at. Ottey got up and started to walk over, before receiving the inevitable summons. But he'd left his office with his bicycle gear before she reached it and strode out of the open area. There was a collective sigh from everyone in the team, including Mackenzie. What the hell had he found? It didn't look like it was anything minor. Ottey quickly grabbed her car keys, coat and bag. She managed to intercept him in the bike shed by the front door of the building.

'Mind telling me what's going on?' she asked, positioning herself between his bike and the exit.

'Nicholas Cubitt didn't kill Brother Dominic,' he said with great authority and the tiniest bit of drama. He always secretly enjoyed these moments.

'What? So where are you off to? Going to set him free?'

'Don't be ridiculous, you know very well I have no such authority. What is more he is still guilty of conspiracy to kidnap,' he replied curtly.

'I was joking,' she said wearily.

'As I think I've mentioned before, a necessary requirement for a joke is wit.'

'Oh, do shut up. Where are you off to?'

'The mortuary,' he replied, despite the fact that he thought she was being unnecessarily rude. 'I need to speak to Dr Hawkins.'

'All right. I'll take you.'

They drove in silence. She didn't want to ask him anything, as she could sense that he was still trying to fully work through whatever it was he'd found.

'DS Cross!' he announced, warrant card held above his head as he walked into the mortuary. Ottey rolled her eyes at Dr Clare Hawkins as the pathologist steeled herself for whatever was about to follow.

'What have I got wrong this time?' she asked wearily.

'Time of death,' Cross stated.

'What of it?' she asked.

'Brother Dominic's time of death. We've all been working on the assumption that it was March the thirty-first. The date of his abduction,' he replied.

'I thought you didn't entertain assumptions,' she replied.

'As a rule, I don't, and what I'm about to say proves why it's unwise to make them during any investigation. However, this one seems to have slipped through unnoticed.'

'It happens,' she said.

'Not to me.'

'You know something, you'd be quite objectionable if you weren't so charming and sweet. Please elaborate,' she asked teasingly.

Cross was stalled momentarily and looked to Ottey for help. She mouthed, 'Sarcasm.'

'You didn't give a specific time of death as it was difficult to determine,' he said.

'I think I gave a twenty-four-hour window, unless I'm mistaken,' she said.

'Correct. On the evidence we were presented with we deduced that Dominic had been killed on the evening of March the thirty-first. After he'd given his killer the information he was after,' Cross continued.

'Okay...'

'But according to your report he had two types of injury, did he not?'

'No. He had several types of injury,' she contradicted him.

'Of course, but essentially there were two main categories – bruising caused by fists, and fractured, or broken, bones caused by some sort of twisted implement which we have yet to find.'

'Correct.'

'The breaks to his bones and the skull were the fatal injuries.'

'Yes.'

'Which has to mean that the bruising occurred at least eighteen hours before. They had time to go yellow. Which as we know means there were two separate assaults, the first of which was on the evening of March the thirty-first, the second at least eighteen hours later at some time on the first of April.'

'Yes, that would make sense,' she replied cautiously.

'It was all in your report, Doctor. We just missed it,' Cross said.

'So, Nicholas Cubitt went back the next day and finished him off?' asked Ottey, thinking out loud.

'That would be a reasonable assumption were it not for the fact that Nicholas Cubitt's phone was being used on the first of April in London,' replied Cross.

'Maybe he didn't have it with him,' Ottey suggested.

'That seems unlikely. We need to find out where Cubitt was when Davis called him on the thirty-first,' said Cross.

'Because if Nick arrived in the second vehicle why would he need to call him?' said Ottey, thinking out loud.

The answer came back a couple of hours later. When Nick Cubitt took the call from Davis, he was indeed in London.

'Which means he wasn't in the second car,' said Ottey.

'Exactly. So, if it wasn't Nicholas Cubitt, who was it?' asked Cross.

When they got back to the office they marched across the open area of the MCU with some purpose. In the car back they had made a call to Nicholas Cubitt's now unemployed secretary Mandy. In their first conversation with her they'd only asked her about the night of the thirty-first when she wasn't able to provide her employer with an alibi. They now asked about the first. Nicholas Cubitt was with her. She remembered. It was April Fool's day. They went to a restaurant for dinner in London, after which he stayed the night with her in her flat. They'd been in a relationship for some time, but obviously not any more.

'Do you think he did it? Killed the monk?' Ottey couldn't help asking her on the speaker phone in the car, even though she knew Cross would be quietly seething at such a speculative and irrelevant question.

'Well, you obviously do. Why would I think any different to the police?' she asked.

'Interesting she doesn't defend him in any way,' Ottey commented after the call was over.

'Lends credence to the alibi she gave him for the first,' Cross observed, while being reminded of the blind faith some people had in the police. A standard he always tried to hold himself to.

Carson came into Cross's office without knocking which was

something Cross hated. Carson definitely did it on purpose at times, thought Ottey.

'What's going on?' he asked.

'Nothing,' replied Ottey innocently.

'Rumour has it he's off on one of his wild goose chases again,' he continued, referring to Cross as if he wasn't in the room.

'It's not a goose chase,' replied Ottey.

'I'm merely putting my files and reports in order for court,' Cross said quietly.

'Really? Is that it?' Carson asked, sounding surprised that his network of office informants had got it wrong.

'It is,' replied Cross.

'Well, that's a relief. Everyone upstairs is pleased we've put this one to bed relatively quickly. I'll leave you to it then,' he said and turned to leave.

'Oh, one more thing you should know before you leave,' said Cross.

'Yes?' replied the now amenable DCI Carson.

'Nicholas Cubitt is innocent of the murder of Brother Dominic Augustus,' Cross said.

'What?' Carson spluttered in disbelief.

Ottey almost burst out laughing. Cross's timing in these situations was always impeccably comic, despite the fact that he had absolutely no intention of it being so.

'Guilty of kidnap, or conspiracy of kidnap and unlawful imprisonment, but not of murder,' Cross summed up.

Carson looked stunned.

'Why do you always do this?' he asked.

'What?'

'Fiddle with things when there's no need to fiddle with them,' Carson said, flummoxed to such an extent that this was the best expression he could come up with.

'If it's any consolation I too thought that Nicholas Cubitt was guilty and was happy for him to be charged,' Cross said.

'It is no consolation. What am I going to tell the higher-ups?' he pleaded.

'You should tell them that in your usual dogged pursuit of truth and the service of justice, no stone is ever left unturned. Even after someone has been charged. Because, to your mind, the only thing worse than an innocent man going to prison for a murder he didn't commit, is the fact that the real culprit is still walking around free,' said Cross.

Carson stood there for a moment thinking that what Cross had just said did, in fact, make a great deal of sense and did have a certain ring to it. Who upstairs could argue with that sentiment?

'Any chance you could write that down for me?' he asked Cross.

54

Ottey and Cross arrived at Coxton Hall later that morning. Charlotte let them in to the house and led them to the kitchen where they sat at the table as she made some tea. Julian and Rosemary Cubitt were walking in the kitchen garden gathering some vegetables for dinner.

'I saw on the news that Nick's been charged with murder,' Charlotte said as she filled the kettle. It was as if she wanted the sound of the water cascading into the kettle to drown out what she was saying. She didn't even want to hear herself say it.

'That's correct,' replied Cross.

'Well, you've made a big mistake.'

'What makes you say that?'

'I know my Nick. It's just not something he'd do.'

'But he's admitted to kidnapping the monk,' Ottey pointed out.

'Really?'

Charlotte seemed genuinely shocked by this.

'Do you find that surprising?' asked Cross.

'Well, yes.'

'Is it enough to make you reconsider whether he could go further and kill a man? The fact that he had him kidnapped, taped to a chair and savagely beaten?' he asked.

'He didn't,' she protested.

'He very much did and what is more, has told us that himself.'

'Why?'

'Well, maybe that's something you can ask him when you visit him in prison, which on past experience, I'm sure you'll do,' said Cross.

Charlotte thought for a moment. She looked like she was about to say something but then had second thoughts about it.

'What is it, Charlotte? Is there something you'd like to tell us?'

The kettle boiled and she poured the water into the teapot.

'Did you see someone use the quad bike on the night of April the first?' Cross asked.

'Yes,' she answered without turning round.

'Who was it, Charlotte? You must tell us,' Ottey urged her.

She turned and was about to speak when Rosemary and Julian Cubitt walked into the kitchen. Him as usual with a walking stick, her with a trug full of colourful fresh vegetables. She handed it to Charlotte who put it to one side. Something Rosemary Cubitt could easily have done for herself, Cross thought.

'Detectives,' said Julian Cubitt. 'Have there been any developments?'

He sat at the table and put his walking stick to one side.

'Nicholas has been charged with the kidnap and murder of Brother Dominic,' Cross informed them.

'Yes, we read that. There was no need for you to come all this way to tell us,' said Rosemary.

A phone rang. Charlotte picked up a handset from the French dresser.

'That's the gate,' explained Julian. 'Probably a delivery.'

'Hello? Hello?' said Charlotte but the phone kept ringing. 'I think the batteries may have gone in this.'

'No, that's the wrong one. I don't know where it's come from,' said Rosemary pointing to another identical one on the sideboard. 'Try that one.'

Charlotte went over, picked it up and answered it. The ringing stopped. She stepped outside to speak to whoever it was.

'We needed to come out because there are one or two things we have to clear up,' said Ottey.

Charlotte reappeared. She looked distinctly worried.

'Who was it, Charlotte?' asked Julian.

'More police,' she replied.

'Really?' Julian commented and looked back at Cross for some sort of explanation.

'We visited Frankie Davis in prison yesterday. Does that name mean anything to you, Mr Cubitt?'

'It does not.'

'He was the man who beat Brother Dominic, taped to a chair, before you discovered him in the kitchen of the cottage on the night of March the thirty-first,' said Cross.

'I did no such thing,' replied Cubitt.

What was more interesting to Cross was the fact that Cubitt's wife didn't say anything, nor react in any way to this information.

'The farmer at the end of the lane who alerted you to our presence the other day has since told us he'd called you to tell you he'd seen a car outside the cottage that night.'

Cubitt still said nothing. Then, 'He was dead when I found him. The monk.'

'Why didn't you call the police?'

'Because I knew who the monk was.'

'Who was it?'

'Alexander Mount.'

'So, what difference did that make?'

'He knew it had to be his son. After all, it had been his cottage. He blamed Alexander for what happened to the bank,' said Rosemary. Julian gave her an instinctive, warning glance. Cross looked at her for a moment then back to Julian.

'Did you blame him?' asked Cross.

'No, of course not. The blame lay fairly and squarely with Nicholas and he's more than paid for it.'

'By going to prison?' Cross clarified.

'That and everything else. He lost everything,' said Julian.

'So, he had a lot of anger towards Alexander,' said Ottey.

'It would certainly seem so. But I have no idea what he was trying to achieve with this course of action.'

'So, you knew it had to be him,' she went on.

'Of course. It was too much of a coincidence. The fact that it was Alex, and the location,' replied Rosemary.

'Unless you had no need to put it together. Unless you already knew,' said Cross.

'How could he know? He hadn't been in touch with his son for years. Not since he's been in prison,' said Rosemary.

'But that's not actually correct is it, Mr Cubitt?' said Cross. 'You'd been in regular contact with him since you reached out to him eighteen months ago.'

'Julian, is this true?' asked Rosemary.

'Yes,' he replied quietly.

'Why?' she asked.

'Because he's my son. Because I'm not getting any younger,' he replied, with an edge to his voice.

'He ruined your life,' she protested.

'For which he has paid dearly.'

'Did Nick discuss his intentions with you regarding Brother Dominic?' asked Cross.

'He did not,' Julian replied.

'Did he tell you he'd discovered Alexander Mount living as a monk at St Eustace's Abbey?' Cross went on.

'He did not.'

'So, the beaten Brother Dominic came as a complete surprise?'

'Obviously.'

'Then why not call the police?' asked Ottey.

'Because I knew that would end with him back in prison and he wouldn't be able to cope going through all that again.'

'So, you decided to cover it up?' she said.

'Yes. I decided to get rid of the body.'

'How?'

'I have a tenant farmer who runs a small abattoir on his farm.

He has an incinerator on the site. I was going to use that. No one would ever know.'

'Did you move it then and there?' asked Ottey.

'No. I went home to think it through. I went back the following night.'

'The first?' Cross asked, just to make sure.

'Yes.'

'How were you going to move the body?'

'With our quad bike and trailer. The trailer has a small electrical winch.'

'So, what happened?' asked Cross.

'I went back with the quad bike and trailer the next night. I winched the body into the trailer and went down the lanes towards the farm. But I had an accident and ended up in a ditch. I couldn't get the body back into the trailer. I was exhausted. So I left him there and that was that. Not my finest moment,' he said mournfully.

They all sat there in silence for a moment, as they digested this information.

'That all makes sense, Mr Cubitt. It's all very plausible,' Cross finally said. 'But a couple of things puzzle me.'

Cross frowned as if he were really trying to see the events of that night as Cubitt had just described them.

'Mrs Cubitt, were you aware of what your husband was up to that night?' asked Cross.

'She was not,' answered Julian before his wife had a chance to.

'He hadn't told you about the body in the cottage?'

'No.'

There was a pause. Charlotte was still standing, unnoticed, by the counter. It was like she was glued to the spot. Cross turned to her and she flinched.

'Mrs Hoskins, do you remember what I was asking you before Mr and Mrs Cubitt returned from the garden?' Cross said.

'Yes,' she replied nervously.

'Who did you see driving the quad bike and trailer away from the barn on the night of April the first?'

The woman hesitated.

'Charlotte?' asked Ottey quietly.

'It was her. Rosemary. Mrs Cubitt was driving it.'

'You're quite sure?' asked Cross.

'Yes. Neil saw her as well.'

Cross nodded slightly and turned back to the table. He looked like he was trying to piece this new piece of information into the narrative as explained by Julian Cubitt. He looked up finally.

'Frankie Davis says Brother Dominic was alive when he left him,' Cross began.

'Well, he would say that, wouldn't he?' said Rosemary.

'He left because he heard another car approach. It was your car, although he couldn't tell us that. The person who could confirm it, though, was the farmer. He saw you arrive and the other car leaving. The next night you went back to dispose of the body, but you discovered he wasn't dead and so you killed him,' Cross summed up.

'Julian Cubitt, I'm arresting you on suspicion of the murder of Brother Dominic Augustus,' said Ottey.

'But he was dead when I found him!' spluttered Cubitt.

'Rosemary Cubitt, I'm arresting you on suspicion of conspiracy to murder. DS Ottey will read you your rights,' said Cross as he left the room.

Poor Charlotte was still standing there frozen. Not knowing what to do.

'I'm going to speak with your husband,' said Cross getting up and leaving. He walked across the grounds to find Hoskins who confirmed what his wife had said. It was Rosemary Cubitt on the quad bike.

'So, what are we supposed to do now?' he asked Cross desperately. 'We've worked here all our adult lives.'

'I don't know,' replied Cross and reflected that the victims of this sequence of events and the consequences for them were wide reaching.

'The property will probably need caretakers,' Cross observed. 'While they're inside.'

'After we've just dobbed them in? I don't think so,' said Hoskins.

'Good point,' replied Cross.

The Cubitts were taken away in two separate police cars back to the MCU. Cross turned to Charlotte in the kitchen.

'Do you have a bin liner?' he asked.

She gave him one. He put on a pair of latex gloves and went to the front and back doors where Cubitt kept his collection of walking sticks. He placed them all in the bag. A couple of them had hefty, twisted handles. He then went back into the kitchen and picked up the phone that hadn't worked for the estate gates. He took off the battery cover. Inside was a sticker on which was written 'Abbey Gates'.

55

Carson was in his usual customary rush to charge Cubitt. He always seemed to do this, but Cross didn't see the point of it. They had twenty-four hours in which to question the Cubitts, before needing to get an extension. What was the benefit of charging them before then? Carson reminded Cross of a schoolboy in class with his hand always in the air first to answer a question, jumping up and down in his seat and grunting with effort to make sure the teacher saw him first.

'I'll get straight onto the CPS about charging him,' he told the group.

'Charging him with what?' asked Cross.

'Murder. The reason you arrested him, George.'

'It would be better to wait,' Cross went on.

'Why?' asked Carson, barely able to conceal his frustration.

'We know that in all probability one of them killed Brother Dominic. The problem is, we don't know which one.'

'What are you talking about?' Carson asked.

'We can't say for certain which one of them it was.'

'You found blood on one of his walking sticks, the twisted end of which would seem to be a match for the injuries the monk sustained,' said Carson, as if pointing out the obvious to a small child.

'The walking stick does indeed belong to Cubitt and would seem to be the murder weapon. But we don't as yet know which one of them employed it to kill the monk. The quad bike is severely damaged down the right-hand side of the machine. We know Rosemary was driving it, so why didn't she receive any injuries in the accident? It's another inconsistency that needs examining,' Cross summed up.

'And because of that you're saying we should hold off charging?' asked Carson.

'Excellent,' Cross replied.

'What?' asked Carson mystified.

'I appear to have made myself clear,' replied Cross, causing a familiar chorus of laughter which Carson was rapidly tiring of.

Julian Cubitt had been joined by his lawyer. A formidable woman in a blue suit with a pearl necklace and matching earrings. Her hair looked like it was so firmly set it would break the teeth of a stainless-steel comb. Cross organised his files then looked up at Cubitt.

'Percy Simmonds,' he began.

'What about him?' Cubitt replied. The conversation now had a very different tone to the ones they'd had previously around Cubitt's kitchen table. He was less defensive, more on the offense.

'He's your family solicitor. Is that correct? The solicitor who provided you with Mrs Ingham here.'

'Yes.'

'How often do you meet with Mr Simmonds?' Cross asked.

'Generally, twice a year.'

'At the house?' Cross asked.

'Yes, he comes over for lunch.'

'And you meet him with your wife?'

'Yes, she's involved in all aspects of our finances.'

'So, never any reason really for you to visit their offices in Bath?' Cross went on.

'No.'

'Then what was the purpose of your three visits there since May of last year?' Cross asked.

'A few things cropped up, that's all,' Cubitt replied.

'Did Rosemary accompany you on those visits?'

'She did not, as I recall.'

People always said 'I recall', when they wanted to imply whatever is being asked of them is of little or no importance to them, Cross had noticed.

'Any particular reason for that?' Cross asked.

'No.'

'Was she aware of the appointment?'

'Probably.'

'But you're not sure.'

'No.'

'Not a problem. We can ask her ourselves,' Cross replied. Cubitt coughed and cleared his throat nervously. 'The last two meetings with Mr Simmonds included a...' he checked his notes, 'Mr Croft.'

'How do you know that?' Cubitt asked.

'Is that correct?' Cross asked, ignoring him.

Cubitt looked nervously at his solicitor, who nodded curtly.

'Yes,' he replied.

'Do you consider yourself to be technically competent when it comes to the internet, with emails and messaging, Zoom calls, all that kind of thing?' asked Cross, seeming to go off topic.

'I get by,' Cubitt replied.

'When it comes to deleting emails?'

'Obviously.'

'So many people think that. Take it for granted. Yet you made a fundamental mistake when deleting emails, which presumably you didn't want your wife to see. Such a simple error, but if it's of any consolation, one so many people seem to make. You deleted your emails to Simmonds forgetting that when you do that, they simply move to a deleted files folder in your mailing app. I find it so puzzling. Who thought that was necessary at the software company? It's as if we can't be trusted to know whether we really intend to delete an email or not. So there's a built-in safety net, a folder that is filled to the brim with emails we thought we'd deleted and exiled to the safety of non-existence. Sent out into the ether as if they were never written. Unfortunately for you, all your emails concerning your secret, well, from your wife, meetings with Percy Simmonds were just sitting there for anyone to find. So we now know that Mr Croft works in the probate department of Mrs Ingham's law firm and that you were making changes to your will. One quite significant one, in fact. The question, though, is who else might have found out by looking in that irritating deleted items folder?'

Cubitt said nothing.

'You altered your will so that on your death Rosemary would be given a year to live in the big house while Weald cottage was restored. She would then move into the cottage and be able to live there for the rest of her natural life, as long as she didn't remarry. She wasn't bequeathed the cottage, as you wanted the estate to remain intact. The estate which you were now leaving in its entirety to your son. Is that correct?'

Cubitt was flummoxed.

'Was it your intention to tell your wife at some point? Or just let her discover it after your death when there would be nothing she could do about it and you wouldn't be around?' Cross asked. 'But the question you really need to ask yourself is, if we were able to find those emails so quickly, couldn't someone else with access to that computer and knowledge of your passwords also be able to find them? Does anyone else have such access?'

Cubitt didn't answer immediately then said, quietly, 'My wife.'

'Ah well, food for thought. Perhaps we should have a break?' Cross suggested, and before he was furnished with an answer, he'd left the room.

'Mr Cubitt, were you aware of Alexander Mount's existence as a monk at St Eustace's Abbey?' Cross began, when they were back in the interview room.

'I already answered this when you asked me at the house,' Cubitt sighed with irritation.

'Mr Cubitt, were you aware of Alexander Mount's existence as a monk at St Eustace's Abbey?' Cross repeated.

'I was not,' Cubitt replied tersely.

'Mr Cubitt, were you aware of Alexander Mount's existence as a monk at St Eustace's Abbey?' Cross said again in exactly the same tone, as if it were the first time he'd asked.

'I just answered that,' Cubitt replied, exasperated, and looking at his lawyer for help.

'Mr Cubitt, were you aware of Alexander Mount's existence as a monk at St Eustace's Abbey?' said Cross.

'What is he doing? My client has already answered the question,' the lawyer asked Ottey, as if Cross wasn't in the room.

'He's simply giving him the opportunity to answer it truthfully,' she replied.

'Mr Cubitt, were you aware of Alexander Mount's existence as a monk at St Eustace's Abbey?' Cross asked again.

'No,' Cubitt replied.

Ottey sighed and pushed an A4 sheet of paper across the table.

'For the tape I'm showing Mr Cubitt a transcript of his texts with Nicholas Cubitt over the past few months. In these texts you can see that your son not only disclosed it to you, but the two of you entered into quite a long thread about it. You express your astonishment,' she said.

'I didn't know he was going to do anything as stupid as this,' he replied.

'These denials, these, well frankly, lies aren't going to look so good for you in court, Mr Cubitt. When you may ask the jury to believe something you've said they may have difficulty, having witnessed how liberal you can be with the truth,' Cross informed him.

Mrs Ingham leant over to Cubitt, causing her pearls to rattle together like a Newton's cradle on a desktop, and whispered in his ear.

'Were you aware of your son's intentions regarding the monk?' Cross asked.

'I knew he was going to the abbey to talk to him.'

'Why was he going to do that?'

'He said he wanted closure.'

'Which is why the identity of the monk in the cottage came as no surprise to you,' said Ottey.

'His identity, no. His presence there and in that condition, absolutely. I was appalled, furious,' he said.

'Did you call Nick?' she asked.

'No. I decided just to clear up his mess and get rid of the body.'

'You weren't curious as to why he'd done this?'

'I thought he'd lost his mind, to be honest with you. Got angry, things had gone too far. Alex had done more than enough damage to this family, I wasn't going to let him do any more,' Cubitt replied.

'Some people, many people, would say that what happened to your family and its business was something you brought entirely upon yourselves,' Cross said.

'Then they obviously don't have a full grasp of the facts,' came the arrogant reply. Cross held his look for a moment, then turned over a couple of pages in his file. He found the page he was searching for and looked surprised at what he found. This, despite the fact that whatever was written on it was in his own hand.

'You maintain that Brother Dominic was dead on March the thirty-first when you found him and you went back the following day with your wife simply to dispose of the body. Unlawfully, I should add,' Cross said.

'Yes,' replied Cubitt.

'Except that's not actually true, is it? It's yet another lie to add to the ever-growing list,' said Cross. Cubitt said nothing. 'You thought he was dead on the thirty-first, presumably because you didn't look closely enough to be able to check. But when you went back on the first you discovered he was very much alive.'

'Barely. He was barely alive,' Cubitt admitted.

'What happened then?' Cross asked.

Cubitt was a little unsure how to answer.

'I can't remember. It's all a bit of a blur,' he replied unconvincingly. 'Look, I'm getting a little tired. Could we have a break please?' he pleaded.

'Mr Cubitt, we know he was killed with one of your walking sticks. The one you had with you that day. It has a large twisted orb for a handle,' Cross continued.

Cubitt said nothing, so Cross piled on the pressure.

'You should also know that we're fairly certain that your wife, with access to your phone and computer, may well have known that you'd changed your will,' said Cross. 'She knew everything was going to Nicholas.'

'In our book, that gives her motive,' said Ottey.

'And you're saying that's why she did it?' Cubitt asked. 'What difference would that possibly make to her situation?'

There was a long pause in the room as they all took in what he'd just said.

'So, you're saying she did kill Brother Dominic?' asked Cross, eventually pouncing on Cubitt's slip.

Cubitt looked at his lawyer desperately. She gave him an imperceptible but encouraging nod. He looked at the ground for a moment, trying to grapple with what to say next.

'Yes. She did,' Cubitt said quietly.

'What happened? Exactly,' Cross pushed. Cubitt drew in a large breath as he recalled the horrific events of that night.

'When we realised he was still alive, I suggested maybe we should call the police and an ambulance. But she told me to think about Nick. He would almost certainly go back to prison,' Cubitt said.

'Do you believe she was really concerned about him? She knew about the will,' Ottey said.

'I don't know.'

'What happened that night, Mr Cubitt?' Cross pushed.

'It was so quick. She reached over, grabbed my stick, turned it upside down and hit him on the head.'

'The autopsy report tells us it was a lot more than just a blow to the head, Mr Cubitt. He had several broken bones in his legs, his arms. His body was covered with injuries he sustained in that attack,' said Ottey.

'She just went berserk,' he said, as if he still couldn't believe what he'd witnessed. 'She kept hitting him, again and again. I didn't recognise her. I tried to stop her but she hit my hand with the stick and just carried on. Why did she do that?'

'Mr Cubitt, are you confirming that your wife killed Brother Dominic?' asked Cross.

'I am.' It was almost a whisper.

'Were you involved at all?' Cross went on.

'I was not,' he said quietly, the reality of all of it dawning on him. That he'd now told the police. 'Why did she do that? Do you know?'

He began to weep, his shoulders heaving in great shuddering sobs.

56

Rosemary had lost a lot of her attitude by the time Cross and Ottey sat opposite her in the interview room. Having mug shots taken against a height board and fingerprints uploaded into a computer often had this effect on people.

'It was obvious Nicholas had killed Alexander. Why? I have no idea.' So Rosemary Cubitt began her interview with Ottey and Cross. 'He still blamed him for everything and possibly was still angry. I know we should've called the police. I suggested it but Julian was adamant we shouldn't. He was still trying to protect his son after all this time.'

'He told us different. He said it was he who insisted on calling the police and you were the one who said no,' Ottey replied.

'He's confused.'

'So, tell us what happened,' Ottey went on, sounding like a friend talking to another after something terrible had happened to them, being a sympathetic ear.

'Well, as you know, we'd decided, rightly or wrongly, well I suppose wrongly, to take the body to the farm incinerator,' she began.

'But you ended up in the ditch. Talk us through how that happened,' said Ottey.

'It was wet, muddy, I lost control and slid in,' she replied.

'Slid in?' Cross repeated.

'Yes, that's right. I skidded and lost control,' she said.

'So, you were on the bike when it went into the ditch?' he asked.

'I was.' She laughed nervously as if this was surely obvious.

'But you weren't hurt?' Cross continued.

'No.'

'How was that?'

'I don't know.'

'You say you went into a skid and slid into the ditch,' said Cross trying to picture the scene.

'That's right.'

'And you were in a normal riding position with a leg each side of the machine?' Cross asked.

'Yes.'

'So, why wasn't your right leg trapped under the quad bike, Mrs Cubitt?'

'I don't know. Maybe I jumped?'

'Maybe you jumped?'

'Yes.'

'It's a strange place to have an accident,' he said.

'Why?'

'Because the footpath at the point of the accident is completely straight. If it'd been on a corner, it would make more sense. Maybe you took the corner too fast, lost the back end and ended up in the ditch. But there was no corner. How could that happen on a straight piece of track?' he asked, almost as if he was trying to figure it out himself.

'I don't know. I lost control.'

'So you keep saying. But the truth is, from our perspective, it just doesn't add up. You see, the tyre marks you left prove that you drove straight into the ditch. No loss of control. No skidding or sliding. You just drove in. Can you explain that?'

'Like I said, I jumped off.'

'What you actually said,' he replied, looking at his notes, 'was that "maybe" you jumped.'

'Well, now I think about it, I'm more sure.'

'So, you jumped because you knew you were going into the ditch,' Cross asked, to make sure he'd got this absolutely right.

'Yes.'

'Because you'd steered the quad bike into the ditch,' Cross said.

'No,' she protested.

'If it were an accident, Mrs Cubitt, you would have stayed on the bike trying to steer it away from the ditch. But you didn't, you just went straight on. Why was that?'

'Like I said, it was an accident.'

'What are you trying to say, Sergeant?' her solicitor asked.

'I don't think I'm *trying* to say anything. I'm pretty sure I actually just said it. It wasn't an accident. The question is why Mrs Cubitt deliberately drove the quad bike into the ditch when she was supposed to be taking it to the farm with an incinerator?'

No one said anything. Cross made a note in his folder, turned a page, read something, then looked up.

'Do you have access to your husband's computer, more specifically his laptop, Mrs Cubitt?' he asked, although he already knew the answer.

'I do.'

'And his phone?'

'Yes.'

'Do you go through his texts?'

'Why would I do that? He doesn't text anyone other than me,' she replied.

'Were you aware that your husband had changed his will?' Cross asked.

'No.'

'That on his death you would have use of Weald Cottage and Nicholas would inherit the rest of the estate?'

'No,' she replied.

'Really? So, this is news to you?' Cross asked.

'Yes.'

'You seem remarkably calm.' Cross turned to her lawyer. 'The reason I'm surprised is that, up until this point, Julian's entire wealth and the estate were going to Mrs Cubitt. Quite a blow to find this has been changed, I would've thought. Less so, obviously, if it's something you already know.'

Cross let it hang in the air, then, with timing worthy of Mark Rylance, stated calmly, 'Unless of course something were to happen to Nick, in which case everything would revert to Mrs Cubitt.'

'Something like being found guilty of murder,' Ottey suggested. 'The murder of Brother Dominic Augustus, aka Alexander Mount.'

'You know your mistake, Mrs Cubitt? You underestimated your husband's love for his son. It's not something that just disappears. It's deeply engrained in a father's soul and, in the end, Julian put it ahead of his love for you,' said Cross.

'After all he did! After what that idiot did? Can you believe that?' She appealed to her lawyer. 'He destroyed everything through his arrogance and stupidity,' she spat.

'Exactly. It must be unconscionable to you, to reward that. After what he did to the family business his father goes and leaves everything to him. Even more unbelievable when you take into account everything you've done for Julian over the years.'

Cross let that hang in the air, then asked, 'Did you know that he'd been in touch with Nicholas over the last few months?'

'No comment,' she replied.

'You crashed the quad bike into the ditch deliberately, something forensics confirm. You wanted the body to be discovered, Nick to be found guilty of murder, go to prison and then perhaps your husband might have second thoughts about his will,' Cross summed up.

'Nick killed him. Why shouldn't he pay the price? Why should we cover up for him? He'd done enough damage to Julian and the family as it was,' she replied.

'Because he didn't kill Brother Dominic,' Cross said undramatically. She said nothing.

'He was alive when you found him,' said Ottey.

'He was killed with your husband's walking stick,' Cross added.

'What happened? Was it Julian who killed him?' Ottey asked.

'No comment.'

'I imagine you're wondering how to play this right now. Has Julian behaved like the honourable husband in his interview? Defended his wife and confessed to something he didn't do? Or did he change his mind once he became aware of the fact that you might have known about the will? That you were losing the estate. Did he then re-examine the quad bike accident and the leaving of Dominic's body in a different light?' Cross mused.

'We couldn't get the body out. We tried but it was impossible,' she retorted.

'I think as you managed to get the bike back out, you could've retrieved the body. The trailer had a winch. But you persuaded Julian you were shaken, perhaps, and that people might have been alerted to your presence by the accident. You had to, so that the body would be found and Nick would take the blame,' said Ottey.

'This is all very well in theory,' said the lawyer. 'But it's all conjecture.'

'Good point and timely put,' said Cross. 'Let's move onto the evidence. We have two eyewitnesses who saw you drive away from the estate on the night in question, as well as your admission. There are also two fingerprints. Your fingerprints. One on the back of the chair the victim was taped to. The other on your husband's walking stick. Which is the murder weapon.'

'She presumably handled her husband's walking sticks all the time,' her solicitor pointed out.

'The fingerprint in question is a bloody one,' answered Cross.

'Did you kill Brother Dominic Augustus on April the first of this year, Mrs Cubitt?' Ottey asked.

'No comment,' she replied.

'It might help you to know that we have a witness who has

stated quite categorically that he saw you do it. Your husband,' said Cross.

Rosemary Cubitt looked stunned. Defeated.

'I don't believe you,' she said.

'I'd like to talk to my client,' said the lawyer before she went any further.

Several hours later they had a signed statement from Rosemary to the effect that she had killed Brother Dominic.

57

A few weeks later, on a clear early summer Friday night in June, Cross found himself in the back seat of a car with Stephen. In the front was Raymond, with Christine driving. They were on their way to St Eustace's Abbey. The father abbot had invited everyone who had worked on the organ to come and hear Peter, the abbey organist, give a short recital. Cross felt that his mother really had no place on this trip then realised she was the only one with a car so said nothing, despite the fact that the temptation to do so was huge. Cross was glad to be in a full car, though, with people who knew each other. It alleviated the need for him to contribute to the conversation. This was to be the first of two such excursions this quartet would make together in the coming weeks. They were going to go up to London to Tate Britain, for a party to unveil the new Lucien Freud the gallery had acquired. It had been bequeathed by Stephen in loving memory of his brother, Dominic Augustus, OSB.

The organ had been regulated by Harrison and Harrison of Durham, a world-renowned organ builder and restorer. Sir Patrick Murphy had paid for it. Unfortunately for Cross this had been done over a couple of weekdays and so he had been unable to observe. He also didn't know how complimentary the people from Durham had been about his work on the organ. One of them had joked with the abbot that if Cross ever gave up being in the police there was a job for him with them.

As they walked to the church the night air was filled with the smells of early summer. Wild flowers added their scent to the pine trees that populated the abbey grounds. Again, the peace of it all struck Cross as such a rare commodity.

Ottey pulled up in her car. She got out with her girls, the younger of whom immediately ran over to Cross, throwing her arms around his waist in an enthusiastic hug.

'George!' she exclaimed to her victim who was now standing ramrod straight, arms held out sideways and paralysed with an inability to know how to respond.

'Why are you here?' was all he could come up with.

'Nice to see you too, George,' said Ottey who had had her fill of George Cross for that day. 'Come on, girls,' she said and led them away up the lane.

'Oh, George,' said his father, shaking his head wearily and walking away with Christine.

'I think possibly I should have stayed at home,' Cross said to Stephen who was now the only walking companion he had.

'Nonsense. You did all the work,' Stephen replied.

'True. Maybe all of *you* should've stayed at home.'

Stephen laughed, which puzzled Cross who was being perfectly serious.

The gathering inside the church was small and intimate. Sir Patrick Murphy was there on his own. No Bates. Cross wondered whether he was still in Murphy's employment or whether being indirectly involved with the case was too much for Murphy to stomach. He sat at the back in a pew on his own, as if unsure whether he belonged there and was welcome. He nodded at Cross as he passed. Cross had already emailed him to thank him for his contribution to the renovation. In truth it was a stiffly worded and formal email but Murphy was grateful, if a little surprised to have received it. Fred Savage and his builders were there, sitting uncomfortably in suits. They looked like they were at a funeral. Ursula Mead was there as well as Mackenzie and Swift. Cross was initially puzzled then remembered they'd spent a day working with him on the organ.

The four of them sat in the front pew.

'Are you going to play?' Stephen asked Cross.

'Absolutely not.'

He had no intention of doing so, although the thought had crossed his mind. This wasn't through any consideration about not treading on Peter's toes, or spoiling his party. He simply hated performing in front of others. It was bad enough playing when Stephen and his mother were listening.

The recital was beautiful. Cross had to admit that while he had some reservations about Peter's choice of music – the programme, as it were – he thought him a very accomplished organist. It was basically like a best hits album of classical organ music with some Bach, Widor and César Franck. The community of monks sat in their stalls to one side of the altar, presumably praying as they listened. In the middle of the recital Cross got up and moved to the centre of the church, halfway back in the pews. He wanted to get a different perspective on the acoustics and tone of the instrument. He was thrilled with it. The voice of the organ suited this small church perfectly. It sounded wonderful. As he sat there, he reflected how the chance to restore the organ and the opportunity to spend time at the abbey had been a real restorative during such an unpleasant case.

At the end of the recital Father Abbot Anselm stepped forward and thanked them all for their work on the organ. He then blessed them and followed the monks as they glided as one out of the side door.

Cross got his backpack out of the boot of his mother's car. Murphy had slipped out unnoticed before the end of the recital and already left. Cross watched as Ottey walked her girls to the car. She was actually in a wonderful mood. She'd found buyers for both her and her mother's flats and the offer she'd made on the house with the granny annexe, as she now called it, accepted. All was well with the world.

'A nice text to her over the weekend wouldn't go amiss,' said Christine.

Cross was about to object and point out that not only did

she not know him well enough, she certainly didn't know Ottey at all. But he was stopped by his father and Stephen saying in unison, 'She's right.'

They said goodbye and drove off, leaving Cross. Mackenzie and Swift came over.

'Been abandoned?' asked Swift cheerily. 'Was it something you said?'

'No,' Cross replied firmly.

'Need a lift anywhere?' asked Mackenzie.

'No,' he replied and walked away towards the abbey house.

Mackenzie turned to Swift.

'Will you never learn?' she joked.

'I know. Mea culpa. Mea culpa,' he replied.

'Oh, let's get out of here before you go full-on Benedictine.'

As Swift drove her out of the monastery Mackenzie turned to look at George walking towards the abbey house. She felt a huge pang. She didn't know why. All she knew was that he often had this effect on her. Cross actually had this effect on most of the people who came to know him.

George Cross knocked on the door of the abbey house. After a minute or so it was opened by Father Magnus.

'Ah, George. Welcome.'

Cross said nothing but went in. The monk closed the door. Their voices could be heard receding as they walked down the corridor.

'Brother Benedict has prepared your room. Will you be joining us for supper?'

'Of course!' replied George as if the idea of *not* sharing a meal with nine monks was completely absurd.

Acknowledgements

M y thanks as ever go to the team at Head of Zeus for their support and for always being readily on hand. My editor, Bethan Jones, for her astute reading and constructive criticism, as well as her love for George and his world. Lucy Ridout for her brilliant notes and eye for narrative. The books benefit hugely from her suggestions. Peyton Stableford, Andrew Knowles, Polly Grice, Ben Prior, Christian Duck and Nikky Ward for all their work in bringing George Cross to the world. Tim Owen KC for his patient advice on all things legal in the book. Dr Amanda Jeffrey, forensic pathologist, for answering too many banal medical questions about the misfortunes which befall my victims. Laura Johnson of Harrison and Harrison, Durham, for showing me around the inner workings of the organ at St Mary on the hill in the City. If I've got things wrong, it's because I lost my beautiful EM Meyrowitz spectacles that day and it is no reflection on Laura – see what I did there? Angela McMahon, my PR, for taking this Harrogate newbie up to the festival and introducing me to the great and the good of the crime world. My social media team Sarah Oldman and Lilly Hill who managed to make this old hack into a viral TikTok sensation with over a million views over a weekend. Dale Gibson of Bermondsey Street Bees for both his advice and providing honey for the St Eustace Monastery honey pots.

The book is dedicated to Brian Worthington, my English teacher at school. His erudition and intellect was responsible for inspiring many when it came to English literature. Driving three of us from Bristol to Cambridge to have tea with his former teacher FR Leavis and his wife Queenie is a memory I cherish to this day. Lastly, as ever to my family. My wife Rachel and my daughters, Bella and Sophia, whose support is incalculable, even when it takes the form, as it so often does, of taking the Mickey Bliss. (George would point out here that it is incorrect to use the rhyming component of a piece of rhyming slang, and that this should be written simply as taking 'the mickey'. My excuse is that you don't often see it written in its full form and I rather like it.)

About the Author

TIM SULLIVAN is a crime writer, screenwriter and director who has worked on major feature films such as the fourth *Shrek*, *Flushed Away*, *Letters to Juliet*, *A Handful of Dust*, *Jack and Sarah*, and the TV series *Cold Feet*. His crime series featuring the socially awkward but brilliantly persistent DS George Cross has topped the book charts and been widely acclaimed. Tim lives in North London with his wife Rachel, the Emmy Award-winning producer of *The Barefoot Contessa* and *Pioneer Woman*.

To find out more about the author,
please visit TimSullivan.co.uk.

The Monk

ALSO BY TIM SULLIVAN

The Dentist
The Cyclist
The Patient
The Politician

SHORT STORIES

The Lost Boys
The Ex-Wife